Katie Galvin lives in Perth, Western Australia. Her childhood love of fantasy and magic followed her into her adult years, resulting in her writing *The Gifted* series. In the rare moments where she's not running her speech therapy business or writing, Katie can be found at the gym, with a coffee in hand or rolling her eyes at her cat's antics.

instagram.com/katie_galvin_writing

Also by Katie Galvin

The Gifted

The Broken

The Divine

THE BROKEN

KATIE GALVIN

One More Chapter
a division of HarperCollins*Publishers* Ltd
1 London Bridge Street
London SE1 9GF
www.harpercollins.co.uk
HarperCollins*Publishers*
Macken House, 39/40 Mayor Street Upper,
Dublin 1, D01 C9W8, Ireland

This paperback edition 2025
1
First published in Great Britain in ebook format
by HarperCollins*Publishers* 2025

Copyright © Katie Galvin 2025
Katie Galvin asserts the moral right to be identified
as the author of this work

A catalogue record of this book is available from the British Library
ISBN: 978-0-00-867919-4

This novel is entirely a work of fiction. The names, characters and incidents portrayed in it are the work of the author's imagination. Any resemblance to actual persons, living or dead, events or localities is entirely coincidental.

Printed and bound in the UK using 100% Renewable Electricity
by CPI Group (UK) Ltd
All rights reserved. No part of this publication may be reproduced, stored in a retrieval system, or transmitted, in any form or by any means, electronic, mechanical, photocopying, recording or otherwise, without the prior permission of the publishers.

Without limiting the exclusive rights of any author, contributor or the publisher of this publication, any unauthorised use of this publication to train generative artificial intelligence (AI) technologies is expressly prohibited. HarperCollins also exercise their rights under Article 4(3) of the Digital Single Market Directive 2019/790 and expressly reserve this publication from the text and data mining exception.

Chapter One

Blood stained the ground beneath my feet. Most of it was my own.

I stared across at my opponent, Brutus, each of us reclaiming our breath as we circled each other. The roundness of his cheeks and wispiness of his beard hinted at his youth. His eyes, however, held no trace of innocence. The Den had no place for such a useless quality. None of Naruzia did.

Sand shifted underfoot as I studied the man, the stench of blood and sweat surrounding us. He bounced lightly on his feet, shaking out bloodstained hands, not bothering to wipe away the red dripping from his nose. Bruises littered his face from his previous fight – a blood bath that almost put my many fights from my time serving as captain for the Naruzian army to shame for sheer brutality. Almost.

'You're a halfway decent fighter,' I said, spitting out a mouthful of blood. The iron tang of it sent my stomach roiling, the effects of the alcohol I'd drunk in the morning not yet worn off. Above high limestone walls, shadowy figures leant forward in anticipation.

He grunted. 'And you're a shit one.'

I almost laughed. Ada, my once second-in-command before she'd been executed for my mistakes, would've laughed along with me. My kills on the battlefield had been second to none. But that prowess hadn't stopped me from losing everything in the end.

Bitterness surged at the same time as Brutus's fist flew. It would've been easy to dodge it. I could grab his arm and twist until something cracked. Or duck under the blow, ramming my fist into his midsection and leave him retching on the ground. If I'd wanted to, I could even leave him as a pile of silver ash, my gods-given Gift of death stealing his life before he had a chance to blink. The audience would've loved any of those. There were few things the wretches who came to The Den adored as much as blood and death.

Instead, I let the blow slam into my cheek. The pain was quick and sudden, my teeth cutting the inside of my cheek. More blood filled my mouth. Behind the high limestone barriers, the audience roared their approval.

Straightening, I met Brutus's glare and swiped at my lips with the back of my hand. My split lip stung. I relished that pain. Relished the swelling of my cheek as I smiled. 'Is that the best you can do?'

A man's ego was so often a fragile thing. My opponent was no exception.

His fists tightened, rage reddening the tops of his cheeks. The Illusioned lights above cast a sickly glow upon his sweat-soaked skin as his arm drew back. My smile broadened in anticipation. This time, I leant towards the blow. Let his fist catch my chin. Let red spray. But the arc of it was too small, too feeble a repentance for the blood that'd spilled the day I'd let my sister die.

More, I thought.

A kick came next, his bare foot slamming into my thigh.

Avoidable, if I had any desire to. It was an impressive blow – swift and solid. Enough so that the divine corruption of my blood almost reared to the surface.

Not yet, I reprimanded it, shoving it back. It might crave death, seeking to follow the nature Dearil had given me with his godly paternity, but I didn't want my pain to end. The hungry power slunk back, simmering in my veins.

The uppercut Brutus delivered next sent me staggering back a step, blood spilling over my lip with stubborn tenacity. There were too many gaps in his attacks. Too many ways I could end this. Even with the delight of pain, with the hope that Brutus would be enough to take me down, every hit I took was a choice. There was no challenge. No thrill of a true opponent. Not like there had been with *him*.

Unbidden, an image of a golden-haired man wearing a sinful smile appeared in my mind as Brutus's next blow found my side. The impact was dulled by the roaring that consumed my senses as I remembered *him*. Him laughing under me after I stabbed him. His lips on mine, and the warmth in my chest. Him promising to protect my sister, only to watch her die because he mistakenly thought I was worth more than her.

Callum. The newly crowned King of Naruzia. The man I'd vowed to kill the next time I saw him.

This time, it wasn't the greedy Gift that surged forward. It was my anger, driving my fist upwards and into Brutus's wrist. Something crunched under my blow, Brutus's scream of pain a beckoning call for the audience's cheers.

And then the anger was gone, shoved down until I found blessed emptiness once more. My smile was painted with blood and hollowness as I said, 'That was even more pathetic.'

I kept that smile in place as he launched himself forward, grasping a handful of my hair and slamming my face into his knee. Blood spurted from my nose, spattering amongst the shadows. It soaked my threadbare shirt in a spattering of red raindrops. Cassie would've been horrified to see such a mess. She'd always been too sweet for the world. Kind, in a way that someone like me didn't deserve. The only piece of goodness that'd manage to hold some of my monstrousness at bay.

But she was dead. Her throat had been sliced open by Liam, the enemy prince who I'd deluded myself into trusting. The pain wasn't enough. It never was.

So, I smiled some more. I stood my ground and waited.

'Fight!' the audience screamed in voices filled with savagery. 'Don't just stand there, fight!'

'Still pathetic?' the man grunted, flexing his fingers.

I raised my fingers, dabbing at warmth spilling from my nose. It stung.

'Yes,' I replied honestly. This whole situation was pathetic. Him. Me. The audience. This whole damned kingdom.

He twisted his head, spitting onto the stone. 'You have guts, girl. I'll give you that.'

'I have nothing,' I said, and my chest tightened in agreement.

'Most grown men wouldn't take a beating like that,' he continued, ignoring my words. Ignoring me. 'But it's time to give it up. Surrender, and I'll finish this quickly.'

'There's no surrendering.'

He glanced around conspiratorially before leaning in. The audience's cries increased, upset by the pause. 'I know The Den's owner. He'll make an exception for you, I'm sure.'

A blatant lie. No one knew who owned this shithole of a fighting pit. A low-ranked fighter like him certainly wouldn't. Even my arrogant handler claimed to have no idea who ran this place.

'There's no surrendering,' I repeated. Just like there hadn't been that day when Cassie died. When I had gambled her life to protect this kingdom I hated and managed to lose both.

A shuddering grief rose in me. I pressed my eyes close, fingers digging into my palm, but there was no relief behind my eyelids. Instead, there was a throne room. Two princes – one from Archin, and one from Naruzia. Liam, who had betrayed me by slicing open my sister's throat. Callum, who had betrayed me by choosing to save me over my sister. And me, helpless. Useless. Watching as the only person who'd made the world endurable die with fear in her eyes.

Even the next hit, slamming into my head and sending my eyes flying open, wasn't enough to rid me of the memories of them.

'Gods,' Brutus said, shaking his fist out again. The audience shouted their disapproval, the blood spilt not enough to satiate. I didn't care. All that mattered was I was still conscious. Still capable of remembering. And I hated it. 'You have to be Gifted to still be conscious.' His eyes narrowed with suspicion. 'You can heal yourself, can't you?'

'No.' The reply was short. Hard, and filled with threat.

He either didn't hear that threat or didn't think to listen. His head bobbed in a confident nod. 'That has to be it. You're Gifted by Vitus.'

Blood roared in my ears as silver flickered in the edges of my vision. *Vitus.* The revered god of life. The god who had inhabited the previous king's body and used my sister's life as an anchor to the mortal realm. The next breath I took tasted of ash and death.

My opponent continued, ignorant of his folly. 'Figures a girl could only win by cheating. Fights are Gift-free. I don't care if you're Gifted by the damned god of death himself, you can't—'

His words choked off as my hand flew upwards. My fingers curled into the soft flesh of his throat. Twisting, I sent him slamming onto the stone. He gasped for breath I refused to allow him as my knee pressed into his chest, my fingers tightening until all it would take was a single wrench and his throat would be torn clean from his body. 'Don't mention his name.'

The man's brows bunched with a mixture of agony and confusion. I eased my grip, just enough. 'Vitus? But—'

My fingers were squeezing again. The god's name thundered through me, a calling bell to every dark part of me – the malice, the rage, the hatred. The emotions swarmed, becoming a tangible, crackling entity in my veins. And there was so much to hate. So many people, mortals and gods, who were out of my reach. But my opponent wasn't.

The silver that flickered in my vision surged over my skin, twining around my fingers and slamming into the man. His eyes lit up with silver as veins bulged and his back arched. It only lasted a moment before he was gone. Crumbled, like a log left too long in a fire, into a dusting of silver ash.

Around me, the crowd had grown silent. Slowly, I rose to my feet, dusting the ash from my knees. The toxicity of hatred and fury remained, unsatisfied with the death it had caused. Fatigue followed, swamping me. All I wanted was oblivion. To forget all my failures.

I tilted my head back, letting the Illusioned lights sting at my eyes. The prick of the audience's terrified stares prickled at my skin. I ignored them. A boy ran into the centre of the arena, giving me a wide berth. He shook as he gestured to me. 'O-our winner is—'

Turning, I strode for the exit before he could utter my name.

Chapter Two

'Cutting it a bit fine, weren't we?' Jaxon Bladditch, infamous scourge of Naruzia and my handler at The Den, leant back in his rickety chair. A cup of wine was held casually in one hand, a glass of amber-coloured whiskey in the other. I took both from him, downing the wine in one go and ignoring his frown. 'When I said, *make it interesting,* I didn't mean get beaten bloody and then kill your opponent in one go.'

I dropped into the chair opposite him. A man seated close by glared. I glared back, twisting so that my cloak folds shifted. All it took him was a glance at the four weapons at my belt and he was turning back to his card game. 'I don't care what you meant.'

Jaxon clicked his tongue, drawing my attention back to him. He raised his hand and a young barmaid hurried over. His smile brightened, teeth flashing amidst olive skin. 'A cup of wine, if you'd be so kind.' The lilt of an Axanian accent, the growing empire across the sea to the east of Naruzia. was as smooth as his words.

The girl smiled, blushing prettily as she nodded eagerly. 'Anything else?'

He draped an arm casually over the back of his chair. 'Not now, but later…'

The trailed-off sentence was enough to stoke the girl's imagination. Her blush slipped beneath her dress's collar. I sighed.

At twenty-four, Jaxon was charismatic, good-looking and a complete scoundrel. The first night we'd met, he'd asked if I had any interest in making some extra coin after participating in a rather bloody bar brawl I'd started. I'd asked if he had any interest in having his throat slit, and he'd doubled his offer of coins. Since then, I'd seen five love confessions and five broken hearts. He'd smiled every time someone had run away crying.

'Make that three wines,' I said, before he could turn it into six confessions.

Jaxon turned his stare on me, the golden-yellow of his eyes gleaming. 'Are we expecting a guest?'

'Do I seem like the sort of person who would entertain guests?'

'Only if it ended in some sort of fight.' He eyed me before his gaze dropped to my near-empty money pouch. It sat upon the sticky table. For most, a fool's decision. For me, a way to invite violence. 'I don't think you have enough coin to afford one drink, let alone two.'

I smiled. He had the sense to tense. 'Actually, make it four wines. Put it on his tab.'

The girl hesitated, glancing towards Jaxon. With a heavy sigh, he nodded. He didn't speak until she had hurried away, swallowed by the bustling crowd. 'You're going to drain my pockets dry at this rate.'

'Unlikely.' I tossed back the whisky. Dropping the empty glass onto the table, I glowered down at it. There was barely a hint of any buzz in my body. Oblivion was a far way off. 'We both know you earnt a fair bit off that fight tonight.'

'Who would've expected the pretty blonde woman to be capable of killing a man so easily?' Jaxon frowned, shaking his head. 'Speaking of which, that disguise will have to be retired. The audience was a little ... *unnerved* by your performance. What was that silver light?' He peered over at me. 'Your Gift?'

I shrugged, brushing blonde hair off my shoulders. As I did so, Jaxon waved his hand through the air. The blonde lengthened and shifted into curls, the colour deepening until they were black. My skin changed next, darkening to deep brown. Scars appeared across my skin, a collection earnt from the mother who had sold me to King Kane for the use of my Gift, from King Kane himself, and a sparse few from fighting in the war. 'You can just make a new illusion. You're always going on about how useful your Gift is.'

Jaxon let out a long-suffering sigh. 'I *can*, but there's only so many different combinations of hair, skin and eye colour I can come up with. How many have you gone through now?'

I stared at him flatly. We both knew there were countless illusions he could weave. Gifted by the goddess Tarina, who ruled over illusions and trickery, Jaxon was particularly skilled. His illusions were impossible to tell from the real thing, making him stand out even amongst other Gifted. It also made him one of the most dangerous liars in Alluvite's slums. 'Where's my cut of the coin?'

Eyeing the empty cups on the table, Jaxon said, 'I think you drank your cut.'

'We both know that's nowhere near the amount of money you scammed off the audience.'

Jaxon pressed a hand to his chest. 'Scammed? I'm hurt. Gambling is an honest trade.'

'No, it's not. Especially when you make sure to make me seem pitiful and weak so everyone except you will bet against me.'

'Fine. It's an artform – one I happen to be good at.'

The barmaid reappeared, quickly placing down the cups of wine before disappearing at the glower I sent her way. 'It's theft.'

Not that I particularly cared. I just needed something to distract myself with until the alcohol could do its work and make me forget everything.

'It's business.' He snatched up one of the cups before I could pull all four towards me. Red liquid sloshed over the edge. 'A business that you readily agreed to be part of after you realised how much your nightly drinking would cost you.'

In the corner, a trio of fiddlers began to pick up a jaunty tune. Cheerful shouts sounded throughout the tavern, grating against my nerves. I took a long draw of one of the wines. 'A business that we agreed; that I would get half the cut for every fight I won. I even agreed to accept my cut at this dingy tavern every second fight at your insistence.' Only because I was in desperate need of the coin.

'Thirty per cent.'

'Yes,' I agreed, placing the cup down and lowering my hand to one of my knives. My finger tapped the hilt slowly. 'It *was* thirty per cent. Then you tried to shortchange me a week ago. Now it's fifty.'

'Any agreements made with a knife to my throat are null and void.'

I smiled, a slow curve of my lips that Jaxon blanched at. 'Then my agreement to not rip out your lying tongue in exchange for coin must also be void, right?' A small pouch of coins dropped to the table in front of me. I tugged it open, eyeing the gleam of silver from within the leather. 'I don't need to count these, do I?'

Jaxon adopted an affronted expression. 'What do you take me for?'

'A liar and a cheat.'

He paused. Opened his mouth, closed it, then shrugged. 'Can't argue with that. However, I happen to value all my body parts and would rather they don't have an unfortunate meeting with your knife.' He watched as I tossed back the next cup of wine. The alcohol was cheap, the taste poor and the bite of it strong. I didn't care. If it tore all thoughts from my mind before the end of the night, it had served its purpose. 'What do you need the coin for, anyway? Surely not just for alcohol. You live in a hovel—'

'It doesn't concern you,' I cut him off. This was a business relationship, nothing more, even if he was the closest thing I had to a friend right now.

I wasn't about to tell him any of what had happened, nor would I confide in him as though we were friends. It had been over three months since Callum and I had returned to the Naruzian palace with the chains of gods in tow at King Kane's orders. Three months since Liam and Kane had summoned Dearil by killing dozens of innocents within the throne room, binding the god in the chains and rendering his power useless. Three months since Vitus used the tether I'd created with my Gift to bind Cassie's soul to her body as a sacrifice, allowing Vitus to secure himself to Kane's body and killing Cassie. Three months since I had warned Callum to stay away from me and vowed to have vengeance for Cassie by finding a way to the godly realm – the only place where I might discover how to kill a god.

Three months, and I had nothing to show for it.

'It very well does if my best fighter shows up drunk or hungover at every fight she's scheduled for.' Jaxon leant forward, his hands wrapping around one of the cups of wine. I stared at his fingers. Wondered how much the coin was worth it to keep putting up with his talking. 'You earn a decent amount from the fights. If you didn't spend it on alcohol every night, you could—'

My knife whipped upwards, its deadly edge pressed to the fragile underside of Jaxon's wrist. He froze. 'You're a tool for me to use, Jaxon. A way for me to earn enough coin to do as I please. Nothing more. Nothing less.'

'We're business partners. You don't need to—' His words cut off in a sharp hiss. A line of red formed under the blade's edge.

'A tool,' I repeated. His throat worked in a swallow as I pushed the knife in deeper. Droplets of blood fell upon the table. It wouldn't be hard to slit his wrist. To let him bleed out and watch as he died. Maybe it'd ease some of the tightness in my chest.

Yet Jaxon did not run away. Instead, he grinned. 'I thought my years as a sailor were bad enough, but it seems being fr—' He took one look at my expression and hurriedly corrected himself, 'Being a *tool* for you to use is far more dangerous.'

I pressed my lips together. The call for blood thrummed through my veins. That wretched power within me wanted death. It'd be easy to satisfy it now. Yet, when I'd needed it to save Cassie, it had failed, unable to do anything against Vitus's power. When I'd sought for a way into the godly realm to grow more powerful and seek vengeance for her death, it yielded no paths for me to follow. No results to ease the heavy sense of failure. In the end, it was useless.

Sudden fatigue washed over me. The blade fell from Jaxon's wrist as I swept up the cup. Tipping my head back, I swallowed the last of the drink. That sweet buzz was finally beginning to take hold. Inside my veins, the crackling of my power abated somewhat. It was as suffocated by the drink as my thoughts were.

Throwing a handful of coins on the table, I turned to leave. Usually, in Jaxon's company, I'd be content to drink until I collapsed. Now, though, all I wanted was to be far away from him and the marks of concern in his expression. He grasped a handful of my cloak. 'I thought it was going on my tab?'

I regretted not cutting his hand off. 'I won't owe favours to anyone.'

'I don't expect anything in return.' He let go of my cloak, sliding one of the silver coins across the table. 'Let me pay. Go buy something to eat. It's a wonder no bones snapped today with how gaunt you're looking.'

My stomach twisted with hunger at his words. I ignored it. 'I don't need your pity.'

'It's not pity,' he said, his finger still pressed to the coin. 'It's an investment. You're my most valuable commodity.'

'I'm not some fool who'll allow myself to be indebted to you.' I'd seen the sort of man Jaxon was. He might be all smiles and charming words now, but I'd watched him drive a knife through the hand of a man who tried to cheat him. A coin now meant repayment later. All I cared for was fighting, drinking and forgetting – not repaying favours.

Jaxon sighed. 'I'm not lying. There'll be no paying me back.'

I flicked the coin. The force sent it spinning out from under his finger. 'The only thing you're good at is lying.'

'And you?' Jaxon narrowed his eyes at me as I began to turn for the door once more. 'What are you good at?'

I didn't look back as I strode for the exit. 'Killing.'

Chapter Three

I didn't bother heading for my 'hovel', as Jaxon had so kindly put it. There was nothing waiting for me there but damp floors, a thin mattress and the smell of mould. The place was little more than a place to sleep for me. It was no home. The only place – the only *person* – I'd ever counted as my home was gone.

Instead, I wove through the streets. The moon dappled a pattern upon the ground, its dim light failing to stand up against most shadows. Passing by those partaking in the lurid distractions of the night, I cut through an alleyway, the voices of others fading into nothingness. My steps quickened as I picked up on the echo of a second set of steps behind me.

Their pace quickly adjusted, the light tread merging seamlessly with my own. I smiled. It seemed someone was looking for a bloody end tonight if they were following me.

That suited me just fine. I was itching for some violence.

Veering off to the left, I opened the door to one of the many taverns I'd acquainted myself with over the past months. A small bell rang to announce my arrival. No one bothered to glance my way as I looped around the crush of bodies, keeping my eyes peeled for any fingers that might dip into my pockets or knives ready to slice my side. The Dagger and Cloak was a tavern of ill repute – one that preferred to ignore any and all crimes rather than bothering to deal with them. Only those willing to gamble their life stepped inside with any significant coin on them.

The thick scent of ale and sweat smothered me as I came to a stop at the bar. Resting an arm on the grimy surface, I lifted a hand to the barkeep. He took one look at me and glanced at the several knife marks left on the wall to the left. 'Here to make a mess again?'

I shrugged. 'You managed to get the blood off, didn't you?'

He picked up a grimy cloth, wiping it on the inside of an equally filthy glass. It did little but smear the marks further. 'It took two weeks to shake the guards from this place. The people here don't like city guards sniffing about their business.'

I shrugged. That guard had been … *unfortunate*. I didn't remember much of what had happened that night. There'd been a dead guard – one who I'd hunted down for his close ties to King Kane, the former ruler of Naruzia – lying at my feet. The sensation of falling into an abyss as I realised my last lead to the godly realm and my last chance at vengeance had been another dead end. And then a desperate need to drink until I forgot everything. 'You don't have problems now.'

'Because someone high up got involved.' The glass clattered as he slammed it down. 'Someone with power, I was told. Enough to control the city guard. Someone who I *don't* want watching my business.'

I stilled. 'Who?'

He shrugged, turning his back on me. 'Don't know. But don't come here expecting a drink again.'

'Money-grabbing prick,' I muttered as he strode away.

Most of the taverns of better repute had already learnt my face. This had been one of the last that'd tolerated my presence. Even so, I knew as well as he did that he wouldn't bar my entrance. It'd cause too much of a commotion, and if eyes were already on the tavern, it'd only make things worse.

I narrowed my eyes at the glorious array of various alcohols lined up on a shelf. My hands pressed to the top of the bar. 'If you won't pour me another, I'll fetch my own.'

A black-gloved hand clamped around my wrist. Anger was quick to answer my summons, filling me with ice as I spun to face whoever had grabbed me. They were either stupid or had a death wish. Either way, they would not be leaving with their hand intact.

I froze, staring at the hooded figure standing next to me. In my disagreement with the barkeep, I'd failed to remember why I'd entered the tavern in the first place. My shadow had finally mustered the courage to approach me.

'I think you've had enough for tonight.' The voice was smooth and melodious in quality. Unfortunately, it was also one that I recognised.

King Callum's personal guard, Deana.

I wasted no time on niceties as I shoved her hand away. 'Get off.'

She reached up, sliding off the hood of her cloak. She was deceptively sweet-looking, with her rounded blue eyes and heart-shaped face. But no one sweet would've earnt the position as King Callum's right hand. I glared at the threads of gold woven into her uniform – a mark of her rise from prince's guard to king's guard. 'Whatever you're here for, the answer is no.'

'Hello, *Deana*,' she drawled, hand slamming back around my wrist as I turned to regard the alcohol once more. 'How lovely to see you, Deana. It's been too long, Deana. How have you been, Deana?'

With a huff, I tugged my hand free. It seemed I wouldn't be getting that drink, after all. Eyeing the exit, I forcefully pushed my way through the bodies. Much to my disgust, Deana easily kept pace.

Cool air bit into my skin as I escaped the clamour. Winter had come on swiftly this year. Holding the folds of my cloak around me, I gritted my teeth against the chill that swept through me. A few drunken revellers teetered their way along the road, one step away from falling into a heap of tangled limbs. From the way the ground rolled beneath my feet, I wasn't too far from doing the same. A cough behind had my teeth gritting tighter.

'He sent you?' I bit out, tipping my head back to glare at the sky. Beyond the crooked rooftops and crumbling eaves, a heavy cloud-covering blocked the stars.

Her stare prickled against my skin as she said, 'He figured you might be less inclined to send me back with my throat slashed like the others he'd sent.' Her eyebrows rose. 'Or to not be found at all.'

Basic morality dictated that decent people would feel remorse at her words. I wasn't decent, and any sense of morality I had scarcely abided by had disintegrated with Cassie's death.

'He should've gotten the message when I sent the first one back.' I strode away from her.

'I rather liked the fourth one you returned to us.' Deana easily kept pace. 'The gouging out of his eyes was a lovely touch.'

I remembered that one. I'd recognised the man's leering stare the moment he'd approached me – the same stare that had scoured over me from his guard post every time King Kane had called me for a whipping. His end had been ... slow.

Deana continued as though I hadn't spoken. 'And the twelfth? Grisly doesn't quite cover it. Not that I blame you. Silla was a nasty woman, at the best of times. Those were far more interesting than the ones that vanished.'

As though recognising the mention of its handiwork, the sleepy Gift in me raised its head. It was too suffocated with the alcohol to do much, but without it, it would've unleashed. It'd become a famished beast since Cassie died, no longer held at bay by her soul. I rarely had the energy to restrain it. Nor did I have the desire to.

'So, what will it be?' Deana prattled on, her cheery voice ill-placed in Alluvite's slums. Even the light seemed to delight in her, lighting up her blonde hair. 'Will you be coming to Callum now or later?'

I stopped abruptly, spinning to face her. 'I warned him.' That sleepy energy thrummed beneath my skin. It might be repressed, but it was by no means gone. 'I told him what would happen if he tried to approach me again.'

Deana waved a hand through the air, unbothered by the anger crackling in my voice. 'People say all sorts of things in the heat of the moment.' She paused, tilting her head to the side. She tapped her finger next to her right eye. 'Your eyes are becoming defective.'

Dammit. I wrangled hold of the unruly power, cursing its poor control. Only two days had passed since I'd paid good coin for someone Gifted in illusions to paint them brown. It seemed my Gift was growing impatient at being subdued. Refusing to acknowledge the change, I snapped out, 'You're a piss-poor king's guard if you're trying to bring me back to him. My threat wasn't a jest – he *will* die next time I set eyes upon him.'

'Even if he had information about how to cross between the mortal and gods' realm?'

Her words rid me of any remaining buzz from my drinking. *Information.* The very thing I'd been searching for.

The anger coiling in my chest mixed with confusion. 'There's no way to access the godly realm.' Callum had to be lying, trying to entice me back to the palace for who-knew-what purpose. I'd searched for months for a way to the godly realm. Left body after body in my wake. All ending in a dead end, my path to vengeance blocked. 'What information does he…' I trailed off, realising too late I'd betrayed my interest.

Deana smiled smugly. She flicked her braid over her shoulder as she said. 'You've been asking about it ever since you stormed out of the palace. It'd be harder for him not to know.'

I uttered a curse so foul that, if I wasn't already on a god's 'to kill' list, I most certainly would be now. 'I was careful.'

'You were.' Her eyes gleamed. 'But I was more so.' She leant forward, and the braid fell back over her shoulder once more. 'I know everywhere you've been for the past few months, Chiara. Every drinking hole, every hidden den, every brothel.' She paused, her gaze flattening with disapproval. 'The Den.'

'I would've known if I'd been followed.'

Her grin widened. My scowl deepened. 'You only knew tonight because I let you.' Ignoring my irritation, Deana hooked her arm through mine and pulled me down the street. 'Come. We're starting to look like lovers having a spat. Let's go meet with Callum.'

It was the part of me that felt something unclench at his name that made me tear my arm from Deana's arm. It was a stubborn little part. One that I had trodden on and sliced at and screamed at, waiting for it to die. Yet it was still there. The part that still cared. The very thing that had led to the ruination of everything good in my life.

I would see it crushed.

'No.'

The bemusement on Deana's face was almost comical. People did not refuse a king. Ever.

There were no invisible chains that bound me to this king, though. I would not bend to the whims of that bloodline. Never again.

'No?'

'No.' My jaw set. Callum had to be lying. 'If you take me back there, I will kill him.'

The lack of uncertainty in my words made Deana's natural elegance drop. She reeled back, shock parting her lips. 'But he's trying to *help* you.'

The silence of the air was sliced in two by my bitter laugh. 'Last time Callum deigned to *help* me, he got C—' My tongue twisted on the name, the two syllables that once gave my heart a reason to beat now unable to pass through my lips. 'He got my sister killed.'

Deana frowned. She lifted a hand as though to grasp hold of me. I twisted out of her reach. I had no desire to be comforted. Comfort was for those who deserved it. 'It wasn't his fault.'

You promised. The words I had once fired at him as deadly as any weapon were fresh in my mind, a constant reminder of his betrayal. Of the promise he broke the moment he let Cassie die. All because saving her meant my life would've been forfeited. 'No.'

The single syllable was all I left behind as I turned and allowed myself to be swallowed by the night.

I'd already uttered three foul curses aimed at the gods that morning. I was bordering on using a fourth as I ran down the street, shoving past the teeming crowds filling each street. My throat was dry and scratchy, pairing well with the pounding headache I'd acquired. I ignored all of it. The discomfort was the least of what I deserved.

I swung around a corner, the thick aroma of meat juices dripping into open flames filling the air from the marketplace. Tongues clicked and heads shook as I sped past the square's occupants. I slowed at my third near-miss of slamming into someone too slow to move out of my way. I was late for the fight already. There was no sense in rushing now.

It'd been a sleepless night of agonised thoughts. Of weighing the truth of Deana's offer. I still believed Callum was lying, but if he wasn't... I frowned, nails digging into my palm. A breakthrough in the path to vengeance was enticing, but the thought of seeing Callum again – no. I couldn't do that. Couldn't endure the confusion of everything I'd felt and everything that'd passed between us.

But wouldn't it be worth it for vengeance? The question wound through my thoughts.

He's lying, I thought fiercely, shoving the question away. He had to be.

A child scrambled out of my way, eyes wide with fright as their mother gripped their shoulder. Where my dark clothes, complete with a smattering of bloodstains, had fit in seamlessly with the night, they were discordant amongst the colours of the day. Everywhere I looked, was a burst of colour – a sunset-orange day dress, or a tunic the shade of spring grass. Ribbons woven in hair and bright bolts of fabric hung from stalls. Once, I might've found the colours tedious, but thought little else of it. Now, I despised them. *Hated* how these people could thrive in this loathsome kingdom. How they could smile and laugh when Cassie never would again.

My sister had loved the brightness that populated Alluvite's streets. She would often talk of buying dresses when she was old enough to venture out into the city alone. When I visited, she'd drag me over to the palace window and point out all those spots of brightness she could see. And then she'd beg me, over and over until I ceded, to tell me stories of the people living amongst the vibrancy. She would never get to buy those dresses. Never get to meet those people or make stories of her own.

Because of cruel gods and capricious royals. Because of me.

The sword I had pinched from a would-be thug thumped my back. The blade didn't quite fit the scabbard I'd slung carelessly over a shoulder. No one gave the battered weapon a second glance. It held none of the fine beauty of my knives or daggers. Finely made swords and well-balanced daggers had no place at The Den. Even a shoddily crafted weapon could still be deadly in my hands.

'Necklace?' The word startled me, my free hand dropping to my dagger. Hungry warmth gathered in my veins before I recognised the toothless beam of old Annie, her years carved deeply into her face.

Of an unidentifiable age, somewhere between eighty and a hundred, the crone was a constant at this particular marketplace. Her age-spotted hands flicked through today's wares with surprisingly lithe fingers. She hoisted up a chain, battered crescent pendant dangling off it. The design was simple, the golden paint chipping away to reveal dull metal underneath.

I sidestepped her outstretched arm. 'No.'

Annie might've been old, but she could be fast when she wanted to. The chain was tossed back onto her pile of various trinkets. From a dirt-crusted pocket, she withdrew a ring inset with a gem.

Gold again. Just like Vitus's power. Just like a king's crown.

I despised the colour.

'What about this?' She thrust it forwards, her other hand fisting on my cloak.

The crackling power in my veins strengthened. It felt like a taunt – a reminder of the thoughts I'd been consumed with overnight. Of the possibility that Callum was perhaps not lying. That I might be nothing more than a coward, too afraid to see him to seek the vengeance Cassie deserved. 'No.'

'Ah, but this is not any ordinary ring.' I raised my brows. The only thing extraordinary about the item was that it hadn't fallen to pieces yet. 'It's said to house the blessing of the King of gods himself.' She leant close, the stench of mould emanating from her clothes. *'Vitus.'*

I tensed at the name, ripping my cloak free of her bony-fingered grasp. Another taunt. Another stab at the possible ways I was failing Cassie even after death. That I was letting my own selfish desire to stay far from Callum win.

My Gift thrummed in time with my heart. *'No.* Get that thing away from me.'

'All right, girl, no need to be rude,' she huffed, tucking the ring back into a grimy pocket. 'Didn't know you were one of 'em heathens.'

I forced a breath in through clenched teeth. Annie's rheumy eyes narrowed as though she were imagining all the suffering I would be enduring in the Dark for my irreverence. That was fine. I was already destined for the Dark, for things far worse.

I took a step away before stopping. 'Do you have anything blessed by Dearil?' The question slipped out before it had fully formed in my mind. A memory flashed in my mind – my father, wrapped in the chains of the gods, his power leashed. Him disappearing as I remained on the throne room floor, holding Cassie tight.

Annie's face dropped into a scowl so thin that her lips almost disappeared into her folds of skin.

'Of course not,' she snapped, shuffling a few steps back. 'Only a fool would want to be blessed by Death.'

I forced a faint smile onto my lips. She paled. 'Of course. Only a fool,' I echoed. I did not waste any more time on her, striding away. Her huff of disgust followed me.

Only a fool would want to be blessed by Death. What did that make the daughter of the god? A fool? A nightmare? Or simply a waste of space?

My money was on the last one.

The backstreets of Alluvite were rarely visited by the crowds that'd been in the marketplace. It was the perfect place to spiral in uncertainty without the annoyance of other bodies crowding me, grating against me. That offer of a ring for Vitus occupied my thoughts. I'd turned down Deana so quickly, but perhaps I'd been wrong. Perhaps I was giving up an opportunity I should've been clutching hold of by refusing to return. Callum might've consumed far too many of my thoughts and pulled on my fury like no other, but Vitus was the true evil. The one who I should be focused on for Cassie.

Tapping a finger against the hilt of my knife, I lost myself to the familiar twists and turns. It was a balancing game – whether seeing Callum again was worth the revenge on Vitus.

No, I warned myself. Agreeing to anything involving Callum was a dangerous path. One I was likely to find coiled with thorny vines waiting to entrap me. Chances were, he knew nothing of use. Staying far away from him was the best option.

Yet, no matter how much I tried to convince myself, that thought didn't quite settle like it should've.

It took a few more twists and turns before I stepped into the darkest alley in Alluvite. Not even the breeze dared to follow behind me. Sunlight did not make it past the crowded-together rooftops. The alley itself was deceptively empty, only a single door to be seen. The rest was all bricks and stones, flat walls and bountiful splashes of crimson adorning the floor. The smells and laughter of the markets didn't make it into the alley.

The stone ground was littered with loose trinkets and oddities. Earnings that the winners didn't want, and the losers could rarely retrieve. Shadows lined every wall and corner. The single, unassuming door sat at the far end, unguarded except for the cowled figure leaning casually next to it. It was an innocuous entrance for The Den.

'Jaxon,' I ground out as he pushed his cowl off before slotting his hands comfortably in his pockets.

'Chiara.' Jaxon returned. He shifted a grey package out from under his arm. 'You're late. Again.' He handed over the package.

I took one look at it and snorted with disgust.

'Really?' I dangled the mask between two fingers as Jaxon raised a hand. Tingling swept over my body. Wisps of black hair at the edge of my vision lightened into wiry brown. My skin took on a pale cast, the scars wrapping around my hands and wrists disappearing. Frowning, I stared at the now unblemished skin. A new body for a new fight. 'Why a mask? I haven't had to wear one in any of the previous fights.'

'It creates character. A persona that the audience will willingly cheer for. Something that you are in desperate need of.' He snatched the mask out of my hand before I could drop it into the dirt and waved a hand at me. His illusion tingled at the skin surrounding my eyes. I raised my brows at him. 'Your silver was cracking through the brown.'

'I don't need an audience to cheer for me.' I snatched the mask back, narrowing my eyes when Jaxon stepped forward as though to help. He held his hands up in surrender.

'An audience who likes you is more likely to bet in the match.'

'Shouldn't we avoid that?' Too many bets on me, and the odds decreased. Jaxon meant less money, which meant I earnt less. And less coin meant I'd have to test the limits of my thieving skills to obtain my night's worth of alcohol.

His lips curved into a smile. 'I never said they'd be betting on you. You'll simply be more interesting for them to watch being pummelled into the ground.' Jaxon tapped the tip of my nose. My Gift surged forward, silver sparks flaring. Quickly stepping back, he grinned. 'That's how we get our coin.'

'If anyone ever catches your trickery, you'll be a dead man walking.' I warned him, brushing the Illusioned hair off my shoulders.

Jaxon's smile was delighted. 'I know.'

I eyed him. It had been that very smile that had convinced me to work beside him. The way that, no matter how wide it grew or how high it stretched, it never met his eyes. It was the smile of someone who held no attachments. Someone who would stab me in the back the moment it suited him.

I liked that about him. Betrayal was easier to bear when I expected it. And I knew now that friendships and camaraderie were not meant for someone like me. Not made for a monster who dealt in only blood and death.

He clapped me on the shoulder. 'In you go. And do try not to come out a bloody mess this time.'

Chapter Four

The fight did not last long. The audience's roars of approval chased me into the alleyway, each step leaving behind boot prints marked with crimson. The sharp scent of iron followed me as doggedly as it had when I'd fought in the war, matting my hair and wetting my cheeks. I slid my sword – even more battered than it had been before – back into its scabbard as I stopped in front of Jaxon.

'I thought I said *not* to come out a bloody mess.' He stared pointedly at the red spattered across me.

I shrugged, dragging the heel of my palm across my mouth. The blood that'd fallen there left a foul taste in my mouth.

The fight had been a quick one, my opponent's arrogance misjudged. I'd meant to take his beating as I had with Brutus. When he'd suggested to his handler that his reward for winning be to have me to sell as a slave, however, he'd signed his own death warrant. I'd left his head sitting in the middle of the arena before stalking out.

I would never be a slave again.

'Still, it was quite a show,' Jaxon remarked, offering me a clean handkerchief. I made no move to take it. 'At least it wasn't your blood this time. You did well.'

'Go fetch my coin,' I snapped back, not caring for his games tonight. 'And it had better be the full amount.'

Jaxon's smile faltered. His eyes dropped to where I'd shoved my hands into my pockets. For a moment, it seemed like he was going to ask something. I turned my head to stare past him before he could try. He was nothing more than a way for me to earn money, and vice versa. Neither of us had need of anything more. At last, he simply said, 'I'll be quick,' before disappearing.

Sighing, I leant against the brick wall, tossing my dagger idly as I waited. My pounding headache was beginning to re-emerge. The fight had been a blessed few minutes of silence, but now that it was over, the blood already drying, thoughts of Callum and Vitus returned with a vengeance.

I watched as the silver of my blade glinted in its upwards twist. *To stay far away from Callum and potentially forego a chance of vengeance.*

The blade twisted on its way down. *Or to meet with the man I'd promised to kill and perhaps gain a chance to slay a god.*

'Interesting company you keep.' I stiffened at the irritatingly familiar female voice as Deana made her way down the alley.

'Leave me alone,' I said, catching the dagger deftly. Deana was unimpressed, eyeing me without a single trace of amusement in her lovely features. That was fine by me. I was far from amused myself.

'You do know who you're working with? Jaxon Bladditch? The heartless rogue?'

'I would much rather the heartless rogue than the callous king. At least a rogue knows what he is.' I straightened, arms folding over my chest. The illusion had begun dripping off me, my scars beginning to wrap their way around me as my skin darkened. 'What is it you want, Deana?'

'I want you to come with me to see Callum.'

'And I want your king to drop dead this second. I don't think either of us is going to get what we want.'

Deana pursed her lips. 'I don't think that's true.'

My knuckles paled on the dagger hilt. It would be easy to end her. A slice across her throat and she'd be drowning in her own blood. Or a blade to her heart to give her a quick end. She might put up a fight – might make me work for it. In the end, though, I knew who would come out on top.

I had killed all the others Callum had sent to watch me and make sure I didn't tear his precious city down. Except that Deana was the closest person I knew to the king. If I killed her, there was every chance Callum would decide to track me down himself.

That was not an option.

'You don't know me, at all.' Fury churned inside, intertwining with my Gift. Hints of silver sparked on my skin in response. Deana was a fool to approach me now, without alcohol to subdue death's appetite.

She merely shrugged. 'Maybe not, but I've seen you with Callum. Hate is a very passionate thing.'

Maybe I *should* just slice her throat and be done with it. I inspected her, searching for weapons. A silver wire was wrapped around her throat – a seemingly delicate necklace, but I knew better. A garrotte. Perhaps she'd be able to provide the challenge I'd so desperately been craving. The out-of-tune whistle and metallic clink of coins halted my hand where it had been lowering to one of my daggers. Deana spun, her cloak whirling with her. Jaxon smiled with the roguish-ness he used on most women. One that promised pleasure and torment in equal measure. Most fell for it within seconds. The aftermath was always a sight to see.

This smile, though, held a hint of sharpness. Like a beautiful piece of stained glass with a jagged edge.

Deana tensed further, until all she seemed to be was coiled

muscle and readiness to fight. 'Leave,' she ordered, her voice a whip in the air.

Jaxon's smile grew. He tossed the sack of coins in the cold night's air, the pieces inside clinking every time he caught them.

'Oh, I don't think I will, lovely.' He stepped forward. 'You see, you may have free rein of that pretty palace you call home. But out here, this is my city. My streets. And you're bothering one of my own.' The sack of coins sailed over Deana's head and I snatched it from the air before the precious metal could land at my feet. In the same fluid movement, Jaxon drew the curved sword he kept sheathed at his side. It caught strands of moonlight in his polished edge.

Deana's face turned stony. Something in my stomach simultaneously tightened and thrilled at the sight of the two of them. Jaxon was a scourge upon the city when he unleashed his sword. I had only seen it a few times, but even I would hesitate to cross blades with him. Deana, I had never seen in action. There was a deadly calm in her, however. The sort of calm that hinted at experience dealing in violence and coming out victorious.

This fight would be far more entertaining than any I might partake in in The Den.

Instead of unfurling the deadly garrot coiled around her neck like a lovely, ornate piece of beauty, Deana flashed her blue eyes at me. 'That's a no, then?'

I shook my head sharply, even as doubt clawed at me.

'I'll see you tomorrow.' With that, Deana stalked away, her shoulder bumping hard into Jaxon as she did so.

Jaxon raised an eyebrow. 'You do attract unsavoury attention, darling. A king's guard? What naughty things have you been up to?' The look I cut him was enough for him to sheathe his sword and raise his hands in defeat. 'No questions. I remember.'

I hefted the weight of the sack in my hand, nodding with satisfaction. It seemed Jaxon wouldn't be going home shorthanded tonight. He watched my fingers curl possessively around the sack. If it was anyone else, the narrowing of his eyes might have marked concern. In Jaxon, the only concern he had was that he would have to find a new champion should I meet an untimely end.

'No judgements, either.' My fingers closed around the sack, pulling it into the folds of my cloak. Jaxon made no move to stop me.

'What, pray tell, are you planning to do with that?' From the look in his eyes, he already knew.

Not that it was any of his business, but I replied anyway. 'Drink.' And then I strode away, leaving Jaxon to his disapproval. Oblivion awaited.

Chapter Five

True to her word, Deana appeared at every tavern or back alley I found myself in the next night. And the next. And the next. By the time another fight rolled around two weeks later, I was considering saying yes, just so that I could shake her presence. I bent down with a groan, tugging on the new boots I'd bought the day before with what little coin I had left. The leather refused to yield, warning of blisters before the evening was through.

Leaving behind the half-rotted carcass of an indiscriminate vegetable, I slipped outside and into the afternoon shade. My stomach grumbled in protest at my foregone meal. I had four hours before I was due at The Den. Enough time to wander the streets and pinch a bit of food from an unsuspecting stall. Jaxon had taught me enough of the streets that I could now mostly escape unnoticed.

With the foreboding grey of the sky warning of impending rain, the market square was empty of stalls. The square offered little in way of protection from the elements. The few brave souls who dared to risk the weather would likely scurry off before long.

Only the permanent fixtures of stalls remained, mostly consisting of those selling food. I strode up to a stall selling meat wrapped in flat bread. The enticing scent of meat roasting over an open flame had my mouth watering. The stall owner, a woman with greying hair and pebble-like eyes, casually turned the meat, hip resting against the greasy wood of the countertop. Across from her, two men, one not much older than I, the other a few years younger, waited for their meals.

The woman listened intently to the men as they spoke of how quiet the Archinian army had been since King Kane had disappeared, the war for conquest of Archin seemingly at a pause with the crowning of the new king. Her head bobbed in agreement every so often. Fat spat in the open flame as it dripped from the meat, but she didn't flinch. Small burn scars dotted her hands like tiny freckles.

I walked confidently up to the stall, hands loose by my side. Nothing quite screamed thief like a slinking body or hidden hands. None of the trio looked up, even as my fingers slipped over the edge of the stall and pulled a thin, still warm flatbread free of its home. Melted butter greased my fingers. I took a small bite as I turned away.

My sure steps faltered as the wind brought the younger of the two men's words to my ears.

'... completely healed with a single look,' he was saying, voice holding the rasp of a pipe user.

My feet stopped entirely. *Healed.* There were only three I knew who were Gifted in healing. Callum, who, based on rumours, had not deigned to use his Gift since he had taken the throne. Liam, whose Gift was pitifully weak in comparison. And the god who'd granted them each their power. I took another bite of the food, pulling a slip of paper from my pocket as though I was reading it. It was blank. A way to seem busy to not raise suspicions.

'That's not possible,' the woman argued, a sizzle sounding as meat juices fell on blazing embers. 'Even Gifted healers need skin contact.'

I turned slightly, still holding the slip of paper, and, as though it contained directions, let my gaze dart around before settling vaguely on the trio. The older man, bearing the same hooked nose as the younger, shook his head vehemently. 'It's true. Single look, and the woman was cured of the cough that was sure to kill her.' He leant forward conspiratorially, eyes flashing with the gleam of knowing. 'She wasn't the only one. A lad, no older than nine, suddenly walking after a fall that was sure to spell his death. And a farmer who was trampled by a bull, healed of his crushed chest.'

A chill swept down the back of my neck, dread tightening in a noose. I stepped closer to the three, slipping the flatbread in a pocket. 'Excuse me,' I interrupted, keeping my voice as soft as its hoarseness would allow. 'You said there were some healings occurring?'

The older man looked me over sceptically. The younger one had no such qualms. He smiled, eyes sliding a little low for my liking before rising once more. I held back the urge to slam my fist into one of those wandering eyes. I needed information. 'Some man has been visiting villages and healing the sick and injured,' he told me.

'Charitable,' I murmured, my nails digging into my skin. 'What did he look like?'

The older man shot me another suspicious look. The younger rambled on. 'He's been covered in gold armour from head to toe. No one knows.' His smile broadened. 'Truly charitable, if he doesn't want any credit.'

Gold was not a colour those aiming to stay away from notice wore. 'No one knows who he is?'

The lady slid their hot wraps across to them, wrapped tight in paper to keep the juices from dripping. The younger bit into his, mouth smeared with thick white yoghurt as he chewed. This time, the older was the one who spoke. 'No.'

Disappointment settled in my stomach. I began to turn away.

'There was something, though.' The words halted my movement. I cocked my head to one side, waiting for the older man to continue. His eyes darted down to where my fingers had unconsciously curled around the hilt of one of my many blades. The man's throat bobbed as he swallowed hard, but he continued, nonetheless. 'His eyes. They were the only part visible. They were said to be made of pure gold.'

I didn't know how long I wandered. There was a vague awareness of the sun dipping lower until the slums were burnished in a golden glow. A sense of shoulders ploughing into me and curses thrown my way. The scents of the market were replaced at some point by that of human filth as I crossed into the shadows of the city. Yet it was all distant, my mind and body seeming disconnected. I could only focus on one thing.

They were said to be gold.

I'd never met a mortal who could heal without touching, nor had I met any mortals with eyes of gold. But a divine being with eyes of that colour? I'd seen that. And while I'd never seen Vitus' power in action, I had no doubt he could heal simply by willing it.

Every turn of a corner, I'd question my decision to send Deana away. I hated the idea of crawling back to Callum. Of accepting his help. But perhaps all I was doing was hiding from a chance at vengeance.

I'd managed, for at least the past month, to build a mental barrier against the thoughts that threatened to invade. Every so often, those insidious thoughts slipped through the cracks, even though most of the time, I managed to force them back. I'd particularly guarded my mind against the four that had vanished from the court room that day.

Liam, the prince who had betrayed me and then torn out my heart.

Dearil, the father I'd never wanted, whom I knew had never wanted me.

King Kane, who had enslaved me for years.

And the god, Vitus, who now enslaved his body.

With one rumour, the barrier I had fortified threatened to crash down.

If Vitus was out healing random people in the streets, I doubted it was for anything as straightforward as charity. I had heard a little of him from Dearil in the past, and had told stories of him myself. And I knew that it was his fault that I no longer told the stories that once came as naturally as talking. That there was no longer anyone I cared to tell stories to. Now he was out there, getting up to gods-knew-what, while I let my sister's memory wither and die. While I chose to ignore the offer of a lesser evil and allowed the greater one to run rampant.

It was that thought, the way it made me shrivel up inside, that devoured me with heavy blackness.

My fault. My fault. My fault.

The familiar refrain that had been beating its steady rhythm the past few months roared in my head, drowning out the noise. I walked through a haze of people and colour without truly seeing any of it. Vitus was out there, plotting, while all I did was wither.

I'd ignored Deana's offer. Placed my loathing of Callum over the vengeance for Cassie's death. *Selfish,* a voice whispered, and it sounded an awful lot like my sister's.

By some miracle, my feet managed to lead me to where I needed to go. Jaxon stood waiting when I turned down the street to The Den. He nodded his greeting. 'You're late.'

I said nothing.

Jaxon lifted his hands, yellow sparking. I pushed past him, not allowing his Gift to touch me.

'Chiara!' he barked. 'I haven't done—'

'I don't care.'

Jaxon stepped around me, blocking my entrance. 'I do.' His eyes flashed with irritation. He was not used to being ignored. 'If they see you like this, someone might one day recognise you and seek revenge. And if you're with me, they'll connect the dots. They'll come after—'

'I don't care.'

Jaxon huffed, folding his arms. 'Stop being difficult. It's just an illusion. An illusion that will save your lovely head from being hunted down as well as mine.'

There was nothing in me, no anger, no rage, no bloodlust, *nothing*, as I lifted my eyes to his. 'I. Don't. Care.'

Whatever he saw in my face, it was enough to make his own expression gentle. 'Chiara—' Jaxon took a step forward as though to offer some meagre platitude. It was a mistake. Quick as a wraith, I spun past him, threw open the door and stalked into the arena. With a muttered curse, he followed. He would do nothing to stop me now. Not when we were in full sight of the crowd. As they always did, the lights beat down with intensity on my cloaked back. The crowd was silent. It may have been the scars that littered my visible skin. It may be that some of the soldiers lounging in the middle rows recognised me. It may have simply been the mix of cheap and expensive spirits that many had imbibed.

It didn't matter.

All that mattered was that I'd failed my sister. Gods, I couldn't even *think* her name. And it wasn't just that those who were responsible for her death still walked the earth. It was all the times before that – all the times I had betrayed my care for her in front of the king. All the times I'd visited her instead of protecting her by cutting ties completely. All the times I had thought that maybe I could become worthy of her love. She had died because I cared for her. Died because I had trusted the wrong men. If she'd seen me as the monster I was – if I'd let her see that side of me, let it scare her away – then she would still be alive. I had failed her, and someone had to suffer for it.

I just hadn't decided yet if it would be my opponent, or if it would be me.

'Careful tonight,' Jaxon murmured as he kept a careful distance from me. 'I received word that a certain right-hand woman of the king was involved in tonight's selection of your opponent.' I assumed I was supposed to follow his gaze as it cut towards the audience. I didn't. 'Whenever that woman meddles, trouble follows.'

There was a beat of silence. I didn't bother repeating my earlier words. From the sigh Jaxon gave as he turned back to the door, he already knew that I had no interest in who'd meddled in my choice of opponent.

The silence stretched thin as we waited, and waited, and waited. Jaxon lounged at the door, eyes narrowing with every passing second. The silence broke, murmurings beginning to echo through the arena. I stood still. I would not leave until my knuckles were bloody.

'Where are they?' Jaxon hissed between gritted teeth. His fingers twitched at his side. He spoke a moment too soon. As soon as the hissed words had exited his mouth, the door opposite cracked open. A man strolled through, unbothered by his tardiness.

My initial instinct was disappointment. The man was unassuming in size and looks. He was about a head taller than me, and twice the girth. While muscled, much of it was covered by ample softness and padding. His skin was tanned and weathered, as though he spent hours in the sun each day. Garbed in practical clothes – a light cotton shirt, dark brown pants and boots slathered with dried mud – he looked better suited to a farm than The Den. Before I could write him off, my Gift surged. It raced through my veins with far more vehemence than normal. It seemed it was hungry.

My eyes met my opponent's as I clenched my fists, concealing the beginnings of silver threading upon my palms. Silver I hadn't willingly called to the surface. The numbness cracked, a coil of dread forming.

When I met his eyes, though, I understood. Eyes that looked almost brown in the darkness, until they were caught by the Illusioned lights. Then, my breath hitched and my hands trembled – with fear, rage or re-remembered grief, I couldn't tell. Because those eyes weren't just brown.

They were fractured with gold.

Chapter Six

'What's wrong with his eyes?' Jaxon breathed behind me. Tension twisted through his words as though he, too, understood what gold signified. Understood and loathed it.

'It's just a fancy new drug,' I said as I focused on the grotesque face before me. I hoped I was right. I didn't want to think about what else might cause the gold webbing that fractured the brown. The sheen speared straight through the whites of his eyes, edging onto his skin like gilded veins. His lips peeled back to reveal blood-speckled teeth beneath. Gold grew in his gums. My dread deepened, sending my heart thudding in my chest.

'There's no drug in this city or any others that can do that,' Jaxon murmured.

I steadied my feet, curling my fingers until my nails met my palm. 'It has to be a drug,' I said, the words scratching against my throat. 'What else could cause such a thing?'

Jaxon did not reply.

'I warned you that you were to die soon, little raven.' There was no inflection in the man's voice, no lilt or emotion. Just endless cold.

The Broken

Little raven. The words hit me like a fist, sending me staggering back a step. Jaxon's hand pressed to my back. A silent warning, no doubt, that I was not to exit before the fight had finished. Especially not when I had entered without one of his illusions. For a moment, I considered damning The Den's rules. There was only one time I had heard that title spoken. Words that had fallen from a god's mouth as he'd smiled at me, my sister's body at his feet and my father in chains by his side. Vitus.

'Who are you?' I breathed, the words carrying through the silence to the man before me. The gruesome smile stretched wider. Yet it never quite reached those gold-stained eyes.

'I am a farmer,' he intoned. Severe shadows circled his eyes. His skin was stretched thin across bone as though he hadn't had a meal in weeks. Deep red combined with dirt was smeared on his shirt.

My breathing quickened as I stared at him. At the corpse-like pallor of his skin. The words the boy had spoken earlier came back to me. *A farmer who was trampled by a bull, healed of his crushed chest.* Healed by a mysterious golden-eyed man. My Gift pulsed in my veins as though confirming the reason it had surged so heartily at the sight of the man. Not because of the life it could devour. Because of what it *couldn't* find.

This man did not live.

It made no sense. Yet, my Gift thrummed with what almost felt like approval at the conclusion I'd come to.

My mouth grew dry as I asked, 'Who do you follow?'

The laugh that came out of the gaping mouth sent icy claws raking down my spine. 'You already know that.' The farmer tilted his head. 'Would you like to talk to him, little raven?'

The only other creature who'd called me by that name.

'Vitus.' The name was so soft, I didn't think it would reach the farmer's ears. Yet from the tilt of his head and the satisfied gleam in his eyes, it had.

'Correct.' This time, it wasn't the rasp of an ageing farmer. It was a deeper voice, one filled with power and malice. A god's voice.

A shudder ran through me. This was nothing like when Dearil had possessed a mortal to speak to me. Not when golden light seeped under the man's flesh, as though threatening to split him into pieces. 'Why are you here?'

That horrid laugh came again. 'I told you that day. You must die. You do not merit enough attention for me to do it personally.'

'Why now?'

'Why not?' he challenged. Not an answer, not truly.

'Answer me.' I stepped forward, hand falling to my dagger.

'I think not.' He swept his hand around, gesturing at the audience. 'Our crowd grows hungry for blood, and I grow bored of wasting time.'

My body stiffened. 'Then fight,' I challenged, pulling my dagger free of its scabbard. Any lingering numbness was gone. I had decided.

Before setting eyes on them, I'd been considering letting the other fighter win. Letting myself see how close their beating could take me to death. But I couldn't let that happen now. Not if it meant letting this follower of a cruel god have the satisfaction of ending me, as Vitus had ended my sister. The farmer didn't lose his smile as I lunged at him, swinging the dagger in what should have been a death blow. Simple, clean, to the neck. Instead of ducking or offering a counter-attack, he lifted a hand.

The blade drove itself into the soft flesh with a wet *thud*. The smile didn't flicker. The man did not falter or rear back. Instead, he curled his fingers slowly around the blade. Let it slice deeper into his flesh. My eyes widened. I tried to pull it back, but the strength of the farmer was too much. Blood flowed slowly – too slowly for the size of the wound. I stared, horror mounting at the flecks of gold invading the red. A faint stench of rot rose as the blood spilt onto the floor.

Drip. Drip. Drip.

I shuddered at the sound, at the memories of blood dripping down the stairs, then pooling on the ground of the throne room, and soaking into my trousers as I cradled my sister in my arms. Nausea swelled. I swallowed, fighting against the horrors that awaited in my memory. The farmer's unnatural eyes gleamed in triumph, as though he could see exactly what was invading my mind. Slowly, deliberately, he lifted his other hand. I scrambled back, relinquishing my hold on the weapon. His uninjured hand closed around the hilt. With barely a wince, the farmer sharply drew both hands down.

The blade snapped clean in two.

'I wished to thank you.' It was eerie, hearing such an ancient, fathomless voice from such an ordinary body. He tore out the half of the dagger still stuck in his hand. More blood dribbled out.

'I don't want gratitude from you.' My fists curled at my sides. The farmer's smile was pure malice. 'I have never done, and never will do, anything to *deserve* gratitude from you.'

'Of course you did. For not killing your own sister before I could, and for the magic you saved for me. Such a pity that your sister had to pay the price.'

For a second, I froze. Then, a tidal wave of blind, unadulterated rage swept through me. With a wordless cry of fury, I thrust forward. There was no blade in my hand, no thoughts except a mindless need to make him suffer. I would rip out this man's heart with my bare fingers, and when the time came, I'd shove it down Vitus's throat. I would carve out the gold-veined eyes and wear them as a trophy. I would—

My fist was centimetres from his face when his hand clamped around my wrist. The gilded threads in his eyes flared with unnatural light. The smile dropped away. Gold gathered at his fingertips, the vibrancy of it stinging my eyes.

Then, there was pain. It was worse than any knife wound, worse than a whip to the back or a fist to the face. Agony swept through me, setting every inch of me on fire. Inside, my Gift curled into a ball, so small and tight I had no hope of reaching it, even if I wished to. And still, the anger, the hatred, surged and consumed me.

'That Gifted boy of mine reminded me of this little trick. The power of death and life cannot coexist in one body.' He lifted his hand, tilting it under the Illusioned lights. I heard nothing beyond. Could see nothing beyond him, too. 'Though this body doesn't hold my power quite so well.'

He stared at me, as though expecting an answer. All I could give him was a hissed-out breath of agony.

'I've been testing it on Dearil. Like father like daughter, it seems,' he said, and I hissed out a breath of pain between my teeth. I couldn't reply, couldn't even shut my eyes. My will had been torn away by the torture. 'Perhaps I should visit that useless boy. Give him my *personal* thanks, particularly after he refused to bend to my will like the other Gifted prince. What was his name?' The pain grew hotter. If I could still move, I might've clawed at my skin to dig out whatever was forcing this suffering on me. 'Callum, was it?'

The name sent a spear of clarity through me.

No. That loathing of Callum belonged to me. Not Vitus. That rage was enough to yank me through the pain.

A surge of energy bolted through me. I tore myself away from his grip and fell to my knees. Silence drenched the space, the crowd's clamour strangely quiet. My eyes lifted to the farmer's. He was smiling again, circling. A spoilt child staring at a newly discovered plaything.

'Such a pity you are a stubborn little creature. Otherwise, you, too, could have joined my growing devotees.' *Devotees*. Vitus was the god of life. There was no telling how many fools would be willing to kneel before him. 'Even if there is only a trace of purity in your mortal-tainted blood, I could have made an exception for you. You could have had a place in the realm I will remake.'

I remained kneeling, fingers pressing hard into the stony ground. I knew what would come next. The only end Vitus could deliver to me.

I was going to die. And there would be no one who would shed tears over it. No one who would mourn me.

I almost smiled.

'Get up.' I twisted to glare behind me. It was Jaxon, who was half leaning towards me, as though about to leap forward and haul me to my feet. Gold light shimmered behind him, drenching the space. 'Get *up*, Chiara.'

Was he, even now, calculating the loss of profit my death would bring? Bitter amusement nestled itself next to my pain and anger. 'You'll find someone else.'

Jaxon only shook his head, face drawn. He opened his mouth. A golden knife flashed by me. It slammed into the stone by his head, the hilt quivering with the force with which it was thrown. 'Stay out of this, boy, or I'll let *her* know exactly where you are.'

Another knife whizzed by, leaving a stinging line across my cheek. A lock of hair fell to the ground. Spinning around, I bit down on a hiss of torment. Warmth spilt down my cheek, red spattering the ground at my knees. Vitus smiled down at me.

'So much weaker than I hoped for from someone of Dearil's blood. I would have thought you would last longer than a minute. Maybe if you had been trained as a god rather than as a mortal...' He crouched down, eyes level with mine. Fetid breath slammed into me, nauseatingly strong. 'No matter.'

His hand snapped forward, thick fingers circling my neck. They squeezed. Air grew thin as I clawed at his unflinching hand.

His smile stretched, the gold brightening, and then the pain found me once more. The tightness at my throat disappeared beneath the flood of agony. The only warning I had that I was in desperate need of air was the dots appearing before my eyes.

Between the spots of hazy darkness, the farmer leant in, his cold lips brushing my cheek. 'Naruzia will be the first to fall. And with it, their king.'

Callum.

My Gift roared to life, tugged awake by the thread of hatred and fury and so much more that entangled me with Callum. *Mine,* it seemed to snarl in feral fury. If he was to die, then it would be at my hand. His soul was mine to send to the Dark. Not Vitus's. My fingers twitched under the overwhelming pain. Twitched, then lifted to a second dagger at my hip.

I smiled with feral triumph as the farmer's eyes widened.

It was surprisingly easy to drive the dagger into the farmer's heart. Flesh gave way, rancid-smelling blood dripping onto me. The fingers around my neck slackened. I shoved harder. Heard bones crack. Meeting his eyes, I twisted. The farmer slammed onto the stone ground as I yanked the dagger free then drove it down again. More blood – too little for any living body – trickled from the wound. And in those last moments, where the gold began to relinquish its grasp on the man, I made sure to keep smiling. Made sure the god watching from beyond the body before me saw the promise in my eyes.

You're next.

And then the gold was gone. The flesh beneath me crumpled inwards, skin wrinkling and greying, chest caving. The stench of rot grew thicker. Wrenching my blade free and scrambling to my feet, I stared down at the body, my smile fading as confusion took its place. This was not a fresh corpse. At best, it was days old, already showing signs of decay. Swallowing back nausea, I turned away, fingers pressing to the throbbing at my throat.

The noise of the crowd rushed back in, the silence shattered by mutterings as eyes peered down at us. Hands grasped at my shoulders. I tensed, my fingers tightening on the dagger. Before I could swing it, Jaxon was spinning me around, his features pallid. 'What in the gods' names was that?'

'I killed him. You get your winnings.' I shoved his hands away. I didn't dare slide my dagger away. Not when it was the only thing keeping my hands from trembling.

'Damn the winnings!'

'You never pass on coin.' My voice echoed in my ears.

Jaxon ignored my words. 'He barely touched you and you crumpled. There was a golden barrier around you and it didn't seem like the audience could see or hear a damned thing. So, I'll ask again – what was that?'

I eyed the crowds. I'd barely noticed the silence throughout the fight. All I'd been able to focus on was the noise. It seemed the god had managed to block off our conversation completely.

The hair raised at the back of my neck. This was what a god was capable of without even being present. What I'd allowed to grow unfettered as I drowned myself in my grief.

'Well?' Jaxon prompted.

'What do you want me to say, Jaxon?' I pushed past him, headed for the door. His light tread followed. 'I did what you wanted. I killed the man. Did I not perform enough for you?' The trembling had begun in my hands. I shoved my dagger into its scabbard before pushing my hands into my pockets. Vitus had finally come, and I hadn't been prepared. Had *let* myself be unprepared. Because it was easier to give up than to avenge my sister's death. Easier to avoid Callum than chase retribution.

I stepped out into the dark night air. Deana was already waiting, as she had been after my last few fights, looking at me expectantly.

A certain right-hand woman of the king was involved in tonight's selection of your opponent, Jaxon had said. Nothing seemed to escape Deana's notice. I had no doubt she'd known exactly what manner of person she'd selected. Had guessed who he'd devoted himself to. Had maybe even known the rage his words might ignite.

I stopped before her, Jaxon halting a few steps behind. She tilted her head, hair falling over her shoulder. 'What will it be tonight? Leave me alone? Go away? I hope the Dark takes Callum and everyone he loves? Does he want me to kill you, or is he just stupid? I'm going to kill the gods-damned king and every last one of his gutless soldiers unless he stops sending you after me?' She smirked. 'That one was my favourite.'

Her smile grew as I shook my head, as though she'd expected my response. Planned for it.

And then I uttered the words that I had no doubt I'd come to regret in the near future. Even so, there was no other choice. Not if I wanted to find passage to the godly realm and discover a way to kill Vitus.

'None of those,' I said. 'I'll come.'

Chapter Seven

When Deana insisted I come to the palace immediately, my daggers came out. I may have acquiesced to Callum's demands, but I'd be damned if I did so with grace. Jaxon had taken it upon himself to follow me home. He now stood, straighter than I'd ever seen him, in my combined kitchen, bedroom and living room. Every so often, he'd give a disdainful sniff while staring at a build-up of dust or a heap of dirty clothes. Nothing belonging to him brushed the walls.

I couldn't fault him for it. He hadn't been wrong when he'd labelled my place a hovel. I could and did, however, fault him for being a raging pain in my ass.

'So, you're trying to get into the godly realm?' Jaxon asked, staring disdainfully down at a dirtied dish lying discarded on the floor.

I glanced over to him, waiting for him to tell me I was insane. If I'd heard someone else tell me they were trying to attempt the impossible, I'd be laughing in their face. Yet Jaxon didn't seem surprised. 'I'm not sure how that's any of your business.'

'Everything that happens this side of the city is my business.'

He eyed me curiously. 'What other secrets are you hiding? I thought your little trick with death – and where that Gift came from – was the extent of it, but it seems my employees have become slack in gathering information.'

'You know where my Gift came from?' I asked sharply as I shoved a bottle into a threadbare bag. It clinked as it landed on the five daggers, six throwing knives, and one, particularly long, lethal knife I'd already stashed in there.

His smile was slow. 'Of course. Only one god can Gift death.'

I stared at him, debating whether to ask whether he knew the exact nature of my relationship with Dearil. The slyness of his smile made me think I'd only get something elusive in response, so instead I asked, 'Why are you here?'

'I would never turn down an invite from you, dear Chiara.'

I threw an incredulous look his way. 'You weren't invited.'

His lips curved downwards as he pressed a hand to his chest, mock-hurt entering his expression. 'And that was very rude of you. I *should've* been invited. Everyone enjoys my company.'

'You can keep my winnings,' I offered as I secured my bag, then tacked on, 'and all the ones you previously cut off my wage.'

'I'm fine.' He picked up a discarded bottle, wrinkling his nose as it hung from two fingers. Only a few drops of liquor were left in it.

'Fine.' I strapped on the last of my blades. 'I'll pay you to go away.'

He looked pointedly around the room. 'With what coin?'

I shrugged. 'I might have some stashed away.'

'With the amount you've been drinking, there's not a chance.' He swiped the bag from my hand, slinging it over his shoulder before I could protest. He strode towards the door with all the confidence of a criminal.

'What are you doing?' I chased after him onto the quiet streets. It was well past midnight, though noises came from most directions. From some, singing and revelry; from others, shouts and curses. The slums rarely had a dull moment once night had fallen.

Jaxon grinned, Illusioned lantern light cutting across his features. 'Why, coming with you, of course.'

'No,' I snapped, grasping hold of the bag. Jaxon's grip didn't budge. 'Why would you?'

The smile dropped from his face. His eyes hardened. 'I heard the name of the god in the arena. I'm afraid his little barrier didn't impact me as much as he likely wanted it to.'

My chest tightened, feet faltering. 'So?'

He stopped so abruptly I nearly walked straight past him. His hand curled around my upper arm, pulling me to a halt. Irritation swirled. 'I've chopped a hand off for less,' I warned.

He ignored me. 'You're not the only one wronged by that god.' The lack of jest in his voice unnerved me. When joking, he was a ruthless bastard. When he was like this … I shuddered to think. 'And you're not the only one seeking vengeance.'

A hint of curiosity pricked at me. Part of me wanted to know more. The rest didn't want to add the knowledge of another's pain to my own. If I didn't know, I didn't care. It was as simple as that. And this miserable isolation – that was the least of what I deserved. Instead of asking, I said, 'Who says I'm going to the palace to get vengeance?'

'I saw the look in your eyes. I've heard rumours and whispers of the Archinian prince, of King Kane and what happened that day in the throne room.' His eyes softened a fraction. 'I am truly so—'

'Don't.' My hand lifted in a sharp movement, cutting off the apology. Sympathy or pity for that day didn't belong to me.

'Besides, it's either you're seeking vengeance or you're wanting to get to the palace for quality time with a certain handsome king.' Jaxon's serious expression turned to a sly grin.

I scowled. 'Our young king certainly has a keen interest in you, doesn't he?'

The curse I shot his way was so colourful it had Jaxon bursting out with laughter. I glared until he quietened down. 'They might arrest you on sight. You do realise you're a criminal, don't you?'

Jaxon sidestepped a body on the road with ease. In the darkness of the night, it was difficult to tell if it was alive or not. Neither of us bothered to check. Either the person was dead, or they would be by morning if they continued laying prostrate like that. Not our problem. 'A criminal with a deal with the crown.'

I raised an inquisitive eyebrow. All he gave me was a secretive smile.

'Sly bastard,' I muttered.

'Look.' Jaxon held up his hands in a show of congeniality. 'How about we make a deal. You allow me to come along.' He glanced down meaningfully at the dagger I had just freed and was twisting idly in one hand. 'And I promise to steal as much of the king's belongings as I can?'

A reluctant smile forced itself onto my lips. I turned my head to hide it. 'Why would I be interested in that?'

'Think about it.' His arm slung casually around my shoulders. For a moment, I let it stay before pushing him away. 'There are undoubtedly precious items there. Things that once belonged to King Kane, and now belong to King Callum. Wouldn't it be like getting revenge against two at once?'

'And how much do you think you can get before you're caught?'

'Enough to cripple the royal vaults for years to come.' There was no jest in his words, no uncertainty.

I allowed my lips to turn upwards. Perhaps I could make use of him in the palace. If not as an ally, then as someone with loose morals and as little care for royalty as I had. I held out a hand for Jaxon to shake. 'Deal.'

The walk to the palace was a quick one, with Jaxon talking the whole way and me steadfastly ignoring him. The weapons we both wore kept most pickpockets and merchants far away from us, and pedestrians gave us a healthy berth. Jaxon led the way through the maze of the slum, his confidence remaining with him as we crossed over to where alleys widened into open spaces and neatly kept gardens.

'You should lose the scowl,' Jaxon said as we passed a couple strolling under the warmth of the sunlight. 'People might get the wrong idea.'

I shot said scowl at the couple as the woman gave a haughty sniff. She blanched, turning towards her partner. Moments later, their steps quickened as they hurried along. 'What wrong idea would that be?'

'That you're marching to the palace to declare war on our beloved king.'

I tilted my head, considering. 'Would killing the king be a declaration of war?'

Jaxon raised his brows as he glanced at me. 'I'm sure you can figure out that one for yourself.'

I smiled, and I could've sworn he shuddered as we came to a stop before the structure that loomed over Alluvite.

The palace was as much of a behemoth as I remembered. It was made of white stone as far as the eye could see, with golden veins snaking upwards, which sent shivers of unease through me. The guards at the gates eyed us warily until I gave my name before stepping aside. One, a young woman with suspicious eyes that countered her bright smile, stared as we made for the marble steps that led to the wooden door. Four guarded the doors. Once, there would've been far more.

My smile vanished. I doubted there were many soldiers to spare after the loss of life in the throne room.

Skulls shattering. Blood pooling. Eyes staring. And one, small neck bleeding and bleeding and bleeding and—

'Chiara.' The snap of Jaxon's voice and the brush of his fingers against my shoulder brought me back. 'You okay?'

'Let's go.' I pulled away from him, forcing my shaking hands into fists.

I focused on the stairs up to the palace entrance. All I had to do was walk in there. That was all. Walk in, meet with the king, and decide whether the day would end in blood. And after all that, figure out how, exactly, I would enter the godly realm and slay a god. If I was lucky, there may even be time to ruin a king along the way.

I steadied my breathing. Jaxon kept stride with me. The moon was slowly sinking in the sky, stars winking out one by one as they felt the threat of the coming day looming. The pebbles beneath my feet crackled as we stepped over them, a few rolling away from my dragging steps. I focused on their movement, the predictability of each step helping to ground me. I had survived a vengeful god. I had faced down two princes – one, for whom I had my own plans of revenge – after Vitus was dealt with – and the other, for whom there was a distinct possibility of death today. I could walk into a palace.

I could, if my legs would just move.

I swallowed, pressing my fists into the sides of my legs. I had frozen a few steps away from the stairs. My traitorous legs refused to follow my commands to move. It wasn't just the press of one memory bearing down on me, though. It was the weight of them all. That day had cracked something open deep inside of me. Something that I had fought tooth and nail to keep closed. Memories both sweet and bitter mingled together in a suffocating crush.

The Broken

The day my adoptive mother had thrown me at the feet of the king and begged for me to be taken away.

Holding my sister and telling her stories until she fell asleep in my arms.

The small twinges of resentment that her existence bound me so tightly to a king I hated.

The first time I held a sword and was beaten for not winning against a veteran fighter.

Watching the prince with his shadowy Gift heal a prisoner, just so he could be tortured again.

The first lashing I had, which left a set of whipping scars on my back.

The cakes my sister handed me whenever I came back to the palace.

Pretending for a bit that I could be allowed a friend in the Archinian prince, Liam.

The most recent lashing, and the first time I had felt the pain of Vitus's Gift warring with Dearil's blood.

My brief belief in the small piece of trust that had blossomed between Callum and me.

The crush of that belief as Liam slashed my sister's throat and Callum let it happen.

'Kill him if you want,' Jaxon whispered. His words were quiet enough that the approaching guard couldn't hear him. 'I'll take the rest of them.'

'And then leave me to hang for the crime?'

Jaxon's grin was answer enough.

'State your business.' The guard who stepped forward was dressed in all black, a wolf's head embroidered into her clothes. I vaguely recognised her reticent glare as the guard who had greeted Liam, Callum and I when we had appeared at the palace three months ago. She eyed my blades as mistrustfully now as she had then. This time, though, there were no attempts to remove them.

She was a fool. I was far more likely to use them now that the hostage who King Kane had possessed to keep me at bay was gone. I didn't answer. Jaxon eyed me for a moment before jumping in with a charming smile. 'Chiara Halnea and her companion. Here to see the king, on orders of the king.'

At the sight of Jaxon's flashing white teeth contrasting with his smooth olive skin, and the nobleman's crest on his expensive jacket, which certainly did not belong to him, the woman flushed. She bowed low. 'Apologies, my lord.'

Without removing his eyes from her, Jaxon nudged an elbow into my side. 'Hear that, Chiara? *Lord.*'

'Not a chance,' I replied, shoving him away. 'You're arrogant enough as you are.'

The woman straightened. 'Please, continue. Lady Deana will be there to meet you.'

I masked my surprise. *Lady* Deana. Unusual for someone with a title to choose a life as a guard. 'Thank you.' I tugged at Jaxon's arm as he remained in place, smile curving up in a way that could only be described as flirtatious. 'Come *on*.'

He grumbled as we went along, the Illusioned jacket disappearing.

'She was twice your age, you idiot,' I huffed at him, pulling him along as a mother might to a resistant toddler.

'So?'

For the second time that night, I cursed him out so soundly he grinned.

As promised, Deana was waiting for us within the sterile hallways of the palace. She'd traded her cloak for a regal cape, attached at the shoulders of her uniform. 'Callum's waiting for you.' Her lips curled downwards as she glared over at Jaxon. 'You, I don't recall inviting.'

He patted my shoulder. 'I received a personal invitation from the lovely Chiara.'

I batted his hand away.

Deana gave me a long look, before sighing and asking, 'Really? You chose to bring *him?*'

Having no desire to respond to the warmth in her voice as she spoke to me, I shrugged. Deana hesitated for a moment before turning. She nodded to two guards who stood watch at the end of the corridor. They swiftly opened a set of wooden doors, ushering us further into the palace.

I eyed the pair as we passed. I didn't recognise either of them. Their features were young – far younger than I remembered any of the palace guards being. Their uniform was plainer than Deana's, too, missing the golden embroidery and fitted coat she wore.

'Brent and Luc are two of our newer recruits,' she said, noting where my attention had turned. 'Most of the palace guards are.'

When I didn't say anything, Jaxon asked, 'Why would new recruits be assigned to palace duty? I thought this was meant to be the most desirable duty a guard could have.'

Deana shot him a glare as we rounded a corner, the stark white of the walls as overwhelming as it had always been. The few staff we passed hurriedly stepped aside, bowing their heads as they did so. 'What would you know about duty?'

He shrugged, his fingers skimming over a plaster-head of King Kane, perched upon a small table. 'More than you'd think. I used to be a guard in the eastern empire.'

Deana drew to an abrupt halt. She swung around, planting a hand on her hip. 'You told me you joined a pirate crew.'

'When I left Axania.' Jaxon eyed the king's head, as though

deciding whether it was worth stealing. He flicked its forehead, shaking his head. 'Why would anyone have such a garish thing made?'

'And you said you were once a blacksmith.'

Turning back to Deana, Jaxon grinned. 'What can I say? I'm multi-talented.'

'You're no older than twenty-five, and you're telling me you've worked three different jobs? Ones which require years of training and skill?' Deana folded her arms, the deep scowl on her features hinting at a history that went deeper than the occasional run-in. 'The only thing you're talented at is lying with that silver tongue of yours.'

The smile on Jaxon's face grew more devious. I stepped in before he could say anything that would end up with one or both of us kicked out of the palace. 'Why the young guards?'

Deana eyed Jaxon for a heartbeat longer before turning her attention back to me. 'We've had to intensify the training of all our new recruits. Too many were sent to war before the Archin royal family called for retreat and locked down their borders. Few have any desire to serve the son of the man who sent them onto those bloody battlefields. It would be dangerous to have men with no loyalty guarding Callum's back. So, I selected the best amongst those who had been training to be soldiers.'

'And the previous palace guards?' I asked as we began walking once more.

'They grew lazy under King Kane. And half of them ended up dead or missing, anyway.' She gave me a pointed look.

I shrugged. 'If they were that important, Callum should've kept his people away from me.'

We fell silent after that. At first, the path we took was easily recognisable. Each step had my chest tightening and my nails digging into my palm. I hated this palace. Hated the life I'd lived here – the mistakes I'd made and the people who'd guided me into making them. The first door to the left would take us the servant's way to the kitchens, where my sister once worked. Three twists along, and the passage on the right took us to a locked door and twisting stairs to the dungeons. Two left and three right turns later, we were near where I had stayed in my brief intervals back at the palace. It was when we passed through an unassuming wooden door, guarded by two more soft-featured guards, that I crossed into unmapped territory. These were areas I had never been granted the privilege of accessing.

'We're not going to the throne room?' I forced nonchalance into my voice as I stared up at the vaulted ceilings. During the day, light would flow freely through the corridor from a large window at the opposite end. Outside, Illusioned lanterns lit up a neatly kept garden. My gaze drifted down, over stern-faced portraits of six different men, all bearing the same thin lips and narrowed eyes. The previous kings of the empire.

'Callum thought you would prefer somewhere else. Besides, he hasn't stepped foot in there since … well, since that day.'

I glanced over at Deana, frowning at the complex mix of emotions on her face. I would not ask why Callum would not set foot in that cursed room. I would not care.

'Where are we going, then?' I asked, just as Jaxon meandered over to where a pedestal sat below one of the king's portraits. A ruby-encrusted brooch sat atop a plush velvet cushion. A relic of some sort?

'The king's wing,' Deana replied before grabbing and gripping Jaxon's wrist. He snatched his hand back from where he'd been reaching for the brooch, rubbing the spot she'd pinched and looking at her pitifully. Her eyes turned icy and her fingers twitched towards the garrotte wrapped loosely around her neck. 'Callum wishes to meet you here.'

I narrowed my eyes at the blind trust she – *he* – was giving me in telling me exactly where Callum slept. It would be easy to get past any defences they had in place, to creep into the king's chambers, watch the way the sharp planes of his face eased while he slept... I shook myself, ridding my brain of the image of him. Of course, I would watch his face to make sure he was asleep before slitting his throat. Nothing more.

The meaning behind the words caught up with me. I stopped suddenly. Deana and Jaxon continued on a few steps before stopping themselves. They turned to stare at me.

'You surely can't mean Cal— the king is meeting us in his *bedchamber?*'

Deana smirked. Jaxon smirked more. It was a good thing they hated each other. Otherwise, they'd make a formidable, merciless team.

'What are you worried about?' Jaxon teased, smirk firmly in place.

'His receiving chambers are just before his actual chambers,' Deana explained.

My cheeks heated. I cursed my disobedient body. Even if my mind had latched onto hatred, it had not forgotten the way his mere presence had set my heart pounding, my blood heating, with more than just anger.

He was nothing but a liar. He'd broken a vow. I would remember that. I *had* to.

Taking pity on me, Deana explained, 'Receiving chambers – it's where he holds all his meetings,' before coming to a stop before a set of doors. She smiled at the three standing there – two women and one man. The tallest of the women snapped a salute. 'Ma'am.'

'Any disturbances, Kailey?' Deana asked.

Kailey shook her head, short brown hair swaying with the movement. One hand rested on the hilt of a sheathed sword. 'No. His Majesty is meeting with Commander Lena now. He also met with the head of the merchant's guild earlier, to discuss rationing of any goods that come from Archin and how to distribute them.

And Lady Rebekah came for an audience earlier – something about the trade routes being blocked between Carishmere and Alluvite so she couldn't get her shipment of silk.'

Deana sighed, her fingers pinching the bridge of her nose. 'We're at a standstill from a years' long war, there've been reports of strange deaths around Naruzia, and *that's* what she came to His Majesty about?' She paused, then lowered her hand before asking, 'Did she leave ... alive?'

The shorter woman rubbed the back of her neck. 'She was alive, but...' A hint of a smile crossed her face as the male guard let out a choked sound, a hand flying up to cover his mouth. 'There were a fair few tears.'

Deana groaned. 'He's meant to be making allies, not more enemies. And you, Arley? Anything to report?'

The man, Arley, shifted. 'Lord Kyron demanded another audience. He wants His Majesty to reopen the investigation into his son's death.'

I stiffened, recognising the lord's name. I remembered his son well – an ass who had ended up as a pile of ashes. One whose disappearance led to the execution of my unit.

Jaxon shot me a curious look, and before Deana could interrogate the guards any further, a female voice from inside the room said, 'As you command, Your Majesty.'

The doors swung open. A tall woman stepped out, her shorn head accentuating sharp features. She bowed at the waist to Deana. 'Lady Deana.'

'Commander Lena.' Deana reached forward, grasping the woman's forearm. 'I trust your talks were fruitful?'

Lena nodded. 'We spoke of stationing the city guard. His Majesty suggested—' She broke off, her sharp eyes swinging in my and Jaxon's direction before swinging back to Deana. 'I'll report to you later, Ma'am.'

My brows raised at the respect in Lena's voice as she

addressed Deana. Judging from the golden emblem she wore, matched with the cape attached to the shoulders of her tunic, she was high-ranking. A commander of the guard, perhaps? Yet she spoke to Deana as though she was her superior.

It seemed Deana wasn't merely Callum's right-hand woman because of their friendship. Deana laughed, noting my expression. 'Don't worry about Chiara. She won't spill any of our secrets.'

Lena stiffened. 'Chiara?' Her attention swung back to me, her eyes narrowing. 'Chiara Halnea?'

I inclined my head, smiling sharply at the suspicion in Lena's eyes. 'That would be me.'

'I've heard of you. The one who threatened His Majesty's life.' Her hand dropped to the sword strapped at her side as she shifted back towards the chambers she'd come from. My smile grew. Surely no one could blame me for spilling blood if she swung first.

'I do hope you're not causing problems for my guest, Commander.'

I froze at the familiar voice. The sharpness to it, threaded with an undercurrent of amusement. Lena stiffened, turning towards the still open door. 'Your Majesty—'

'No one is to harm Chiara.' The amusement fell away, replaced by ice. 'You might be the commander of my guard, but you are not irreplaceable. Do not forget that.'

Lena flushed. She stared at the door, then at me, before forcing her hand away from her blade. 'Yes, Your Majesty. My apologies.'

Offering me one final warning glare, Lena turned and strode down the hallway.

Deana grinned at me as she shoved the doors open wider. 'You do love to cause a scene, don't you?'

I didn't respond. I couldn't. All I could focus on was the voice that called out, 'Come in.'

I'd thought I'd carved it into my memory – braced myself for the way it had my heart quickening and my skin prickling. But hearing it in person again – gods, I *hated* it. Hated that it wasn't only fury and loathing that coiled inside me. My fingers fell to the comfort of my blade. Lifting my chin, I stepped past Jaxon and into the luxury of the receiving chamber. I had options. And if I didn't like what Callum had to say, I would kill him.

The room was far lusher than any of the boxes at The Den. It was lined with a plush, grey carpet that ran wall-to-wall. The soft threads gave way beneath my boots, the soles leaving indentations as I walked forward. Deana had already thrown herself across a chaise, head propped up by one arm as she tossed a chocolate she had snagged off a serving platter into her mouth. Two red-velvet armchairs sat next to the chaise.

And opposite, lips twisted in a familiar smirk, green eyes gleaming, Callum sat. He was every bit the indolent king as he quirked an eyebrow.

'Would you care to tell me,' he drawled, 'why all my men are ending up dead?'

Chapter Eight

I folded my arms and glared. 'I warned you not to follow me that night. That goes for your men, too.'

His eyes slid to Deana. 'But not my women?'

My anger churned at the insufferable smirk on his face. I'd forgotten how easily he dug his way under my skin. 'I killed plenty of those, too.'

His smile only grew. 'Oh, I know.' He tilted his head. 'I enjoyed the fingers you left behind from Eva. It was very ... *artistic*.'

'I'm glad you found it entertaining,' I bit out.

'I find everything you do entertaining,' Callum said. 'I always have.'

This was a mistake. I should never have come back here. 'You're as much of a bastard as ever, it seems.'

'And you're as enchanting as always.' He raised his brows as his gaze dropped to where I'd grasped hold of one of my knives. 'Already planning regicide? I'm disappointed. I thought you'd be smart enough to get the information first, *then* kill me.'

'Oh, go to the Dark,' I spat, even as my fingers uncurled. He was, unfortunately, right. I needed that information.

The Broken

He chuckled, dark, low and completely infuriating. 'One day, Captain. One day.'

Deana shifted. 'Please don't tempt fate.'

Callum uncrossed his long legs and pushed himself to his feet. He flipped over the stack of documents on his desk. 'Fate's been after me for a long time. I doubt a few taunts will quicken its coming.'

I raised my brows, eyeing the overturned documents. 'Afraid I'll steal your secrets?'

'I'm sure you'd find something in the kingdom's running that could be used against me.' He barely glanced at Jaxon as the thief came to a stop beside me. When I didn't deign to respond to his comment, he continued. 'So, what will it be? Killing me or information?'

I smiled back, my Gift crackling to life in my veins as it sensed the spike of viciousness. 'There's plenty of time for both.'

'Hmm.'

The noncommittal sound stoked the flames within my chest. 'You don't think I can?' I stepped closer. Deana sat up, her legs swinging around the side of the chaise. The casual brushing of her fingers against her garrotte was the only warning she gave. She might have brought me here, but she did not trust me with Callum's life. At least one of them possessed a droplet of common sense.

Callum only smiled. 'Oh, I know you can. I just don't think you will.' His legs brushed against the table between us. Slowly, he reached down, plucking a grape from its stem He rolled it between his fingers, his eyes never leaving mine, before letting it drop back onto the plate. 'Leave us, Deana.'

'Your Majesty—' Deana started, rising to her feet.

'It was not a request.' Callum's gaze cooled as it moved to her. She hesitated, muttered something about idiot kings under her breath, and then sighed in acquiescence.

'Please don't kill him yet,' she whispered as she passed me. Despite the light tone, there was a tightness at the corner of her lips that marked her displeasure. 'It will make such a mess. I'm terribly fond of this room.'

'Deana.' The name was said as a long-suffering sigh. The corner of Callum's mouth kicked upwards, pushing at the scar that ran over his lips. 'You're not saying anything rude about your king, are you?'

Deana grinned back. There was an ease between them – a hint of the friendship they had shared since they were young. Callum had once told me that Deana had been the card his father had used to keep him in line. The only friend he'd allowed himself to have – a connection back to his humanity.

For me, it had been my sister. But that connection didn't exist anymore.

'I would never dream of it,' Deana said as she strode for the door, her cape fluttering behind her. 'Speaking ill of you would be considered treason, Your Majesty.'

Callum sighed as she left the room, shaking his head. 'It's never stopped her in the past.' His eyes cut across to where Jaxon had not taken a single step towards the door. 'Did you not hear me? Leave us.'

'You don't command me.' Jaxon's voice was icy beneath the mask of his smile. Callum might be a king, but Jaxon ruled the criminal underworld. Neither were used to yielding.

'Go,' I said to Jaxon, tilting my head in the direction of the open door. His brows furrowed. I thought he might refuse again and I'd have to force him out. Instead, he brandished a dramatic bow.

'Always at your service, my lady.'

'Jaxon.' I didn't mean for his name to mimic the same tone as Callum had used with Deana – fond exasperation. There was nothing in me that remotely resembled Callum. And nothing left in me to feel *fond* about anyone. Jaxon flashed me a cocky smile, spared Callum an unimpressed once over, then left the room with a flourish.

'He's loyal,' Callum commented as the door shut behind Jaxon, sealing us in. I pressed my lips together, dropping into the chair opposite one he took up. My knife rested upon my knees. There was nothing to read in Callum's expression – no pleasure or irritation. His blank mask was perfectly in place.

'More than you,' I shot back, fingers tapping on the knife blade. Sparks of silver skittered across the blade's edge, my Gift rearing to life. 'And no, he's not. Jaxon wants something, so he's using me to get it.'

'Interesting choice of company.' One corner of Callum's mouth twisted upwards. His emerald eyes glinted in the glow of the light, a perfect complement to the golden hair that was currently pulled away from his face. No circlet sat on his head. King Kane had worn his crown almost constantly – a reminder that he was king. That one wrong move might wipe out an entire family line.

And yet Callum managed to look more regal for the lack of it.

'Has it been so long that you need to study my face with such intensity, Captain?'

I stiffened, but I refused to let my gaze shift away from him. My fingers dug into my legs. 'Don't call me that.'

'What? Captain?' He raked his fingers through his hair. 'I suppose you aren't truly a captain anymore, are you? You're no longer chained to the Naruzian army.'

'No longer chained to your cursed bloodline,' I corrected. 'You will stop calling me by that title.'

'Yet, here you are, still barking out orders like you're on the battlefield.' His finger tapped slowly on the arm of his chair, eyes glittering with wicked amusement. 'Yes, I think *Captain* suits you quite well.'

My jaw gave a throb of protest as my teeth ground together.

Unable to hold his stare any longer, I began to inspect the room. The walls were as white as the corridors, with a few tapestries hanging depicting several of the gods. There was one of Kerta, riding a horse into battle; Kyrah, leaning over a pool to divine an unknown truth; Vaya, lulling beings into a deep sleep. Two spots were bare, a chunk of the wall chipped. I frowned. The damage looked suspiciously like someone had taken a sword to it.

'Akmad and Vitus,' Callum clarified.

The god of darkness and light, who had Gifted his father. And the god of life, who had Gifted Callum.

'I couldn't have them in here.'

It struck me, then, who this room must have belonged to before it fell into the hands of the present king. 'These quarters were your father's?'

I cursed myself the moment the question sprang to my lips. I didn't care about Callum, or who these quarters might have once belonged to. Even so, my gaze couldn't help but be drawn to him as the silence stretched on. His face had frozen into an expression so cold, even I felt its chill.

'They were, once. He liked to use this room for his … lessons.' Callum's smile looked forced, the corners too high and his eyes too dull.

My scrutiny fell to the scar that cut across his lips. The only mark, he'd once told me, of the damage his father had wreaked on his body that Callum had been allowed to keep. The rest of his beatings had been forcibly healed away by his own Gift. Just as it had with Vitus's puppet, my Gift surged through me, filled with indignant anger. *Mine*, it thrummed in a consuming rhythm. I didn't care that he had once been hurt. That he had been broken and reforged, just as I had been. I cared that it wasn't me that had done it.

I forced all of it back. 'What did you want to bring me here for?' I asked. 'If not to let me kill you.'

Callum lifted a goblet of deep red to his lips, drinking deeply before answering. When he lowered it, his smile had faded. 'I know what you're looking for.'

Deana had alluded to that. Still, I asked, 'How?'

'Deana is good at many things, but what she's best at is remaining unseen and gathering information.' He raised his brows at my frown. 'She's been trailing you for months.'

My fists tightened. How much had she seen? And how much had she told Callum?

My cheeks heated with a mixture of rage and humiliation. 'Why send the other guards?' I retrieved my own goblet and filled it to the brim from a pitcher of wine. 'You could've had Deana approach me from the start.'

Callum barely blinked as he said, 'Presents.'

'Don't talk in riddles,' I warned, my Gift responding to my annoyance. It pressed to my skin, my veins growing incandescent beneath the wrappings of scars. I was a glass bottle, and all it would take was the right fuse for me to explode. With Vitus's Gift in his blood, my own Gift would barely touch Callum. It would be everyone else residing in the palace who'd pay the price of my fury.

I drank the wine in one go. My Gift slunk back down into a little ball.

Callum raised a brow but didn't comment. 'My father's guards,' he clarified.

Understanding dawned. I had recognised every single one of them, remembered the ones who had held me down, who had lifted the whip against me, who had pressed a knife to my skin when I was disobedient. I had refused to even consider that Callum might be sending them deliberately, gift-wrapped packages for me to take my anger out on. My wrath roused once more. It wasn't a fair or righteous anger. Yet I could not stop the seething that Callum knew me well enough to understand that

that was one of very few 'presents' I would actually enjoy. 'I would've killed anyone who was connected to you.'

'Yet Deana returned alive.'

It irked me how easily he saw through my lies. 'Only because she'd be too much of a hassle to kill.'

'You'd have found a way.' Callum ran his eyes over me, his gaze settling briefly on my knives before it flicked upwards. 'You've always been talented at achieving what most would consider impossible.'

My skin prickled with how intensely he studied me. 'Talented at killing, you mean.'

'No, Captain,' he said slowly. 'I don't.'

Discomfort skittered at the hint of what I might've described as warmth in anyone else's voice. 'Tell me why I'm here.'

Callum sighed. 'Can't we just enjoy a few—'

'No.' I rose to my feet, my braid falling over my shoulder as irritation swelled. 'If you're not going to give me straight answers about why I'm here, then I'm better off finding the closest tavern and spending the night there.'

Callum shifted, his smirk disappearing. 'We found someone who might know how to access the other realm.' He leant forward, fingers steepling. For the first time, I noticed the depths of the shadows beneath his eyes, as though he'd had as many sleepless nights as me. 'One of the few guards we didn't send out to you finally caved.'

I frowned, irritated that Callum had been able to get answers where I hadn't. Though perhaps if I, too, had had access to the depths of darkness the palace dungeons possessed, I would've had the same outcome.

Callum continued. 'He said there was a woman who liked to brag about how she knew a way into a place ordinary mortals couldn't dream of. That she'd received something from the godly realm once and knew the secret to how to reach there.' He paused.

'That there's some elusive concoction that can separate a soul from a body.'

'I have an easy way to do that.' I tapped one of my knives. 'No need to go chasing mythical concoctions.'

A ghost of a smile flitted over his lips. 'You are rather skilled at that, but this is different. The man said the separation is temporary. That the woman spoke of how she heard of it from another. No word on what this mystery concoction is, of course, but apparently, it'll allow the separation just long enough for one to cross the barrier between realms without being sent back.'

I scoffed. 'She sounds like nothing more than a woman who liked her wine too much and the truth too little.'

'I'd agree, if I hadn't recognised the name he spoke.'

I slowly lowered myself back to my chair. 'Who?'

Callum leant forward, hands clasped. His eyes flicked down to the knife I'd rebalanced on my legs then came up to meet mine. That look was enough to twist my stomach. He had barely seemed to notice my blade until now. Had not seemed to think I would use it until we'd approached this topic.

'Madame Tussant.' Everything in me froze at the name. It was a name that'd once plagued my nightmares. One that I'd flinched at every time I'd heard it. Callum's eyes held me steady in their gaze as he continued. 'Your mother.'

Chapter Nine

My first instinct was to stand up, turn around and walk. Keep on walking until I was as far away from this man as humanly possible.

Even hearing the name of the woman who'd sold me to King Kane was enough to yank memories, nearly as terrible as those of Cassie dying, to the surface. Memories of dark rooms and fists. Of being told what my future as a courtesan would be through painful encounters. Of me protecting Cassie from it all, until the day my Gift had run rampant and killed her. Of using my Gift to hold her soul in place until that final day when I lost her to a god.

I was tempted to escape through the closed doors behind me. I would have to contend with Deana, but it would be doable. In the other direction was a window that was likely three storeys up. Both were preferable options to hunting down the woman I hadn't seen in years. And both would take me away from the king before me.

My second instinct was to drink.

I gave into this, pouring myself another cup of wine. Droplets sloshed over the edge, spattering on the base of the cup. Callum watched as I tipped my head back, draining the glass. I slammed the goblet onto the table, then refilled it and drank again. It didn't take long for the gentle warmth of the wine to spread from my belly into my mind, suffocating some of the trepidation that had wound around me. 'She's lying. She has to be.'

'Is she?' Callum studied me, my skin itching wherever his eyes touched. What did he see with those inscrutable eyes? And why did I suddenly want to hide? 'You're half god, Chiara. It's entirely possible that she's telling the—'

'No.' I slammed down the cup, letting the metallic clang ring through the room. 'She has to be lying.'

Sighing, he leant back. 'I think we both know there's every chance she does know a way across to the godly realm.'

'That woman knows nothing but a need for power.' I shook my head, the allure of the wine contending with the sweet temptation of a plate of abandoned fruit sitting to one side of Callum, who hadn't touched any of it. 'She was trying to garner attention. To make herself look important.'

'Chiara...' Callum began, his hand lifting as though to reach for me.

I curled my hands into fists. 'You don't know what she's like.'

'I don't,' he allowed, 'but I know you. And I know that this reaction isn't because you don't believe her.'

Anger stiffened me. 'You know nothing about me.'

Callum eyed me, his lips flattening for a moment before he shook his head. 'Fine. Then consider this: they may only be boasts, but we both know that she did receive something from the godly realm.' His hand dropped. 'You.'

The air was too cold, Callum's presence in front of me too consuming. My Gift crept closer to the surface, prodding for any breaks in the protection of alcohol and my own flimsy restraints.

'We both know she's the last lead either of us have,' Callum said, far too softly.

My eyes slid away from his. He was right, and I hated him for it.

Yet again, I was letting my own cowardice get in the way of vengeance for Cassie.

'Take one of the rooms.' Callum's voice was surprisingly gentle. 'Take a day, a week, a month to consider.'

I laughed. 'Deana must've gathered the rumours about the golden man bringing back the dead. We might not have a month.'

'I don't care,' Callum said, his jaw setting in a stubborn line. It was surprising how familiar a sight it was, as though our brief time together had carved itself deeply into me. 'I'll make time.'

'Commanding time itself now, are you?' I laughed again. 'My, how arrogant you've grown in your rise to power. What will you be claiming next, Your Majesty? That you control the gods themselves?'

He looked away, his lips flattening. 'We both know I can't do that.'

A brief, heavy silence fell. We did both know that.

I broke the quiet first, not wishing to share memories with Callum, no matter how macabre they might be. 'Deana planned for me to fight that golden-eyed man in the Den, didn't she? She must've known he was one of Vitus's followers, and that his being there might incite me to come here.' My eyes narrowed. 'Was it at your orders?'

Callum smiled. 'I'm sure you did just fine.'

'Just fine until the bastard started using a Gift awfully similar to yours, Your Majesty,' I snapped. 'I'm sure you remember how well it went the last time you used your Gift on me.'

His smile vanished, the air seeming to steal the chill from his expression. 'I knew nothing of any Gift.' His knuckles blanched. 'Were you hurt?'

Anger was a living beast, and it threatened to destroy

everything within sight. *One day,* I promised, even as I said, 'What do you care?'

Callum tensed. 'I do care, Chiara. I—'

'It doesn't matter.' The only thing that did was retribution. Callum's lies could wait. Even if I couldn't sense any insincerity in his expression. 'I only brought it up to prove that Vitus is beginning to act. Time isn't on your side.'

A muscle in his jaw ticked. 'I don't care. As I already said, if you need time, I'll find a way to make time. This has to be your decision.'

Your decision. I hated the cruel trap of being given a choice. Choices were what got people hurt. Killed. Especially choices made by me.

But Vitus was out there, Liam likely by his side. And perhaps I hated Callum and despised the woman who'd never truly been my mother, but those two – I would shred my soul into tiny pieces if it meant inflicting on them even a fraction of the pain Cassie must've felt.

'If I do this,' I said at last, clasping the goblet between my hands and a droplet of wine dribbled onto my finger, 'it's not because we are friends. We're not allies. We never will be.'

Callum's blank mask returned. 'Of course not.'

'This isn't redemption at the end. I won't be forgiving you.' Forgiveness wasn't for the likes of us.

The mask momentarily faltered, a flicker of hurt and then resignation crossing his features. 'Did I ever ask for your forgiveness?'

He hadn't. And loathe as I was to admit it, I was grateful for it. He wouldn't have meant any apologies he spoke. Not when he'd told me himself that he did not regret his choice.

I placed the cup on the small table and pushed up off the seat. I was done with this conversation. Done with him for the night. 'I'll do it, but not tonight.' Not when I was too far into my drink and hadn't yet mustered enough courage to face my childhood tormentor.

'You'll stay here.'

I frowned, unsure if it was a question or command. 'I'll be going home.'

'No, Captain.' Callum's features slipped into the mask of authority. Of a king. 'I will not have you disappearing into that city once more.'

If a smile could be a weapon, then I was certain mine was the sharpest of knives. 'Afraid you'll lose me? If I wanted to vanish, I'd vanish.'

'No,' he said, brows drawing inwards as his voice lowered. 'I'm worried you'll lose yourself if you go back there.'

'I have no need for false concern.'

'Good,' Callum said, his wicked smile sliding back onto his features. And, gods-damned me, the part of me I hadn't yet managed to destroy heated at the sight of it. 'I'd never dare provide anything false to you.'

'Except for false promises.'

The smile crumbled. I was good at that, it seemed – drawing those smiles out and then smashing them to pieces. It should've felt like a victory. Instead, I only felt more hollow.

'You will stay in one of our rooms,' Callum repeated, more firmly this time.

'Fine,' I conceded, purely for convenience, of course.

'I'll request the staff stay away from your quarters. There'll be a guard at the end of the corridor for your security, but that's it. You'll be safe from them. From everyone.'

My hand closed around the door handle. I turned to stare at the king. He was still staring at me as though I held the answer to a question he had not yet figured out how to ask.

I put all my malice into my smile. 'And they'll be safe from me?'

He didn't hesitate. 'Yes.'

'If you think that, you know nothing.'

With that, I stalked out and left the king to his isolation.

Deana showed me to my rooms. She was delighted to announce that they were directly next to Callum's.

'These used to be his rooms, in fact.' Deana smiled impishly as she showed me around my quarters. They were far bigger than any space I had ever called my own. I stood still in the centre, discomfort rattling down my bones. Part of it was due to the sheer size of the room – all the directions an attacker could approach me. The rest was because of the damned bed, pushed up against a stone wall. Thick white blankets, endless cushions and a gauzy canopy. A bed that Callum had once used.

Skin flushing, I quickly turned my attention to the rest of the space. A small dressing table sat to the right, a bottle of wine perched on top. On the other wall, a window opened out onto a golden railed balcony. Pale curtains flapped in the slight breeze, letting cool air drift in.

If Deana noticed my discomfort, she didn't comment. Instead, she pushed open a large, ornately carved door to reveal the silver-veined marble room within; a tub, big enough to fit myself, Deana and likely two more, with a large wash sink and toileting area to the side. The scent of lavender and vanilla floated into the open space.

'The bathroom,' she explained unnecessarily. Pulling the door shut, she pointed to a third door on the opposite side of the room. It was shut, a brass key inserted in the lock. 'And that door will take you to Callum's quarters, if you desire.'

I ignored her suggestive look. 'Not a chance.' Not unless I

somehow lost sight of my plans for vengeance against Vitus and killed him during the night.

Deana simply shrugged. 'It locks from this side. And his, of course.'

Foolish. So incredibly foolish to allow me unrestricted access to his chambers. Lock or not, I'd be able to get in. I seated myself on the end of the huge mattress. It sunk beneath my weight, its softness tempting. I could only imagine the cost of it. I patted the blankets, marvelling at the quality of the fabric. Selling a single blanket could likely give me enough rent for my room back in the slums for a number of months.

Deana watched with faint amusement. 'Comfortable, isn't it?'

I did not allow myself to return her smile. 'Where will I find Callum when I'm ready to find Madame Tussant?'

Her smile turned sly. 'I'm sure wherever you are, he won't be far.'

'If he tries to keep tabs on me—'

Her laugh cut me off. 'That's not quite what I meant. When you're ready, tell one of the staff to fetch me. Or you can go to Callum yourself – he'll be in his receiving chambers, or in one of the meeting rooms with the nobles, if he's in the palace.' She glanced at the locked door. 'If he's not in there, then you can always try his bedchambers. I'm sure he'd love—'

'I'm tired,' I interrupted, fingers curling into the blankets as I tried not to follow her gaze.

Deana nodded. 'Brent will be on duty tonight. If you need anything, ask him.' Her expression darkened. 'I'll likely be spending the night dealing with the pest you brought into the palace.'

I almost pitied Jaxon as the door clicked shut behind Deana. Throwing myself back, I let the colours swim into a blur around me. Sleep. I needed sleep.

But every time I closed my eyes, I saw my mother's face. Her beauty turned cruel by a sneer. Remembered the feel of her blows on my body. Running my fingers over the lines on my arms, I wondered how many of my collection of marks belonged to her. Fewer than they did to King Kane, I was sure, but far more than anything I'd earnt in battle. She'd been careful, though. Always so careful to maximise the suffering while minimising the permanency of the damage.

Damaged goods don't sell well, she'd always whisper as she'd led me from the small room where Cassie and I had fended for ourselves out to the main rooms of the brothel.

A shiver of childhood terror crept through me. Dragging a hand over my face, I sucked in a deep breath. That fear made me far smaller than any other. A child trembling before the woman who claimed to be her mother, desperately trying to keep her attention so it didn't wander to Cassie.

A bitter laugh escaped me. In the end, none of that mattered. Cassie had died despite everything I'd done. Because of everything I'd done.

And now I was putting off vengeance. I sensed that, if I were to march up to Callum and demand we go this night, he'd accept. Yet, try as I might, I couldn't quite convince that creeping fear to loosen its grip on my body or mind.

Pathetic, my own voice whispered scornfully inside me. I agreed with it.

Desperate for a distraction from my thoughts, I turned on my side. Stared at the door with its brass key. Turned onto my back once more. All that did was draw a wholly different set of thoughts – ones that were equally troubling, if not more so. Callum would be sleeping on the other side of that door sometime soon. Tantalisingly close. Easily accessed. Would he be as defenceless in his sleep as most were? I didn't think so.

Should I kill him? Be rid of him and the irritating space he occupied in my mind, day in and day out? Letting out a frustrated breath, I threw an arm over my eyes. No. I needed him alive for the time being. Best to leave him be until I'd secured my way into the godly realm. Satisfied that I'd made the right choice, I tried to relax. And then I waited for sleep to come. And waited. And waited.

After some time had passed, the presence of the locked door seared into my thoughts, I threw myself to my feet and headed straight for my bags. Yanking the bottle of spirits free, I ripped the stopper out with my teeth.

If I wasn't going to sleep tonight, then I could make damned well sure I wiped my mind of any annoying thoughts. And hopefully wipe away the sight of Callum's infuriating face in the process.

Chapter Ten

Dawn made its sleepy arrival in its usual aggravating way, cheerfully forcing itself past the darkness of my room. Smears of pink and orange blurred at the horizon past half-drawn curtains. Spears of pain dug into my head as I moved. Sweat beaded, gathering in my hair as I went through a range of exercises. Swallowing the nausea that threatened to rise, I did not allow myself to stop. No matter how terrible my body might feel, I'd be damned if I let it fall into a sorry state. If I wanted my vengeance, then I needed to at least have a decent physical form.

Jaxon, who had let himself in at some point during the short burst of sleep I had fallen into, was sprawled across the bed. He propped his head up, staring at me.

'You're making me tired just looking at you,' he drawled, eyes flicking over me.

'You could join me,' I offered through pants. My arms trembled with strain as I completed my last push up before I staggered up to my feet. The sleeveless tunic I wore was plastered to my body, my hair a mess of curls. Wiping sweat away with the back of my hand, I sank back into a chair.

'I think not.' Jaxon stared disdainfully. One would think I had just suggested he roll around in mud.

'Don't you have somewhere to be?' I asked, tugging my tunic over my head. Jaxon huffed in annoyance as he looked away, then waited until I'd signalled I was dressed before turning back.

He sighed, his nose wrinkling as I threw the dirty clothes onto a growing pile on the floor. He flopped back on the sheets. Strands of sunlight honeyed the olive tones of his skin. 'I'm bored,' he said for what had to be the twentieth time since I had dragged myself up from where I'd collapsed on the floor the night before.

Beginning to work my fingers through the greasy strands of my hair, I eyed him. 'And what, exactly, am I meant to do about that?'

He rolled onto his stomach, shifting so he was looking directly at me. 'The fighting pit won't be the same without you, darling.' An offer wrapped in a comment.

'No.'

A playful pout appeared. 'Aren't you bored?'

'I've been here one night, Jaxon.'

'Exactly. Someone like you must be tiring of all … this?' He waved a lazy hand at the splendour of the room. I cast my eyes around. My sister would have loved it. The fine clothes stashed away, the bed that could easily fit a family, the balcony with its gilded railing.

It didn't matter what she did or didn't love. She was dead.

'I don't,' I lied, setting into the task of braiding my hair.

'If you're not going to do anything about the king's offer today, the least you could do is earn me some more money.'

'Who said I wasn't?'

He eyed me sceptically. 'You're telling me you'll hunt down dear old Cal right now and tell him you're prepared to see Madame Tussant?'

I hesitated, pricks of pain hitting my scalp from where I'd pulled my hair too tight. 'How do you know that?'

'I have my ways.' He raised his brows. 'Well?'

Securing the end of my braid with a leather tie, I pressed my lips together. Last night, I'd had every intention of marching up to Callum and announcing that I'd hunt Madame Tussant down today. But no amount of alcohol was enough to banish the memory, the fear, of living under her rule. And no amount of alcohol could convince me that seeing Callum this morning was a good idea. 'I might go today.' If I could convince myself to stop being such a damned coward.

Jaxon made a noncommittal sound. Annoyance surged. When had he started acting so familiar with me? What made it even worse was that he was right. It was highly unlikely that I'd muster the courage to face Callum or my mother today.

Irritation clenching my hands, I strode over to the balcony and stared down at a guard in black armour patrolling the gardens; striding through blooms of pinks, purples and orange, careful to step around the newer shoots. Even from this height, I could see the morning frost coating the tips of petals and the spread of grass.

'Callum would go for you. If you asked,' Jaxon said softly. Deciding what to say.

I knew. I had seen it in Callum's eyes, the first night. Seen the silent offer behind the smirks and jibes. And I'd hated it. Hated that he saw my weakness. 'I won't take anything from him.'

'Except a fine room and food and clothes?'

Before I could say anything, there was a knock at the door. I twisted, ready to send whoever it was away, but Jaxon was up first. He dodged my attempt to grasp hold of him and flung open the doors to reveal none other than Callum standing at the threshold.

My shoulders stiffened. I narrowed my eyes. 'What happened to giving me time?'

Callum's lips curled into a smile, the dark cut of his clothes stark against the white of the corridor behind him. 'I came to see if you needed anything.'

My fingers curled. 'I don't.' When he didn't move, I folded my arms, fighting the urge to step away from him. 'Is there something else that you want?'

There was something odd about his expression. Something about his smile that bordered on lazy instead of hinting at the wickedness I'd once enjoyed seeing in his expression. 'I want you to decide.'

'Decide what?' I stepped back, twisting and walking into the room so I wouldn't have to look at him anymore.

Jaxon watched as Callum followed me in. 'Decide if you will continue to be a coward or if you'll actually do something about what's happening out there.' Callum gestured to the city beyond the gardens. By now, the markets would be buzzing with people and The Den would be getting cleaned of any blood from the previous night's fights.

I whirled, nearly crashing into him he stood so close. Yet, my Gift did not stir as it usually did in his presence. 'Such a different tune to what you sang last night, Your Majesty.'

Callum's jaw hardened. 'There's been more of the golden-eyed devotees in the past two days.' The green of his eyes seemed to shift as he stared down at me, a strange tinge entering them.

Anger flared. I yanked a dagger from its sheathe and drew it across his throat. Jaxon made a startled sound as Callum staggered back, hands flying up to his throat. No blood appeared between his fingers as he stared.

Turning to Jaxon, I slammed the dagger back into its sheathe. 'If you're going to use your illusions, at least make them believable.'

Jaxon frowned as Callum's figure flickered, then vanished in bursts of yellow light. 'That *was* believable. I've already tricked a handful of guards and plenty of servants with it.'

I said nothing. Didn't point out how the colour of his eyes was a shade off, or how his smile didn't cut as sharply as it should've. Nor did I tell Jaxon that Callum had insisted on calling me *Captain* since he'd brought me back to the palace along with Liam months ago.

I hated that I even noticed those differences.

Jaxon sighed. 'Those golden eyed followers of Vitus are killing people, Chiara. Killing families. Children. Innocents.'

Pain flashed briefly across his face. *You're not the only one wronged by a god. And you're not the only one seeking vengeance.* Perhaps he, too, had lost someone. A sibling or a parent. A lover. I wondered it, but I did not ask. As much as he seemed to delight in prying into my business, Jaxon was an expert at evasion when it came to himself.

Besides, I reminded myself, I didn't care.

'It's not my business,' I shot back. 'Not my people.'

Jaxon's face softened a little. 'No, because you won't let anyone become yours. Cassie—'

'Don't.' I didn't want to know how he knew her name. Inside, the silver beast rumbled in warning. 'Don't say another word.'

At whatever showed on my face, Jaxon raised his hands. Still, he tried again. 'I didn't know her, but she likely would have wanted...'

Silver lashed itself onto my fingers like vines as my fists tightened. My barely-there restraint faltered. 'Get out.'

'You need to commit to your plan for revenge,' he warned, the yellow in his eyes brightening 'Before you kill someone. Or yourself.'

My control disappeared. A whip of silver lashed out. It headed straight for Jaxon's chest. Horror filled me even as the light connected. I hadn't meant to, didn't want to kill him. But my control had never been strong. Not even before I had lost everything. My breaths rasped through me, hand stretching as though I could recall the silver. It was far too disobedient. There was a flare of light, silver and yellow battling each other for control. The silver won out. Jaxon's body consumed by it.

'No,' I whispered, limbs trembling as I stepped towards where he had stood. 'No.'

I couldn't breathe. In that moment, it didn't matter what I had told myself – that people don't matter. That I no longer cared who lived and who died, so long as Vitus and Liam ended up on the list of the dead. All that mattered was that Jaxon was gone. Killed by my own hand. Jaxon, who had glued himself to my side like a parasite. Who had worried when I came out of fights too bloody, even if he pretended not to. Who had perhaps been a friend, even if I was too terrified to admit that he'd become that.

I'd known I shouldn't get too close to anyone. Yet, here I was. Remaking my past mistakes.

There was a crack, like thunder splitting the skies in two, and the silver rescinded. But there was no warming of my skin, no brush of death against my soul. My terror faltered. Faltered, then transformed into rage as I spied the yellow words burning on the wooden floor.

Make a decision. 'Asshole!' I shouted at the closed door. Jaxon merely chuckled, the sounds of his steps fading as he walked away, disappearing just as the illusion of him had.

He had known what I might do if provoked. Known and planned for it, just like Deana had the night before. And, damn him, he had proven himself right.

It was far past time to visit Callum.

Chapter Eleven

'I'll go.'

If Callum was surprised at my abrupt entry into his study, he didn't show it. He pushed the document he was working on to one side, ink dripping off the sharp tip of a quill. He appraised my clothing. 'Now, I presume? Given you're dressed like that.'

That consisted of form-fitting black trousers and a short-sleeved tunic. A weapon's belt circled my waist, four daggers slid into their scabbards I looked every bit the daughter of Death. I wasn't sure whether I hated that I resembled even a fraction of my absent father, or if I relished the delicious darkness of it all.

'Certainly not next year,' I sniped back, folding my arms over my chest. 'Where does *she* now reside?'

I couldn't bring myself to utter her name. To err near the memories of my childhood – the pain and suffering. Near memories of Cassie.

But I would have to face them all soon enough.

'Oh, no.' The smile on Callum's face was unnerving as he rose, unfurling to his full height. I tried not to study it. Tried not to notice how *right* it looked compared to Jaxon's illusion. 'I'm not telling you that.'

Irritation built. 'Why not?'

'Because you're an explosive right now. I have no doubt that one good jibe from that woman will make you blow up.' Callum moved to the front of the desk, leaning against it. Of their own accord, my eyes travelled down his tailored grey shirt that revealed muscled arms, to where his dark coloured pants outlined every muscle in his legs. 'And there's no way I'm letting you near my people if you're liable to kill all of them. You go with me, or you don't go at all.'

My eyes snapped up to his, outrage making my teeth clench. *His* people. How quickly he'd claimed them for his own. 'I wouldn't kill innocents.'

'Wouldn't you?' Callum stepped forward. Flames of anger were beginning to take shape in his eyes. 'Tell me, Chiara, how many *innocents* do you think died during the years you protected your sister?'

My breath hitched. The words hit far harder than I cared to admit.

Too many. There had been too many naive children, who had no place in the midst of battle, whose lives I had ended. Some had been at the end of my blades. Some had been mercy killings, as they bled out in indescribable pain. I'd lost count of how many I'd killed after the first handful of battles. Figured that over fifty kills at the age of fourteen was enough to mark me a monster, and monsters did not keep score.

But some of their faces – I didn't care to speak of how they appeared in my fragmented nightmares. How I'd sometimes wondered who they had left behind. And I'd never let myself consider it – the numerous lives I was destroying to save one.

The ever-present comfort of anger rose. 'You think I'm the only one who killed innocents? What about you? I know all about your healing, Your Majesty. Those who were lucky enough to receive your services in the dungeon.'

Callum stiffened. 'I'm well aware of what I did.'

'Are you?' I asked, cruelty twisting my words into something ugly. 'What do you think is worse – cutting down someone in battle, or healing them over and over again until their mind breaks from the torture they're receiving?'

'I never said I didn't do those things,' Callum said coolly. 'But you can't tell me you've never hurt an innocent, either. And you definitely can't try to shame me for worrying that you might do it again.'

My fingernails dug deep. Sharp pain accompanied a spilling of warmth onto my palm. 'Yes, I'm cruel. I'm villainous. I'm all of those things.' I took in a deep breath, trying to ease the wrenching of my heart. 'But at least I'm not a coward.'

My words cut towards him like daggers.

He straightened, his eyes darkening with a rage that matched my own. 'Coward?'

I smiled, every bit as malicious as I had just promised. 'Yes. A coward.' I stepped forward until we were almost chest to chest. 'At least I admit I'm a monster – and don't pretend to hide behind a mask of honour.'

Callum's dark laugh was absent of kindness. 'When did I ever pretend to have honour?'

'When you acted as though sacrificing my sister's life for mine was worth it.'

His eyes glinted with feral anger, and something darker. 'I don't pretend that was a just choice. If I were a good, decent man, I likely wouldn't have made that decision.' I opened my mouth, about to find a new way to slice him to pieces, but he continued before I could. 'But I'm not a good, decent man, Chiara. And I'm not a coward.'

'What are you, then?' I bristled with barely-leashed fury, the air thick with tension. We were two knives, held at the other's throat.

'A fool.' His expression softened. He sighed, leaning back as he dragged a hand over his face. 'I'm a fool with a heart I can't control. One that has decided it wants someone it shouldn't.'

'I don't want it.' I slammed a hand against his chest. He didn't flinch. The dim lighting of the room accentuated every shadow, every straight line of his face. 'I don't want a single piece of your wretched heart.'

His smile was a wicked curve, his scar white against his tanned skin where it curved up his cheek. 'Now who's being a coward?' He angled his face towards mine. My pulse quickened as I realised just how little space existed between us. 'You hide your feelings behind drinking and blood. You hide your own heart from yourself.'

'I don't want you.' My hand fisted in the material of his shirt. It did not push him away or pull him nearer. It simply held, trembling in the soft fabric. 'I loathe you.'

'I don't think you do.' His finger hooked under my chin, his eyes raking over my features. 'I think you hate it that you don't loathe me.'

The anger that blazed through me was so wild it burnt my very blood with its heat. Yet I did not pull away. It was as though I was suspended, frozen in the tension between us. At this distance, I felt I might be able to see his pulse under his skin if I looked hard enough. I wondered if it was as unsteady, as feral, as my own. How easy it would be at this distance to slash a blade across his throat.

But I didn't need him dead. I needed him to see he was wrong.

I wasn't sure who moved first. I pushed onto my toes, my hand wrenching him down by his shirt. His fingers slid up my jaw, pulling me towards him. And then our lips were colliding, our breaths merging as we kissed. There was nothing gentle or sweet or kind in the action. We were two blazing fires, crashing into each other with a force that could destroy both of us. His hand tangled in my hair, our bodies pressing together. I couldn't tell who stole whose warmth. Twisting my hand, I gathered more fabric in my hand. We broke apart for just enough time to breathe before our lips met once more, hungrier than before. This ... this was power and fire and fury.

His lips were as unyielding as the rest of him. Where every past touch and kiss and moment I had shared with a man had been the other bowing before me, letting me lead, Callum did nothing of the sort. His body pressed against me, pushing me back until I was flat against a wall.

I wasn't one to bow. I met every one of his touches: the fiery trail of lips on mine, on my throat, further down. The smell of sandalwood and the coming rain - *his* smell – was dangerously intoxicating as I grasped him tight. Every kiss was domineering. Heated, as though to see which of us could draw more need from the other. His hand fisted tighter in my hair, his lips finding the vulnerable parts of my throat. My pulse quickened under his touch. I curled my hand around his jaw, forcing his lips back to mine. They were warm. Firm, his enjoyment written in the slight curve of his lips under mine.

This was its own battle. A battle that we both fought with passion, neither of us willing to give in to the other. I would not concede defeat as I caught his chin in my hand, pulling him back up as his lips found my collarbone. I yanked him up, my lips finding his once more. I would not yield. Not when warmth pooled everywhere on my skin, deep in my belly, desire filling every pore.

But it wasn't enough. I needed more. Needed him.

I knew then that I had made a mistake. Deana had been right, all those nights ago.

Hate was a very passionate thing.

I shoved him backwards, breathing hard, my skin heating. The smile that graced his lips made my eyes narrow. My heart thrummed beneath my skin. For the first time in months, I felt *alive.*

'Your loathing is an odd thing,' he murmured, taking a step back. And before I could regain my breath enough to explain – to claim that my heart did not race and my blood had not warmed – he turned and strode from the room.

It took me more than an hour to move from the spot that I stood in. More than an hour to cool the heat in my blood that did not just belong to my wrath. More than an hour to finally allow myself to see reason, and to process each piece of information. *I had kissed the man I hated.* Fact. An undeniable, detestable fact that I would very much like to scourge from my mind. Especially the feel of his hands against my skin, and those hot, trailing kisses that had awoken heat deep inside. Unbidden, my hand rose to brush against my still tingling lips.

I snapped it back down before such a foolish action could occur.

I could admit to myself that the idea of Callum dying was … not as pleasant as I'd thought it would be, that I didn't want him dead as much as I had thought. But that was all there could be. Callum and I – we were not a pairing that was made to last. And while I could admit a part of me understood his choice, I couldn't find it within me to forgive him for not choosing Cassie.

There was only one path forward for me. One littered with blood and revenge. My heart had no place on that road. Once I'd gotten what I needed from the king, I would distance myself so fully that I never again succumbed to my desire.

Emboldened by my decision, I stalked out of the room, ready

to locate Callum. I didn't have to look far down the pristine white of the corridor. He sat, one leg bent and the other draped lazily across the floor, opposite the door. His head was tipped back, resting against the wall behind him, as his chest rose and fell in even breaths. I paused, studying him. With his shirt parted and hair tousled, he didn't look like an untouchable king. He simply looked like a man.

It was a dangerous thing to see him as.

I shifted forward and his eyes snapped open. Any illusion of ordinariness vanished. Shadows speared through the emerald colouring of his irises. The darkness launched onto his skin, wreathing his hands and arms. It swelled, his breath audibly hitching, as his gaze darted around the corridor. A tendril of worry wormed its way into me. This was not the collected king I knew, nor the passionate man I had been trapped with earlier. He looked young. Vulnerable. My hand lifted towards him before I realised what it was doing. 'Are you—'

At the sound of my voice, the haziness disappeared. 'Are you finished musing about all that's wrong in the world?' he asked, rising as though nothing had happened.

Fine. If he wanted to pretend he was fine, then I would act the same. I had enough of my own problems. He could deal with whatever plagued his sleep himself. 'I wasn't musing.'

One side of his lips quirked upwards. A hint of a dimple appeared. 'Of course you weren't, my lady. Such a woman as yourself would never deign to do anything so common as musing.'

'Gods, you're insufferable.' I shook my head, annoyed. 'And what was it you were doing?'

'Musing.' His eyes glimmered with amusement, but the smile did not quite meet his eyes. 'I've never claimed to be anything but common.'

Gritting my teeth, I began striding down the long corridor.

One of the guards from the day before – Kailey, I thought her name was – bowed respectfully as we passed. 'We're not friends. I'm not engaging in this *banter* with you.'

'Trust me, Captain. I know we're not friends.'

'I told you not to call me that.'

'What would you prefer I call you?' I didn't need to look at him to picture his slow smile. 'I can think of a few names. How about—'

Having no desire to hear what titles he'd thought up, I said, 'What happened in there – if you breathe a word of it—'

'You'll slit my throat while I sleep.'

I stopped in the corridor, turning slowly to face Callum. Behind him, hung an imposing portrait of a long-gone ruler. The lighting accentuated the too thin, too-small features of the man. The only resemblance he held to Callum was the golden hair. 'Oh, no,' I said, smiling just a little. 'I wouldn't slit your throat. That would be far less painful than what I have planned.'

When Callum smiled back, it was every bit as edged as mine. My damned body reacted, heat crawling over my skin. It was normal, I reminded myself, to appreciate a creature made so beautifully. To admire its form. But anything more wasn't made for someone like me. And Callum certainly wasn't.

'I look forward to it,' he said in a voice filled with wicked darkness.

I twisted my body around to face the seemingly never-ending corridor. 'I'll let you come.' The words came out so fast they jumbled together.

'What was that?'

Gods, how I would love to cut up that pretty face and watch it bleed.

Liar, something deep inside me purred.

Idiot, I hissed back, shoving that silly voice away. 'I said, I'll let you come.'

'So gracious, my—'

'I swear, if you say "my lady" one more time, I will end you here and now.'

'I was going to say, my captain,' he lied through his teeth.

'That's even worse.' Ignoring the amusement dancing in his eyes, I continued. 'I take the lead.'

Callum turned the corner ahead before I did, his arm brushing against mine. I hastened my pace. He matched it easily. Sunlight poured through the tiny windows, dappling the marbled ground in gleaming rays. It would have been pretty if not for the coldness of the place. 'Of course. I can't imagine you'd have it any other way.'

I didn't respond. Not when I knew the truth. If we were to ever lose our sanity again – if he were to touch me, to kiss me, as he had back in his study – then there was every chance I might let him take the lead. Let him have control, even if only for a moment.

And that thought was far more terrifying than any mortal, or god, could be.

Chapter Twelve

The Rose and Crown, my mother's most illustrious brothel, had not changed since the last time I'd been there, as a child. Ivy crept up the walls around a doorway shielded only by a transparent fabric. Thick incense twisted onto the street. The sweetest of scents often hid the worst of stenches. I recalled well enough the back alley, filled with the rotting corpses of both children and adults who'd displeased a customer or lost their value. My mouth was painfully dry as I reached for the curtains. Sounds of pleasure threaded through the air, undercutting the gentle music playing. My fingers shook, grasping a handful of the silky material. I didn't want to set foot in this foul place. Didn't want to face whatever memories lay inside.

'It's your last chance to let me handle it on my own,' Callum murmured behind me. 'You can wait here.'

Most of me rebelled at even touching the pearlescent door handle. The rest of me rebelled at the thought that I could be so weak. I shot a glare over my shoulder.

Callum's face was coated in thick shadows by his deep cowl. 'I'm not so pathetic that I need a man to do my work for me.'

'No one's saying you're pathetic.' His hand moved towards me before stopping, centimetres from my cheek. He sighed as I shifted away, dropping his hand back to his side. 'But everyone needs to lean on another at times.'

I turned back to the door, wrenching the curtain aside. 'Not me.'

I stepped into the warmth of the interior. A glowing hearth was barely visible through the tangled bodies. Hazy light soaked the air, several censers holding burning incense hung from wooden beams. I stepped over a row of lush floor cushions, thankfully absent of the bodies that sprawled across much more of the room. It was easy to spot the courtesans, their practised movements smooth. They moved amongst the patrons with ease, fingers trailing over bared skin and sensuous smiles offered to the tempted. When coin was flashed, the courtesan would stop, either leading the client to one of the curtained alcoves, to a set of stairs at the back of the room or, for the more daring, to a spot in the open.

I averted my gaze from the courtesans as I led Callum through the heated bodies, not wishing to deal with their advances. Nor did I wish to see how young they all were. There were a few who I did not manage to keep my attention from. A man, the faintest wisps of a beard hinting at a recent exit from boyhood. A woman who flinched even as she smiled at her customer. A girl, no older than fifteen, who had caught the attention of two men with greying hair.

'This can't be legal,' Callum breathed. With the closeness of everyone around us, his body was pressed flush to mine, warmth seeping through my clothes.

'Aren't you the king? You should know what's allowed in your own kingdom.'

'A title thrust on me, and one I'm apparently terrible at.' He lapsed into silence. I glanced back at him to find his eyes scouring the faces of those around us with muted horror.

Reaching up, I tugged his cowl back down from where it'd almost revealed his golden hair. His eyes fell to mine. 'It's as legal as your father made it.' My hand fell away from his cloak, his face shadowed once more. 'And as legal as you allow it to continue being.'

'I didn't know,' he said hoarsely as we continued on once more, narrowly avoiding a child with a tray of drinks in her hands. 'My advisors … the nobles didn't say anything.'

'Why would they?' I eyed the stairs at the back, which were lavishly carpeted in golden fibres. Mother did always have indulgent tastes. 'Who do you think these upper-end brothels are patronaged by?'

'Dammit,' Callum bit out with enough viciousness that I almost looked back at him again. 'A few months at being king, and I'm already failing my people. I should've known. Should've done something about this.'

I didn't reply. I had no right to. I *had* known, and I'd done nothing about it.

Instead, I said, 'She'll be up two storeys. I imagine her study is still up there. Or, if she's not there, she'll be in her bedchambers.'

'Did you live up there?' Callum asked.

'Sometimes.' It was the only answer I gave. As we reached the bottom of the stairs, two figures emerged from the shadows. Both were bronze-skinned men – twins, from the looks of them – their skin oiled with something smelling of the forests to the west of Alluvite, dark hair slicked back. Wicked-looking swords hung by their hips. They were nothing short of beautiful, like warriors from ancient tales. Untouchable.

Or untouchable for anyone who didn't have copious amounts of gold to spend to purchase their time.

'No one upstairs,' one intoned. Ice crawled down my spine at the flatness there. Only the barest hint of the same lilting accent as Jaxon betrayed his Axanian empire heritage.

'Unless you pay,' the other finished.

Callum stepped to my side, his hand atop his sword. I caught him by his wrist before he could do anything foolish. To bring a sword out here would bring the wrath of my mother down on us. They might be pretty to look at, but plenty of my mother's workers had been forcibly trained to deal with troublemakers. Her displeasure would end with a bloodbath – one Callum and I would survive, but many of the workers wouldn't. Part of me also quaked at the memory of my mother's fury.

Foolish things, emotions. I would have carved them out long ago if I could.

'We're not here to pay.' My voice was clearer than I had thought it would be, despite the odd feeling of another, smaller, version of myself, one that was weak and still unformed – trembling deep inside. 'We're here to speak to Madame Tussant.' I paused, then spoke her true name. 'To speak to Gabriela Halnea.'

The first of the bronze men smiled, but it was wooden, as though he was a puppet whose expressions were controlled by another. 'It's a bold thing, to demand such an audience. Unless you are here for work, she will not see you.' His eyes swept over me. Nose wrinkling at the plain black of my clothes and then the hints of scarring at my collarbone and backs of my hands. He clicked his tongue in disapproval. 'And even if you are here for work, she does not take in scarred strays.'

The second nodded his agreement, his eyes sliding to Callum. 'You, though – I cannot see your face, but she can work with the rest of you.'

Here for work. My heart stuttered. Fingers curling towards my palms.

A hand slid into mine, warm and anchoring as his fingers squeezed. My next breath came easier as I forced a casual smile onto my face, even as I cursed myself for allowing myself to borrow Callum's strength. 'I am here for...' Despite everything, despite the stakes, I couldn't make the words come out.

'We're here as investors.' Callum stepped in smoothly, shifting forward so his body half covered mine as though he could protect me from the onslaught of memories. I stared at him, torn between shoving him away and allowing him to stay where he was. His grasp of my hand didn't waver, the tightness the only thing from letting me sink into that version of me that I wanted to eradicate from existence.

I'm supposed to hate him, I reminded myself. But if this – allowing myself to be held up by his quiet strength – was how I'd face my mother, then so be it. I waited a heartbeat longer before ripping my hand from his grip. Casting my eyes to the side, I watched the young girl I'd seen earlier slip through the patrons with her glasses of wine. Gods, I needed that. My eyes flicked down, then, to the girl of ten holding them. Liquid sloshed precariously as she ducked and weaved, managing to evade hands that reached for things other than the glasses. She was a pretty little thing, with wavy brown hair and a spattering of freckles across her nose.

The thought of a drink suddenly disappeared as I fought to swallow down the nausea that surged. I knew better than most what happened to pretty little girls in this place.

'You don't look like investors.' The second brother scanned us over doubtfully as I turned. 'Either you pay your way for one of the rooms, or one of you puts yourself up for sale. There is no other way to go up.' His hand shifted to his sword, his twin mirroring the movement.

Callum's own knuckles whitened on the hand that held the sword. 'We can pay handsomely,' he tried again.

The second brother, the shorter of the pair, considered us again. He took in the fine cut of our clothes, Callum's simple yet well-made sword, the polished, well-kept boots. 'There's an auction later,' he said at last. 'You can invest by buying one of the girls.'

His hand shot out as the serving girl passed us. She yelped, dropping the tray. Red liquid splashed over the floor, over my boots. I held back my Gift at the sight of the wine. It looked an awful lot like blood – like the coming of death. But I wasn't going to let my Gift take control. If there was to be a fight, it would be far more to slit throats and let chaos reign. My fingers edged towards my blades.

'This one will be well-priced,' the guard offered, shaking the girl enough that tears welled in her eyes. She didn't make a sound. 'She'll be hard to break in, but that's half the fun.'

Just like that, I was done.

Done with being in this place.

Done with the memories.

Done with everything.

Callum didn't try to stop me as I stepped forward, gripping the creature with as much force as I could muster and letting it show. Not much, just enough to let the silver crack through my Illusioned eyes, to let sparks dance along my fingertips.

'Tell my mother that her daughter is home.' My voice was a low, deadly thing, sharper than any blade a mortal could wield. 'And if we don't go upstairs right now, there will be a repeat of the last time I set foot in this place.'

And with the way my Gift was twisting through me, this time there would be no survivors.

Chapter Thirteen

It took all of two minutes for one of the now-pale guards to run upstairs and then race back down to let us know that my mother was waiting for us. He led us up the winding staircase. My steps slowed when we approached the first floor. Sounds snuck free from the door barring entrance to the landing and onto the first floor. Some were sounds of pleasure. Others, sounds of pain. I tensed at a loud crack, followed closely by a muffled sob. Callum stepped between me and the landing, pausing as I had. He didn't say anything. He simply waited, as though he knew that anything – a comforting word, a gentle touch – would be enough for me to snap and kill everyone in this miserable brothel.

I forced steel into my spine and continued. Not for the first time, I silently cursed Callum for seeing far more than I wanted him to. We wound our way upwards, the stairs falling darker with each step we took. When our guide reached the second landing, the wooden door was wide open, revealing a golden-coloured carpet trailing up to heavy velvet curtains. My mother's chambers were through there – a study and receiving rooms at the front, her bedchambers tucked behind. The layout was not dissimilar to the king's chambers I'd seen. She'd undoubtedly copied it. She'd always viewed herself as a queen, lording it over those she'd enslaved at her brothels. I began to turn down the hall but the guide did not stop, he continued on.

My heart stilled as I faltered. He paused a few steps up, unbothered by the shift of the stair's state into neglect. Wood creaked under his weight, splinters of wood peeling away from the handrail. He did not speak. Instead, he waited, his figure cast in deep shadows.

'Aren't we going to her office?' I asked.

'No.'

The air seemed to thin around me. I stared up that narrow staircase. There were less Illusioned lights, darkness far more prominent. It made it easier to hide what went on in the upper level. Easier to disguise the stubborn bloodstains. I swallowed, my heart quickening.

A hand brushed against my back. 'You don't have to go,' Callum said as the guide turned and disappeared into the darkness.

I sucked in air, held my breath long enough that my chest began to burn. In that moment, all the unreasonable fury, that had begun to abate towards Callum, roared back to life. How easy it would be if he told me I had to proceed. If he coerced me into it. Instead, he'd given me a choice. And, right now, that seemed like the greatest cruelty of all.

But I wouldn't allow myself to be weak. Gritting my teeth, I squared my shoulders.

'I do,' I answered him at last. Not for me. Never for me. But for my sister, for her abandonment as a child, for the things that would have happened to her if we weren't sold off, I would face my childhood nightmare. Face her and show her the monster she began to create. The monster King Kane and Liam had completed.

My eyes roamed over the walls, each glance sending a new

throb of pain through my jaw. The wood of the stair rail was littered with long scratches, left by those who had just been bound into their contracts. The ratty carpet hosted its own tears and stains. Some were rust-coloured droplets, other puddles or smears. Too many bodies had been dragged down these stairs, left behind by those who'd proved to be unpliable. If I had studied them well enough, I might've been able to name the owner of a few. Stephanie, the fifteen-year-old who had once snuck Cassie and I a sweet. Beth, who had sung us to sleep to cover the sounds from the rooms below. Oscar, whose gentle hands had taught me how to bind my own wounds when I was five. They had been the first to teach me the dangers of caring about others in this world. The first to teach me grief.

My fingers brushed over a particularly deep gouge. I remembered that one, too. How my nail had been torn half off in the process of making it as I'd been dragged up the stairs to where my mother had given me a beating for some act of disobedience. There were more of my marks, my memories, scattered about. The tales of all the times I had refused to be broken. Of how I had clung to survival for my sister, making myself the target so she never would be. It was almost laughable that the sole person I'd survived for had been the one to leave me so broken in the end.

Caught in my own thoughts, I faltered on the next stair. Warm fingers pressed to my lower back. 'Steady,' Callum murmured, his breath warm against my cheek.

A breath shuddered through me. His touch was ... *distracting*. Warm. Secure. Everything this place was not. It was shamefully difficult to step away from his lingering touch. Even so, I managed. The distance between us increased as I hurried up the stairs.

The stench of urine, vomit and blood thickened as we emerged onto the third floor. The guard stood at the landing's door. His hand rested on the hilt of his sword as he stared emotionlessly at us. Satisfied that we were caught up, he pushed open the well-oiled door. I stared down the narrow hall. The shadows swamped the place. There were no Illusioned lights, only flickering candles lighting the way. The candles flickering barely gave enough light to see the way forward. On each side of the hall, four doors were tightly closed, bolted from the outside.

Our steps echoed through the space as we passed the doors. Unlike the first floor, there were no sounds from any of the rooms. Callum and I strode along, not a single sound emerged from any of the rooms. Only the smells betrayed that the rooms were occupied. I hoped the occupants were merely sleeping.

I knew most of them were not.

'What is this?' Callum whispered. The same horror from earlier filled his voice.

I swallowed, trying to breathe in as little of the stench as possible. My stomach was already tied in knots; I feared anything else might have me losing my breakfast on the floor.

There was no inflection, no intonation in my voice as I spoke. I would not let him pity me. 'It's where the workers are sent first. Where they're branded and bound to a contract. Where they're trained.' I hesitated, then added, 'Where they're punished.'

His breath caught. 'Did she do that to you? Brand you?'

I shrugged, hiding the knotting of my stomach under a mask of indifference. 'She did. I don't think its visible anymore, behind all the other scars. It was on my back.' I sensed the tension in Callum's body as we strode past door after door. Sighing, I said, 'If it bothers you that much, you can tell my mother you'll be healing those kept in there. Even she can't disobey a command from the king.'

His steps faltered. I glanced back, brows bunching. His lips were pressed together, his skin pale, save for the shadows that were laced at the edge of his eyes. Before I could prod him about what was wrong, our guide announced, 'Madame is in here.'

Any thoughts about Callum's lack of response vanished as I turned around, watching as the door at the end of the hall swung open. The room behind it had not changed much over the years. No window, no bed, no toilet facilities. Just a dirty blanket and a pillow stuffed in a corner. The only difference, was that someone had gone to the trouble of dragging up a wooden chair with a straight, strong back, a scarlet fabric draped over the wood's base.

Its occupant would have been described as beautiful in her prime. Still could be now. Greying blonde hair pulled up in a hairstyle so extravagant it could have belonged on a true queen. Her skin, though beginning to crease, remained mostly blemish free. Rouge stained her cheeks and lips, her golden gown dripping off her like molten metal. A slit ran high up her thigh, leaving the entire length of her leg exposed. She smirked the moment she set her eyes upon me.

'When I heard my daughter had come to visit,' Gabriela Halnea, the esteemed madame of half the brothels in Alluvite, began, 'I'd rather hoped it was dear Cassie.'

I flinched involuntarily – at her voice, at the name, at the memories.

My mother's lips stretched into a smile. 'Then I remembered the rumours from a few months back. That you had managed to kill my only *true* daughter.' The hand steadying my back was the only thing that kept me from crumbling to my knees. This time, I didn't have it in me to move away. Seeing those features, so similar to Cassie's, yet worlds apart, twisting into a malicious smile had sent all the strength rushing from my body.

My mother unfolded her legs languidly. Her eyes ran down my body, tongue clicking with displeasure at whatever she saw. 'Such a pity,' she tsked as the guard closed the door behind us. 'If you weren't such a feral creature, you would've brought me plenty of coin. Even with those scars.' She paused, staring at the lines that poked above my collar and beyond my sleeves. 'Maybe even because of them.'

Again, I recoiled. I couldn't speak. If I were to part my lips, I feared all that would come out would be the wordless screams I had flung her way as a child. I hated this – the way she reduced me to that state.

'We're here for information.' If Callum's voice could be given form, I imagined it would've been as icy daggers. My mother's eyes flicked over to him, her smirk growing into a smile of pleasure.

'My, my,' she crooned, at last rising to her feet. She circled around us like a predator sizing up its prey. 'You certainly have been keeping fine company, pet.' Her hand lifted, pushing off my hood. Cold fingers hooked around my chin. It felt nothing like when Callum had held me there the night before. Red painted nails dug painfully into my flesh, sharp enough that warmth welled beneath the cruel points.

I didn't pull away. My breath rattled out of me, hundreds of the marks upon my body – both seen and unseen – seeming to flare with the ghost of pain. Still, words refused to come.

'Tell me, Your Majesty, has my monster told you all the naughty things she's done?' Her eyes flicked back to Callum's. The rustling of a cowl being pushed back sounded, and her smile stretched. 'That's better. No point hiding faces amongst friends.'

'I have no interest in anything you wish to tell me.' Callum's voice was flat, though I knew better than to think it was emotionless. It was the voice he used when he felt far too much. 'Chiara gets to decide what I do and don't know.'

My mother's eyes cut back to me, and for a moment, they blazed with rage, her nails digging deeper. The vitriol was wiped away a heartbeat later as she chuckled. 'I think I might tell you anyway. Consider it payment for whatever it is you've come here for.'

Steel rang. 'The only payment I'll be—'

'It's fine, Callum,' I cut in, wishing my voice didn't rasp as much as it did. 'She's vindictive. This is the only way we'll get the information.'

My mother's eyes flattened, displeasure briefly entering them before she pasted on another smile. 'It seems you remember me well, pet.' She looked to Callum. 'She was such a disobedient child. So ungrateful for all the opportunities I gave her. Chiara would have been the finest courtesan in the city. In the kingdom, even.' Her laugh was nasty. 'Can you imagine? This ruined thing, once the future jewel of my brothel.'

I stared at her red-painted lips as they moved. Let her tease and humiliate, and she would grow bored. Fight it, and she would retaliate.

'I fed and clothed her. Began training her. And then one day, she turned on me. Killed every single one of the people in here. She even killed her own sister with her monstruous power.' Tears welled in my mother's eyes, turning them prettily glassy with feigned grief. 'And now she's killed my only true daughter again.'

Twisting her wrist, my mother forced my face to turn to Callum's. Her cloying perfume filled my nose, choking me. 'So, before you ask it, Your Majesty, is this worthless creature worth your question? Your time?'

There was no flicker of power in my stomach, no pull to destroy everything. There was no place for my Gift here. Not when the words she spoke were true. I *had* killed Cassie. Twice. Once, by allowing my Gift to flare out of control when we were children. And again, by not being enough to save her.

Callum's eyes were filled with nothing but icy rage, his eyes shot through with black, shadows writhing beneath his skin. It was suddenly hard to gain breath for an entirely different reason to fear as he levelled that glare at my mother. 'She is worth everything. And she's certainly worth more than you.'

Everything stilled in me and then roared to life. I finally yanked away from my mother as she gaped at him. I was drowning in the same disbelief I saw in her eyes.

She is worth everything. They were words I might've spoken about Cassie. Would've whispered to myself as I committed atrocities to keep her safe. But he'd just spoken them about *me*. And that ... that didn't make sense.

Somehow, I managed to rip my eyes from Callum to look at my mother. 'We want to know how to access the godly realm. And we heard you've been bragging that you know a way. Some concoction that separates the soul from the body.'

'Why should I tell you, you little brat?' My mother spat the words out as she reclaimed her seat, though with far less grace than she had before. Anything beautiful about her had disintegrated with her expression. It was an ugly one, twisted with years of malice and resentment.

Callum's laugh was low and wicked. 'Because if you don't, you're going to suffer.' There was a promise in those words as his hand fell to his sword.

My mother did not balk. Instead, she threw her head back and laughed. 'You can't touch me. Your father signed a contract. He agreed I could run whatever schemes I wished, employ as many as I wished, so long as I didn't interfere with the crown.'

The shadows upon Callum's skin entered his words as he smiled. 'My father is gone. And contracts can be destroyed as easily as they are made.'

'Only a few months into your reign and you're already making such lofty threats.' She sneered. 'You really are your father's son.'

Callum's knuckles whitened around his sword, but his smile didn't slip as he tilted his head. 'Who said I was to be the one to make you suffer?'

My mother's attention flicked to me. I held her stare. Made sure she watched as my hand dropped to my weapon's belt, locating my favourite dagger. I was not a child any longer. I would not be cowed by her. And so, I let a little of the monster into my smile, into my eyes, as I stepped forwards. Silver graced my skin, tiny starbursts of light that danced over my fingertips. My smile only grew as she seemed to spy that monster. As she paled, and the tip of my dagger drew a bead of blood at her lovely neck.

'M-my guards,' she gasped, her body pushing back in the chair. I didn't let her escape the dagger's sting.

'Won't hear a thing,' Callum assured her. 'And if they do, if they even care, I'm sure we can deal with them.'

My mother's eyes were now full of true fear. There was violence in Callum's voice. And there was certainly violence in me.

'One more chance,' he warned, stepping up to my side. 'Before Chiara does to you what I'm sure you've done to her. Tell us how to get to the godly realm.'

The silver at my fingers leapt towards her. She cried out, jerking and deepening the cut at her throat. The sparks dissipated before they touched her. 'I don't know,' she gasped, her voice a tremulous mess. She no longer looked a queen.

Callum shrugged, turning away as I slowly slid the dagger down the delicate column of her neck. It halted just shy of cutting her bodice. 'Wait!' My mother's fingers were claws against the arms of the chair, but she didn't try to defend herself. She knew better than to touch where my skin was glowing. 'I don't know, but I do know someone who might.'

'Well?' Callum prompted when her voice failed her. 'If you're finding it hard to speak, perhaps Chiara can—'

'There was a boy!' she gasped. 'One not much older than you are now, who brought you. Claimed he drank something to get here. Said you were a gift from the gods. I would've never taken you in if I knew the truth. Knew that you were a curse more than a gift.'

'Back on track,' Callum ordered.

The hatred in her eyes swerved for a second to him before coming back to me. 'I don't know his name. His voice had the sound of the eastern empire.'

'Not helpful enough. Chiara, feel free to cut something vital.'

'Wait!' Another shriek, desperate as I reached to hold down a hand. 'There was something else. His eyes! His eyes were strange.'

Callum strode forward, leaning over my shoulder to glare down at the shaking woman. 'How so?'

Her chest rose and fell with great gasps, each shuddering inhale bringing her skin closer to being pierced. Fear had swallowed her whole. 'Yellow eyes,' she said, the sounds merging in a desperate bid to please Callum. 'He had yellow eyes. And his name was ... Jack. No, no, Jason. Something like that.'

My dagger retracted as a different kind of anger raised its head. One less sharp, but no less potent. Callum and I exchanged a glance. There was only one we knew with yellow eyes. One, it seemed, who was more of a liar than even I had suspected. And even if it didn't quite make sense, I knew it wasn't a lie. My mother might be vindictive, but when she was truly scared, she was a coward.

Callum nodded. 'Thank you for your help, Madame Tussant. It's been most informative.'

She sagged, blood trickling down her neck. 'I've given you your information.' Her head snapped up, eyes narrowed, lips twisted into a snarl. 'Now, get out of my brothel.'

Callum turned to me. 'Well?'

'Well, what?' I shoved my dagger back into its scabbard. I'd have to give it a thorough cleaning later to rid it of her stain.

'Will you do it, or shall I?'

I lifted my hands, considering the silver sparks there. They had not abated since they'd first sprung to my skin. My Gift knew what I wanted. Knew that the moment I'd resolved myself to come here, there was only one way this ended. One way I could begin on my path of vengeance for Cassie.

'Are you deaf?' My mother rose to her feet, her shadow looming large. 'Get. *Out.*'

'I hope the Dark is as monstrous an afterlife as it seems,' I said as I lifted my hand towards her, fingers curling around her chin in the same way she'd held me earlier. My Gift didn't surge. Not immediately. There was enough time for understanding to blossom in her eyes. For her to try to pull away from me, and the stench of urine to fill the air as her golden gown became wet with her fear. And just enough time for my lips to curl into a smile.

Then, silver light flared. It filled the room, crackling power raising the hairs on my arm. She screamed – short, high, and agonised. If not for his Gift from Vitus, Callum would have been screaming beside her. The light rescinded, leaving behind a scattering of silver ash.

'Huh.' Callum toed the pile of silver that lay where Madame Tussant had stood only moments before. 'I thought you'd draw it out.'

The sparks on my skin submerged back into my body. 'Oh, I would have done,' I stared at the pile that had once been my mother, 'but my sister wouldn't have wanted that.'

'What do you want done with the brothels?' he asked, already turning away from her remains. In spite of my attempts to quell it, a smile tugged at the corners of my lips. How my mother would've raged if she'd known how quickly the king had moved past her death. To know she was beneath his notice. Beneath my notice, too, as I turned from her. 'I can burn them all if that's what you wish.'

I hesitated. Did I wish that? There would be a degree of satisfaction to it, but without my mother here to watch her empire razed, it seemed somewhat pointless. I shook my head. 'No. Give it to the workers. Free them from their contracts.' We began walking down the corridor. I hesitated as we passed the nearest door. 'There'll be some who need medical attention. Plenty who'll be beyond even your help.'

Something tightened in Callum's features. He did not look at the door. 'There's non-Gifted healers at the palace and scattered around the city. I'll send someone for them.'

I studied his profile, eyes narrowing. For the first time since I'd come to the palace the night before, he refused to look at me. 'Can't you heal them? The worst of them, at least.'

As though in answer, the shadows beneath his skin deepened. 'I can't.'

I lifted a hand towards him, not quite touching. 'But—'

'I can't, Chiara.' The use of my name was jarring. He glared down the corridor. 'I wish I could, but I have my duties to see to. Duties that could see more dying from starvation or crime if I neglect them. They'll survive with the non-Gifted healers.'

My hand fell away. I stepped back, dipping into a shallow bow. 'Of course, Your Majesty.' Straightening, I smiled with all the venom I could muster. 'After all, how could a mere commoner expect your personal tending? I should be honoured to be in your presence at all.'

His head whipped towards me, shadows twisting within the green of his irises. 'That's not what I meant.'

I brushed past him. My chest burnt – with anger, with embarrassment. Of course he wouldn't heal them. I should've known better. And why had I even asked? I was not meant to care about anything aside from my vengeance.

'Don't let me take up anymore of your valuable time,' I said. 'It seems I've inconvenienced you enough as it is.'

'Chiara—'

But I was gone, door to the landing slamming closed behind me, before he could say anything else.

Chapter Fourteen

By the time Callum came downstairs, I had released enough of my anger to have a swift, abrupt conversation about what needed to be done. It took all night to clear the brothel of patrons and to inform the workers they were free of any indentured service they had left to complete. Most stared, hollow eyed, when they were given their leave. The rooms on the third storey had only been filled with corpses: bodies left to rot until someone new came along. The rest had long since been broken, souls destroyed so thoroughly I doubted they would make it through winter.

But when they were told the Madame had perished – even the most broken turned to hide their smiles.

Callum and I exchanged clipped words but, as the night wore on and the full cruelty of the brothel was revealed, he grew quieter and my mood fouler. I could only imagine the thoughts churning through his mind. The conclusions about me he must be coming to as he corralled the non-Gifted healers and sent them to those who were the worst off. By the time dawn painted the world in golden hues, we were headed back to the palace. Every so often, Callum would turn towards me, lips parted and a look of unbearable sympathy in his eyes. And every time he did so, I sped up, whatever he wished to say lost as the distance increased between us.

We reached the palace entrance. Callum paused, turning to me yet again. 'Chiara, I—'

'We made a mess of that brothel. I'm sure you need to sort things out,' I said, refusing to meet his eyes.

'That's not what—'

'I'll leave you here, Your Majesty.' I ducked past the hand he reached out to me, fleeing into the palace's depths like the coward I was. I debated going into town and finding the cheapest, vilest liquid I could find. The type that burnt the throat and wiped the mind. The sort that could leave me dead if I drank too much. Perhaps if I did, my skin might stop crawling as it had the moment we'd set foot in the brothel. Maybe I'd forget that look in Callum's eyes – one of sympathy and concern. A look that I neither wanted nor deserved. It took all the strength I had not to succumb to the temptation.

But I had a job to do, and a liar to confront.

First, I visited my rooms, changing from the black clothes that reeked of the brothel's incense. Digging through my wardrobe, I found an unadorned pair of white linen pants and a sky-blue shirt, with long sleeves that cinched at the wrists. My cloak stayed on, though. As suffocating as the scent was, the various compartments contained a number of my much-needed weapons. I was still debating which of them I would use against Jaxon when I found him.

I had quite a few to choose from. Three daggers, including my favourite, in my weapon's belt. Four hunting knives, more suitable for animals than humans, but not entirely out of the question. Two smaller throwing knives in case he made a run for it. And tucked into my hair, two slender pins that were currently holding back my curls in a bun but that would easily be able to push through an eye and straight into the brain.

Satisfied that I had enough of an armoury on me to draw out answers from Jaxon, I stalked out of my room and almost crashed into Deana. One look at her flushed cheeks and irritated expression warned me she was on the precipice of fury. Given she was storming from the direction of Callum's chambers, I had a fair guess what might be causing it.

Her eyes narrowed further as they settled upon me. 'Would you care to tell me where you've both been?'

I tilted my head towards the closed doors down the corridor, where I imagined Callum must've disappeared into. 'Didn't you ask Callum?'

Deana snorted, flicking her hair over her shoulders. 'Wherever you went, it's put him in a foul enough mood that he told me if I didn't stop knocking, he'd send me to work in the laundries for the next five weeks.' Her eyes widened with horror. 'Have you seen what that does to one's hands?'

She lifted her own hands as though to show they were indeed worth more than laundry duty. Her pale skin was callused in all the places that marked someone who knew how to wield a weapon, but not in any of the places of someone used to hard labour. A lady, one of the guards had said. I could see it, in the way she walked with her shoulders back, her smooth skin and the cut of her clothes, that she was a mark above other guards and soldiers.

'How terrifying,' I deadpanned.

Deana nodded earnestly, then paused, taking in my clothing. 'You look different in that. Nice. Less, *I'm going to murder your entire family*, and more, *I'll murder only you*.'

It was easy to keep the twisting emotions out of my voice as I said, 'Thank you?'

She beamed. 'You're welcome. In return, perhaps you can now tell me where you and Callum were all night?'

I took in her own garments. She had lost her king's guard uniform, replacing it with a day gown of midnight blue. The laces pulled tight at her midsection, accentuating her curves. 'Callum allows you to wear that as a king's guard?' I asked, sidestepping her demand.

Deana snorted again, a sound I had never heard from a noble. Her hand brushed over the soft-looking material, smoothing it. 'Callum doesn't *allow* me to do anything. Besides, clothing is an armour in itself. I'm the least threatening a person can be. A lady.' She widened her eyes, sweetening the smile on her lips. The perfect picture of a guileless noblewoman.

'That's ... smart,' I said, and meaning it. I generally viewed my gender as nothing more than an obstacle. It caused no end of annoyance when I was underestimated, again and again. Yet Deana turned it into a strength, honing her femininity into a weapon. I was a little intimidated by it, and by her.

She sighed, reaching over and linking her arm with mine. I tensed but did not pull away. How long had it been since anyone had treated me so casually? Jaxon didn't count – I often questioned his sanity. And Callum ... well. There was an entirely different problem with him.

'If His Majesty refuses to exit his room,' Deana said. 'I suppose you'll have to fill my time instead.' Her eyes sparked with mischief. 'So, what will it be? Dancing? Spying? Sparring? All worthwhile pursuits for well-bred ladies such as ourselves.'

I opened my mouth to protest, but the words didn't come. Because, despite knowing better, I yearned for female company. I hadn't had it since my second-in-command, Ada, had died at King Kane's orders. Besides, I rather thought Deana would delight in what I was going to suggest.

'I think I can do better than that.'

'Oh?' Her eyebrows raised, lips tipping up into an expectant grin.

'How would you like to see Jaxon's balls nailed to a wall?'

The glint in her eyes became wicked delight as Deana began pulling me to the palace exit. 'You do know how to spoil a girl.'

As we strolled the streets of Alluvite, Deana seemed to find joy in every other shop window. There was a dress she told me we must go and try, some food we would have to come back to purchase, and jewellery that would look spectacular with a gown she had. Every time she tried to show me something, I turned my eyes away. I had never had much interest – or enough coin – for shopping. The only times I had ever walked through these streets, eyes scanning the trinkets and wares, was to find something for my sister. Small pieces of the world I could bring back to her. Now, seeing the vibrant colours and lush fabrics, that empty place inside of me grew, along with the ache for a drink.

The sun was breaking through the clouds, combatting the chill of the air as we made our way to where I suspected Jaxon would be. The streets narrowed and grew darker the further we went from the palace. Clothes became more threadbare, voices roughened and speech turned vulgar. Despite looking out of place in her fine dress, Deana smiled brilliantly at every coarse curse she heard.

'How does a lady become a king's guard?' I asked, when at Deana's insistence we paused at a small pastry shop. She studied each pastry with a keen eye. Finally, she settled on a layered, flaky pastry filled with chocolate. Ordering two, Deana answered as we waited for the baker to wrap them in paper. 'With great difficulty.'

Taking the package the baker offered, Deana handed me one of the pastries. I closed my eyes, in raptures at the way it crumbled in my mouth, the chocolate a melting pile of goodness. Gods, it had been some time since I'd had anything other than bland mush and almost rotted fruit.

'I was betrothed – a match arranged by my parents when I was ten years old.' Deana's voice lost its typical lightness as we walked down the streets. 'He was twenty years older than me, and not a good man. I was visiting the palace with my parents one day and ran into him. He tried to corner me…' Her throat worked on a swallow, the brightness in her eyes dimming. 'He never got a chance to do anything, though, because a little golden-haired boy came around the corner and demanded he unhand me. The man laughed. He said that even a prince couldn't stop him from taking what was his. Callum replied that I was his property, that I was to be his spymaster, and that to touch me would be a crime punishable by death.'

'What about the king?' I asked, reeling a little from her ordeal. 'Didn't he deny it?'

Deana laughed, the light re-entering her face.

'That was the beauty of it. Callum said it was the king's decision and decree. He knew that King Kane would not name his only son and heir a liar, and thus draw doubt on Callum's lineage and succession to the throne – which would risk the stability of the royal line and provoke assassination attempts. He might've hated Callum, but he loved the power of being king. There was no way he'd risk that.'

'What happened with your betrothed?' I knew men. Knew what they were capable of if they believed themselves spurned. Liam's face flashed through my mind, his hands pressing against me, his knife cutting my skin as he leant over me, threatened to do things to me. A shiver ran down my arms.

Deana's smile was a cold, brittle thing. 'He was given a coveted position in the army as recompense and posted on the Archin border. Last I heard, he'd vanished when everything went to shit. He undoubtedly knew he'd be stripped of his rank as a general once Callum was crowned king. Callum had even been talking of execution for war crimes. Rumour has it the man fled to Archin to pledge his loyalty there.'

My blood went cold. 'A general?'

Before rumours of a complete purging of the army's command had started, a month or so back, there'd been plenty of generals out there; most of them detestable, some of them barely competent, and a rare few actually useful. There was only one I knew of who would have been likely to have done anything heinous enough to warrant Callum's order of an execution.

Deana's eyes slid to me, to the way my skin blanched and my fists tightened, before she nodded slowly. 'General Tizan,' she said. 'I take it you've met him?'

The sight of his arrogant smile as he'd sent me to deliver Liam back to Alluvite filled my head. 'He killed my friends,' I breathed. 'And sent me my second-in-command's head.'

Deana's hand curled around mine, squeezing tight. 'One day,' she promised, intensity thrumming through her words. 'One day, we'll find him. We'll make him pay.'

I swallowed hard. Gods, I'd missed female companionship. The possibility of a friend. Maybe it was a wretched, selfish thing to do when I remembered so clearly what had happened to my other friends. But I hadn't slept for over a day, my emotional stamina was drained dry, and I was a wretched, selfish creature. I couldn't find it within me to muster the defences I'd been maintaining for months. To banish Deana's warmth so I could drown in my own isolation. So, I squeezed her hand back.

By the time we reached The Den, I had learnt enough about Deana to know she was an indomitable force. It was a wonder I hadn't ever run into her in my years training in the palace. A wonder, and yet not. From the sounds of her prowess, I suspected King Kane had deliberately kept us far away from each other.

Isolation was a key weapon in the old king's toolkit, a form of suffering to ensure I stayed his loyal dog. And Deana was the sort of person you could never feel isolated around.

She had trained, Deana told me, between the ages of ten to thirteen with the other guards before it was discovered that she really did have a knack for spying. Callum called her into his personal retinue, and she began to build networks around the city. There was, she informed me, an informant in almost every brothel and tavern in the city, and many in the other towns around Naruzia. Deana's mother and father had been cold and distant since she was a babe, becoming more so once she'd shunned the betrothal. Both had died in a raid from Archin years ago. Deana hadn't attended either's funeral.

Deana didn't ask any prying questions. She didn't try to get me to talk about my sister, or the drink I downed every night. She didn't push me to tell her about my father, or Vitus or Liam. Instead, she chattered away, leaving silences for me to fill – quickly filling them herself when it was clear I wouldn't. When we reached The Den, she dragged me away from my usual entrance and led me through the spectator entrance, cutting a path through the crowd to seats draped in shadows, near the wall surrounding the arena.

'As excited as I am to see Jaxon lose his favourite part,' she whispered as we settled into our seats, pointedly ignoring the ogling of the man to her left, 'Why, exactly, are we nailing his balls to the wall?'

I regretted the next breath I took as the stench of the space slammed into me. The air here was too familiar to the rooms on the upper level of the Rose and Crown. Blood and bile coated the floor and walls.

It wasn't easy, opening my mouth and allowing the words to come forth. To expose even a hint of the truth. 'That information you found, about my mother,' I began slowly, watching as Deana nodded her head. 'That's where we were. At her brothel.'

And despite knowing she was dead and had suffered, despite freeing the poor souls chained to that place, a small part of me still flinched at the thought that I had been back to that place. Deana's arm brushed against mine. 'And?'

'Apparently, whoever knew how to access the godly realm had yellow eyes.'

Deana's attention swung to the arena below. Her hands fisted on her skirts as she glared down at the currently empty space. The stands were almost full, signalling a match was soon to begin.

'That bastard,' she seethed, her words filled with venom. 'That lying, conniving *bastard*.'

I raised my brows. I was angry, but the rage that seethed in Deana's voice spoke of resentment that had built up over years. The sort that came after betrayal. I recognised the fury, even if it had now become something different. Something softer and yet far less palatable. 'What, exactly, is between you two?'

'I don't know what you mean. He's a low-life criminal who somehow weaselled his way into a general pardon for past and future crimes – provided no innocents are harmed in his dealings. And now he owns plenty of places like this.' She swung her hand wide, gesturing to the ugliness of The Den.

I bolted upright in my chair, staring at her. 'Jaxon *owns* this?'

She gave me an odd look. 'Of course. Didn't he spend most nights here with you over the past few months?'

'I just thought this was a convenient place to scam money off others. He told me he was a handler for the fighters.' I sat back down, folding my arms in irritation. 'He could definitely have paid me more.' Deana's smile didn't quite reach her eyes as I studied her. 'And you're definitely not telling me everything.'

She opened her mouth, no doubt to protest any further connection with Jaxon, but was saved by doors slamming open.

The first one in was a woman with hair shorn close to her head. She wore what looked to be lightweight, black armour that moved sinuously as she walked. Golden chains were wrapped around her waist. A chill ran down my spine. The chains were eerily similar to the chains that Liam manipulated Callum and I to deliver straight into King Kane's awaiting hands. Dearil was likely still bound by them.

'I want that,' Deana whispered, pointing at the armour. I nodded in agreement. It was a fine creation. The woman came to a stop at the edge of the arena. She did not deign to look up at the audience. Either she didn't know the benefits of appealing to a crowd, or she didn't need their approval to back up her fighting skills. From the unwavering focus in her eyes and confident tilt of her head, my money was on the latter.

Around us, audience members clamoured to make their final bets. Deana's eyes flicked to a squat grey-haired man, who accepted coins with greedy eagerness. 'Should've brought Callum's money.' She touched the pockets of her dress with a frown.

'You haven't even seen the other person yet,' I said, not bothering to check my own pockets. If there'd been any coin in there, I wouldn't be spending it on a worthless bet.

Deana smiled. 'I don't care. My money's on her.'

Seconds ticked into minutes. The opponent still didn't show.

The Den seemed to have a problem with punctuality.

Leaning back, I folded my arms and scanned the audience for any sign of Jaxon. It was too dark to make out much; shadows cloaked most features. People crowded together, shoving for the front of the audience area or scrambling for the back where coin changed hands. Sometimes, it'd be for a bet. Other times, a package would be passed back – drugs, weaponry, anything that the city's guard would usually crack down on.

My gaze caught on one figure standing on the opposite side of the pit; too far back to make out anything other than a tall frame that could only belong to a man, and a straight-backed posture. Nothing like how Jaxon, laggard that he was, would stand. Yet my attention was pinned on him, and how the other silhouette seemed to give him a wide berth.

And even though I could see nothing of their features, I could've sworn I felt their eyes meet mine.

'Deana,' I whispered, nudging her side.

She twisted, her skirts rustling. 'You find him?'

I shook my head. 'Do you see the man on the other side? The one at the back? You don't think ... Callum wouldn't come without guards, would he?'

Deana stiffened, needing no other explanation. 'He would.' She let out an annoyed huff. 'Do you know how many times I've told him he needs to bring guards with him? He's far too confident in his own skills. All it'll take is a lucky blow, and we'll be a kingdom on the brink of war without anyone to lead us.'

I pressed my fingers into my palm. 'Would he have followed us?'

Deana was silent for several long moments. Someone dropped a bottle behind, glass shattering as a fight broke out to our left. The audience were becoming impatient. At last, she said, 'No. Not if he thought you'd be unhappy about it. Unless, of course, he thought there was a risk that someone would get hurt.'

My cheeks heated as I shifted, looking away from who I was now certain must be Callum. 'Why's he here?'

'If he was with you when you found out about Jaxon, he likely figured he'd find out the truth by himself.'

'He has people for that,' I argued. I could still feel him making his presence felt to me. Still feel his eyes on me, while my own were involuntarily being drawn back to him. I forced my focus back to the pit. 'He has *you*.'

'But he knows Jaxon is close to you,' Deana said, as though it should've been obvious. 'So he likely wants to find out the truth before getting anyone else involved.' She began to rise. 'I should go—'

'No.' I grabbed her wrist, dragging her back down. A man to her right grunted as she knocked into him, but one sweet smile of apology from her made him too flustered to do much more than blink at her. 'Don't.'

Deana frowned. 'But—'

The arrival of the other fighter saved me. The door below creaked open, a slim, lithe figure slipping through as Deana sighed and sat back down. I frowned. Jaxon always guarded the door to protect his investments, and make sure said investments didn't flee. Yet there was no sign of him. Instead, the contender meandered his way further into the arena. His cloak of scarlet, dripping down his body like a waterfall of blood, shielded his features from view.

'Do you see Jaxon?' I asked Deana, who was staring across at Callum with a small crease in her brow. 'He's always here.'

She opened her mouth as she shifted her attention downwards. Opened, then closed, then opened again. By the time she gathered her thoughts enough to speak, it was no longer confusion that creased her features. It was anger. 'That asshole better not get himself killed before we can tear him to shreds.'

I followed her glower back to the arena just as the other contender pushed back their cowl. I took in the smile first – wide and ready to cause chaos. The thick, black hair perfectly styled. And those damned eyes. Bright yellow and promising trouble.

'Gods,' I breathed. 'What is that idiot doing?'

Jaxon pulled a curved sword from his cloak, allowing the fabric to pool around his feet after he'd unclasped it. A design of curling leaves and flowers shimmered yellow beneath the Illusioned lights. Designs from Axania, he'd once told me, drawn by someone he'd once known. He hadn't elaborated past that, and I hadn't asked.

There was a breath of silence and then, the fight began.

The woman was as strong and agile as I had imagined, darting towards Jaxon with enviable speed. The darkness flowed with her. It hounded her every step, wreathing her with shadows. My stomach lurched at the sight, at the memory of the last person I had seen wield shadows Gifted by Akmad. The night Cassie had died, when King Kane had sent dozens of palace staff falling to their deaths.

Jaxon didn't flinch as the shadows crashed into him. The entire audience plunged into the same blackness, annoyed murmurs arising. There was the sound of metal against metal, a grunt and then a sharp cry of pain.

Fingers found mine in the darkness. 'Can you see it?' Deana asked, her voice hoarse as her nails dug into my skin. 'Jaxon. Is he – is he all—'

As quickly as it began, the darkness fled, bathing the world in light once more. Deana's hand dropped away as she exhaled. The woman was now directly in front of Jaxon, golden chains swinging with practised ease. One blow would be all it took. Blood dripped from his nose onto the ground, infusing the stone in its vibrancy. Deana half rose, but I gripped her arm and dragged her back down. Interference was paid for in blood.

Jaxon smiled tauntingly. 'Is that all you've got?'

The woman's chest rose with a sharp inhale at the clear challenge. Her chains swung, light reflecting off their golden lengths. Deana's hand found mine once more, gripping me tightly. I had been right. One blow was all it took. Just not from who I'd expected.

Even as I, as the whole crowd, flinched at what was sure to be the end, Jaxon moved.

He ducked, twisting under the swinging chains, the

momentum of which left the woman unsteady on her feet for no more than a heartbeat. That was all Jaxon needed. He struck with the lithe speed of an asp, swinging his blade hard at her neck. The yellow carving flared brighter as they neared her neck. She didn't have time to duck, or do anything but widen her eyes and part her lips. Blood sprayed through the air as Jaxon's blade sunk deep, finding its way to just above her armour. He smiled with vicious triumph as he yanked it free. More blood spilt. It dripped to the ground, coating that well-made armour as she fell to her knees. He didn't bother watching as the woman pressed a hand to her neck: a futile attempt to stem the flow of blood. Her eyes lifted, pupils blown as she searched the audience for somebody to help her.

No one did.

And when she collapsed, her death warming my skin, the crowd broke into a roar of approval. Jaxon grinned, lifting his arms in the air, and the cheering grew louder. Blood coated his hands and cheeks. Here, brutality and blood paved the way for greatness. And this – whether they knew it or not – was their king.

'Who will be next?' His voice easily cut through the cacophony of claps. Everyone fell into dead silence. Jaxon's smile grew vicious, then amused as the silence stretched. 'No one? Not one of you is brave enough to challenge me?'

Someone coughed. Another let out a nervous laugh. But there were no takers.

Jaxon nodded his approval. 'It seems you've learnt your lesson.' He kicked a foot into the side of the woman's body, tilting his head towards someone unseen. Moments later, two adolescent boys ran forth. They grasped the woman's wrists and dragged her corpse away. 'Next time someone wants to whisper secrets about me and mine, don't let me find out.'

I understood then. This hadn't been a fight. It had been an execution.

He spun slowly, eyeing the audience one last time. He slid his sword away with a violent ringing of steel. 'If no one else will fight me, then we're done here.'

He was still smirking as I shook off Deana's restraining hand. Rising to my feet, I spared a quick glance across the audience. Callum had shifted closer to the front. Enough so that I caught a glimpse of his frown as I strode down the stone steps and vaulted over the wall, landing softly on my feet behind Jaxon.

The crowd fell silent once more.

'I'll challenge you.'

Chapter Fifteen

Jaxon hid his shock well, his momentary confusion vanishing behind the mask of his condescending smile. The crowd watched with bated breath, waiting to see what his next move would be. Waiting to see what punishment my impudence would bring.

'This spit of a girl wants to challenge me?' Jaxon called up to the crowd, waiting until their laughter came before hissing to me. 'What, exactly, do you think you're doing?'

I smirked, mimicking the exact expression Jaxon had worn before. 'What does it look like?'

Jaxon's smile tightened. We circled each other, neither of us withdrawing our weapons. Not yet. 'It looks like you've got a death wish.'

'Oh, it's not me who has a death wish.' I grinned, showing all my teeth and forcing myself to keep my focus on Jaxon. To not think about who was watching from above. 'I made a visit to my dear mother today.'

'Mother?' Jaxon's brow creased. There was a fleeting moment of confusion, and then panic.

'Madame Tussant,' I elaborated. The panic cleared, replaced with relief. The bastard was somehow *relieved* by what I had said. Why? What other secrets was he hiding? My teeth ground together. Focus. I needed to focus on my task. On getting answers. 'She had some interesting things to say.'

Jaxon winced but didn't answer my unspoken question. The audience had begun to murmur at our whispered conversation. I continued on. 'How about a bet?'

I could see the crime lord in his eyes as they narrowed, calculating, figuring how to twist this to his advantage. 'Go on.'

'No use of Gifts. Just sword against sword. I win, you tell me what I need to know. You win…' I trailed off, inviting Jaxon to finish the sentence.

'A favour,' he suggested, voice loud enough that the closest audience members shouted their approval. Gambling outside of the pit was exciting, but inside was entertainment. His eyes were sharp with cunning as his voice lowered. 'And I'll offer you the same, in addition to whatever secrets you want. If you win.' He grinned. 'You won't. Not without your Gift.'

A favour. It was a dangerous thing to offer him. No matter how friendly we were, Jaxon would not hesitate to use the favour to his advantage. Even if it meant hurting me, hurting others, in the process. For a moment, I hesitated. My eyes lifted before I could think to stop myself. Callum, was now at the front of the audience, almost directly opposite where Deana was sitting. The light caught disapproval in the set of his features as he shook his head sharply.

I looked back to Jaxon, unable to hold Callum's stare. He'd seen too much the night before. Maybe Deana was wrong. Maybe he was here because of that sympathy I'd seen earlier. Because he no longer thought I was capable of protecting myself.

Ignore him, I ordered myself, even as I sensed it was an impossibility. I'd never managed to carve Callum from my mind, even in the months we spent apart. I certainly wouldn't be able to do so now.

'Well?' Jaxon prompted when I didn't speak.

His offer might just be a new way to bind myself to another's whims. I still needed those answers more than I needed to avoid being involved in sticky situations. And I could always find a way out of being under his thumb if I needed to.

After all, favours only belonged to the living.

'It's a deal.' I sketched a shallow bow before withdrawing two hunting knives from their scabbards. Better suited for animals as they were, it would make winning all the more satisfying when I brought him down.

Jaxon withdrew his blade once more in a fluid movement. It was a beautiful blade, the curved edge glinting a shade of silver brighter than I'd ever seen on a sword. One time, when he was almost as deep into his cups as I was, he had told me it had been crafted by a master forger in Axania. Another thing I had not cared to ask more about, even when I saw the shadows in his eyes.

'My people won't be very happy if this doesn't end with one of us dead,' Jaxon said conversationally, beginning to circle. *My people.* The words were telling of his power.

I shrugged, letting my knives swing by my sides. 'I'm sure you already have some entertainment lined up for later in the evening to smooth things over should one of your fights not be taken well.' From the gleam in his eyes, I had guessed right. 'And if I don't like the information you give me, then they'll get their share of blood tonight.'

'No Gift means no using your fancy magic to improve your swordplay,' he warned, victory already gleaming in his eyes. 'It wouldn't be fair if the daughter of death started—'

'So you do know about my father.' I'd guessed as much but had never been able to confirm it.

'I trade in secrets. Of course I know.' He waved a hand as

though to brush aside that information. 'No Gifts. You said it yourself.'

I frowned as though I hadn't already planned for that. My Gift was well and truly locked away, courtesy of two swift drinks from small flasks I had tucked away in my cloak. We began at the same time, neither of us needing to confirm the other ready. I spun, my knife slicing for his neck. He launched himself backwards, letting out a wild laugh before lifting his sword in a swing of his own. Metal clashing as I parried, slid my knife along his sword as I lunged inwards, elbow driving for his throat. Before I could connect, Jaxon lifted his forearm. He grinned at the impact. I twisted, one knife, shoving at his sword while the other drove for his midsection. He did not falter. His sword flipped, the flat of it meeting my blade.

Before he could counter-attack, I jumped away. We eyed each other, circling with predatory intent. It was like a game. A step forward from him, one backwards from me. A lunge from me, a twist away from him. Most other male fighters I'd faced relied on brute force, big sweeps and powerful movements. Those were always the easiest to defeat.

But Jaxon – he moved like a dancer. Every movement, every twist and turn, was part of a choreography with an end I couldn't quite see coming. For every one of my thrusts, there was a counter. Every lunge, a dodge.

But he still wasn't quite as good as Callum.

I almost looked upwards. Jaxon took the opportunity, lunging towards me.

I fell back, feet slipping on the stone. The time I allowed Jaxon to see the sweat beading on my forehead, the slight tremble in my hands. I fed him the truth he wanted to see – that without my Gift, I was no more than ordinary with blades. He pushed his advantage. His sword swung in from the side. It collided with my knife, hard and accurate. I didn't have to fake the clenching of my teeth at the reverberations that sent tiny shockwaves up my arm. My fingers struggled to hold on to the hilt as I narrowly dodged another blow aimed at my neck.

Jaxon smiled tauntingly, believing himself a cat playing with a mouse. 'You could've just asked for information,' he said, stepping forward as I stumbled back. My back collided with the wall behind me, the rough stone scratching at my skin. Jaxon was good. Better than good. He moved as though he'd fought for years, for longer than some of the most experienced soldiers I'd ever fought with. It wasn't hard to see how he might have clawed his way to the top of the underworld, how he might have succeeded as a pirate. 'I might've even told you. It would have been less painful that way.'

When I grinned up at him, his smile was a mirror image of my own. 'This way is far more satisfying.'

He was ruthless in his attack, swinging again and again. I dodged one, blocked the next, but the third came so quickly, I didn't have time to do anything but lift one hand. The flat of his blade slammed into my wrist with a cracking sound, sending a pain sharp enough that my fingers sprung open. One of my knives clattered to the ground.

'You're good enough, even without your Gift, I'll give you that.' Jaxon smiled as I glared at him, lifting the remaining knife. 'But it's time to concede, Chiara.'

'Don't condescend to me.' I kicked the knife away, sending it spinning to the other side of the arena. 'If you're going to fight, use the sharp edge of your blade.'

'I would if we'd agreed you could use your Gift.' He swung his sword like a pendulum as I stepped back, giving myself breathing room. 'But I have no desire to kill you. And that's what I'd do if I didn't hold back.'

Cocky asshole, I thought to myself as I smiled sweetly. 'You're forgetting something.' I switched my knife to my other hand.

Jaxon raised a brow as we circled each other. 'Do fill me in.'

'My Gift might've been what helped me begin killing. But I've trained, hour after hour, day after day, year after year. I have been beaten and broken and whipped every time I failed.' My smile grew vicious as a kernel of suspicion entered Jaxon's expression. 'It's not my Gift that helps me win now.'

I brought my impractically sandalled foot up, driving it into Jaxon's stomach with all my force. He let out a choked wheeze as he bent double, stumbling back a few steps. He coughed, barely managing to straighten before I launched into my attack, sweeping into a series of parries and blows he barely kept up with, his sword finally moving with his full skill. His eyes were wide, his skin beaded with sweat.

We were back in our game. Only this time, I was leading it, and I planned to win.

I thrust again and again, careful movements made to test limits, test strength. He met them all. But with each parry, his strength weakened, his feet finding it harder to maintain their ground. All it took was one misstep from Jaxon. I veered to the left, aiming my knife for his side. The sword swept down to intercept. I grinned, and realisation entered Jaxon's eyes. The knife arced through the air, landing securely in my other hand. I swung upwards. Within seconds, the point was under Jaxon's chin.

'Concede,' I whispered, both of our chests heaving, sweat running down my back in thick beads that clung to my shirt. My heart beat wildly in my chest – not with fear, or adrenaline, but with excitement. How long had it been since I'd had a living opponent truly draw a sweat?

Not that long, a voice whispered, dredging up memories of Callum. I glanced upwards as Jaxon's sword fell to the ground in surrender. But in the shadows of the audience, there was no wicked gaze ready to meet my own. Callum was gone.

Good. That was good, I tried to convince myself. I didn't want him here.

Wrenching my attention back to Jaxon, I raised my brows. 'Well? Will it be surrender, or should we find out how many body parts you'll lose before you give me my information?'

There was a heartbeat's hesitation, and then he threw his head back and laughed.

The crowd was silent for a few moments, caught between laughing with Jaxon at a joke they could not understand, or demanding I slit his throat. With anyone else, they would already be calling for his blood. But fear had crept through their ranks the moment Jaxon had cut into his previous opponent's neck, which stilled the calls for more blood to spill. I decided for them. Sheathing my blade, I offered a single nod to the audience. There was a beat of uncertainty, then the cheering started. Blood might be what they were after, but we had put on a fine enough show that they didn't thirst for it tonight.

'You truly are a surprise,' Jaxon said as he brushed past me to the door behind. I narrowed my eyes, falling into step with him. If Deana wasn't already waiting for us, I knew she'd find her way to the alley quick enough.

'And you owe me answers.'

Jaxon nodded, his only sign of agreement. I pulled my cloak around me, bracing myself for the cold outside. As predicted, Deana was leaning against a stone wall. Her skirts swayed in the breeze as she straightened. Jaxon faltered, whirling to me.

'Really? You brought her?' I smiled at the scowl he wore.

'Of course she brought me.' Deana pulled her hair back into a ponytail, quickly securing it before the wind could whip any more strands across her face. 'She knows you're a sneaky, two-faced bastard and that you deserved me heckling from the sidelines.'

Jaxon's eyes narrowed. 'Always a pleasure, Deana.' He glanced around. 'And where is that king of yours, Chiara? I could've sworn I sensed an arrogance big enough to fill The Den before.'

I frowned, struggling not to defer to Deana for an explanation. It didn't matter that Callum had been there. That he'd disappeared before we'd finished our fight.

'That arrogance would've been yours,' Deana said drily.

'We made a deal,' I interrupted before things could progress to childish squabbling. I kicked a crate over to Jaxon. It slammed into his shins, earning me a pained grunt. 'Sit and start talking. What did Madame Tussant tell you?'

I sat down upon a second crate, watching his expression carefully. There was no telling what lies he'd attempt to slip into his words.

'That you know a way to travel to the godly realms,' he said, and a burst of anger skittered through me. I forced it down. Answers first, rage later. 'You knew that I was searching for a way through. You're correct on both counts,' he said slowly, no hint of apology in the words.

I barely stopped myself reaching for my knives. 'And you didn't think to tell me? If you'd told me, I wouldn't have—' I broke off, shaking my head sharply. *Wouldn't have to have gone back to the place my nightmares started.* Deana's gaze prickled at my skin, her brows drawing together at whatever expression lay upon my features. Jaxon sighed, leaning forward to rest his forearms on his knees. Dried blood painted his fingers and his boots as he scrutinised me. 'I had to know.'

My heart quickened, a mix of fury and trepidation squeezing my insides. My voice was deadly quiet as I replied, 'Had to know what?'

Jaxon's gaze met and held my own. 'Had to know if you had given up.'

The Broken

I reeled back, shoulders hitting the wall as the crate clattered across cobblestones. *Had to know if you had given up.* He didn't need to elaborate. 'Why?' I bit out, with enough venom that Deana tensed. 'What business is it of yours whether I—' For the second time, I choked off the words before they could pour out. The words rattled through my head regardless. *What business is it of yours whether I've given up on living?*

Jaxon watched me carefully, measuring my reaction. Planning his response accordingly. 'If you went there, if you came out, I knew you would be able to continue. If not...' He trailed off, shrugged, then continued. 'It's dangerous information to possess. No point yielding it to someone intent on dying.'

Deana shot forward then, her eyes blazing. She did not reach for a weapon. Instead, red light shimmered between her hands. Within seconds, a knife formed, the blade long and fine. Perfect for gutting open the man before us. I stared at the crimson hue of the weapon. She had to be Gifted by Kerta, goddess of war. Even amongst the ranks of Kerta's Gifted, those who could form weapons from thin air were highly coveted.

'Don't speak to her like that,' Deana warned, the blade's tip centimetres from Jaxon's throat. He didn't raise his eyes to her, but his shoulders were tenser than I'd ever seen them. It was as though every muscle was fighting against an urge to tilt his head back to study her.

I hesitated, debating whether it would be worth the mess to see Deana truly nail his balls to the wall, before stepping forward. 'He's right,' I said. Deana opened her mouth to protest, but I shook my head. 'He's an ass, but he's right. Information like that ... if it got to the wrong people, it could be cataclysmic.' We already had one god on the loose, and that ... that had destroyed everything important to me. Who knew what more slipping between the realms would do. 'No sense sharing it until he was sure I would complete the journey.'

Deana huffed. The knife lowered but did not disappear as she leant against the wall beside me. I turned back to Jaxon. 'So, how do we do it?'

Jaxon's smile was sly: a fox through and through. 'If I tell you here, little birds might steal the secrets away.' As he said it, a pebble dropped from the roof above, clattering against the ground. My eyes shot upwards. I caught a glimpse of a child, brown hair loose and wild, as they scampered over the roof tops.

'One of yours?' I asked, returning my attention to Jaxon.

He shrugged. 'That one was, but there were more than one. I have enough enemies to know no street is without its ears.'

'Later, then,' I said. Deana crossed her arms, her weapon finally disappearing in a fine red mist. Mistrust narrowed her eyes. I rose, offering a hand to Jaxon as a peace offering. He took it, hauling himself to his feet.

'One thing doesn't make sense, though,' I said quietly, scanning the rooftops for the ears he'd mentioned. The palace would be relatively safe to talk openly. Even so, the question pressed on me, begging me to let it out. 'My mother said a young man, not many years older than me, dropped off a babe at her doorstep. At first, I thought maybe it was a relation – I've not met any other with your eyes, but perhaps a brother or father might have.' I paused. Jaxon was silent, assessing. 'But then she said your name. Or close to it.'

Another pause. Deana led the way a few steps ahead, but the tension in her shoulders gave away her eavesdropping.

'I was the one to bring you,' Jaxon confirmed.

'That doesn't make sense,' I repeated. 'How could you be the one to drop me at that place if you're only a few years older than me now?'

His smile was jesting, but his tone was deadly serious as he answered, 'Because I've been this age for three hundred years.'

I stared at him as Deana's steps faltered ahead of me. I should be laughing now, accusing him of being insane, or running far, far away. Yet there was no amusement in Jaxon's eyes. No hint of a lie.

'How?' I breathed, heart thundering in my ears.

Amusement was there in his eyes. 'Gods have children more than you think. Surely you didn't think you're the only halfling out there?'

Chapter Sixteen

Not the only halfling out there. The words thundered through me as we walked back to the palace in silence. I had never considered the possibility that the abomination of my parentage might not be a one-off. I observed Jaxon the whole way back, though he walked apart from Deana and I, barely looking at either of us. As much as I wanted to fire questions at him until he begged me to stop, I didn't dare to, not in the open, or at all. Instead, as we strode past the palace guards, I distracted myself by arguing with Deana.

'We don't *have* to involve him,' I said, stepping into the sterility of the main corridor. Someone had placed fresh roses on a side table, several petals scattered at the base of the vase.

Deana sent a deadpan look my way. 'He's the king.'

'I'm with Chiara,' Jaxon quipped from behind us. We turned matching glares on him, signalling *shut up* in unison. He held his hands up, falling back a step.

'He's the king of the *mortal* realm. And only part of it,' I said with all the confidence of someone whose argument made little sense. 'We're talking about going to the *godly* realm.'

Deana sighed, her skirts brushing over the marbled floor as we turned a corner. 'I know you vowed to kill him and all, but I'm the one who'll have to deal with all the whining if you were to suddenly vanish.'

I eyed her. 'I could kill him now and save you the whining.'

Deana laughed. 'Oh, I doubt you would do that.'

I crossed my arms and scowled. 'It's just ... surely we can wait until after to tell him?'

'Tell me what?'

My body tensed even as my skin warmed. Callum's voice was deceptively mild – pleasant even – as he appeared from a doorway on the left wall. His eyes tracked over the three of us and our mismatched clothing. Deana, who grinned at me in her gown. Jaxon, who sketched an exaggerated bow in his scarlet cloak. Me, in my crumpled white trousers and cropped blue top. His gaze dragged over me the longest, pausing on a splatter of blood at the hem of my trousers before lifting to my face.

'Would you care to tell me why you thought offering up a favour to a criminal was a good idea?' Callum asked, and Jaxon had the gall to look offended.

'Would you care to tell me what you were doing out of the palace without guards?' Deana asked sharply, shifting in front of me. When Callum only folded his arms, she sighed and swept past him, her head high in the air. I made to follow, but his hand snapped out, curling around my upper arm.

'Chiara—' he whispered, as Jaxon slid past and shot me a roguish wink. I glared at him, stoutly refusing to look at Callum.

'Jaxon has information,' I said shortly, pulling myself free of his grasp, trying to ignore the lingering warmth from where he'd held me. 'And don't grab me like that again if you want to keep that hand.'

I hurried after Deana before he had a chance to say anything else, catching him exhale – a short, irritated sound – as his booted steps pursued us. The room Deana led us to was a familiar one. It was as unadorned as the rest of the palace. A large, wooden table took up most of the room, eight chairs of dark brown pushed in around it. The wall furthest from the door was occupied by a bookshelf that spanned wall to wall, containing tomes of long-forgotten history. A map, discarded and collecting dust, sat in the middle of the table. My feet carried me over to it, my fingers trailing the familiar lines and landing on the circle around the Niguran forest.

I swallowed hard, shoving my sudden, overwhelming grief down before it could take hold. The last time I'd been here, I'd been naively making plans. Plans to retrieve the chains of the gods, despite knowing, deep down, that they would be used for evil. Plans for my sister's freedom. Plans that had ultimately led to her demise.

Callum appeared beside me, but I ignored him and stalked around the table, slamming myself down into the seat next to Deana. I didn't want to see whatever was written on his face. Jaxon took the chair opposite me. He propped his feet up on the table and kicked his chair back so far, I thought he would tumble off.

A chair scraped, and Callum settled in his seat. 'So?' The word was full of expectancy and command. Deana glanced at me, eyed my scowl, and began talking.

'It turns out that our lovely house guest here'—she pointed an accusing finger at Jaxon, who smiled innocently—'has been lying.' She paused, then amended, 'Lying more than we thought.'

'Is that so.' The chill of Callum's voice was felt as surely as a winter's wind. Jaxon rocked forward until all four chair legs were firmly secured on the ground. His feet remained on the tabletop, the map crinkling beneath them. Deana scowled.

'Your spymaster is exaggerating.' Jaxon pushed himself back

again and Deana's jaw tightened. 'I've simply been ... *omitting* details.'

'Is that so,' Callum repeated. His hand yanked Jaxon's chair back, pushing it firmly to the floor with a *thud*.

Jaxon sighed, rolling his eyes theatrically. 'If you *have* to know—'

'We do.'

'I may have a way to enter the godly realm. A concoction, as Madame Tussant has spent her time bragging about.' His yellow eyes slid to mine, locking on. 'Though it won't be easy.' He rocked back again. 'Especially not if you want to go with the lovely Chiara, Cal.'

Deana's foot kicked out so swiftly that no one had time to react. It hooked around one of the chair legs, pulling viciously. One moment, Jaxon was leaning back, as relaxed as he always was. The next, he was tumbling off, legs straight up in the air and his cloak a swirl of red around him. The crash ricocheted through the room as Jaxon landed, grunting at the impact. He slowly righted himself, staring at Deana with an unreadable expression.

'You will address him as Your Majesty, or you will not address him at all.' Deana's voice was icier than I had ever heard it. Enough that it made me wonder what, exactly, her role as spymaster involved. What deeds might be committed in the shadows.

'That,' Jaxon said, his tone matching Deana's, 'was decidedly uncalled for. Besides, *she* doesn't have to call him Your Majesty.' He jerked a thumb at me. I glowered at him, not wanting to be brought into whatever the mess between them was.

'That's because I like her a lot more than I like you,' Deana bit back.

'As much as I'd love to see Deana rip you in two,' Callum interrupted, as Jaxon opened his mouth, 'would you care to tell me how you know this?'

Jaxon sent one last glower at Deana before turning to the king, sliding his usual smile back into place. 'Oh, you know. Same old, same old. Born to a goddess, spent my childhood in the godly realm learning to do all manner of wicked things, came back here, travelled, delivered a baby – you were very cute, by the way'—he directed at me, and I debated the merits of punching him now versus later—'to a godforsaken place under the order of the child's father.'

The only sign of his shock was Callum's slow blink as he processed what Jaxon had said. 'Your … mother?' he asked haltingly, as though his tongue was struggling to put racing thoughts into words.

Jaxon smiled smugly, but there was a bitter edge in his eyes. 'Did I forget to mention? I'm cursed with the goddess of illusions and stories as my mother.'

'Makes sense that you've such a silver tongue if Tarina's your mother,' Deana muttered.

A moment of shock was all Callum took to digest the information before he nodded resolutely. 'Well, then. How do we get to the godly realm?'

My heart gave a strange lurch at the thought of Callum completing what was sure to be a perilous journey to the other realm.

'You're not coming,' I told him.

Callum raised his eyebrows. 'Are you the one with the information?'

I pressed my palms to the edge of the table as I leant forward, readying myself to rise to my feet. 'No, but I am the one who is going to—'

'Children, children.' Jaxon threw an arm in front of Callum, drawing my glower. 'Please, settle down. And to answer your question, Cal—' He shot a pointed look at Deana before his expression darkened. 'With great care and difficulty.'

'That woman said that this mystery concoction separates body from soul.' Callum studied Jaxon. 'And I've studied books on the godly realm. They suggest that the only way for a mortal to pass through is to be sent to the Gates for their final judgement.'

'Is that what you've been doing in the library the past few months?' Deana asked, twisting towards Callum. 'Studying the godly realm?'

'Studying the passage to the godly realm,' he corrected.

I stared at Callum. 'Why?'

His brows drew together as though he was confused as to why I'd even ask. 'Because Deana told me that's what you were looking for.'

Shifting back on the chair, I tore my focus away from him, my cheeks warming. He said it so easily. There was no shame in his words. No embarrassment. Only calm confidence, as though it were perfectly natural for a king to study for a way to help someone who'd sworn to kill them.

'Nothing living with mortal blood can go between the realms with the barrier up. Even gods can only send their spiritual essence, and only for a few moments. Unless, of course, they bind themselves as Vitus did to Kane's body.'

My shoulders slumped. 'So, it's not possible.'

'Oh, no. I never said that.' As one, all three of us frowned at Jaxon, who smiled. He let the silence stretch out until Deana half rose from her chair, fists clenched, then he hurriedly continued. 'It's simple, really. All you have to do, to travel between the realms, is die.'

Chapter Seventeen

Callum launched to his feet at Jaxon's announcement, his chair rattling behind him. 'No.'

Jaxon kept his eyes on me. Waiting.

Understanding dawned. 'This was the whole point of your little test, wasn't it? Why you didn't just tell me you had the information?'

'If you do this, you have to *want* to come back.' He paused, brows drawing together before he asked, 'Do you?'

Callum stared, confusion scrunching his expression. I ignored him as best I could as I considered Jaxon's question. I wasn't sure I would have been able to say a confident yes a few days before.

I wasn't even sure I could give a confident yes now.

'It's not happening,' Callum said, no room for yielding in his voice.

'It's not you who needs to be worried.' Jaxon did not move his eyes from me as he spoke to the king. 'You have your fancy Gift. Your body will likely repair itself within moments. Repair my lovely form, as well.' Callum flinched, but Jaxon ploughed on.

'And it'll take a few days for me to find the right poison to stop us actually dying, so you'll have time to prepare. I don't have any preparations to make – you'll be doing all the work, after all – but…' He trailed off, before shifting his attention back to me. His meaning was clear. There was only one amongst us who could not be touched by Callum's Gift.

'Gods dammit, it's not me I'm worried about!' The words cracked through the room, shattering any response I was beginning to formulate. My heart picked up a notch – in fear, in rage, in so many emotions I couldn't untangle them. I twisted my head until I was staring directly at him. Callum's fists trembled where they pressed onto the table. A muscle ticked in his jaw.

It easiest to grasp hold of the rage. 'You said before it wasn't my decision to make whether you come or not. But you also don't get to decide for me,' I said.

'I'm not trying to decide for you.' He paused, shook his head and said, 'Or maybe I am, but it's not my intention. You have a habit of throwing yourself into danger, though, with very little thought for yourself. You need to think this through, not rush into it.'

'I've been thinking on only this since the day Cassie died,' I said, my throat tightening as it always did when I spoke her name. 'This is the chance I've been looking for. I'm not going to throw it away for you.'

'Not for *me*. For yourself.' Callum stared at me, the shadows under his eyes pronounced under the light. 'Please, Chiara. I can't do anything if this goes wrong. Jaxon isn't talking about the possibility of injury. He's talking about death.'

'If that's my fate, so be it.' I didn't look away from him. He'd seen too much weakness in me the night before. 'But I will not let your fear stop me from going.'

Callum sighed, dragging his fingers through his hair in an

aggravated motion. 'Why is it that the person I want most to listen to me is perhaps the only one in this kingdom who won't follow a king's commands?'

'If it makes you feel better, I wouldn't follow your commands, either,' Jaxon piped up unhelpfully.

Everyone ignored him. 'Is this because of last night?'

Callum frowned. 'I'm not sure—'

'Don't bother lying. I saw how you looked at me. The pity.' The word tasted sour. 'And I saw you in The Den. I saw you leave before the fight was over. Was that all it took? A glimpse into my past, and you've decided I'm too weak to do anything.'

Callum's expression twisted with what almost looked like pain. 'Chiara, I don't—'

But whatever he was about to say was thankfully cut short by a knock at the door.

'Expecting someone?' Jaxon asked cheerily. He'd settled back into his feet-up position, though all four chair legs remained steadily on the ground, and he kept a close eye on Deana. Callum didn't shift his gaze from me as I rose so I could do something, anything, other than look at him.

Deana beat me to it. She opened the door a crack to reveal an older man of about sixty. He ran a trembling hand over thinning white hair, his chest heaving in a too-tight shirt ill-suited for his frame. A line of sweat gathered in the moustache at his trembling upper lip.

'M-my lady,' he panted, attempting to bow. Deana steadied him when he almost fell on his face. 'I was told His Majesty would be here?'

Deana nodded, swinging the door open wider to reveal Callum. I could still feel the prick of his eyes, then their absence as he reluctantly turned them on the man at the door.

'Steward Terrion,' Callum said in surprise. I peered closer, finally recognising the man. He had been a trembling, quiet man in the old king's presence, responsible for the daily tasks in the castle and announcing visitors as they arrived in the palace. Looking at his quaking figure now, it seemed not much had changed.

'Your Majesty.' Again, the steward tried to bow. Deana leapt into action, ushering him forward before he could embarrass himself further and shake so violently he split in two. 'There's news from Archin. I came as soon as I heard.'

I watched Callum's face tighten, a change imperceptible to most. Other than that, there was no outward sign of worry. 'Have they finally broken the temporary truce?'

It had been talked about in the city. Whether Archin would press its advantage with the old king gone and the new one so untested. The raids that would surely come, the influx of refugees to the towns closer to Alluvite as they fled the savagery that was always brought. Yet, nothing had happened.

The steward's head shook rapidly, threatening to pop the button done right up to his chin. 'No, Your Majesty. Not the borders.'

Callum waited. When the steward made no move to expand on his explanation, he pinched the bridge of his nose and said with longsuffering patience, 'If not that, then what?'

The steward's hands fluttered around him. 'Oh, yes, Your Majesty. Apologies, Your Majesty. There is word of a coup.'

My heart jumped to my throat. I knew what was coming, knew what he would say, and I should have been able to brace myself for it. Instead, I wanted to scream at him to stop, and to scream the same at Deana as she placed a reassuring hand on the man's arm, nodding at him to continue. His pallor faded as he focused on her kind features, a contrast to my glare, Jaxon's sharp smirk and Callum's indifference.

Deana was the only one gentle enough to calm the man in a room full of wolves.

Terrion swallowed, his throat bobbing under his collar. 'Nearly the entire Archinian royal family is dead.'

Even Jaxon paled at that. King Kane had ensured Archin was our enemy, and yet, there had remained hope that the war might end with a new king. Callum might have been able to, with time, come to some sort of truce. But if they were dead…

The king and queen. The heir, who sounded like he cared more about gambling and women, yet hadn't seemed a tyrant. Two princesses, told to be sweeter than honey in their countenance. The youngest no older than ten.

Gone.

'Who?' My voice was little more than a rasp. The steward turned to me, his brown eyes rheumy with shock that I was daring to speak in the presence of the king. I wondered if Terrion recognised me from the times he had entered the throne room to deliver some message as I knelt on the floor, my back a bloody mess. He had averted his eyes every time.

'Who?' I demanded again when he made no move to answer. I didn't want to know. I had to know. The steward blinked again.

'Answer her,' Callum snapped, impatient.

The steward coughed, cheeks flushing a deeper red. 'Apologies, Your Majesty.' Everyone seemed to bite down on a sigh at that. 'It was the youngest son, Your Majesty. K— Prince Liam.'

My breath caught at his name and at the title he had been about to voice.

King Liam.

I shook my head, the movement driven by horror. A man like that as king. A man who saw people, women, as objects. Who had smiled when slicing a blade through the throat of an innocent. Sitting on a throne with a god-possessed tyrant by his side.

The Broken

Archin was about to become a nightmare, and the rest of the mortal realm would surely follow.

A sharp pain in my arm broke through the dark swirl of my thoughts. Blood welled beneath where my nails dug into my arm to stifle the trembling of rage. There was another question I needed to ask, yet I couldn't bring myself to utter the words.

Callum had no such qualms. 'How.'

The smile that promised all manner of deadly things was enough to get the steward in motion, regardless of whether the king approved it or not.

'The reports we were getting were ... confusing.' Terrion's eyebrows bunched together, as though he was trying to puzzle how people believed such things. 'They said he led an army. An army of golden-eyed warriors.' His features pinched further. 'There were even rumours of...' He trailed off, casting a glance at Callum worriedly before continuing, 'Well, Your Majesty, of your father. Only *golden*.'

My gaze collided with Jaxon's and then Deana's. Both had seen that golden-eyed warrior in The Den. Seen what he could do. Silence settled over us. Shame spiralled through me. I had given up for over a month. Given up on vengeance and stopped fighting to find a way to end Vitus and Liam.

This was the consequence.

'How many died?' Deana asked quietly, her skin pale under the light. One hand wrapped around her garrotte, the other clenched in her skirts.

The steward swallowed again, hands clasping together tightly. His eyes drifted to the floor. 'My Lady, perhaps this is not a topic to be discussed before a delicate woman such as yourself.' He clearly did not count me as a lady. That was fine by me. I barely counted myself as human these days.

'How many.' There was no room for debate in Callum's words.

Another swallow. A bead of sweat rolled down the steward's

jaw. 'The reports are coming in at this stage, Your Majesty, but from what we've heard, thousands. Thousands are dead.'

I sucked in a breath. Thousands. Thousands of soldiers, slaughtered on entry to the city. Slaughtered for doing their job; killed, in part, by their own prince. I had killed many on the battlefields, but this felt different. Unnatural, unjust. How were mortals expected to go up against a god's army?

'I didn't know there were that many soldiers left in Archin.' I spoke without realising I had, the thought popping to my lips as I remembered reports from my time as a captain in the Naruzian army. Our spies had reported that much of Archin's forces were depleted.

The steward slid his watery eyes to me. His lips trembling, his skin paling so much that I feared he was on the brink of death. Deep, dark circles beneath his eyes, like bruises. 'Not just soldiers.' He swallowed before parting his lips, but no words came.

Callum walked over to a pitcher of wine and filled a glass. He strode over to Terrion, shoving it into his hand. 'Drink that. It'll help.'

That Terrion didn't pause to thank Callum before gulping down the wine spoke volumes of how shaken he was. He continued, 'They slaughtered everyone in the city who didn't bow. And then they slaughtered everyone else. The most able-bodied men, the ones who could fight – I heard that they weren't killed, though. They were changed, shifted into … *things* with golden eyes. Reports are that they have been sent to the border under the eye of your former general.'

A ragged breath left Callum's lips as he almost collapsed into his chair. His eyes sliced through with shadows as he stared mutely at the steward. I could see the words in there, a reflection of the ones flowing through me.

My fault. My fault. My fault.

If only I had continued searching for a way to destroy Vitus. If

I hadn't let myself become what I was now. And the biggest one of all – if I hadn't hesitated for that single, vital moment in the throne room. If I had been strong enough to let my sister go, instead of allowing her life to be used to bring a wrathful god into our world.

This was all my fault, as much as it was Callum's. More so. I was used to bloodied hands, but this – this was wading, swimming, in a sea of blood. And most of it belonged to those who were as innocent as my sister had been.

'The children?' Deana asked reluctantly, eyes glassy with tears. I placed a hand against the back of a chair and braced myself.

'Dead.' The word was a whisper from Terrion. 'At least one thousand.'

One thousand children, slaughtered for not bowing to Liam and Vitus. For being deemed useless. Most of them wouldn't have been able to comprehend the weight of the decision their parents had made in refusing to swear fealty. One thousand innocents, gone. And if Dearil wasn't there to usher their souls to the next world…

'Did they burn the bodies?' The question from Jaxon was so abrupt, so strange, we all turned to face him with a question in our eyes. His usual glib expression was now hard. What invisible scars that likely lined his soul? Three hundred years he'd lived, he'd said. In those years, how many children had he seen slaughtered?

The steward's lips pressed into a thin line before Callum's hard stare hastened his answer. 'Not that I—'

Callum cut in before the man suffered a heart attack. 'Thank you, Steward Terrion. You may go.'

The poor man looked like he was about to burst into tears as he fled the room. Callum turned to face Jaxon, who was watching after the steward with an unreadable expression.

'Why did you ask that?' Callum asked reasonably. Not accusing, just interested. Assessing.

Jaxon turned to Callum. He opened his mouth, then closed it. Shook his head once before saying, 'I'll be heading into the city to put some pressure on those I've sent to hunt down the poison we need. The sooner we enter the godly realm, the better.'

'Why?' I asked, my finger tapping against my leg as I fought against the suffocating press on my chest.

Jaxon's jaw tensed. 'I need to speak with Kerta before I say anything.' He said the goddess's name casually, as though she were a distant relative rather than a divine being. 'There's no sense in planting ideas in your head if I'm wrong.' He dragged his hand over his face. 'Gods, I hope I'm wrong.'

I turned to Callum, searching for … something. A plan? Cutting words to slice through the danger we faced? Even if it shamed me to do so, I couldn't help but seek his quiet reassurance.

Instead, he sat, pale-faced and staring off, as though seeing the sight of the massacre in his mind. The sight of Callum so shaken sent a bolt of dread through me. Enough of one that my chest tightened further, my airways contracting. I closed my eyes, and all I could see were images of thousands of children's bodies. Killed then discarded, not even given the dignity of burning. What had happened was nothing like a battlefield, where suffering was found on both sides no matter who won. It was an extermination.

Suddenly, I couldn't breathe. Couldn't do anything but turn and, like a coward, race from the room. And when I finally reached my chambers, my breath little more than thin wheezes, I shut the door. Rested my back to it and slid to the floor. Crumpled into a ball and pressed the heels of my hands against my eyes until they stung. Turmoil raged inside. There was too much to think about. Too much to regret. Enough that I would drown in it if I let myself. I only waited long enough to regain the strength to push myself up. Then, I drank.

The intrusion of light from the corridor was an unwelcome one. I attempted to blink the haziness from my vision, but it only sent the room spinning faster. The ceiling was a blur of shadows and light. Lifting the bottle, I frowned at it and tipped it upside down. Only a few scant drops dripped onto my cheeks.

'You look terrible.'

Scowling, I threw the bottle to the side, hearing something crash as I forced myself to roll onto my stomach. I'd been so close to forgetting everything. A few more mouthfuls, and I might've found all my fear, all my guilt, gone. 'Go away,' I grumbled, peering at Callum as he stepped into the room.

'How much have you had?'

'Not enough.' I groped around beside me, fingers landing on another bottle. Letting out a cry of victory, I conquered the swaying room to rise into a seated position. 'Stop frowning. This'—I waved the bottle around—'is none of your business.'

Callum's frown deepened. 'I think it's very much my business, given that's my wine you're drinking.'

Forgetting the bottle I held in my hand, I attempted to push my hair out of my face. Instead, I only succeeded in hitting myself in the face. I glared at the bottle accusingly. 'Stupid.'

He snatched the bottle away from me before I could react. 'I hope you're not talking about me.'

'That's mine.'

Callum turned the bottle, eyebrows raised. 'The bottle with the royal insignia on it is yours?'

I started to nod, then stopped, fearing my head might fall off my shoulders. The thought of my head disconnecting caused a giggle to escape. How nice it would be to not be weighed down by my own mind. Adopting a serious expression, I said, 'Yes. Finders' keepers.'

'I'm not quite sure how that works.' He disappeared from my vision for a moment before reappearing, the bottle gone when he crouched in front of me. His brow creased, as it did whenever he was perplexed by something.

I laughed, fingers pressing to the crease. 'I can read your face like a book, you know.'

His fingers curled around my wrist, thumb brushing the fragile skin on its underside. My smile grew. His touch was warm – even warmer than the drink had made me. 'I somehow doubt that.'

'I can.' I shifted onto my knees, leaning towards him. 'You regret me coming here, don't you?'

'I'd never regret anything to do with you.' He gently tugged my hand away from him but didn't let go where he held me. 'Why do you drink so much, Chiara?'

My amusement vanished. 'Why do you care?' I began to lean away from him, but the world was moving too fast. I surrendered to the fall as I began to tip backwards.

A hand behind my neck stopped me. Gently easing me upright, Callum met my eyes. 'I care.'

I snorted. 'You pity me. I saw that look in your eyes after we visited my mother. You think me pathetic. Weak. It's why you left during the fight, too. Because you didn't want to watch me lose.' The words came out with far more hurt than I wanted.

He inhaled a ragged breath. His thumb brushed down my cheek. 'I'd never think you pathetic.'

Another snort from me. If I had full control over my limbs, I might have turned my back so I didn't have to look at him. 'Right.'

Callum's fingers slid from my wrist to encircle my hand. 'I was furious. So violently enraged by what that woman had done to you, I worried if I looked at you for one more moment I would go and burn down every brothel she owned. And, when I was done with that, I'd hunt down every person who ever hurt you. I was furious at The Den, too. Furious that Jaxon had lied to you, that you'd bother negotiating with him. And I left because I knew you wouldn't want me there once you won.' Pure fire flared in those lovely emerald eyes as he clutched my hand like a lifeline. 'But never once did I think you weak or pathetic. If anything, it only reminded me of exactly how strong you are.'

Not ready to give up on my anger, I replied, 'Then why didn't you hunt those people down?'

'Because it's your vengeance to have. Not mine. And as much as I want to tear down the entire city if it meant no one would hurt you again, I won't take that from you.'

I inhaled sharply at the heat in his words. For a moment, I felt that thread I had sensed a few times before – the one that connected me to life, that tugged and reminded me that my death had not yet come. No one had ever held such anger on my behalf. Maybe it made me a wicked, evil creature, but part of me revelled in it. Revelled in the fact he would gladly kill anyone, destroy anything, for me. And that terrified me.

I stared down at where his hand held mine. 'Stop.'

Callum raised his brows. 'Stop what?'

'Stop pretending to care.'

'No.'

A breath hissed out between my teeth. 'No?'

'No, Chiara.' His eyes flicked over my face. 'I've lived a life where my every breath has been dictated by my father. I built a wall around myself, just as you've done. And I would do almost anything for you. But to stop caring, to stop feeling – that is one of the few things I won't do.'

My heart thudded. I didn't know what to do with what he had

said. All I knew was that I needed to stop him talking before those walls he spoke of crumbled. My hand wrenched free of his and circled his neck, my nails digging into his fragile skin. I glared up at him. Waited for him to fight me off as we both knew he was capable of. Instead, he only smiled.

'Do it.'

My fingers trembled. A little more pressure and he wouldn't be able to sneak in breath to fuel his words. Beneath my touch, I felt his pulse race, synchronising with my own. 'You're an infestation.'

'An infestation?' The laugh that rumbled through him vibrated through my fingertips. 'I don't think I've ever received such a high compliment from you.'

I glared at my fingers, ordering them to tighten. I wouldn't kill him – I'd already decided our future would end in a parting rather than with his death – but I could leave him unconscious. Let myself stand alone once more, just as I'd done for most of my life. 'It's not meant to be a compliment.' I leant closer, pressing my fingers deeper into the smooth column of his neck. He tilted his head as though to allow me better access. 'You invade my mind in every waking moment. You're like a gnat that's buzzing around that won't leave me be. It's – it's infuriating.'

His lips twitched. 'Another fine compliment.'

I focused on his rapid pulse. No human could tame their heart, yet I didn't think it was fear that sent his racing, just as I knew it wasn't fear that had mine spiking. 'I should kill you and be done with it.' A lie, but I needed to rebuild my defences. Needed him to believe me nothing more than a monster.

A wicked gleam entered his eyes. 'Then go ahead, Captain.' His smile – gods, it was a thing crafted of all things dark and dangerous in the world. Something that made me see red. Something that made my entire body heat. 'Kill me.'

His fingers pressed harder against my own. My hand jerked of its own accord, loosening before I could pinch his airway shut. 'You can't do it.' There was a taunt to his words.

'I can.' I glared at my traitorous hand. *Do it*, I willed it. *Do it before you give in.*

'If you were going to, I would've been dead the day you left the palace.' Callum's breath coasting across my cheeks as he angled his face towards me. We had both risen to a kneeling position, my hand at his throat and his holding it in place. Locked in a strange embrace neither of us pulled away from. 'Tell me why you drink.'

Maybe it was the alcohol. Maybe it was the exhaustion that settled over me. Or maybe it was the closeness – the way each of his breaths brushed my skin, every heartbeat felt beneath my fingers – that finally destroyed my defences. 'Because I failed.'

'Failed at what?' His brows drew close. 'Killing me?'

'All those people who died in Archin. Those who'll die here.' The room blurred. This time, it wasn't the drink. 'Her.' The word was a broken whisper.

The hand on mine jolted as Callum inhaled sharply. 'Gods, Chiara. You can't mean—'

'I thought I would be the monster in everyone's story but hers. But in the end, I was the monster in her story, too. The one who let her down when she needed me the most.' Bitterness twisted everything inside me. Suddenly, I needed that hand at Callum's throat to be around my own instead. Needed it to claw out my guilt, my shame, and leave it spattered in crimson hues upon the floor.

Callum's hand tightened, refusing to release me. His eyes darkened, shadows growing amongst the green. 'Let me be the monster of your story,' he said, his voice sharp and brittle and ... angry. Angry at me. 'Rage at me. Curse me. Fight me. But never—' His free hand lifted, cupping my cheek with a gentleness at odds with the rage in his eyes. 'Never make yourself the villain.'

'But I am.' My eyes bore into his. 'I am the villain. Every night, I kill and I kill and I kill. And do you know what I feel while I'm soaking my hands in blood?' I don't give him a chance to answer. 'I *enjoy* it.'

The anger faded, replaced by a crooked smile. Fondness crept into his expression, like someone looking at a child who has just admitted that they enjoy the sweets they aren't allowed to have. 'I didn't say you weren't cruel, Chiara, or that you weren't the wickedest person I know. You're certainly that.' His eyes drifted downwards, lingering on my mouth. My cheeks warmed, my breaths shallowing as I found my own gaze lowering. 'But you're not evil. You're not a villain. You're the kind of cruel this world needs. The kind of cruel *I* need.'

I stared up at him. At the way his lips parted a fraction. At the strands of golden hair that fell upon his brow. At the challenge that burned in his eyes. And then my hand was shifting, sliding behind his neck and tangling in the tousled strands there. I pulled him downwards as his hand fell to the small of my back, tugging me upwards. We were of one mind. One desire, each of us burning with anger and desire. And all the things we'd both been taught not to feel.

The moment our lips met was more than anything I had ever felt before. It was not the fight of last time, nor the gentle kiss I had once shared with Liam. This was fire and need, want and desperation. Callum was the air I needed to breathe, the water I needed to drink. My lips parted in a gasp as he wrapped his other arm around me, pulling me flush against him. Everywhere he touched was warm, our bodies melding together as though they were made for each other. My fingers dug harder into his hair. The scent – his scent – of sandalwood and the coming rain surrounded me. My veins were filled with molten desire, and his touch was the fuse that would set me alight. His fingers curled around the side of my waist. More. I needed more of him.

Even as I thought it, Callum gently eased me back, the hand that had been pulling me closer now holding me in place as I resisted. He smiled, his scar only adding to the wickedness of his expression.

'Not right now, Captain,' he whispered into the tension-riddled air. 'I will not have you when you're only half in your right mind.'

Every part of me was ablaze with want, the walls I had built well and truly ruined. He'd had the nerve to stoke the embers of a desire I had thought stamped out, only to be the one to pull away.

'You're a bastard.' Irritated, I attempted to create some distance between us. Instead, I leant too far. The room began spinning again, my body becoming weightless.

Callum caught me before I crashed onto the carpet. Cradling me to his chest, he rose to his feet, lifting me up with him without the slightest hint of effort. Pressed against his chest as I was, I could feel his heartbeat. Feel every rise and fall of his chest, the tension in every part of him.

He wanted me. I could feel it. I scowled up at him. 'That's not fair.'

'What's not fair?' Fingers combed through my hair, pulling strands off my face.

Sighing with contentment, I closed my eyes. Any coherence had disappeared from my mind, the alcohol truly setting in. 'You can't kiss me like that and then stop.'

A soft laugh sounded. 'I thought you wanted to kill me.'

'I don't think I'd like that.' I cracked open an eye, peering up at him. 'I'll find a more creative way to punish you.'

Callum's smile was a dark thing, edged with promise. 'I'm sure you will, Captain. But not tonight.'

Huffing out a breath, I flipped onto my other side, eyes shutting once more as the room spun wildly. There was a long silence as I tried to keep some semblance of a filter in place. I lost the battle after a minute of valiant fighting. 'I don't hate you.' My fingers pressed into the mattress. 'But I don't … I don't think I deserve to feel anything else.' My breath stalled as I waited for Callum to say something. To brush it off, or tease me, or agree.

Instead, there was only silence. Indignance swelled. I twisted around, ready to stagger to my feet and demand some sort of answer. But when I did, all I found was shadows. Callum was gone.

Chapter Eighteen

By the time my pounding head and roiling stomach abated enough to allow me to slip out of bed, the sky was already golden with the afternoon rays of sun. The wine I'd drunk so liberally the night before had allowed me to slip into a dreamless sleep. When I'd woken, my splitting headache was second to the shame of the kiss. I'd sworn to myself that I wouldn't allow myself to touch Callum like that again. To need him so desperately. And yet, it had been me who'd initiated that kiss. And he'd been the one to pull back.

Cheeks aflame, I glared at myself in the full-length mirror perched against the far wall. My hands bunched into the skirts of the dress I wore, trying to shove away the memory of his fingers pushing against my back, curling into my side, his lips on mine as he deepened the kiss, as I reached up and—

Giving my head a sharp shake, I released my fists from my dress. There was a brutal simplicity to its design that I admired – the sheer fall of the skirts, the sharp cuts of the bodice that left plenty of scar-riddled skin exposed. I could understand why Deana had said dresses were a kind of armour. And I wanted this – this separation from the person I had been last night. Wanted to be someone who knew how to navigate the machinations of kings, and held control over their own traitorous emotions.

Eyes rising, I brushed my fingers along the ring of greenish-purple bruises that still circled my neck from my last fight at The Den. Perhaps Callum would wear his own chain of bruises today. Something about the thought of that – of something I'd marked on his flesh, on the fragile skin at his neck – had my cheeks deepening in colour.

'Gods,' I muttered, turning from the mirror. I needed a distraction. Not just from that, but from the thought of Archin, too. All those people, dead. The kingdom we'd fought so hard against, wiped out in a day. How long until Naruzia was wiped out, too? After shoving a dagger into a thigh scabbard cloaked by my skirts, I strode from the room. A young man with pale hair grinned at me, leaning against the wall. 'Afternoon, my lady.'

'Not a lady, Harris,' I replied brusquely. The guards who were on rotation outside my room were a cheery lot, though I questioned the sanity of some, considering how easily they acted around me. It didn't surprise me that Deana had chosen them.

Kailey straightened next to him, her braid falling over her shoulder. She smiled but kept her hand close to her sword. She, at least, had some sense. 'Begging your pardon, my lady, but we were given clear instructions by the king's new advisor that we must address you as such.'

My eyes narrowed. 'Newest advisor?'

Harris nodded eagerly. 'I can't remember his name – the lord who's been living here.'

'The lord who's been living here,' I repeated slowly, suspicion starting to build. I hadn't spent much time walking the palace corridors, but surely Callum or Deana would've mentioned if a lord had been staying within the palace walls. All nobility, aside from Deana, had manors scattered across Naruzia. 'This lord told you to address me as my lady?'

The guards nodded in unison.

'What does he look like?'

Kailey's brows bunched. She glanced over my shoulder, her gaze locking onto someone. 'He's rather handsome.'

'I am, aren't I?' Jaxon's cheery voice sounded.

Turning, I glowered at Jaxon. 'Do you ever stop lying?'

'Lying?' He tilted his head, brows drawing low. 'Whatever could you mean?'

'You tell me, *Lord* Jaxon.'

A smile bloomed. 'Ah. That.' He shrugged. 'Well, it's only a matter of time before Cal sees sense and grants me a lordship.'

At the irreverence with which Jaxon spoke of their king, Harris inhaled sharply while Kailey shifted. Shaking my head, I grabbed Jaxon's arm and hauled him away from my guards. 'I'm surprised Deana hasn't stuck a sword through you for lying to her guards.'

'She tried to,' he said with a wince. 'But I convinced her it's the best way to explain the presence of a criminal and'—he cast me a sidelong look before settling on—'*you* in the palace.' His attention shifted downwards, brows raising. 'You're dressed up.'

'And you're…' I trailed off as Jaxon's jacket came into focus. A brilliant clash of colours, the dusky tones of a fading sunset meeting beautifully with his olive skin, silver buttons gleaming on the front. His trousers were comparatively plain, serving to accentuate the fine make of the sword strapped to his side.

'Dashing? Fabulous? Handsome?' Jaxon grinned wickedly. 'Why, thank you, my dear. I *am* all those things.'

I rolled my eyes. 'What I am is bored.' A lie. The itching on my skin wasn't from boredom, but from the need to do something. Anything, to stop feeling so useless.

A smile lit up his face, and I regretted my words. 'Finally, you admit it.' He leant, his elbow nudging at my side. 'You miss The Den.'

I shot him a sidelong glare. 'What I *miss* is not being confined to a stuffy palace with a stuffy king.'

Jaxon's smile grew knowing. We passed a maid running a feather duster over an empty side table. She nearly dove back through the nearest door in an effort to avoid us. 'Ah, so it's about our dear Cal, then.'

'No, it's – That's not—' I took in a calming breath. 'I need air.' Needed to clear my head so I could focus once more on bringing Vitus down. Jaxon had said it would take a few days to make the preparations for the godly realm. I had to be ready before then.

Jaxon's steps did not falter as we twisted around a corner. 'I saw Cal this morning,' he said conversationally, though I could feel him studying me from the corner of his eye. 'He seemed rather on edge.'

I frowned. 'Of course he would be after the news we received yesterday.'

'I don't think that's all it is.' Jaxon paused by a window, staring out over the rooftops of Alluvite. 'I overheard him in a meeting with Commander Lena and three of the army generals.'

Leaning against the wall beside the window, I frowned. 'Overheard?'

Jaxon's shameless smile didn't reach as high as it usually did. There was an edge to his eternal amusement that had my own nerves tangling. Maybe he was also caught in a web of horror and shame over Archin.

'Eavesdropped,' he corrected. 'They were discussing the best way to set up defences should our enemy turn their attention here. There was lots of discussion and plenty of threats, but Callum seemed to be rather calm about it all. The moment he stepped away from them, however, his expression changed. He seemed …

frustrated. Hurried out to the courtyard without so much as a greeting.'

'I'm not sure why you're telling me this,' I said, frowning. 'The king's mental state is none of my concern.'

'So you don't know what might have put him in such a mood?'

My mind filled with flashes of my fingers on his neck, then his lips on mine, his hands wrapped in my hair and— 'No.'

Jaxon sighed. 'I'd believe you if you weren't wearing an almost identical expression to the one he was wearing.'

'I'm not wearing any particular expression.'

'You look furious.'

'I'm not,' I snapped.

He raised his brows. 'So you're not scowling at me like you're considering whether using your Gift might be a good option right about now?' As my scowl deepened, Jaxon clapped me on the shoulder. 'Mortals have emotions, Chiara, as much as you like to pretend otherwise. Get used to them.'

'I'm not a full mortal,' I muttered. 'Neither are you.'

His laughter was strained. 'Gods, I wish I was. I envy them their short lives. If I'd died like one, I wouldn't be having to deal with all of this now.'

I stared at him, searching for a hint of insincerity. There was none. And, for the first time, it occurred to me that those years he'd live – they'd be the same I'd one day endure if I wasn't killed first.

'How long do half gods live?'

Jaxon shrugged. 'It changes, depending on the strength of the divine blood in our veins. Someone like me? I'd probably approach a thousand years and still have a few centuries to go.'

The thought of all that time sent a shudder through me. Hesitantly, I asked, 'And me?'

He studied me, lips pressed together and brow furrowing. But rather than answer straight away, he then turned to look out of the window. Stared to the north, where Archin lingered somewhere beyond the horizon. 'I don't think you want to know the answer to that.'

'I do,' I insisted, even as a chill settled over me. Gods, I didn't want to live for centuries. Didn't want to see people wither. But maybe that'd always been my fate – to watch those around me die.

Jaxon sighed. 'Based on your divine blood, I'd say—' He broke off, the acrid scent of smoke hitting him the same time it did me. His brow furrowed as he leant forward, shoving the window open. Tendrils of grey wove through the air before us as he stuck his head out.

'Is there a fire?' I asked, trying to catch a glimpse of the city beyond him. Fires weren't unusual in the slums, though they were usually contained quickly by the city guard.

Jaxon pulled his head back in. 'The smoke seems to be coming from the front of the palace.'

The front of the palace. The courtyard? Where Jaxon said Callum had headed.

Oh, gods. My heart pounded fiercely as I threw myself into a sprint, several guards scattering out of my way with startled shouts as I powered past them. They didn't try to stop me. Reason warred with fear as I moved. There was no reason to think Callum was in any danger. No reason for me to care, either. But what if there'd been some accident or an attack? Was he injured? Dead? The thought felt like an untethering – a shattering of any barrier between myself and my emotions. Fear bolted through me as I skidded around the palace walls and arrived in the eastern courtyard.

Any worry disappeared underneath a surge of fury as I skidded to a halt underneath a sky tainted with brownish-grey smoke. Callum was nowhere to be seen. Instead, several guards worked to throw boxes of wines and spirits into a raging bonfire.

The Broken

One of them lifted his head at my arrival. He took one look at my heaving chest and clenched fists and blanched.

'The king,' I bit out. 'Where is he?'

'I ... In his receiving chambers, my lady,' the man stammered.

I didn't pause to thank him, whirling around and stalking back into the palace. Servants scattered and guards shifted, but none dared step in my way. Even those outside Callum's chambers stepped aside as I burst in.

'What in the gods' names do you think you're doing?' I demanded.

'I tried to stop her,' Deana called behind me. It was a lie. She'd seen my fury, smirked, and pointed to where the king was working.

Callum glanced up from where he stood at his desk, hands planted to either side of a map. Sections of it – most of Archin and some of the northern-most towns in Naruzia – had been marked in red ink. For a moment, curiosity struck and I began to shift closer, then remembered I was furious with him.

'Good evening.' He returned his gaze to the map.

'Don't give me that.' I jabbed an accusatory finger at him. 'What are you doing?'

Slowly, Callum removed his hands from the edges of the parchment, allowing it to curl back up. 'I presume you're speaking about the bonfire.'

'Bonfire?' I seethed. I spun to the window, gesturing at the dying flames. Someone shouted a warning below. A few seconds later, there was the sound of shattering, and the flames flared higher. The fire was massive, undoubtedly due to the fuel the soldiers were feeding it on the king's orders.

'A bonfire.' He didn't bother hiding a smile.

'That's not a bonfire, asshole.' I stepped closer, only the desk separating Callum from my wrath... His eyes gleamed. 'That's ... that's—'

'A good use of the bottles of liquor *I* own? The ones I found in my cellar?' There was a flash of teeth in his smile as he came out from behind the desk.

Trembling took hold in my fists. I stared at the fire. Any hope of forgetting today – forgetting the child Vitus had selected to remind me of Cassie – was quickly vanishing 'You had no right.' I balled the front of his shirt in my hand 'No. Right.'

His hand caught around mine. 'I won't have you drinking yourself to death before I make use of you.'

'I'm not yours to *use.*' I ripped my hand free of his. The emotions I'd shoved down since hearing the news of Archin were a tangled mess. They needed an out. Someone to aim at. Someone who could take it.

And Callum had offered himself as the prime candidate.

My fist cocked back, then shot for his face. He barely blinked, catching the fist deftly once more. But my anger was not done. Not yet. Perhaps not ever. A distant part of me knew what I was doing was wrong – that the trembling in my hands was not from rage, but desperation. A need for the drink I had become so pathetically reliant on. But I wasn't ready to admit it.

'Chiara,' Callum warned as I drove a knee upwards. He dodged, before pushing me backwards. My back collided with the wall. He pressed the hand he still held into the wall above my head, catching my free one before it could hit him.

'Let me go,' I warned. There was a quake to my voice that I despised. A hint at that desperation, trying to claw its way out.

I needed to forget. To find sweet oblivion and drown in it. My heart began to pound faster. As it quickened, my Gift began to awaken. Anger and dread entangled as it stretched, testing the limits of the chains I used to restrain it.

Callum, unaware of the beast within, studied me. 'Are you going to hit me?' My narrowed eyes answered for me. 'Then, no.'

'You don't understand.'

'Then, explain it.' I twisted my head away, unable to bear his gaze any longer. He sighed and his hands came away from mine. 'Are you upset about the fire, or about Archin?'

Both. Neither. 'Archin has fallen, and countless died because we hadn't moved quickly enough.' My stomach clenched as guilt twisted through me. No, not *we* hadn't moved. *I* hadn't.

'It's not your fault.'

My attention whipped to Callum. 'I don't know what you're talking about.'

'You mean you're not rotating a hundred, *what ifs?* right now?' He raised his brows. 'Because I know I have been. What if I'd sought you out sooner? What if I'd dedicated more time before now searching for a way to bring Vitus down?' He smiled, the twist of his lips bitter. 'Trust me when I say, I carry this burden as much as you do. More so, even. But punishing myself for it does nothing to bring back the dead.'

'I know that,' I snapped.

'Do you?' He glanced pointedly down at where my nails were digging into my palm. 'Because that's not what it looks like to me.'

'It's just … I feel so…' I trailed off, unable to find the words to explain as I glanced at the smoke wafting through the air outside.

'Helpless?'

Just as he'd done countless times before, Callum managed to capture everything I struggled to understand in myself in a single word. Fighting the instinct to do as I usually did – spit out something vitriolic and run away – I dragged my eyes back to him. Candlelight had set a soft glow upon his features, highlighting the concerned furrow in his forehead. The sight terrified me. Concern was not something that belonged to me.

'Is it really so bad to go a night without alcohol?' he asked.

Silence fell for some time before I at last answered, 'Yes.'

'Why?'

'My Gift.' Already, I could feel my skin itching, my breath

tightening. My skin prickled with sweat despite the cold night air around us. 'Drinking … tethers it. Calms it.'

Callum considered me for a few long moments before nodding. 'Gifts can be terrifying things.'

Surprise jolted through me. 'Not your Gift, though.'

A melancholic smile curved his lips. 'You wouldn't think so, would you?' I frowned, but he continued before I could work out what he meant. 'Have you considered that it's the edge and the coming down that leads to your Gift lashing out?'

I had, a thousand times over. A million, even. And every time, it was the threat of my memories returning, of the nightmares and waking with sweat-soaked skin and fear pounding in my heart, that kept me from abstaining. 'It's not an option.'

Callum caught a lock of my hair between his thumb and forefinger. 'That's not how you heal. This form of forgetting – it'll kill you.'

'I'm not sure how that concerns you.' I pulled my hair free from his grasp.

His expression intensified. 'Because watching you slowly kill yourself will end me.'

My body shuddered at that – at the thought of him dead. Just as it had before, when I'd wondered if he'd been harmed by the fire. It seemed my foolish heart had not been as strong as I'd believed it to be. Ignoring it, I said in a voice so quiet it was almost lost, 'I never asked you to watch.'

'I've never had a choice but to watch you, Captain.' He leant in, then gazed down at me, and I looked up at him. 'You captivate me.'

'You…' I swallowed, shaking my head to clear it of the pleasant warmth spreading through me, and failing.

Callum stepped back, giving me space to breathe. 'You can keep drinking if that's what you desire. But your vengeance will be hard to come by if you've drunk yourself into an early grave.'

It took longer than it should've for the words to sink in. *Vengeance.* Everything I wanted. The only thing that gave me purpose. And I knew he was right. Had always known it, from the moment I'd first grabbed a bottle and drowned my sorrows. Yet I hadn't wanted to admit the comfort the drink brought was an obstacle in my own path.

'You have a choice, Chiara.' Callum took yet another pace back. A chill that I hadn't realised was present until now crept over my skin. 'If you're still in the palace come morning, I'll take it as agreement that you're choosing your vengeance over forgetting.'

My heart thudded in my chest. Another choice. I was being given too many recently. To go from a life where every big decision was forced upon me, for better to worse, to this. I was trapped under the pressure of getting those choices right. And this choice tore at me. The dilemma of forgetting all my pain with the drink versus choosing a path of vengeance for my sister.

Callum left without another word, shutting me in his receiving chambers. I stayed there for some time, oscillating between the two choices.

The choice came surprisingly easily. A few horrible nights, a few terrible weeks, to get vengeance. I could do that. For my sister, for those I had left behind. I would endure it, until I didn't have to anymore. I headed to my chambers, decision made.

As soon as I was there, I collapsed on my bed and let myself fall into sleep.

That night, the nightmares returned.

Chapter Nineteen

I was in the throne room.

The marble floor was slick with blood beneath my feet. My legs struggled to hold my weight as I waded through the red. Bodies piled up around me. There were faces I recognised – a combination of servants and guards, adults and children. The rest were indistinguishable, features disappearing underneath decay and rot.

Amongst the bodies, there were those that tore off parts of my heart. A body without its head, the uniform of a soldier cladding a woman's body. Within arms distance of the body, a blonde, braided head sat, eyes wide and accusing. Ada. A boy was next to her, no older than fifteen. Caden, our unit's youngest member, whose eyes had once been so full of life and hope.

My breath raked through my throat. There were other faces I recognised, too. Some, I felt nothing but a distant sorrow for. Some, I smiled at the sight of. The man I had once killed on the battlefield with my Gift. Mercenaries I had slain with a smile on my face. Arlen, the nobleman I had once reduced to dust. My sister's minder, head caved in.

'These are your fault.' The voice was chillingly familiar, echoing around the room. I spun, nightdress twirling. Behind me, Liam stood, *brown hair slicked back. In his hands, a red haired ten-year-old shook, trembling like a rabbit that knew it was about to be hunted down. Her brown eyes were wide and wet with tears. She lifted her hands, curling them around where Liam held a knife to her throat.*

'Cassie.' Her name rattled through me in a hoarse whisper. She was alive. I could still save her. Could change her fate. My hand twitched towards my weapons.

'All of it,' Liam sneered. 'Every single one.' He gave a vicious smile, then wrenched the knife across my sister's neck. I screamed, the sound of it shaking the room. Marble cracked beneath my feet, silver light spilling out. Blood pooled at Cassie's neck, dripping down and staining her white nightdress crimson.

'Your fault,' Liam repeated, eyes flicking down to my closed fist. I glanced down. In my hand, a dagger was clutched, stained red with blood. Horrified, I stumbled back. My feet tangled on a body and I fell backwards, crashing hard onto the floor. The dagger flew out of my grip. And then there was something new in my hand — something heavier. Nausea surged as I stared at my sister's head. At her unblinking, accusatory eyes, staring up at me.

With a hoarse cry, I dropped it. It rolled once before stopping, eyes fixing on me. The disembodied head opened its bloody mouth. 'Your fault.' Her voice was just as I remembered, sweet and sure. 'Your fault. Your fault. Your fault.' The voice turned into a shrieking that pierced my ears, pierced my heart.

'No!' I cried, flinging out a hand. Silver light speared the air, covering everything, dissolving everyone into dust, until there was nothing and no one left except for me, and—

I awoke with a gasp, hauling myself upright. My pulse thundered, my chest rising and falling in desperate gasps. Silver light stung at my eyes, viciously bright.

'It's okay.' A hand pressed to my cheek. I leant into the touch, struggling to orientate myself with the here and now. 'You're here. You're safe.'

I grasped hold of the hand. Held it tightly as though it might tether me to reality. But then I blinked, and I was back in that room, my sister broken on the floor, this silver light destroying everyone and everything except those I wanted it to...

'Tell me one true thing.' His words broke through the circling of my mind.

'Wh-what?'

'Tell me one true thing,' he repeated.

A breath worked its way down my throat as recognition finally struck. *Callum.*

'I'll go first,' he said. 'I feared I would never see you again after that night. That you'd disappear and leave me a shattered man.'

I stared at him, uncertain how to respond. He sat on the edge of my bed, one leg crossed under him as he leant towards me. His eyes were filled with concern, and his golden hair was tousled, as though he had been roused from a deep sleep. My eyes drifted downwards to his bare chest, then lower to a well-defined stomach. Even his body was sharp and focused, just like him.

'Your turn,' he prompted when I said nothing.

I clung to him, fearing I'd lose myself to memories if I let him go. 'I only came back so I could kill you.'

A deep, low chuckle sounded. 'I said one *true* thing, Captain.'

The silver light receded. I opened my mouth to lie again, but something else spilt out in its place. 'I'm not capable of love.'

The hand upon my cheek froze. 'That's not true. You loved Cassie.'

I pulled back. 'I did. But loving her – *losing* her – it broke something in me.' I could feel plenty of other things. Desperation. Concern. Desire. Just not love.

'You're not broken.' Callum's voice was fierce. 'And I don't think you're incapable of love. You're just scared of it.' If I wasn't so exhausted, I would've been enraged by his words. As it was, all I felt was mild irritation. He continued. 'That's a conversation we can have when you're better rested and less likely to act rashly when you hear what I have to say.'

I exhaled, flopping back onto the bed. Teetering on the precipice of unconsciousness, I almost let myself fall. That was when I remembered the silver light.

I jerked upright, nearly cracking my head on Callum's nose. 'My Gift,' I gasped, 'I... Did I use...'

Callum's hands lowered to where mine were tangled in the sheet, every finger curled in my anxiety. 'I moved Deana and your friend out of this wing as soon as I felt your power,' he reassured me, loosening my fingers one by one as he traced gentle circles on the back of my hands. 'The guards and servants were also asked to leave for the night. I suspected this might happen. No one was hurt.'

My chest loosened. I lay down once more with an exhale. 'Thank you,' I breathed into the pillow, twisting my head to meet his eyes.

His lips curled into a smirk. 'I didn't quite catch that. Did you say—?'

'Get out now. Before I do really kill you.' Despite the venom I forced into my glare, I couldn't stop some amusement slinking into my voice.

Callum chuckled softly. 'Sleep.'

It was an easy instruction to follow. Reconnected to reality, my head pounded fiercely, and nausea twisted as the alcohol worked its way out of my system. Despite that, fatigue smothered me. The mattress shifted as Callum made to leave. My sleep addled mind panicked at his absence. He was going to leave, and I was going to be alone again, just as I had always been. Except this time, there was no drink, no forgetting, when the darkness closed in. When I was left behind as I always was. I grasped his hand in mine, halting his steps.

'Stay,' I murmured, not looking at him as I spoke. My cheeks warmed at the pitiful word.

The fingers in mine twitched. 'You mean you won't kill me if I do?'

I did not speak. Didn't dare put to words the confusing mess of feelings and thoughts that muddied inside me. To explain that the hate and anger that I had directed towards him because it was easier than directing it solely towards myself had disappeared days before. No, not disappeared. Shifted into something far hotter. Something that demanded to be felt, to be satiated. Need and desperation, and other things I dared not consider for too long.

A pause, then a weight settled next to me. His fingers brushed strands of hair back from my face, their touch leaving warmth in their wake. 'I'll watch over you. You can rest.'

'That's not why I want you to stay,' I mumbled into the pillow as I began drifting off to sleep. 'And there are things even a king can't protect me from.'

'I know that better than most.' His voice was sad. Sad, and so terribly, terribly lonely, in a way that was achingly familiar. 'But I'm going to try anyway.'

For four days, I stayed in that bed, chained by my own choices. I lay awake during the day, shaking and sweating, barely mustering the energy to relieve myself. At night the nightmares would visit again. Every time I found myself lost in a blaze of silver and sorrow, it would be a hand on my face and my name spoken gently that would bring me back. Every time, Callum would stay when I asked, helping scare the nightmares away. No one else came, kept away by the volatility of my Gift. Only Callum could withstand the touch of my Gift and live.

The withdrawal hit hard, my body craving the alcohol I'd stolen away from it. Some nights, I would cry and plead. Others, I would scream that I hated him. And there were a few nights where I was so lost in memories and withdrawal that I'd say barely anything at all. No matter what I did, though, he never left. And I never asked him to.

On the morning of the sixth day, I mustered the strength to dress myself and leave the rooms. The pounding of my head had dispersed, and I no longer felt like every step would send me running for the bucket that had been a permanent fixture by the bed. Instead, my stomach gave a pang of hunger as I opened my door. Callum waited outside as though he'd known today would be the day I emerged. The light dusted his features in gold. He glanced over me before nodding his approval.

'Breakfast?' was all he said, head tilting down the hallway. I hesitated. It seemed wrong, to have wasted these days and now be pausing for a meal. Callum seemed to sense my uncertainty. He smiled as he said, 'You won't be able to do anything if you collapse from hunger.'

I eyed the shadows undercutting his eyes. 'And how many meals have you had over the past few days?'

'Enough as my time allows.'

From what I'd seen before my six days locked in my chambers, time allowed for no such trivialities for the king. Where Kane was content to force others to do his bidding and let parts of the kingdom fall to ruin, Callum seemed to constantly be going between meetings or dealing with documents and letters. Yet, he'd still found time to stay by my side when I'd asked him to. I relented, nodding as I ran my fingers through my knotted hair.

Callum offered me an arm. I took it, not trusting my exhausted legs to hold me up. We made our way slowly down the corridor. Angling his face towards me, he asked, 'How are you feeling?'

'Like I was run over by three horses.'

Callum smirked. 'Not entirely out of the realm of possibility, given how you ride.'

I nudged my elbow into his side. He merely laughed, and the sound heated my cheeks. This was … nice. Teasing. Being teased. It also felt immensely dangerous, how natural it felt to lean on him for support. I focused forward as we rounded a corner and through a door. A servant bowed low as we passed, a feather duster held in his hand. It was not the stiff-backed pose I'd seen many offer King Kane as they attempted to hide their trembling hands and fearful expressions. The bow was deep. Respectful.

Callum smiled. 'Good work as usual, Joseph.'

I glanced at him, surprised. His father had never bothered to remember the names of his king's guards, let alone mere servants. Joseph straightened, a weathered hand rubbing the back of his neck. 'Thank you, Your Majesty.'

Halting, Callum asked, 'Has your daughter recovered from her illness?'

Joseph nodded, his expression brightening. 'She has. All thanks to the healer you sent.'

'Good to hear. Carry on as you were.'

'Yes, Your Majesty.' Joseph did not lose his smile as he returned to his work, focusing on his dusting as though his life depended on it.

I waited until we were out of earshot before saying, 'That was friendlier than I'd expect of you.'

'I've found people work harder when they believe they're valued.' The corridor began to curve, several windows allowing the morning light to stream in. 'It's simply a different manipulation tactic to the one my father used. The fear he brewed – it would've eventually led him to being killed. There've been plenty of assassination attempts already. This is far more effective at keeping people in line. They realise that those who side with me will reap the benefits, and those who don't ... well, that's where the fear comes in.' His wicked smile faded quickly as he added, 'And I'd rather not rule the way my father did.'

I considered him – the hard set to his eyes, the tightness at his jaw. Even the arm under my fingers had tensed. At last, I asked, 'Do you miss him?'

Callum inhaled sharply. Shadows had begun to pierce his irises, like his own Gift was trying to rise to the surface. Some wounds, though, couldn't be healed. 'I hated him. Hated what he had done, what he stood for. But he was my father.' He blew out a long breath. 'I miss what he might have been.'

'I can't say I'm sorry he's gone.' I trailed a finger along the white wall, not meeting Callum's eyes as we reached a familiar wooden door. He pushed it open, allowing me to go down the stairs first. *But I am sorry he wasn't who you wanted him to be.*

I didn't speak the words, but Callum seemed to hear them, nonetheless, nodding once.

I knew what it was to have a parent who never showed you love. Who shoved you down, again and again, until you forgot that your legs knew how to stand. It was that Callum – the child who grew up in such a cold place – that those silent words were for. An understanding between two children who'd grown up knowing nothing but rage and violence.

Callum's hand steadied me as I reached the bottom of the staircase. 'I'm sorry, too. That your mother wasn't who you deserved.' He eyed me curiously. 'She was your adoptive mother, wasn't she?'

'Unfortunately.'

'Do you know anything of your real mother?'

'No.' And I didn't care to. Any parent I had ever had had abandoned me or abused me. She was no different.

Following the scent of freshly baked bread, I stepped into the kitchens. I braced myself as I entered. The ghost of my sister lived here. It was in the memories that swamped me – the little dustings of flour that always dirtied her face, the sweet treats she took such pride in, the beaming smile she always wore here. The kitchen was far darker without her laughter filling it.

The kitchen staff fell over themselves to bow before Callum. He treated them as he had Joseph, with a smile, before sending them away. Waiting until they'd all left, I asked, 'How much time have we lost?'

Callum's hand brushed over my shoulder as he manoeuvred past me, heading straight for the stoves. 'Not much,' he said over his shoulder. 'Jaxon has been in and out of the palace, hunting down this poison he needs. Deana has been gathering information, but barely any news has gotten out of Archin.'

I read what he wasn't saying. Not many – if any – of her spies had survived the massacre. 'And in Ballaronia?'

'There doesn't seem to be any movement of concern from the Archinian capital. I've sent three units to the Archin border over the past few days, including a Gifted of Kyrah's who can convey messages over some distance.'

The mention of a Gifted of the goddess of divination gave me brief pause. They were a somewhat rare breed, and I hadn't been aware Callum had any at his disposal. 'And the reports they've sent?'

'Nothing other than minor skirmishes with bandits. Everything seems relatively normal.'

'For now.'

'For now,' he echoed as he fetched a small pan. He moved around the kitchen with practised ease, checking the flames on the hob before placing the pan atop it. An egg cracked, the sound of sizzling filling the room.

'King and personal chef?' I asked, sliding onto a stool at the wooden bench. Callum glanced over his shoulder, smiling.

'My mother taught me the basics. She told me a man who knows his worth should be able to cook a basic meal.' His lips twisted wryly. 'That was directly after my father had threatened to beat me if he caught me watching the cooks work again. It was a woman's job, he said, not a prince's. I find it's a way to calm my mind.' He laughed drily. 'Though it hasn't seemed to have been helping much recently.'

I studied him as he cooked, his movements confident. But there were deep shadows under his eyes, and his skin was pale his features drawn.

'You look exhausted,' I said.

'That's what a full day of planning with General Jakob does to me,' he said, his voice gravelly. A hint of guilt pinched at me. A full day of strategising, and a night of me selfishly demanding his time.

'Jakob?' I frowned, trying to drag the name from my memory. Of the four generals in charge during my stint in the army, I couldn't recall any Jakobs.

'Jakob Alridge. He replaced Tizan,' Callum explained, the food sizzling away. 'He was a captain – a good one, who isn't afraid to speak his mind. I figured someone like him was needed to wrangle the other generals into line.'

I nodded. None of the others were as bad as Tizan, but they were all old and stubborn. Some fresh blood would do them some good. 'Were your talks successful?'

Callum sighed. 'Somewhat. We can't attack Archin or Vitus, not with so little information about him. But we've set up units at the larger towns as a defensive measure.'

It was the best plan they could've come up with. Any offensive moves now would likely be suicide. 'What about Alluvite?'

'I met with Commander Lena two days ago.' I recalled the

stern-faced woman I'd met upon entering the palace who had eyed me so mistrustfully. 'Most of our city guards will be redirected to the streets and have been given strict instructions to be alert. They'll be delivering daily reports.'

'No wonder you look so tired.' Not that I looked much better.

Callum smiled ruefully. 'Turns out being a king isn't as easy as lounging around all day.'

'You seem like you're doing all right.'

He flipped one of the eggs onto a plate. 'I don't know if I'm doing all right, but I'm surviving.'

'That's the most important part.'

'My mother used to tell me something similar.' He sighed, staring down at the food he'd prepared. 'That surviving to see another day comes first, and everything else comes when it can.'

I studied his features – the complicated mix of sorrow and fondness in his expression. Perhaps it was that he had put up with all my vulnerability, had listened – no matter what hate-filled words I spewed at him – that had me saying, 'Tell me about her.'

Callum's eyes flicked up to mine, surprise crossing his features. 'My mother?'

I shifted on my stool. 'That's who you were talking about, wasn't it?'

A hint of a smile curved his lips upwards. The warmth in it momentarily took my breath away. All I'd done was ask a single question about himself, but his expression was like I'd just offered him a precious treasure. 'She was kind. Too kind for this place. Her father was a lord who oversaw the eastern territories. She was forced into the marriage at sixteen.'

I shuddered. Sixteen, and married to that tyrant. I might've been sent out to the battlefield far earlier, but the thought of that future – of being chained to a throne, freedom and choice stripped away – was far more terrifying.

Callum continued. 'She had me at seventeen. He broke her by

the time she was twenty.' Another egg went into the pan, the shell shattering a little more violently.

'And what was she like? With you?' I prompted.

Callum's smile emerged again, even brighter. And this time, something in my chest warmed at the sight of it.

'When we were alone, she would tell me stories, not unlike the ones you used to tell your sister.' I quirked an eyebrow and Callum's grin turned sheepish. 'I might've eavesdropped once or twice.'

'Of course you did,' I muttered.

'She used to pretend we were pirates, or rulers of distant lands. Any story, any possibility, as long as my father wasn't there. Tarina had Gifted her with storytelling, and her stories would paint such vivid images.' His face darkened, the plate he'd fetched thudding onto the benchtop. 'As soon as we left her rooms, she would change. Become duller. By the time I was five, the stories didn't come anymore. It was like she was there, but not.'

He placed the bread and eggs on the plate in front of me, watching intently until I took a bite. The simple meal was bliss. I tried not to let the enjoyment show on my face, but from the gleam of his eyes, Callum spotted it anyway. I wrinkled my nose at him even as my cheeks warmed.

'I loved her, and she was a wonderful woman, but she was soft. Too soft.' He took a deep breath, a rolling pain behind those shuttered green eyes. 'I learnt the day she threw herself from a window that I needed to harden myself if I wanted to survive.'

The creaminess of the eggs turned to dust as I swallowed them. He had been so little, too young, to watch his mother broken like that. Ripped from him by the king, and then by her own choice to leap from her tower. 'I've always wondered,' I mused at last. 'If it is better to have a parent you hate or lose one you love.'

Callum was silent for a few moments, then said, 'I think the latter. If it wasn't for her, I would be more of my father than I already am.'

'Callum.' At the sharpness of my tone, his eyes darted up to mine. Gods, there were such depths of pain in there. He needed someone who was capable of lessening that pain. Who knew how to heal instead of hurt. If I was something else – if *we* were something else – perhaps that could've been me. But we were not. He was a king, and I was little more than a broken blade – still sharp enough to cut, but not much use for anything else. So instead of giving my thoughts breath, I remained silent. Tried to ignore the tightening of Callum's lips and the twisting pain in my chest.

'Who's ready to die?' The cheery voice jerked both our attention towards the door. Jaxon only offered a lazy smile as he perched on the stool next to me, leaning across to snatch up my bread.

I stole the bread back, glaring at him.

'What are you doing here?' Callum snapped, the intensity in his voice changing to one of annoyance. Jaxon shrugged merrily.

'I figured you'd want to travel to the godly realm as soon as possible.' Jaxon stretched, arms reaching up and out as he twisted to the side. 'Before Vitus wreaks havoc.'

Callum leant forward. 'You have the poison, then?'

Jaxon plucked the bread back out of my hand, ignoring my frown as he ate the rest of it. He lifted his hand as though to pat my head with fingers coated in crumbs.

I ducked away. 'If you even think about doing that—'

'You'll cut off my hand.' He then proceeded to do it, anyway, mussing my hair and earning an elbow to his stomach. 'I think you need to be a bit more original with your threats.'

'Asshole.'

'I'd be using far stronger language than that to describe him.' Deana's voice joined us as she peeked around the corner. Her lilac shirt clung to her, accentuating her broad shoulders. She eyed my remaining eggs hungrily. I pushed them her way, earning a put-out look from Jaxon.

'What poison does one consume to die and end up in the godly realm?' I asked as Jaxon brushed a few crumbs from his shirt front.

'There's a rare plant, Dragon's Snare, that can be brewed in a very specific way to bring the drinker to the brink of death. The plant is the only one to grow on both sides of the barrier. It forms a link of sorts between this realm and the next. Theoretically, the connection is enough that if you die and are resuscitated, your soul is able to stay put in the godly realm for some time.'

The line between Callum's brows deepened. 'Theoretically?'

Jaxon was already on the search for more food as he answered Callum. 'It worked with me.' He swiped an apple from the bench, tossing it in one hand. 'But it *is* called a poison for a reason. Fatal all the time to those without a Gift; fatal most of the time to those with one. And there needs to be one person left behind to make sure the bodies left don't die.'

Deana stood up. 'Someone needs to stay behind?'

Jaxon smiled. 'Did I forget to mention that? And by my count —' He stopped, made a show of looking at me, then Callum, then back at Deana, 'You'll be of the least use in the godly realm.'

'No. Absolutely not.' Deana's irritation switched to Callum. 'If I can't come and make sure you don't get yourself killed, then you're not going.'

'Chiara can watch over me,' Callum volunteered.

Deana scoffed. 'What a fantastic idea. Let's have the person who gets into as much trouble as you be your protection.'

'It's not trouble if I know I'll come out on top,' I said.

Deana jabbed her fork at me. 'And this is why you're as bad as Callum! All it takes is one time where you overestimate yourself.'

Callum rested his forearms on the bench as he leant forward. 'But it's not an overestimation if we always win.'

Her fork clattered onto the plate. 'Gods, the arrogance between all of you is astounding.' Callum smirked, Jaxon beamed, and I shrugged. Deana sighed, pinching the bridge of her nose. 'There is no way in this realm or any other that I'll let—'

'Deana,' Callum interrupted, his tone now reasonable. 'What would you prefer? That I go, or that I stay here, and get up to all sorts of unkinglike things without you to watch me?'

Her lips twitched, she was not convinced.

Callum added, '*Dangerous* things. I've heard stories about the city – thugs roaming each night to take advantage of those out there. What sort of king would I be if I allowed that to continue? Or maybe I'll head to the Archin border to see the damage – I've been saying that I should, and you've been the only one who's convinced me not to.'

Deana's irritation died down a little at the words, though she still looked unsure. 'Can't Jaxon watch over you instead?'

'Would you really trust him?' Callum asked. Deana sighed in response, which was answer enough.

'I'm going with you,' Jaxon inserted almost casually. He looked up at the silence that followed his declaration. 'What, no, *oh, how fantastic!* No, *Jaxon, what would we do without you?* How about, *Jaxon, we are eternally grateful for your assistance and upon return will grant you a lordship and half the kingdom?*'

Deana laughed. 'I wouldn't trust you with a single house. I also don't recall you being invited.'

Callum collected the plates, placing them in a large tub for washing. 'He's not wrong.' Jaxon's lips parted, and Callum quickly continued before Jaxon could stir up any more trouble. 'About coming along. Not the rest. He's the only one who has been over there, and the only one who might know where loyalties lay.'

I glanced at Jaxon. 'Are there any gods that would side with Dearil?' Worry dug its claws into me. If there weren't, then had these months been a waste of time? Had I been optimistic to believe there was any chance at vengeance?

His expression turned thoughtful. 'Some might. Many of the gods bored of life long ago and chose death over an eternity in the godly realm. There's only a handful that remain. Akmad will side with Vitus.'

'I doubt Evania would,' Callum said, speaking of the goddess of peace who we had met in the Niguran Forest after collecting the chains King Kane had ordered us to collect. 'She seems to have a history with Vitus. And not a good one.'

Jaxon grimaced. 'Evania is … *difficult.* She might not side with Vitus, but it doesn't mean she'd side with us. It wasn't only gods that left their marks on her in her time chained up in the forest.'

'What about your mother?' Deana asked.

Jaxon's hands formed fists. 'She'll side with Vitus. We should pray we don't run into her over there, or else our souls will be in danger.'

'What happens if our souls are harmed over there?'

'Same as here. If you're injured, your body is injured. If you die, you die. Only your body will still be alive, and your soul likely won't exist at all anymore, so…' He trailed off, not needing to finish the sentence. If our souls didn't exist, there would be no eternal rest or torture in the Light or Dark. It would simply be nothingness. Wiped from existence, the only sign we'd ever been there at all the shells of bodies left behind.

I stood, stretching my sore muscles. 'I guess we'd better not let our souls die, then.'

'Exactly.' Jaxon reached into the pocket of his coat, withdrawing three vials of amber liquid no bigger than a thumbnail. 'So now we've gotten all that out of the way, where are we going to die today?'

Chapter Twenty

'For Callum and me, the process is simple. We take the poison, die, and Cal's Gift will heal us up,' Jaxon explained as we walked down the corridors of the palace.

Callum frowned. 'Is that the only way to make it across safely?'

Two guards stepped forward to open the doors to Callum's chambers for us. Jaxon replied, 'It's the most reliable way. We could also wait for a god's goodwill to haul us back from the brink of death, but gods and goodwill don't typically coexist.'

Callum bolted the door behind us. Light spilt through an arched window, bathing the room in a soft glow. 'Perhaps it's best you don't come along, Jaxon.'

'What happened to, *Jaxon's help is invaluable, and we won't survive without it?*'

'I don't think anyone's ever said such a thing,' Deana muttered. She took up residence on a straight-backed chair, eyeing Jaxon suspiciously as he leant against the far wall. 'But the criminal's right. Much as I'd prefer to be going along, there's no way just you and Chiara are going.'

Turning to the window, Callum ran his fingers through his hair. His shoulders were visibly tense, his back rigid. 'We don't know that the healing will work.'

Jaxon clapped him on the shoulder as he passed by, headed for the bed. He flopped onto the edge of it. 'It'll work. I've heard all about your Gift. It's far stronger than most – a little poisoning should be easy.' He fell onto his back, arms folded behind his head as he studied the ceiling. 'Besides, if you don't, Mother dearest will try to fetch me, and I don't quite feel like a lecture from her today.'

'Then you'll survive even if I don't heal you,' Callum said, relaxing a fraction.

A line appeared between Jaxon's brows. 'Well, yes,' he said slowly. 'But as I've already said – I would really prefer that doesn't happen.'

'And if my healing doesn't work on myself?' Callum pressed.

Jaxon threw another confused look at Callum, briefly lifting his head. 'I suppose Mother wouldn't leave you drifting. She'd drag you into the godly realm to deliver you to Vitus, to prevent the piece of his power being lost in the in between with your death.'

Callum nodded resolutely. 'Good.'

'*Not* good,' Jaxon said, falling back. 'That's my point – if you don't heal us, it might be very, very bad. So make sure you do.'

'What about Chiara? Callum can't heal her.' Deana asked. Three sets of eyes turned on me – Deana's concerned, Jaxon's thoughtful, and Callum's filled with too much to decipher. I frowned at the scrutiny, my fingers toying with the hilt of my dagger.

'Chiara's a special case. Daughter of death and all, she should theoretically be able to have some control over her own soul.' His expression shifted towards solemnity. 'All she needs is the will to not pass through the Gates into what waits beyond.'

Callum stiffened. 'I don't like the theoretical.'

'We're wasting time,' I said sharply. 'Where's the poison?'

Jaxon reached into his pocket, retrieving a small vial. I snatched it out of the air when he tossed it to me. The glass was surprisingly cool to the touch as I made my way over and sat myself on the opposite side of the bed to Jaxon. He patted the space between us, tossing a grin Callum's way. 'Better get comfortable, Cal. You wouldn't want to hurt that pretty head of yours by taking a nasty fall.'

I didn't look at Callum as he settled next to me, but I was aware of every movement he made. His arm brushed mine, warmth spreading through the spot of contact. Eager to distract myself, I lifted the vial to the light, pretending to examine the liquid. Yet as I did, I found my attention drifting to the room beyond. I'd never been in Callum's personal chambers before and curiosity ran deep. It was an odd mix of designs. Severe slashes of black tableware, stark against the white of the walls clashed with the dove-grey rug that was plush beneath my feet. A side table stood next to the bed, containing a glass of water. Several books were stacked on top, the top one overturned so the cover was hidden. The black and white I could only guess to be King Kane's décor choice. The books and rug, however, must've belonged to Callum.

'I didn't know you were a reader,' I said offhandedly to Callum, my fingers closing around the vial. Despite my request to hurry things up, my heart beat quickly in my chest. *The will not to pass through the Gates,* Jaxon had said. The will to survive. I possessed that.

Didn't I?

Deana laughed, a tension-riddled sound, as she eyed the books in the corner. 'He used to be more of one before he nearly burnt down the royal library. Books are now smuggled out to him, courtesy of yours truly.'

'You nearly burnt down a library?' Jaxon sounded impressed.

A glint of amusement entered Callum's eyes, the only sign of good humour I'd seen since Jaxon had thrown me the amber liquid. He held his own vial loosely in one hand, seemingly less fascinated by it than I was. 'What Deana failed to mention is she was right alongside me, and it was her who overturned the candle onto the papers of the old curmudgeon who works there, after he refused to let her read a book that he said was *too serious for a lady*.' He shifted his body, leg brushing against mine, to look at his spymaster. My fingers twitched tighter around the vial. 'I was the only one they caught. Her book smuggling days are penance for her crimes.'

Deana smirked. For all her casualness, her eyes tracked each of us like a hawk, ready to leap in at the slightest sign of disaster. 'He deserved it.'

'He did, but the books certainly didn't.'

I let them continue their easy banter, recognising it for the distraction it was. The stopper wiggled easily out of my vial. The smell of too-sweet, overripe fruit hit my nose, with an underlying scent of something bitter and pungent. My nose screwed up. I pushed the stopper back in, pausing the onslaught. 'Are you sure this is safe to drink?' I asked dubiously.

'Yes, Chiara, the bottle of poison is completely safe to drink.' Jaxon lifted his vial in the air, twisting it each way. His lips curled into a grin as he winked at me, reaching across Callum to clink his vial against my own. 'No time like the present. See you on the other side.'

Without another word, Jaxon threw his head back and tipped the entire contents of the vial down his throat in one swallow. I started, half rising off the bed. Within seconds, his skin whitened and sweat dripped down his face. A breath rattled out of him. 'Better go soon, Your Majesty. Trust me when I say you don't want my mother to be the one to find me while I wait for you.'

As soon as the words left Jaxon's mouth, the paleness extended from his skin to his eyes, a ghostly white film covering his irises. The bottle slipped from his grip. It clattered to the ground as Jaxon's chest rose on a final inhale. And then, as easily as a gust of wind snuffing out a candle, he was gone.

We stared at his still body. 'It's a wonder he survived twenty years, let alone over three hundred, with that reckless streak,' Deana said at last. 'My vote is we leave him here and go have something to eat.' Her tone was only half joking.

Her expression soured as Callum copied Jaxon's actions, throwing the liquid back himself. His face screwed up. 'Gods, that's disgusting.'

The process was slower on Callum, the poison counteracted by his Gift. My knuckles ached from where I clutched at my own vial as I watched, unable to move. Something in me twisted as shadows pulsed beneath his skin. Agony that had not been present in Jaxon flared in his eyes. His entire body tensed. I lurched forward, but he held up a hand. 'It-it's fine,' he croaked, his voice brittle.

'This isn't right,' I whispered, staring as a pallor began to appear upon his skin. 'Jaxon wasn't in pain. This isn't—'

'Chiara,' Callum interrupted, his hand settling upon where mine was pressed into the mattress, trembling at the touch. 'I'm fine.'

The pulsing shadows stuttered and then vanished. His pallor spread, creeping up his arms, over his neck. Callum turned his paling face towards me, a weak smile flitting over his face. And then, just like Jaxon, he was gone.

I stared at the two bodies. Something in me pulled taut, almost painfully so, before relaxing. Tremors coursed up my arms. Dead. They were both dead. And there was only one way to check that their souls had survived. I lifted the vial to my lips.

'Bring them back safely,' Deana pleaded as I tipped my head back.

'Both of them?' I asked, trying not to breathe in the stench as the amber liquid ran down my throat. It burnt on its way down. Unpleasant, but not the sort of pain Callum seemed to have experienced.

Deana's eyes steeled, her back straightening. 'All three of you,' she ordered.

There was no time for panic as the fire spread, covering my throat and filling my mouth. I heaved in one final, rattling breath. Then, I fell into oblivion.

I was hurtling through darkness. Or maybe I was crawling through light. It was difficult to tell. The world flashed between black and white, silver and gold, an onslaught of all colours at once and then nothing at all, direction a meaningless concept. My hands stretched out to grab hold of something, anything. Instead, only air slipped through my fingertips. I could hear nothing, yet whispers and screams filled my mind. All of them were desperate pleas. People begging for life. The warmth of death choked me, filling me with all their emotions. Fear, guilt, despair, fury. And in some, only peace.

A silver cord wrapped itself around my wrist, sinking into my skin and whatever it was that lay underneath. Its tangibility kept me tethered to myself. An inbuilt instinct warned me that to lose the cord would be to lose myself. My stomach lurched as the movement of my soul slowed, a black gate rising high in the distance. *Hurry*, the silver line seemed to pulse, its brightness intensifying even as shadows crept close. *Go back.*

I stared down at the approaching objects. This far out, I couldn't make out much. Only an imposing wall of both white and black, and thousands upon thousands of tiny lights, shoved together in a group. The scent of smoke and jasmine swallowed me – a soothing scent, one that I'd only ever experienced when souls left their bodies. The emotions from before swelled higher. And that peace – it latched onto me. Sung to me. Soothed me, even as the cord pulled tighter.

I wanted that peace, more than I'd ever wanted anything.

Yes, the spots of brightness whispered into my mind, voices young and old merging together. *Surrender to death. Close your eyes and let it come. Easy.* The word jolted through me. Had anything ever been easy for me? I was tired. So damned tired, all the time. All I had to do was close my eyes, let my soul complete its journey, and—

'It's not your time.'

My eyes snapped open as my momentum came to an abrupt stop. The cord still connected me, the Gate still called to me, but I was suspended in between. Stuck before a light so brilliant I could not make out a face. But that voice – that sweet, youthful voice – I could never forget.

'Cassie?' I whispered, staring at the light in disbelief. It couldn't be her. She was gone. Far away from me and the calamity I brought.

The light hovered closer. Its warmth flooded over my skin. 'It's not your time,' she repeated.

'It—' Grief welled, choking me. I understood, now, what that gate was. What all those lights were. The gates to the Dark and Light, and the souls that awaited judgement. And this was Cassie's soul – pure. Brilliant. 'It wasn't *your* time. It should've been me that died that day. Not you. You didn't deserve that end.'

Cassie's laughter rippled through the air, batting away the screams and pleas in my mind. 'Silly Chiara. It was my time years ago.' The light shifted closer, and something that almost felt like arms wrapped around my neck and squeezed in a hug. 'Thank you.'

Pain radiated through me. She was thanking me? After all I

had done to her? All I had failed to do for her? Guilt swarmed through me. *My fault.* All her suffering had belonged to me. Not to Callum. Not even to Kane. 'You should hate me.'

The warmth came away from my neck. I could picture the quizzical frown Cassie would've worn in her body. 'Hate you? Why?'

Anger bubbled through me, seeking to tear me to bits. Not at Cassie. At myself. 'If you'd never met me – if I'd never attracted Mother's ire, or been taken in by the king. If you'd never been my sister—'

'Then I would've died before I turned two.' Fingers coasted over my cheek, the faint scent of cinnamon and sweetness following their path. 'I wouldn't have survived the beatings Ma gave you, Chiara.'

'But I killed you.'

'You saved me,' Cassie interrupted, her voice firming, and a wisdom I had never heard in her before entering her tone. 'I understood things when I died the second time. All the ways you protected me.'

'I failed you,' I whispered, my voice raking through my throat. She didn't understand. Didn't see all the ways I could've done better.

'You gave me happiness.' The warmth pulled away from me. 'And now it's time you found your own.'

Impossible, I thought. But I'd never been able to say no to Cassie. So, instead, I smiled weakly and said, 'I wouldn't know where to begin.'

'Begin by not blaming yourself for my death.' Her light moved towards the silver thread. There was a pause, and then she giggled, the strange wisdom to her voice disappearing as she added, 'And there's the new king.'

I stared at her, my jaw slackening. 'What?'

For a moment, I thought I saw a flash of red behind the

brilliant light, and a sliver of warm brown eyes glinting with mischief. 'Are you in love with him? You told me stories about love when I was little.' She sighed wistfully. '*Oh*, it'd be like a storybook come to life. A commoner and a prince get married, and then—'

'*No!*' I sputtered. If I was in my physical body, my cheeks would've been blazing red. 'Of course not. He's a…' I trailed off, searching for a milder word than the ones I usually used to describe Callum. 'We're not well suited.'

'Really?' She drifted away from the silver thread. 'I think he's in love with you.'

'Cassie!' I scolded before glancing down at where the other souls bunched together. My brow furrowed. 'Is this the Light?'

'No.' Her warmth brushed over my hand like fingers curling through mine. 'The Gate won't open.'

I stared at the looming wall at the end of the tunnel we were in. It stretched far beyond where my eyes could see. One half was made of pure white. The other of pure black. Power more fathomless than any even a god could possess called to me, a constant hum that matched the melody of my own Gift. Ancient instinct warned me that this was not the way things should be, with souls crowding outside it. That if too many souls gathered without being permitted entrance, the balance of all the realms could be thrown askew. 'Is something…' I trailed off again, then, 'Dearil is responsible for sending souls through, isn't he?'

'I'm not sure.' Cassie's light floated in a circle around me before coming to a stop before me once more. 'But waiting feels … bad. Like when I ate too many cakes and my body got all itchy.'

A faint smile curved my lips. It had been on one of the rare occasions where we had been together. Cassie's minder had given us some brief privacy, and Cassie had used it to drag me to the kitchens. She'd been bouncing off the walls all afternoon. My smile quickly faded.

The Broken

This was wrong. I didn't want Cassie to be stuck here, waiting to pass on. She deserved so much more than to be caught in limbo. But Dearil was not here. He wouldn't be able to come for some time, if he ever returned to this strange in-between place at all. 'There's no way to open it?'

'I can't do it.' Cassie paused, then added in a quieter voice, 'But you can.'

My attention whipped back to her. 'Why do you think that?'

I could picture her shrug. 'Don't know. Just do.' She giggled, and my chest warmed. 'You always know how to do things.'

A laugh broke free of me. It was such a typical Cassie response. The one person who had never viewed me as a killer or a monster. Who had only seen me as her big sister. Her family.

And now it was time to let her go. I turned to the Gate. My Gift moved by itself, called by a knowing that seemed built into my blood. I might not have known what to do, but the power in my blood did. An image of the Gate opening sprung to mind. I willed it into being. Imagined the souls shifting through, one by one, finding their place in what awaited. The two sides of the Gate began to shift, their size shrinking until they were no bigger than a regular doorway.

I stared as the first of the souls moved towards it, undoubtedly guided by the same ancient knowing I possessed. Most headed for the white. A few were dragged into the darkness, their shrieks cut off as they were swallowed whole. The sight of it sent emotions warring through me – unease that I'd so easily managed such a thing, and an instinctual satisfaction. *This is right*, my Gift hummed. *This is what we're meant to do.*

Cassie laughed again, her warmth brushing over me as phantom arms squeezed me tight. 'I need to go, and so do you. I love you, Chiara.'

I swung towards her, panic flooding me. I couldn't lose her again. Not when she was so close. I clutched at her warmth, at her brightness, but it only slipped through my fingertips. The cord around me wrapped tighter. My attention whipped to it. It was what was tethering me to my body. If I cut it, maybe I could grasp hold of Cassie. Maybe I could—

'Silly,' Cassie said, her voice sad as fingers curled around where mine had reached for the thread. 'There's no place for you amongst the dead.'

'I don't want to leave you,' I choked out, pressure building at my eyes.

'You don't have a choice.' She pressed fingers to my cheek. 'I always wanted to be a part of your stories. Tell some about me, won't you?'

'I will,' I whispered, and I thought I saw something resembling a beaming smile amidst the light.

'Good. Then go.' And then she was shoving against me, the thread at my middle tugging me back the way I'd come as she hurtled towards the Gate of white. I watched even as I flew backwards. Watched as, for a moment, the brilliant light faded and a red-haired girl with bright eyes and a wide grin lifted a hand in farewell.

My breath was ripped away from me as I flew through the cacophony of colours until there was only silver and black around me. As suddenly as the cord had pulled me away, it vanished entirely, the weightlessness melting away with it. My back slammed into icy ground. I blinked once, wetness dampening my lashes. I knew without having to look. Cassie's soul was gone.

I struggled to my feet, swiping away the wetness on my cheeks, and took in what lay before me. Black walls stretched as far as the eye could see, lights glittering on its surface. I brushed my fingers against it, then quickly yanked my hand back when it throbbed against my touch. The lights shifted as though pulsing in time with a heartbeat. I followed them with my eyes to where the light was thickest. Gold, rose, silver, violet, crimson – and a number of other coloured lights – wove together into thick bars that speared through the floor and ceiling. The air crackled with energy. I peered beyond the bars at the small room beyond, housing a surprisingly ordinary desk, chair and bed. Humming sounded as I shifted a step closer. The lights brightened, seeming to call to me as my hand lifted to touch one of the bars.

'I wouldn't recommend doing that.' I whirled to where Jaxon leant against the wall behind me. His hair was mussed and his skin a shade paler than usual, but he looked otherwise fine. 'You'll find yourself thrown several metres back. Those lights are designed to repel the divine.'

'Where's Callum?' I asked, my eyes scanning the shadows surrounding Jaxon.

'You're not going to enquire after my health?' He shook his head. 'I'm hurt.'

I narrowed my eyes. Jaxon grinned.

A hand closed over my shoulder. 'I'm here, Captain.' I turned, finding Callum frowning down at me. 'What's happened?'

I stepped away from him, looking away. 'Nothing.'

'Liar,' he breathed, reaching up and brushing a finger over my cheek. 'You've been crying.'

I stared at the lights threading through the walls. 'It was nothing. Just an encounter with a soul.'

'Whose soul?' Jaxon asked.

'Cassie's,' Callum said without hesitation.

Surprised, I glanced up at him. 'How did you know?'

He smiled sadly. 'There's only one person you would cry over, living or dead.'

I stared at the gentle light that coated his features, painting him in pale beauty. It was unnerving how easily he saw through me. How easily he always had.

'Do you care to explain why we were forced to endure a summons from a goddess?' Jaxon drawled as he turned to Callum.

I frowned, inspecting Callum. He hadn't healed them when he'd brought them here. Suspicion coiled through me.

A pulse ticked in Callum's jaw. 'I'm not sure.'

Jaxon smiled, but it didn't reach his eyes. 'You need to work on your lying skills, Your Majesty. If you weren't going to be of some use by healing us, you might as well not have come.'

The lights on the cell bar throbbed as Callum shifted, casting us all in their ethereal hue. 'You seemed certain someone would make sure we didn't die.'

'Yes,' Jaxon said, no small amount of exasperation in his voice, 'Certain my *mother* would be the one to haul me into this realm. Which, as I said, was why you needed to be the one to heal us.'

Callum's stony stare didn't falter. 'My Gift takes a while to work when it's fighting off death. I sensed someone leading us here, and decided to save my Gift in case I needed it later.'

'If you suspected that it would take long enough for a god to lead us to this realm, then you should've told me *before* I risked my hard earnt separation from my mother.'

'Then Chiara would've gone alone.'

I folded my arms, irritated; a discomforting sensation coursing through me with each throb of lights from the cell. 'You should've let me if you didn't think you could make it here.'

Callum turned his attention to me. 'It's too dangerous for you to go alone. And I was certain I'd make it here, even if it took a little longer than expected.'

Jaxon threw up his hands in frustration. 'Getting caught by my mother would've been dangerous! You're lucky it was someone else who got us out. If it had been Tarina, we'd already be locked away somewhere.' He frowned. 'Though I'm not sure I want to know who retrieved us.'

'I have faith in your ability to cheat and lie your way out of any problem if I took too long to heal us,' Callum said.

'Why does that sound like an insult?' Jaxon asked with a frown.

'Because it is.' Before Jaxon or I could further protest Callum's decision, he said shortly, 'We should get moving.'

The wall of black stretched on for some distance. At one end was a bolted door, the lock complicated enough that I doubted Jaxon would be able to figure it out. The other end revealed nothing but almost complete darkness, lit only by the strange lights in the wall.

'Where are we?' I asked Jaxon.

'Your father's home.' He gestured at the cell. 'Or it was, until he was summoned to the mortal realm and bound with the chains of the gods.'

I stared at the cell. It was small, even by mortal standards. And, if the stories were to be believed, Dearil had been locked up by Vitus decades ago after he had been stripped of his title of king of the gods.

'It's not overly impressive,' Callum remarked. He idly drew a finger along the black stone. The tip came away coated by a shimmering mix of silver and black.

'Not all of us are used to the royal lifestyle,' Jaxon said. 'And I wouldn't spend too much time touching those walls. The lights in there are the souls who needed more dire punishment than what the Dark can offer. An eternity trapped in stone, unable to move or speak.' He smirked, looking pointedly at Callum's dirtied fingertips. 'And that silvery dust is all that remains of the souls that have wasted away into oblivion.'

Callum stared at his finger then wiped it on his shirt. 'I meant that I thought the godly realm would be more alive. Magical.'

Jaxon stared at the empty cell. 'This is their dungeon. Or whatever is the godly equivalent of a dungeon.' I shivered, the air seeming to grow icier as I stared back at the tiny, cramped place my father had spent year after year in. It was a wonder he didn't go mad. Forced to live down here, alone except for the souls to keep him company … it was a cruel punishment. Jaxon continued, voice hardening. 'This is pleasant compared to what lies above. Beyond all the prettiness and colours.'

'I don't doubt it.' Callum murmured softly.

Without another word, the three of us turned back to the straight tunnel. The darkness seemed to creep closer, taunting us with its shadows. I tried to muster up a show of courage. Tried, and failed.

It was Callum, the one who perhaps had the least going for him in this place with two half gods by his side, who stepped forward. 'Shall we?'

Neither Jaxon nor I said anything as we followed Callum into the dark.

Chapter Twenty-One

I wasn't sure how long we walked through the corridor. At times, the air seemed to thicken around us, our movements growing sluggish. At others, it shoved at our backs and quickened our steps.

'It's the fluctuation of time,' Jaxon informed us after Callum questioned him about it. 'There's no linearity to it in the godly realm. It moves as it wishes to.'

'You speak about time like it's sentient,' I said, tipping my head back to stare at the ceiling. Long stalactites dripped down, their black surfaces glistening with moisture. Yet there was no wetness anywhere else in the space – only along the pointed lengths. Small beads of silver glowed beneath the ones I passed under. Yellow and gold emanated from the ones Jaxon and Callum were closest to. They wrapped around them.

'It is, in a way,' Jaxon said as though this should've been obvious. 'Most things in this realm are. The walls, plants. Some gods even believe the air to be a conscious being.'

My steps quickened at that.

'This stone has sentience?' Callum asked, tapping a finger along the black.

'That stone's more like a vessel to hold the souls I told you about. It's obsidian. Stronger than anything in the mortal realm, but still not strong enough to kill a god.'

'Then what is?'

Jaxon turned his eyes on me. 'That's what we're here to find out, isn't it?'

After that, we fell back into silence once more. It may have been minutes or hours or days that we walked before we heard the footsteps. They came from the darkness before us, echoing down to reach our ears. My skin prickled, my Gift stirring. Whoever was coming our way was powerful. I scoured the space around us. There was nothing but smooth surfaces and an unending stretch of tunnel. No places to hide, no corners to duck behind.

'What do we do?' I whispered. The clicking of the footsteps approached with alarming speed. Callum's hand dropped, but his weapons had not travelled with his soul to the godly realm. Pressing his lips together, he curled his fingers into fists.

Jaxon stared at the fists with an amused twist to his lips. 'That's not going to do anything but piss off whichever god is coming.'

A god was coming for us. The ludicrousness of it struck me all at once. Our enemies were not beasts or mortals. They were divine beings. Creatures only spoken of in stories, blessed with power beyond belief. I almost laughed. When Cassie had told me to find my own happiness, I didn't think she meant going to war against such beings.

'You're the one Gifted by Tarina.' Callum crossed his arms across his chest, staring down at Jaxon. 'Cast an illusion.'

Jaxon smiled deviously. He waved a hand before his face.

Shadowy wisps coated it, the shape of it hazy. 'One step ahead of you, Cal.'

'Look.' I lifted my own hand before Callum. It was wrapped in the same silky darkness as Jaxon's, the black dripping off it like swathes of fabric. I pressed that hand against the wall, ignoring the way the soul lights leapt through the obsidian towards me. It all but disappeared as the black merged with the stone.

There was a brief pause in the approaching footsteps before they resumed. We pressed ourselves up against the wall. It was a strange sensation. I looked to the spot next to me. From the press of his arm, his fingers brushing over my own, I knew Callum was there. Yet, no matter how hard I looked, I could only see the never-ending stretch of the wall.

The click of shoes continued. I had heard Deana's heels often enough to recognise the sound; light, feminine, and likely deadly. Praying my breaths weren't too loud, I stilled my body. The tenuous nature of the illusion made every movement, every tiny sound seem like it might shatter it entirely. If I could have slowed my heartbeat, I would have.

Click. Click. Click.

I pressed my eyes shut and counted my breaths. *Pass us by*, I silently ordered.

Click. Click. The footsteps halted.

An airy voice tsked. 'Really, Jaxon, your mother taught you better than that.'

My eyes flew open. I had heard that voice once before, and it had been as distinct then as it was now. Tinkling, sweet, but not wavering in its strength. Evania, goddess of peace. Jaxon let the illusion drop, his features already twisted into a grimace. Callum tensed beside me. Evania stood, resplendent in a rose gold gown that fell in waves of shimmering glitter and brought out the pretty blush on her cheeks. Her rose-coloured eyes were steely as she regarded us. Her head tilted to one side, silver hair cascading over one shoulder.

Jaxon's grimace transformed into a cocky smile and he gave a shallow bow. 'If I had known it was you, my lady, I wouldn't have tried.'

'Don't lie, boy.'

His smile tightened. 'I'm three centuries old. I think I've outgrown that title.' He eyed her warily. 'Why is an esteemed goddess meeting lowly beings such as ourselves?'

Evania flicked her hair off her shoulder. It spilt down her back in pale waves, each strand perfectly in place. 'Because I sensed three foolish souls wandering where they should not. One found their own way here'—she glanced at me, and I fought the urge to back away from her stare and the power rolling through the air—'but two needed someone to fetch them. It was all rather tedious.'

My attention shifted to Callum. Catching my eye, he smiled, but I did not miss the rigidity of his body. He hadn't healed himself or Jaxon, then. But why? Had I been right in my guess about Vitus?

'And you did it out of the magnanimity of your tiny heart?' Jaxon pressed. Even I was taken aback by the abject lack of respect in his voice.

Evania's smile grew cold. 'Do not deign to know the minds of gods.'

Jaxon laughed, clapping his hands together. 'It was Kerta's instructions, wasn't it?'

Evania glowered at him for several silent seconds before clicking her tongue and focusing on me. I forced my feet to stay still, to not slide back at the full weight of the goddess's stare. 'We have met,' she said.

It was not a question, and I dipped my head in a shallow nod, not taking my eyes off her. As prettily wrapped as she was, Evania had been able to manage the chains of the gods with ease – chains that had nearly sent me collapsing beneath their power when I'd held them. I didn't dare find out what she could do with the power that lived in her.

Her eyes slid between me and Jaxon, considering. 'You're growing the trail of males you possess.'

My lips twitched downward, a denial perched on my lips. I wasn't sure, though, how the goddess would take me telling her she was wrong.

Callum didn't hesitate. His own lips had curved into a smile of wicked delight at the words, as though possession by me was entertaining. 'Only in the sense of loyalty, my lady.' His eyes slid to Jaxon, who nodded in hearty agreement. 'I'm afraid I'm the only one of us who completely belongs to Chiara.'

A pity our blades didn't travel with us. Callum certainly could do with one embedded in him right now. Evania didn't smile, but I could hear the amusement in her response. 'That is good. That pairing'—she flicked her eyes between myself and Jaxon again—'would be very twisted, even by mortal standards.'

I frowned, opened my mouth to ask why that would be so wrong, but Callum jumped in before I had a chance. 'And our pairing?' he asked.

I gaped at him. He smiled shamelessly back.

A ghost of a smile touched the goddess's lips. 'Some pairings are forged before paths are set.'

Great. This goddess had clearly attended *Cryptic Messages from Gods: How to talk to mortals* along with my father. 'Come.' Evania waved one of her elegant hands, and familiar rose gold sparks appeared. Though instead of transporting us to wherever she intended as they had upon our last encounter, this time a door of rose-gold light appeared. Behind it, I could make out the faint outline of steep, curving steps. 'We must leave this place.' Without any further explanation, she headed for the stairs.

'Gods, she's always such a nightmare,' Jaxon groaned.

Evania's shoulders tightened. 'I heard that, Jaxon Bladditch.' Any of the lightness fell away from her voice, replaced with utter disdain. 'And next time you speak about me in such a manner, I will make sure your mother is aware that you are here. Now come.'

There was no question as to whether to obey the command. At this stage, it was either continue down the straight corridor for eternity or follow an eccentric goddess to a strange place in a dangerous realm.

'She likes me,' Callum whispered as we followed the goddess through a doorway that had magically appeared. I scoffed, shooting him a look over my shoulder. He lifted his shoulders. 'I can't help it if I'm likeable. And if my pairing with you is already forged, then we might as well…'

'Do not,' I hissed, digging my nails into the back of the hand he had offered to climb a step that was far larger than mortal standards, 'Finish that sentence.'

With the smirk he gave me, he didn't need to.

The space the stairs led through was a riot of colours. Rainbow-coloured light cascaded over us, the faint sound of a breeze rustling through leaves filling the space. Despite it, I felt no such breeze on my skin. Every breath I took carried a new scent – spring grass, then blooming flowers, then baking bread. It took a few minutes to hike up the steep stairs. By the time we reached the top, even Callum was panting with exertion. I glanced down at where we'd come. Where there had been colour before, now only shadow remained, the arduous stairs vanishing.

'It's like climbing a mountain,' Jaxon moaned as he collapsed at the top. The rose-coloured carpet there disappeared moments before his cheek hit the floor. He yelped as he collided with stone.

'Get up,' Evania snapped, glowering down at him. The moment Jaxon was on his feet, the carpet sprung back into existence. She waved a hand, and a second arched doorway appeared before us.

'Does this place exist? It's just ... disappearing,' I asked, fingers trailing along the increasingly translucent stair rail as Evania paused at the doorway.

She twitched her head to one side like a curious bird staring at a worm, trying to decide if it was worth the effort. 'Of course it does.'

My cheeks heated at the *silly mortal* inference. 'Before you did whatever you did to make it appear.'

'Of course it didn't.'

Jaxon smirked at me, nodding along like he knew it the whole time and I hadn't seen him staring at the vanishing stairway with the same puzzlement.

'Hurry now, children.' Evania ushered us through the doorway. This time, there was no hint of what might be held beyond the rose-gold light. As I stepped through, tiny pinpricks pressed against my skin, tingling cascading over my limbs. Bells chimed in my ears – once, twice, then once more. The light swallowed me in its pink hue as the scent of freshly bloomed flowers filled the air, lingering for only seconds before the light disappeared.

We stood in a chamber far finer than anything I had ever encountered in the mortal realm. To one side, a bed made of pure silver stretched across an entire wall. Green vines draped to either side, shielding much of the bed from view. A tiny golden bird jumped from one vine to the next, singing a light song as it went. On the opposite end of the room, a sheet of water stood suspended. Fish darted through the vertical pond, bubbles rising and falling with ease. A few swum upside down. Their scales caught every hint of light, shining it back tenfold like small lanterns.

'This is extraordinary,' Callum murmured as he stopped next

to me. I followed his gaze upwards, taking in the chandelier woven of rose petals, their reflected light spilling out from small blooms.

'Of course,' Evania said, a hint of pride in her voice. 'These are my chambers.'

'Come here, Chiara,' Jaxon called, ignoring the dirty look Evania sent his way. Once I was sure I wouldn't be struck down by her for heeding his call, I strode over to where he stood by an arched window. He smiled, tilting his head towards it. 'Welcome to the godly realm.'

My jaw slackened at the sight I beheld. Row upon row of trees stretched as far as the eye could see, their golden and silver bark shining under the light of two suns. Leaves of every colour broke free of their branches, floating in whichever direction they saw fit. Many rose upwards, disappearing into an indigo sky. Others fell upon ground that glittered like diamonds. As soon as they left the boughs, a new tree sprung into place. There were no buildings to be seen, other than several small ones scattered at the base of wherever we were.

'This is...' I stared, shaking my head. There were so many words to describe it. Beautiful. Opulent. Extraordinary. Cold. Rather than risk pissing off a goddess, I said, 'There's no animals out there.'

Jaxon's smile faded. 'Ah. That'd be because this realm was never meant to house life. Anything you see that lives came from the mortal realm.'

I twisted, staring at him. 'What do you mean?'

'He means that this realm was never meant to belong to the gods.' I whirled around at the sound of Evania's voice. She'd moved to the centre of the room, where a raised section of the floor was covered in a massive expanse of soft blankets and cushions, surrounded by a tame ring of fire that crackled merrily away. There were no logs nor coals for it to burn through. 'This is our home. Our prison, too.'

'Prison?' I shifted away from the window, brow furrowing.

'Stop being dramatic, Evania,' Jaxon sighed as he came to a stop next to me. 'You know as well as I do that the separation of the realms was done with a majority of the gods in favour.'

'*I* was never in favour of it,' Evania said, lifting her chin.

'You voted for it.'

'You weren't even born, child. What could you know of what I voted for?'

Jaxon's expression took on the unbearably smug look I hated. 'Kerta told me.'

Evania's cheeks flushed. She huffed, settling herself amongst a mass of silver-tufted cushions and neatly arranging her skirts around her. 'Enough of the idle gossip. Sit down.'

Callum and I obeyed, stepping towards her. Jaxon stayed where he was. I reached three steps away from the circle of fire when one of the flames licked out at me. Startled, I staggered back, Callum's arm sweeping in front of me as though he could shield me from the heat.

A sharp bang sounded behind us. Evania smiled as a woman strode into the room. She made a sharp gesture with her hand, and the flames sunk back to their previous, sedate state. Red hair streamed behind this woman. Not like Cassie's, which had been more the colour of cranberries. This was the red of blood and ruination. Several locks sparking with the very same flames that had just lunged towards me as she stalked for Evania. Her every movement was lithe and calculated, in a way that reminded me of Deana. Elegantly designed armour clung to her, shimmering as it seemed to remould itself with her every move. She took a knee before Evania, taking a pale hand in hers and pressing her lips to it. Carvings of the same roses that littered the room were scattered across the metal pieces.

Evania beamed, her hands moving in quick movements. The woman rose to her feet, her armour barely making a sound.

'Kerta apologises for the misbehaviour of her flames,' Evania said, her fingers pressed casually to the woman – the goddess's – thigh. 'They have a habit of reacting when they sense power nearby.'

Kerta turned around, offering an apologetic smile. My eyes widened at the sight of her. The woman before us looked nothing like the goddess of war and justice as depicted in the myths and in sculptures. Her face was a mess of scars. Her nose was bent at an odd angle, half of it crushed close to her face. Purplish-red marks twisted across her features, the skin was tight and malformed. Her brows were patchy in places as though the hair had struggled to regrow upon the scarred skin. There was none of the endless beauty spoken of in the tales. Kerta was, if put bluntly, hideously scarred.

And yet she did not shrink from our collective gaze. She stood tall, the sword at her side shifting into a spear, and then leaping to over her shoulder and forming a bow and quiver. Her eyes, the same fiery red as her hair, flashed with amusement. Awe struck me. This goddess was a warrior.

Kerta sat beside Evania, a hand resting upon Evania's knee. Her hands lifted, making strange motions in the air. They twisted and curved, a kind of dance that seemed to tell a story I couldn't decipher. Evania had no such difficulty, casting us a sly look and letting out a tinkling laugh.

Evania translated the hand movements for us. 'It took you long enough.' From the way those flamed eyes locked on me, it seemed that the sentence was directed at me.

My brow furrowed. 'Long enough for what?'

'Dearil told us to expect his daughter months ago. He told us you would surely come immediately.' Kerta's scarred mouth quirked up in a smile, her hair writhing around her as though made of flaming snakes. 'It seems you have made the honest god a liar.'

I bit down on my back teeth. A wise voice within me warned me it would be foolish to narrow my eyes as I was doing now, but I ignored it. 'Cryptic messages to come home without any reason doesn't tell me much. And this is not my home.' I folded my arms. 'Why did he want me here?'

The impertinence in my voice was enough to make Evania's expression grow as frigid as a frozen river. The other goddess, though, opened her mouth and let out a sharp bark of laughter. The sound was harsh and discordant, but it was warm.

'I'll grant that you have a foolish streak of courage to speak to me that way, girl.' From the wrinkle of Evania's nose as she translated the signs, she didn't agree about the courage part. 'Before we get to that, though, I believe young Jaxon was telling the tale of our realm.'

Jaxon laughed before Evania had finished translating. I glanced at him, surprised as he began to sign back to Kerta, speaking as he did so. 'I lay no claim to being a great storyteller, my lady. I'm afraid that Gift of Tarina's did not pass down to me.'

Smiling, Kerta turned to Evania and raised her brows expectantly. Evania frowned. 'I see no reason why I should.'

Kerta flattened her hand, placing her fingertips on her chin, before drawing it away into a fist. The other goddess sighed. 'Fine. Since you said please. And I suppose it's important to understand why Vitus is the way that he is.' Kerta patted Evania's knee before settling back. Jaxon meandered his way over, dropping down beside me, while Callum leant forward. 'Vitus loved mortals once. Cherished them, even, far more than any other god did.'

'Vitus did?' Callum asked dubiously, exchanging a glance with me. We had both seen what had happened in the throne room – the bodies left behind to call Dearil to the realm and entrap him, all as part of Vitus's plan. And the stories since then – especially the razing of Archin – were not the work of a mortal-loving god.

'I said he loved mortals *once*. But the divine were never meant to play amongst humans.' She sighed. 'Mortals loved us, too, far more than they do today. They would pray to us. Bequeath gifts and sacrifices to us. Our numbers were close to a hundred back then.'

Shock jolted through me. Hundreds of gods? I knew of less than ten that existed in the present day.

Kerta caught my surprise, and she began to sign, Jaxon picking up the role of translator. 'Time has dwindled our numbers. Many have chosen eternal rest over the centuries that stretched before us. A few have been killed in skirmishes between us – or were executed by Vitus, or even Dearil before he was imprisoned. All minor gods, of course. Ones whose disappearances wouldn't matter to the balance of things.'

'Why separate the gods from mortals if everything was going well?' Callum asked.

'Because we grew too comfortable.' Evania ran a hand down her flowing skirts, tiny petals scattering down the path her fingers traced. 'We began to grow too fond of the mortals. The balance grew unsteady as we began to show too much favour to certain mortals, and great disasters appeared. Earthquakes. Giant waves come to sweep away villages. Cyclones that did not belong in the areas they struck. The casualties were in the tens of thousands.

'Dearil used his power to slice off the in between – a place that exists between the mortal realm and the realm of the dead.' She swept a hand towards the window, where the leaves continued to fly free of the gold and silver trees. 'A place where life does not naturally occur but can be sustained. All the gods were ordered into the realm. Most were happy to go, seeking to protect the mortals. Some refused – most of those were executed by Dearil. But one – one could not be left behind.'

'Vitus,' Callum guessed.

Kerta nodded solemnly. 'He was a different god then, and he had found a lover amongst the mortals. A woman by the name of Alexia – a halfling born of Kyrah. She was sweet. Kind, in a way that most fail to be. And she loved Vitus as much as he loved her.'

Jaxon shifted beside me. I glanced at him, frowning at the tension in his expression. 'Did you know her?'

'I wasn't alive back then,' he said shortly. 'But I know the fate of Kyrah's children.'

Kerta cast a sad look his way. 'It's the fate of most halflings, child. Those born between realms are not destined for long lives, despite the longevity their blood should grant them. You know that.'

Turning his head, Jaxon twisted his fingers together before saying softly, 'Knowing that doesn't make it right.'

'Did Vitus stay with her?' I asked. I couldn't picture it – Vitus caring for anyone other than himself. A man who could sacrifice an innocent child had no place loving.

Evania's rose eyes darkened. 'He did not. Dearil dragged him over the border to this realm, and sacrificed some of his power to erect the barrier. He begged Dearil to let him through. Tried to give up his divinity. But Dearil worried that there were no mortals that could bear the power of a god. All Vitus could manage was the briefest visits – no more than five minutes every year. It was enough time to find out Alexia was pregnant with twins – *his* twins. To see them grow to four years of age.

'But the mortals grew restless. They wanted someone to blame for the absence of the gods, and all the suffering wrought before the gods disappeared. So they turned on the next best thing – the halflings. The year the twins were to turn five, Vitus visited the mortal realm, only to find the burnt bodies of his family.'

Horror twisted through me. I remembered Cassie's weight in my arms. The grief as I stared at her lifeless face. The knowledge that I'd never see her alive again, and the hatred that had blazed through me because of it. 'Gods,' I whispered, hand pressing to my chest. 'That's awful.'

Kerta nodded. 'It drove Vitus over the edge. He hated Dearil after that. Locked himself away for a century. And when he emerged, he vowed that the mortal realm would one day pay for the murder of his family.'

Part of me empathised with the god. If I had his power, gods knew what I would've done in that situation. But he had killed Cassie and treated her death as though it were nothing more than a stepping stone in his grab for power. That was unforgivable.

Yet I couldn't stop the niggling voice in my mind asking, *are you really any better than him?* I knew the answer. No. I wasn't better than him. I'd kill anyone I needed to for my goal. And if I couldn't be better, than I'd need to make sure I became a whole lot worse.

'How do I kill Vitus?' I asked bluntly.

Kerta let out another discordant laugh, breaking the tension in the room. She rose to her feet, signing: 'Come. We can discuss that while we walk.'

There was no explanation of where we were headed as both goddesses swept from the room, the three of us trailing behind. The pair were mismatched in all obvious ways – height, stature, beauty, clothing, even the way they walked. Where Evania floated, Kerta was firmly rooted to the ground, prowling like a great beast on the hunt. And yet, both walked without a single falter in their steps. Evania adjusted her longer strides to meet Kerta's, walking perfectly in sync.

I couldn't help but glance down to where Callum had adjusted his own pace to meet mine.

'Everything okay?' he asked.

Cheeks warming, I focused forward. 'Perfectly fine.'

The hallways outside the room were beautiful. Every wall was covered in paintings, art, colours swirling together in bright murals. The depicted scenes followed the journeys of the gods and goddesses – Evania, with a crown of flowers in her hair, hand resting upon a mountain lion's head as a rabbit perched on her shoulder; Kerta, with her sword drawn and arrows shooting towards her; another god I recognised as Maya, goddess of the hunt, deep in a forest. As I stared, the colours shifted, the shapes formed transforming into new scenes. A bird fluttered through the paint. It alighted upon the painted shoulder of a yellow-eyed goddess as she sat next to a cloaked god with silver eyes gleaming through the shadows.

Before the scenes could change again, Evania and Kerta were striding onwards. The paintings became arched windows. Light fractured where it streamed through, forming rainbows upon the ground. Clouds curled their way across the indigo sky. There were no trees out of these windows. Instead, water trickled over sharp-tipped stone. Shells were embedded deep into the glistening stone. All at once, the water pulled back, revealing deep, shadowed crevices between each point. A flash of white caught my eye.

'Is that—'

'The bones of the minor gods,' Jaxon confirmed. 'There have been at least three who chose the sea as their final resting place, and those rocks are greedy things. They kept hold of the remains the moment the gods' lives left them.'

I shuddered, turning away from the view. My skin crawled as I thought on what Jaxon had shared earlier – that there was a sentience to most things in this realm. There was no sign of any other gods as we walked. Every footstep echoed back at us. Relief flooded me with every turn we made, only to find the hallways empty. We'd been lucky so far. I didn't know enough of the politics between gods to know who to trust. I wasn't even sold on Kerta's and Evania's apparent trustworthiness. Gods were capricious beings. There was no telling what they sought to gain by helping us.

'Your father has feared Vitus's attempt to bring down the barrier between our world for eons. He knew of Vitus's hatred for mortals.' Kerta signed, her hand movements followed closely by Evania's translation. 'But recently, he has feared it even more. Vitus has been growing impatient, and his followers restless.' Kerta's eerie, red eyes slid to me. 'And Dearil feared for the daughter he'd left there.'

I bit down on my tongue to keep the sharp, slicing words that rose from pouring out. To question where that fear was as I was being abused by the woman I had been left with. When I was a slave to the very king who worked with Vitus to allow his entrance into the mortal world. When I learnt that the only thing to expect from anyone in the mortal realm or any other was pain.

A crease appeared between Kerta's brows as though all those words were painted across my face as clearly as the scenes around us. 'There are rules, child, that govern the gods. Rules and laws more ancient than the existence of your world. If he had brought you here sooner, any god could have questioned your place in our world. A single mistake, and you would've been killed. And if any went after you, Dearil wouldn't have been able to stop them.' Her shoulders lifted in a dismissive shrug. 'He was caged. He had enough power to inhabit the mortal realm by possessing a mortal, but not enough to visit fully unless called upon with ancient rituals. Certainly not enough to bring a child back with him.'

It was an odd thing to consider, that gods were as bound by rules and regulations as mortals were. Divinity only stretched so far it seemed, and gods were not the omnipotent beings they pretended to be.

Kerta continued with her hand signs, turning her flaming eyes ahead once more. 'When he sensed the rising dissent amongst us, though, he sought to bring you here to ready you for the war to come.' The muscles across her back tensed. 'He didn't expect you to be so obstinate. Nor did he expect that war to come so soon.'

'War?' Jaxon cut in, eyebrows raised. 'This place is as boring as it was last time I was here.' He tugged on the end of a tapestry that seemed to be woven from threads of silver. A thread broke in his hand. Before it could disappear into his pocket, Evania snatched it away.

'Last time you were here, you burnt my favourite garden to ashes.' Her cool tone was belied by the anger lining her pretty features. Tension crackled in the air, Evania's hair shifting despite the lack of breeze.

Jaxon's throat worked in a swallow, his eyes shifting away. Surprised by his silence, I raised my brows at him. He grimaced in response.

'War has been brewing for centuries, boy,' Kerta signed, her eyes hard. 'But gods seldom fight each other unless we're sure we'll win. We hide behind careful words and sly smiles. The real war – the bloodshed that is destined to occur – will be up to the mortals.'

'The Gifted,' I guessed.

Kerta nodded. 'Our Gifted were carefully selected at birth. Given tiny seeds of our own power – power that we do not get back until the day they die. Seeds that also make them the perfect vessels for hosting our full might, should any of us perish and upset the balance of the realms.'

'How?'

Kerta turned her fiery eyes on me. 'We make a gamble, based on a multitude of factors, as to who is most likely to serve us. Family, natural inclination to hosting certain powers, temperament. Kyrah's divination allows us to watch those we consider worthy. Sometimes, it goes well. Sometimes, it doesn't. Your king and Vitus are a perfect example of a kernel of the power placed in the wrong mortal.'

Callum tensed beside me. His expression turned shadowed, his jaw feathering. Reaching out, I brushed my fingers against his, not wanting to draw attention to his discomfort around the goddesses. He jolted, his face angling downwards. I tilted my head. *Everything all right?*

The shadows disappeared. His lips curved upwards as he smiled, chin dipping in a nod. I began to pull my hand away. Before I could, his finger hooked around one of my own, squeezing for a heartbeat before releasing. The warmth in my cheeks crept down my neck as I hurried my pace.

'What happens when you make a mistake?'

'We cannot take our Gift away from a mortal. Once they possess that kernel of power, that is theirs to keep.'

'You just leave them with the Gift?' It didn't sound like something Vitus would be willing to do.

There was nothing kind in Kerta's gaze, nor in the movements of her hand. 'No.' She held my gaze. 'We take it back by other means.'

My stomach clenched. It didn't take a leap of logic as to how the gods would take back that Gift. If there was no living being to house the power, then the power would go back to the god. My skin chilled at the thought. 'Would Vitus try to do the same? Take back what he considers his?'

'Gods are patient beings,' Evania said. 'Eventually, he will, but if your king serves another purpose, he will be content to wait. That droplet of power won't make much difference.'

I exhaled, relief flooding me. As though sensing my thoughts, a small smile curled the corner of Kerta's lips. It quickly faded. 'Vitus seeks to merge with his godly body in the mortal realm. At the moment, his physical essence exists in the barrier between the realms. It is slowly moving through though, searching to reunite with Vitus's soul. Once he regains his full power, though, there will be very little that can stop him.'

'Then we have to find his physical body,' Callum said, his voice far calmer than I could muster. 'Destroy it before it reaches him.'

'Impossible,' Evania snapped, waving long fingers through the air in a dismissive gesture. 'The ritual and sacrifice used to bind him to a mortal body also scattered his physical body into tiny fragments. There's no way to destroy them. They will fly to his soul, one by one, until he is whole again.'

'If you seek to stop him,' Kerta added on, 'it's his soul that will need to be destroyed. Not his body. And you must be quick about it.'

'Quick with what?' Callum asked, voice low. We'd shifted closer once more, the brush of his arm against mine a comfort in this strange realm.

Evania let out an exasperated breath. 'Have you not been listening, silly boy?'

Callum merely stared at the goddess, unbothered by the insult. There was a defiance in his eyes – a refusal to bow before their divine presence. As with anything Callum encountered, they were merely a barrier in the way of whatever it was he wanted. And right now, he wanted answers. Evania sighed again.

Even before she spoke, a noxious combination of dread and anticipation twisted together inside me. Wanting to finally take the next step in my path, and a cowardly desire to hide from what was to come.

'Quick with training Chiara to destroy Vitus.'

Chapter Twenty-Two

Callum stopped short, drawing the rest of us to a halt. Irritation flared in Evania's features as Kerta gently tugged on her elbow when she attempted to continue walking. The pair signed, their bodies shifting so none of us could see the full movements of their hands. At last, Evania threw her hands up in frustration before turning to Callum.

'You can't be serious.' His flat voice perfectly mirrored his expression.

Evania's brows lifted. 'I certainly am.'

Kerta looked unamused by the whole situation while Jaxon watched with unabashed interest. Callum, though, looked downright murderous. His eyes were thinned, his body tense with barely leashed fury. 'Your goddesses,' he gestured between the two of them, 'Vitus is as much your problem as he is ours. More so. You deal with him.'

Kerta had the decency to grimace sympathetically. Evania narrowed her eyes right back at Callum. 'You cannot expect us to kill Vitus.'

'Why not?' Where another might tremble in the face of a

goddess, Callum only seemed to harden. 'You must've had an inkling of what the chains did when you helped us take them from the Niguran forest. Did you know that they were to bind Dearil to the mortal realm? That it would lead to Vitus taking on my father's body and beginning this so-called war you speak of?'

Evania flinched at the mention of the chains and Kerta slid an arm around her waist. The goddess of war curled her fingers inwards, bunching the material of the dress as Evania shifted into the touch. Her voice softened as she said, 'I didn't know they would be used on Dearil. If I had, I would've struck you both down, Dearil's daughter or not.'

Guilt pricked at me. It would be easy to blame Evania – to claim she was the one who had failed to stop Vitus. That if we hadn't received her help, then we would never have brought those chains from the forest. Dearil would never have been bound, Vitus never bound to King Kane. And Cassie would still be alive. But I had played that game before. Chosen to blame Callum – blame myself – for Cassie's death. All that waited down that path was pain.

'It doesn't matter,' Callum snapped. 'Risk your own lives if you want to stop this war, rather than using us – using *Chiara* – like a plaything.'

'Callum,' I said softly, pressing my fingers to the back of his hand. He was visibly trembling from the anger that coursed through him. 'I think we should—'

Evania interrupted. 'We're not talking about Kerta or I.' If disdain were a tangible entity, we might have filled an entire bowl with the amount dripping from her voice. 'We're talking about the extremely slim likelihood that the girl isn't as useless as she looks and can save your little realm.'

The wrath in Callum's eyes grew. Kerta moved, stepping in front of Evania. Her fingers flicked in quick signs as shadows began to darken Callum's glower. 'It's about balance.' She tilted her hands side to side like scales, before allowing them to come to rest at the same height. 'We are designed in pairs. For war.' She gestured at herself, at her scars, flames and ever-shifting armour, 'There is peace.' She stepped back, coming back to Evania's side before swinging a hand between Callum and I. 'For life, there is death.'

I refused to look up at Callum – to see if her words had rung the same unwanted cord in him as they had me. As though that pairing were natural.

'We do not have the power to destroy other gods. And, even if we did, our premature involvement could very well destroy the balance in this realm. The very essence of our world and yours would crumble. We would save nothing.'

'And how is that any different for me killing him?' I asked, finger tapping impatiently upon my now folded arms. 'I might only be a halfling, but there's still divinity in me.'

'There are two ways a god can die.' Evania held two fingers before her. 'The first is the god killer – a knife crafted at a time when our numbers were over a hundred, imbued with a drop of every god's power.'

'Great,' Callum said coldly. 'Then find the knife, and you can use it.'

Evania glared. 'The knife has been missing for centuries.'

Jaxon sighed. 'Of course it has.'

'And the second way?' I asked.

'You momentarily tip the balance in favour of death,' Kerta signed. 'Overpower him with your Gift by taking him by surprise. It will be difficult – near impossible – but there's a chance. Without the knife, the only way to kill a god is at the hands of an opposing divinity.'

'But killing Vitus would upset the balance permanently, wouldn't it?'

Kerta shook her head. 'Divine power did not always belong to the gods. Once, it belonged to beings more ancient than us. It has existed and will always exist, for far longer than any alive have. If it's freed from the vessel of Vitus's body, it'll simply seek a new one – a Gifted mortal whose body has been primed by a seed of that very same power. Providing they are strong enough, they would ascend to godhood.'

'And if they're not strong enough?'

Evania shrugged. 'Then they will die, the power will be let loose, and it will wreak havoc. So the vessel will need to be strong enough.'

I hate gods. The ease with which Kerta and Evania communicated this information had irritation building inside me. 'Kill Vitus and everything is solved, then. Sounds easy.'

Evania nodded sagely, the sarcasm going by unnoticed. 'It does sound that way.'

Patience was a virtue I needed to work on if I was to interact with gods on the regular.

'One problem,' I said. 'Vitus is the king of gods – he's had centuries to hone his power. I'm a seventeen-year-old—'

'Eighteen,' Callum interrupted.

I shot a look at him. 'What?'

'Eighteen,' he said again, slower this time. 'You turned eighteen three weeks ago.'

I had? I stared at him, bewildered. Before I could ask how he knew that, Evania cleared her throat. She turned a critical eye on me. 'Even if you had centuries to practise, I have my doubts that you'd be capable of taking Vitus down. You'll most likely die.'

'Fantastic.' I turned, staring out the window as the water washed back over the stones. The gods' bones disappeared once more, leaving only the pretty shells showing on the surface. How many more dark secrets did the beauty of this realm and its occupants conceal? Twisting back around, I continued. 'So, our options are down to a knife that disappeared years ago, or me dying.'

'That's right,' Evania said cheerfully, ignoring the frown Kerta sent her way.

I bit back a sigh. It didn't seem like I was going to be fulfilling Cassie's wish of finding happiness anytime soon. 'Even if I had the power for it, my Gift doesn't work on Vitus, or any of Vitus's Gifted.'

'It worked on the Ankuran man you fought at The Den,' Jaxon pointed out.

'Ankuran?' I stared at Jaxon, the word unfamiliar. 'What's that?'

He winced before turning to Kerta, his hands shifting in rapid signs. Kerta's expression grew increasingly shadowed as she watched the movements, the flames at her hair intensifying. Evania paled as she translated Kerta's response. 'Ankurans are creatures created by Vitus. Creatures of half-life, whose souls are gone but whose bodies are brought back to life.'

'The gold-veined man,' I guessed, remembering the opponent I'd fought in The Den, who had led to me seeking Callum out in the palace. The one whom my Gift had recognised as dead, even as he moved around.

Jaxon nodded. 'I didn't want to bring it up until I was sure. It was a concept Vitus experimented with in the years I lived in this realm – creating creatures whose only desire was to fulfil his bidding. Creatures whom he could inhabit as he wished.' He shuddered. 'Back then, it was just an idea. All his experimentations were failures, and there were few he could test it on in this realm. Mostly the halflings killed by their parents. But Kerta's just confirmed it – Vitus succeeded in creating one a few years before he inhabited Kane.'

Evania's voice shook as she said, 'They're horrific creatures. Aberrations of nature. Ones that can both temporarily host Vitus –

or anyone he chooses to send to briefly occupy the body – as well as mindlessly carrying out Vitus's demands without him having to send his consciousness through.'

Callum inhaled sharply. 'The golden-eyed army,' he said, and the same horrific understanding slammed into me. The army that had razed Archin.

At the time, I'd thought little of it other than them being Vitus's followers – beings he'd somehow lent his power. But they weren't. They were his victims, their souls left to linger in that space I'd found before the gates to the Light and Dark, their bodies used as puppets.

'It's why I asked if their bodies had been burnt,' Jaxon said quietly. 'If they haven't…'

'Then Vitus's army will grow every time he kills,' Kerta finished.

We all fell into heavy silence. How were we supposed to face something like that? A god, who could bring back any he murdered? Any casualty would just be another tool for Vitus to wield against us. The odds were impossible.

A sharp clap of hands drew my attention towards the goddess of war just as I began to spiral. Kerta watched me carefully. 'The most important thing is to focus on bringing Vitus down. Your Gift doesn't work as it should because you haven't tipped the scales in your favour. Even so, it can cause immense pain. If you use your Gift on him and cut him deeply enough, he'll be briefly incapacitated. You can then focus on overwhelming him.' She paused and tilted her head. 'The Ankurans are Gifted by Vitus in a warped way, too, so you could use your Gift against them.'

I frowned. 'Be that as it may, I don't want any power of Vitus's.' Once he died, that power would search for a new vessel. The thought of allowing the same power that had consumed Cassie's life in my veins had ice trickling down my back.

Evania let out a tinkling laugh that scraped my frayed nerves.

'Not you, foolish child. Your body is half a god, already carrying the essence of Vitus's opposite. Your only job is to kill him.'

Her eyes slid to Callum, raking up and down his body. They hovered for a good, long while. It was more scrutinising than leering, but the inexplicable urge to draw a blade on her still surged. *Control*, I reminded myself. Breathing in, I pushed down the small knot of anger in my chest. I had no claim to Callum. No reason to feel so angry.

Maybe, if I kept thinking it, I would stop wanting to rip the goddess's eyes from her head.

Callum had frozen, his fingers pushing against the smooth skin of his wrist. A wrist he had once told me King Kane had shattered before forcing Callum to heal it. His expression, however, was entirely blank. The carefully curated mask of a king who knew emotions were the greatest weapons that could be wielded. 'No.'

A delicate eyebrow rose. 'No?'

'I won't have Vitus's power. Find someone else.'

Evania's lips curled with disdain. She stared down at Callum, still waiting for him to grovel at her feet. 'It is not a mortal's place to defy—'

Kerta placed a calming hand on her shoulder. 'It must be one of Vitus's Gifted. His power would destroy anyone else. And you, child, were created to be the strongest of his Gifted. The perfect specimen. He thought to entice your father to offer his body up by granting you a Gift second only to his own. Most other mortals, Gifted or not, would not withstand the force of power that he houses.'

'There must be others.' Callum's fingers flexed at his side.

'There's one. He'd struggle more than you, but he'd surely survive,' Evania said. Her voice was light, her smile pretty, but there was a glow of annoyance in her eyes. 'The other prince.'

Callum and I snapped out *no* at the same time. The other

prince – Liam – was not an option. Replacing a cruel god with a malicious one would help no one. There was only one choice. Only one person I trusted enough to carry the burden.

I opened my mouth, readying myself to find the right words to shred Callum's resolve. His gaze met mine. Under the hardness there was a layer of vulnerability. I could do it, I realised. I could say something cruel and cutting, remind him of the sister I had lost from his broken promise. I could threaten his friends or his kingdom. I could get on my knees or plead. I suspected I could even just ask him, and he would force himself to do it.

I could, and I should, but … but I wouldn't. Ignoring the prick of eyes on me, I offered Callum a rare smile. Some of the hardness abated. His life had been dictated by threats and cruelty. There had been so few choices in his life, just as there had been in mine – so few paths that didn't trek through blood. And yet, he had been the first to truly offer me a choice. I wouldn't take away his now.

'Your choice,' I said softly, stepping towards him. 'No one else's.'

Evania clicked her tongue with disapproval, already moving towards the door as she said, 'Come with me. I have something to show you.' She glared at me as I moved with Callum. 'Only the king.'

'His name is Callum,' I snapped. Silver skittered across my skin, its brightness matching my fury. 'Stop addressing him like he's a chess piece for you to move around.'

Rose sparks shot her skin in answer to my Gift. 'I will call him as I see fit. He is a mortal, and I am—'

'Chiara,' Callum interrupted, paying no heed to the growing anger in Evania's features as he failed to acknowledge her. 'It's all right. I'll go with her.'

I whirled. 'You can just say no – there's no sense in playing her games!'

He smiled, twisting a lock of my hair around his finger. 'I'm playing no games. I only think it's fair to hear her full reasoning before making any decision.'

My anger deflated as quickly as it had grown. I'd been thinking with the same stubborn rage I always did, while Callum had been thinking as a king. I pressed my lips together. 'Fine. If something happens, don't blame me.'

'Of course.' My hair sprang back into a loose curl as he let it go, his finger shifting to under my chin. He tilted my head back until I was looking at him. 'Thank you.'

I swallowed, cursing my body's betrayal as blood rushed to my cheeks. He was close – close enough that all I could smell was sandalwood and the coming rain. 'For what?'

'For trying to defend me, even if I don't need it.' A wicked glint appeared in his eye. 'Does this mean you like me now?'

I batted away his hand, scowling. 'Go aggravate a goddess instead of bothering me.'

'I haven't even begun to bother you, Captain.' His fingers curled around my jaw this time as he leant in, pausing a hair's breadth away from my lips. His breath skated over my skin. 'Though I'm beginning to think you find me less of a bother and more of a—'

'Please stop before I have to burn my eyes from my skull,' Jaxon said loudly.

I sprang away from Callum, cheeks aflame. One of my hands drove into his chest. Instead of falling back, he caught it, laughing. He lifted my hand to his lips before I could stop him, pressing a kiss to my palm. His eyes gleamed with wicked promises as he gazed up at me. 'To satiate you until next time.'

Before I could respond in what would surely have been a violent manner, Callum straightened and followed Evania through the door. I stared at his broad shoulders – at the way the tension crept back into them moments before the door shut between us.

A finger poked into my forehead. 'You're going to give yourself premature wrinkling if you keep frowning like that.' Jaxon grinned at me. 'Are you perhaps worried about our Cal?'

'I'm...' I trailed off, pressing my lips together before sighing. 'Yes.'

Surprise flared in Jaxon's eyes. Kerta stepped forward, her hands twisting through the air before Jaxon could probe any further. This time, Jaxon translated the movements, albeit with far more reluctance than Evania had. 'While they are away, we will go to my training arena.' Kerta's smile was a calculated creation, the edges curling up whilst still maintaining a reservedness as she waved a hand at the opposite wall. Colours peeled away from each other, spreading to the side. In their place, a set of brass-coloured doors appeared. 'It's time to see what your Gift can do.'

What I could do, it turned out, was not very much at all.

I hissed with frustration as my Gift remained dormant. Across from me, Kerta raised her brows in expectation. 'The power of gods is far unrulier than that of Gifted mortals,' she signed, Jaxon translating. 'Every one of us has a different trigger. Something that will help draw out the power. You need to find yours.'

Being experts in vagueness and calling it advice must be in the job description of gods. I had had my share of frustrations with Dearil's cryptic messages in the past. *Feel it in your blood. Coax it forward. Hold your hands just so.* So far, all her shared wisdom had resulted in nothing but mounting irritation. Where my Gift was usually eager to spring to the surface, now that I actively called upon it, it was reluctant to. If it had been a sentient thing, I would've described it as sulking. Every time I reached for it, it would fall back into its stubborn slumber.

'I'll give a demonstration,' Jaxon said from where he'd

sprawled across a bench that seemed to be entirely carved from shimmering rubies. Despite its appearance, it sank beneath his weight in the same way a cushioned chair might. Flicking his hand through the air, Jaxon crafted tiny butterflies that flitted in the space between us. He waved his hand again. The butterflies twisted into soaring flames. Heat radiated off them, and the thick scent of smoke permeated the air. Another flick of his fingers, and they became a replica of his smugly smiling face. The copy waved jauntily at me. It disappeared in a puff of yellow smoke when my dagger whirled through its forehead.

'That was rude,' Jaxon complained, his fingers brushing against his own forehead. I smiled, finger tapping a second blade I'd plucked from an assortment of weapons carefully placed along the far wall. He laughed.

A hand whacked the back of my head. I spun, glaring at the goddess.

'Focus,' she signed.

Again, Kerta lifted her hands in the air, turning them at perfect angles. Twin swords appeared. Each glowed with flames that sliced the air as they fell into her outstretched hands. They were a strange sort of beauty, in the same way water flooding the streets and stealing those too weak could be beautiful. Undeniably lethal, but extraordinary. I mimicked her movements. Mine were jerkier, fingers not twisting in quite the same way. My eyes remained fixed on my hands as I awaited the silver glow.

Nothing.

Kerta grunted, swords disappearing once more.

'I'm not some old, cranky goddess who's been doing this for years.' I muttered under my breath, turning my head just enough that she couldn't see my lips. Jaxon kindly took it upon himself to translate, then avoided meeting my glare. He didn't manage to avoid the hilt of the blade I sent spinning his way, the end of it slamming into his shoulder hard enough to force a wince out of him.

Kerta's lips curled in a dangerous smile. She twisted her fingers again, as though pulling invisible threads towards herself. This time, a bow and arrow appeared, made of brilliant scarlet. Quicker than my eyes could track, Kerta nocked the arrow, drew, and let it fly. A sharp, stinging pain swept over my ear. With a hiss, I touched my earlobe. Wetness came away on my fingertips. Turning, I stared at where the arrow shaft quivered in the wall, cracks spiderwebbing out from its tip. A small cloud of dust settled upon the ground. 'I might be old, but that doesn't mean I can't remember what it is to be young and ignorant.'

I narrowed my eyes at her, wiping my bloody fingers onto my trousers. 'How do I do this, then? Nothing seems to be working.' This godsdamned Gift had ruined everything worthwhile in my life. My shoulders sagged, a frustrated breath leaving me. 'All I want to do is learn to control it so I can destroy Vitus.'

Feeling my anger, my Gift sparked. Tiny flares of silver crackled down my fingertips. Before I could grasp hold of them, the silver disappeared. Jaxon clapped, impressed at the string of profanities that exited my mouth in a violent burst.

Kerta exhaled. Her scarred fingers grabbed mine, skin rough but warm. She tugged me back around to face her. 'That is why this is so hard for you. Some, like your friends, have Gifts that create. They are easy Gifts to have. They come as easily as the water flows.' Her fingers flicked between us, first pointing at me, then herself. 'Others, like us, have power that destroys. It is not always easy.' There was tension in her face as she continued signing. 'This sort of power isn't about control. Attempting to control it only chokes it. If that happens, then our Gifts rebel against us.'

'Then how do I fix this?'

Kerta took my hands, gently easing out the fists I had curled them into. 'Our Gifts only come when we accept them as a part of ourselves. Accept their destruction, but also accept that new growth can come from such ruin. There is beauty in war. It took me centuries to learn that war can bring good.'

'Like what?' I asked, doubtful. War, to me, had always been a tool wielded by those with power to subjugate those with none. Battles might be where I thrived, but the wars themselves – the machinations of kings and nobles, the clinging to power – were nothing but a competition of corruption and greed.

Kerta, though, smiled, her eyes brightening in their shade of red as she signed. 'Many things. A chance for new lives. Opportunities to come together after centuries apart. *Freedom.*' She eyed me critically, taking in the scars that wrapped over my skin. 'And there is beauty in death, too. Without death, lives hold no meaning. They meander through time without purpose. With death, though, hope exists. Desires come to life. There is nothing more beautiful, or more enviable, to beings like the gods than that which is finite.' The flames in her hair flared, matching the intensity in her eyes. 'You should know that more than anyone, yet you run from both life and death.'

'I don't.' I tugged my hand free. 'I've never feared dying.'

Kerta watched me like one might eye a curious specimen, all shrewd observation and uncomfortable awareness. 'Maybe not for yourself, but for someone else?'

The echo of my earlier panic when I hadn't seen Callum upon arriving in this realm resounded through me. I pushed it aside. 'There's no one left that I care about enough.'

'Hmm.' Kerta eyed me for several long moments. 'We'll see. For now, though, you must accept the destruction your Gift offers if you desire control.'

Unbidden, my eyes dropped to her scarred skin. What destruction had she endured? Smiling, Kerta retracted her hand, running a thumb over twisted flesh. The touch was almost fond.

'I was once as young and foolish as you.' She must have seen the surprise in my eyes, because she let out that deep, discordant laugh. 'It's true. Even gods were young at one time or another. We grew as mortals do, only the mistakes we made cost us far more. At the time, I thought I was indestructible. I was not.' There was no resentment or bitterness on her face as she signed. Only acceptance and faint humour. 'I made a mistake. A terrible, awful mistake that cost me more than just my beauty. Another god died – a minor one, Corinios, whose pitiful power stood no chance against mine when I lost control. He was a friend.'

My lips pressed together. I knew something about losing friends because of my own reckless behaviour.

Kerta wasn't finished. 'But my mistake also granted me something. It gave me my soul-bond.'

I mimicked the movements her hands had made for the last word. They began apart and drifted together before my fingers intertwined. My sign looked childish compared to hers, movements put together like puzzle pieces that didn't quite fit. It was enough, though, for a genuine smile to spread on her lips and a nod of affirmation.

'Soul-bonded.' Her eyes slid towards Jaxon, pity entering her expression. He gave no reaction. 'Gods are different from mortals. Where you marry, and can marry many times over, we are born as half of one soul. When you find your other half, it's—'

'Magic.' Jaxon spoke the word as I had once heard a devout worshipper of Vitus breathe a prayer. 'Magic like no Gift, no power, could ever possess. A sense of rightness that nothing can replicate.' He was looking at his hands, and for a moment, I thought I saw an Illusion of a band of metal around one finger. 'No two soul-bonds are the same. Some are perfect matches, like the meeting of the ocean and the river. Others complement each other and feel more like the pieces designed to slot together perfectly. Some are more … chaotic.'

'Chaotic?'

He nodded. 'Think of a forest fire during a gale.'

'That sounds awful.' As devastatingly destructive as my Gift.

Shaking his head, Jaxon drew a knee up, resting his elbow on it. 'It's not. It's the opposite of that. There can be chaos but underneath it all, there's a ... centre. A place of belonging. Of home.'

Kerta nodded in confirmation. 'It's beautiful. I found my soul-bonded because of my wounds and torment. Because of my Gift.'

I thought of the ethereal, blonde goddess who Kerta had stepped in front of so protectively. 'Evania?' Kerta's smile was one of confirmation. I snorted, thinking of the other goddess's beauty, matched only by her arrogance. 'I'm not sure if congratulations or condolences are in order for that one.'

Kerta, surprisingly, didn't strike me down for the insult. Instead, she twisted her lips wryly. 'It took a long time for me to realise Evania was my soul-bonded. She can be ... difficult. As can I.' She looked at me knowingly. 'I imagine your soul-bonded finds you an acquired taste as well.'

I froze. 'I don't have a soul-bond.' I couldn't. Not when Kerta wasn't wrong about the latter part – acquired taste was a polite way of describing me. *Apathetic. Cruel and cold and hard. Unlovable.* All accurate words that had been thrown at me since I was a child. Words that kept others as safe as they kept me.

Her lips twitched upwards. 'Of course you do. Anyone with a god's blood does. I have Evania. Vitus had Alexia, ill-fated as that affair was. Even Jaxon—'

Jaxon's fingers cut through the air in a sharp movement. I did not need to understand their signed language to know what he'd said. *Enough.* The pity in Evania's eyes grew as he turned to me, his smile tight and eyes flat. 'Having a soul-bond isn't always a good thing. It's a tether to the soul. And damaging, breaking that tether can be ruinous.'

'Like when Alexia died,' I guessed, a complex mix of emotions sweeping through me.

Kerta nodded. 'Vitus could be cold before, but afterwards – that cruelty became unfathomable and indiscriminatory. His soul was left in shreds. It is rare for any being to recover from the snapping of a soul-bond.'

'I don't see how this is helpful to me,' I said to Kerta, lifting my currently ordinary fingers in the air. 'I still can't bring my Gift to the surface.'

'Acceptance,' Kerta signed to me, Jaxon returning to his dutiful watch of her hands, his expression back to a practised mask of faint amusement. 'Accept your Gift, and you can control it. And if you can control it, if you can get close enough to Vitus, then maybe you can kill him.'

She made it sound so easy. Simple, like it should be as natural as breathing. Or perhaps she believed it as natural as living. I'd always struggled with that, too. I lifted my hands before my eyes, watching them. *Come on*, I whispered to my dormant Gift. *If I'm to have any chance of vengeance, any chance of justice, I need you.*

Nothing. Not a single spark of silver. Only cold emptiness inside me, and the vague sense of that terrible *thing* that only came out when it wanted.

'Damned Gift,' I snarled, hands curling into fists. I wanted to hurl myself at something, taking my frustration out in the only way I knew how – with blades sharper than the annoyance slicing at me. I had been born and bred to become something I was exceptional at – a killer. I was not used to failure. I certainly was not used to incompetence. Yet, here I stood, acting as a barrier to my own vengeance.

'Disappointing.' If the cockiness in Callum's voice hadn't alerted me to who our intruder was, the stirring of my Gift and the faint scent of sandalwood and rain would've.

'Fantastic. I have an audience to my failure now.' I dared a glance over my shoulder, finding Callum resting a shoulder against the wall, arms folded and eyes focused solely on me. His lips kicked upwards as our eyes met, but his eyes still retained tendrils of shadows. 'I take it your chat with Evania didn't go well?'

'I said I'd consider what she's asked of me,' Callum said shortly, then forced his expression to relax as he strode over to me. 'I take it your training isn't going well, either?'

I folded my arms. 'It's going fine.'

He glanced over to Jaxon, brows raised. Jaxon grinned, kicking at one of the daggers at his feet. 'There've only been two attempts made on my life, so I suppose it's going as well as it could be.'

'Those weren't attempts on your life,' I said sharply, glaring over my shoulder. 'I never *attempt* to kill.'

'You're not meant to be killing at all,' Jaxon translated as Kerta's fingers shifted. 'You're meant to be focusing.'

'And I haven't killed,' I pointed out before turning my attention back to Callum. He'd shifted even closer, the warmth of his body brushing against my skin. I did not back away. 'What's convinced you to consider taking on Vitus's power? You were adamant about it being a no before.'

'Evania showed me something.' Callum's expression grew grave. 'A future, if Vitus isn't stopped.'

'Well, Cal,' Jaxon drawled, somehow managing to wedge himself between us like an overprotective brother might, 'Let's hear the full extent of it.'

I rolled my eyes at Jaxon's positioning but did not push him out of the way. The physical barrier between Callum and I was a safeguard I needed. Callum cast a stony glance at Evania, who floated over to Kerta. There was an absolute comfort between the goddesses – in the way Kerta's shoulders relaxed and Evania's stony stare softened. No, I realised. I would never have a soul-bond. Such comfort – such relief – it was beyond me. I ignored the pang of envy.

'I saw what could be.' Callum spoke quietly. 'What might come if I refuse this burden.'

Kerta let out an exasperated grunt, staring pointedly at Evania, who smiled, wide eyed and innocent. 'If Kyrah doesn't want me to use her divination mirror, she shouldn't leave it where it's so easily found.'

'In her chambers, inside a locked cabinet?' Kerta signed, unimpressed. Evania only offered a beatific smile in return.

'What did you see?' There was none of Jaxon's usual flippancy in his voice.

Callum stared at Jaxon for a long time. His expression was grave. Haunted.

'Death,' he finally whispered. 'I saw the death of the mortal realm.'

Chapter Twenty-Three

Oh, gods. The death of the mortal realm. Death had never been foreign to me. It was an inevitability, a symptom of holding mortal blood. But this... I was here for vengeance, but how many sisters would die if Vitus were to win? Daughters and sons, friends and lovers? Wiped out to satiate the wrath of a god. The mortal realm had suffered from their own wars. But a war of the divine would tear the realm into shreds.

'There were hundreds of thousands of corpses. Some were scattered on the ground. Others had a worse fate. Their eyes were golden and they – they killed any mortals they came across.' Callum's throat worked in a swallow. 'The mortals left alive were slaves. They had it the worst.'

I didn't ask what he meant. I was well aware of the sort of existence one could have at the hands of a depraved mortal. A god, though with centuries, if not millennia, of living – the cruelties a being such as that could conjure up were unimaginable.

'How does it start?' Jaxon asked hoarsely.

Callum glanced away. 'With my refusal to do this.' My eyes narrowed. There was a lie in those words – in the tightening of his lips and twitch of his fingers. I opened my mouth to press him further but he was already turning his back on me. He stretched his hand towards Kerta. 'Can I have a sword and two knives?'

She stared at him, blinked once, and then the requested weapons clattered at his feet, red power glinting along their edges. Callum smiled, a challenge glinting in his eyes. 'Let's spar.'

I frowned, eyeing the weapons at Callum's feet. They were beautifully crafted blades and a large part of me yearned to pick them up. It wasn't the time, though. There was no telling how long it would be before our presence was discovered by another god and we were forced to return to our mortal bodies, which meant all the time we had needed to be focused on me learning how not to be so useless with my Gift.

'No.' I began to turn back to Kerta, hands lifting to recommence what we had been working on.

'Are you scared?'

My eyes shot up to meet Callum's, catching the smirk that raked over his lips. I should have kept turning to Kerta, giving Callum no response but my back. And perhaps I would have, had I never fought him before. But I remembered his skills. Recalled the thrill of responding to his lithe movements, the sword an extension of himself.

'Hardly.' I scooped up the knives. They were perfectly balanced. 'Fine. Let's spar.'

'Cal, I don't think—' Jaxon started, arms crossed over his chest, but Kerta silenced him with a sharp wave. She watched intently.

'Good.' Callum watched me with the same anticipation in his eyes that I felt. 'Don't worry. I'll go easy on you.'

He gave me no time to respond before lunging forward. If I thought the memory of his fighting was thrilling, it was nothing on seeing it in action. Every limb, every muscle, worked in tandem with his blade. He swung in a wide arc that I blocked with both knives, the impact jarring. His grin widened. He spun, the sword arching under my knives. There was no holding back as I dropped my right hand. Metal clanged, the sword deflected. My other knife aimed for the underside of his throat.

Callum laughed, his forearm slamming into my wrist. A bolt of pain shot through me at the impact. My fingers threatened to spasm. Instead, I forced them to tighten. This was nothing like the fights in the Den – fights where I had complete choice over how many blows connected. Callum was every bit the fighter I was. Any misstep would result in my loss. And that knowledge was electrifying.

I ducked under a lunge at my shoulder, rolling and coming up behind Callum. He was already waiting, his sword an answer to my knives' sweep. Again and again, we swung, perfectly matched even when in opposition. Every blow that met my knives sent tremors racing up my arm. Every lunge of my own had Callum's eyes brightening. Gods, he was strong. Fast, too. But it was the cunning in every movement that was his most dangerous skill. His face betrayed nothing. Every strike skimmed past me, my shirt earning new rips.

He thrust at my side, and I parried with a knife, spinning around him. The kick I aimed at the back of his leg hit nothing but the air. The momentum of it carried me forward a step, and then I was whirling, ducking under the blow that would have taken me in the upper arm if I'd been any slower. My breath was coming heavily now. I didn't miss the sweat trickling down Callum's forehead as I balanced one of the knives in my hand, letting it spin at his head. He twisted to the side at the last moment. If he hadn't, it would have landed dead centre in his forehead.

'That could've killed me.' There was delight in his words. Pure, utter delight.

The bastard was *smiling*. And godsdamn it all, I was grinning back.

It was hard to tell which of us was the child of Death in this moment. Callum lazily brought up his sword as though it required no more effort than breathing. I lifted my remaining knife in answer. Shorter, yes, with less reach, but not any less deadly.

This time, I sliced at his arm. Instead of twisting away, he stepped into my blow. My heart stuttered, my knife swinging to a stop moments before it drove through his flesh. The flash of victory was the only warning I had as Callum wrapped his fingers around my wrist, pressing them into the nerves until my fingers spasmed open. My knife clattered to the ground. Cursing viciously, I drove my free hand forward. He sacrificed his sword, the sound of metal hitting stone ringing loud. He twisted, spinning me around and wrapping his arm around my waist. My breathing hitched at the warmth pressing into me.

'Yield,' he whispered, breath skating over my neck.

A laugh bubbled up through me before I could stop it. The arm at my waist tightened. Gods, how long had it been since I had lost to someone in a fair fight? Too long. Or perhaps never. Even when I was young, the fights I'd been forced into had never been fair. But Callum had beaten me.

'Look at your hands,' Jaxon said, his voice awed.

My gaze shifted downwards. Silver crackled over my fingers, wrapping between them like fine threads. As I stared, it moved upwards, jumping up my arms, and then sparking in my vision. Warmth flooded every vein. This was what power felt like.

'Gods,' Callum said, voice hoarse. 'You're magnificent.'

His words rumbled through me as I let myself be enveloped in his warmth. I couldn't stop another smile lifting my lips. There was a naturalness to the way he held me. A rightness. And every selfish part of me wanted to stay in his embrace.

'See?' Kerta signed, Evania reclaiming her spot as translator. The words sent the smile fleeing from my expression, blood rushing to my cheeks. 'Acceptance. It's the key to control.'

Callum's arm around me loosened. I forced myself to step

away, warmth lingering where he'd touched me. Acceptance, Kerta had said, as though it were easy. I only hoped she referred to acceptance of the deadly power running through my veins. Because acceptance of the other thing – of what existed between Callum and I – seemed a far more dangerous endeavour.

Kerta spent the next hours running me through my paces. My Gift grew increasingly willing as time flew by. It came the easiest when one of the others offered to spar, silver flowing naturally down any blades Kerta crafted. Fighting had always been a part of me. When I thought of my Gift as an extension of that blade, the power would spring to my fingertips, ready to be used. And when I sparred with Callum, his sword flying past me as quickly as my blades did him, the power surged.

I still lacked control, according to Kerta. My Gift lacked any sort of directedness – that, Kerta told me, required a still mind. Her tone indicated that that was something I did not possess. Some time after a bored Evania disappeared, she held a hand up to pause my training. Silver flickered upon my skin before sinking back below the surface. She lifted a hand, a heavy tome appearing in one hand. Jaxon leant forward, interest sparking in his eyes. Her other hand lifted over the cover. Red light rippled from her fingertips, arcing and wrapping around the book, then condensed. The air around us turned still and heavy. A heartbeat later, the book disappeared.

Something thudded to my left. I turned, finding the book at Jaxon's feet. He eyed it mistrustfully.

'Your Gift comes from Dearil,' Kerta signed. 'It should be strong enough to move an item – take it from one place and put it in another.'

'I can do that with my hands and feet,' Jaxon grumbled behind me.

Ignoring him, I asked, 'How is that possible?'.

The book reappeared in Kerta's hand. 'A god's power comes from the threads that create the realms. And, in turn, we have a small amount of control over those threads. Some gods can create wards and barriers by manipulating those threads. Vitus has undoubtedly done that wherever he's placed himself to protect himself from unexpected attacks. Others can cut off fragments of realms, as your father did. We're not really moving the items. Instead, we're bringing two threads together and decreasing the distance.' The book was replaced by a sheet of pale fabric. Kerta grasped the two corners of it, pulling the material taut before pressing the corners together. 'Just like that.'

'You make it sound so simple.' It was a habit of gods, I realised: taking the extraordinary and turn it mundane.

She smiled. 'It is, in a way. But manipulating the realm's threads is draining. A powerful god can move an item like a book no more than seven times. I can only manage five. And the more that needs to be transported, the more power is drained. People are particularly tricky to move about. Dearil can manage to transport four others with himself three times, but no more. He was always the most talented at realm manipulation. Vitus can do the same twice.'

Taking in a breath, I nodded. 'How do I do it?'

The book reappeared. Kerta pushed it into my hands. 'Simply manifest where you want the book to go. Call upon your Gift and visualise it pulling the location towards you. If your power shows, you only have to push the book through to where you're picturing.'

I eyed her dubiously. The power in me felt too new, too raw, to do anything more intricate than killing. 'Can't you just do it if we ever needed to go somewhere urgently?'

Kerta shook her head. 'I would have to be present to do it. It takes a large amount of energy for us to cross the realms, and even then, we can only stay for a few moments in the mortal realm.'

'Evania was able to do it in the Niguran forest,' Callum pointed out.

The flames in Kerta's hair flared, her expression darkening. I stepped back, clutching the book as tension rose around us. 'That was a special case. Evania was driven by wrath and resentment, and what she did to help you cost her. She spent days unconscious afterwards.' Driven by the wrath of what Vitus had once done to her, chaining her to a tree in that forest and letting her be attacked. Hatred for the king of gods filled me. Kerta remained still for several moments, seeming to grapple with her rage. Her hair returned to its normal colouring as she signed, 'Give it a go.'

I sighed, studying the book. It couldn't hurt to try. Closing my eyes, I called my Gift, picturing in my mind the space next to Callum. Let my power gather around the book like a net, moving, pulling—

There was a short cry of pain. My eyes flew open. I had moved the book well enough, shifting it across the room. I had also managed to rip it into hundreds of pieces. Jaxon was pressing a hand to his head, a piece of the hard cover in the other hand. Around Jaxon and Callum, paper littered the ground like the snow I had heard people speak of that fell on the mountains to the west of Axania.

'Let's not try it with people,' Jaxon suggested unhelpfully.

'What did I do wrong?' I asked, staring at the ruined tome. Kerta glanced at the book, then at me.

'You threw your power at it. You need to—'

But whatever she was about to say was cut off by the doors slamming open.

Evania rushed in. Her rose-gold gown more rumpled than

before. That was the only sign of her distress as she said, 'Tarina knows.'

Jaxon jumped to his feet, his features paling. His hands balled into fists as Kerta signed something. No one translated. However, from the sharpness of her movements, that wasn't necessary. We had several choice words in our realm that matched hers.

'She felt her son's power and is demanding to see him.'

Jaxon's face grew stormier. 'No,' he bit out. 'I will not see—'

'And I would not advise it,' Evania snapped back with equal venom. 'If she sees your two companions, she will either rip them to pieces or bring news of it back to Vitus. And she will not be so quick to let you free of her grasp this time, boy.'

Callum spoke before I did, voice grave. 'We need to go back.'

Kerta stared at me for a moment and then nodded sharply. I could see it, though – she didn't think I was ready, or that my Gift would be enough to kill Vitus. That made two of us. Even so, she signed, 'Use your Gift. Coat your blades with it. If you hit the right spot and put in enough power – there's a chance. A chance that his power will rebel so fully against yours that Vitus will shatter.'

A chance. It was not the certainty I'd hoped for, but I knew the truth well enough. There was never certainty when it came to war and tyrants. The only absolute was the eventual death that hounded us all.

'How am I meant to do that?' I asked, narrowing my eyes and setting my jaw. 'I can barely summon my Gift to my skin without a struggle, let alone send it to one specific point.'

'There is no time to teach you.' Kerta's mouth was a slash across her face. 'You will teach yourself, or you will die.'

And with those words of reassurance, the goddesses ushered us from the room.

The return to the mortal realm was easier than the exit. Jaxon retrieved identical vials from those we had taken earlier from what he labelled his *private storage* – a spot behind a loose stone. An emergency plan, he had told me when I had questioned why he even had them.

All it took was a single sip, and I was gone. This time, I grabbed the silver thread that shone in the darkness before I had a chance to drift closer to death. Let it wrap its warmth around me, let the tiny shadows that glistened within pull me towards the mortal realm. A flash of light, silver mixed with dark, and my soul plunged back into my body.

Chapter Twenty-Four

Waking from death felt the same as waking up following a long night of drinking. My limbs were heavy, every muscle seeming to protest movement. A fierce pounding in my head beat out even the worst of my hangovers. For a moment, I lay in the darkness, eyes shut tight against the outward world. Soft material caressed my skin, much smoother than any bedsheets I had ever owned. My hand stretched out, fingers brushing against a still hand.

Worry beginning to sprout, I forced my eyes open. The world I'd left had been bright, flooded with daylight. Now, it was dark. The ceiling above was indiscernible amongst the shadows, the swirling designs that laced the edges melding with the night. There was no sound or sign of any other life in the room. My lips pressed together into a tight line as I forced myself upwards. Air hissed between my teeth at the ricocheting pain that raced from my head down my neck to my spine.

It truly was a hangover, without any of the happy effects of alcohol from the night before.

Swallowing down the bile that rose in my throat, I forced my head to twist to the side, ignoring the throb of pain that followed. Through the heaviness of the dark, I could make out the outline of Jaxon's profile. In stillness, his face was unnervingly soft. Black lashes fell on olive cheeks, his usual conniving grin gone. My eyes tracked down to his chest. I watched, waited, until I saw the slight shudder of fabric as it rose and then fell.

Alive.

The motion of twisting my head the other way sent another bout of nausea racing through me. My body screamed for rest. I ignored the urge to lie down, to close my eyes and sleep. I had to check. Had to know if Callum had also made it.

I stared at his chest, my own heart thudding. Seconds began to tick by.

One. The chest remained still.

Two. My eyes lifted to Callum's face, seeking any sign of life. Any flicker of movement.

Three. A stirring to my other side, signalling Jaxon reviving. Callum remained still. As still as Cassie had been as I clutched her to me, her lifeblood soaking my clothes.

Four. I lurched into motion, my aches fading away into nothingness as I jumped to my feet. My hands fisted in the front of Callum's shirt as I leant closer to him.

'Don't you dare,' I hissed, my hair spilling around us. 'Don't you godsdamn dare, you bastard.'

I pressed my ear to his chest. There was no answering thud or steady rhythm of his heart. The warmth of him I'd felt in the godly realm was gone, cold stillness left in its place.

'Is he...' Jaxon's rasping voice trailed off at the furious glare I cut his way.

'If you die,' I said, placing the heels of my hands into Callum's chest and pressing down in a swift rhythm, waiting to feel something. Anything. 'I will hunt your soul down and kill you twice over.'

There was no response. No snarky comment, no raising of the eyebrows. No glimmer of wicked amusement as he opened his eyes. My own heart beat fast enough for the two of us, erratic and wild. I kept at the compressions, struggling to keep the panic at bay. My Gift was utterly useless. I felt no soul, no warmth of death leaking out from Callum. Nothing to grasp hold of and tie to his body. I had no healing power. No way to save him.

I was going to lose someone again, and I could do nothing about it.

'I will hate you forever for this. You don't get to choose to die. You don't get to leave me.' Pressure built in my eyes, my breath catching. I leant down, pressing my forehead to his. My eyes shut. 'I will...'

Whatever threat or promise was about to jump from my lips never came. My throat swelled, choking back the sob that was edging its way up. Somewhere between leaving the palace and now, I'd forgotten to hate him. Forgotten to guard myself against him. And if I lost him now, it wouldn't just hurt. It would ruin me.

My Gift flickered in my veins, but its melody was no comfort. Not when it could do nothing to help me.

A hand touched my cheek, brushing away tears that had fallen upon my cheeks. I jerked backwards, my eyes snapping open and meeting a set of green ones.

'You do care.' Callum managed to add an infuriating smirk, though it trembled at the corners.

There was a pause, our breaths mingling in the few centimetres of space between us. Then my fear twisted, becoming white-hot fury. I attempted to wrench myself away. Callum was quicker. A hand snaked behind my neck, the other grasping my arm.

'Let go of me,' I ground out, pushing against his chest. My arms were all but trapped between us. Callum's grin widened. 'I said, *let go of me*, you worthless, good for nothing bastard.'

'Why?' As he talked, my traitorous eyes drifted away from his, down to those wickedly curved lips. I could remember how they felt against mine. Confident and completely sure. Just like everything else Callum did. 'You were upset with the thought I might have died. Don't you want to remain here to make sure I'm fine?'

Upset didn't begin to encompass the raging emotions that had tried to swallow me whole. I was too lost to my anger to admit it, though, as my eyes snapped up at his. 'I was upset that I wasn't going to be the one to kill you once this is all over.'

His hold was unyielding as he tugged me closer to him. 'Are you sure that's what it is?'

My scowl shifted into a sweet smile. 'You're right,' I murmured, giving into the pressure of his hands. I let my face angle towards his, lips nearly brushing as I said, 'I was upset I wouldn't get to do this before you died.'

Callum's eyes lit with an intense eagerness. I dipped my head lower, letting my lips press against his. His eyes shut, his arm wrapping around my waist. For a moment, there was nothing but him. His lips, his touch, his skin.

Nothing but him until he reared away, cursing colourfully as a hand flew to his mouth. I clambered to my feet, Jaxon grinning with fiendish amusement. I smiled innocently at Callum, the coppery taste of blood filling my mouth.

'You bit me.' There was shock in Callum's voice as he rose to his feet, mingling with the same wicked delight as when we'd sparred.

I stepped forward, my finger jabbing towards his chest. 'I'll do much worse if you ever think about dying on me.'

The shock increased. His hand fell from his lips, revealing dots of blood. 'You were actually worried about me?'

Behind, a door opened then closed, Jaxon disappearing from the room with some excuse about going to visit The Den. I folded my arms. A candle flickered to one side, the scent of fresh flowers filling the space from where someone – Deana, most likely – had arranged a bunch. 'Tell me the truth. Did you heal yourself to come back here?'

Callum hesitated.

It was all I needed. I stepped forward. 'You *idiot*. You should never have come with us. What would you have done if Evania hadn't fetched you? You would've *died*.' I shook my head, my Gift sparking with my anger. 'I should've gone alone. Should've—'

Callum caught my hand as I went to shove his chest again. 'You're not the only one who gets to take risks, Chiara. It was too dangerous for you to go alone. We didn't know what waited in the godly realm.'

I glared. 'This wasn't a risk. It was suicide!'

'Yet, here I stand. Alive.' His touch slid further up, gently encircling my wrist and lowering my hand. My cheeks heated with a combination of fury and the warmth of his fingers pressed to my skin. 'Jaxon seemed sure Tarina wouldn't leave us there. As I said in the godly realm, I was also certain Jaxon would have a way to get us out of trouble. And I've had dealings with gods before. I know they never resist the chance to meddle in mortal affairs.'

My frown deepened. 'How did you get back here? Evania led you to the godly realm, but she couldn't have brought you to the mortal one.'

Another hesitation. He glanced down at our entwined hands, his brow furrowing. 'You,' he said at last. 'I reached out, and there was a silver cord. It was *you*, Chiara, that led me back to the mortal realm.'

I shook my head, pulling myself free from him and pacing away. 'That doesn't make sense. I'm no god. I—'

'I know what I felt,' Callum said firmly. 'I know *you*.'

Part of me cowered at those words. The rest shivered with delight.

Halting, I swung around. Callum had seated himself on the edge of his bed, shadows carving themselves deep under his eyes. Right now, he didn't look like a king. He looked like a man. An exhausted, vulnerable one.

And that terrified me far more than any king could.

'Why didn't you heal yourself?' I studied him. In the godly realm, I'd been too overwhelmed with everything that'd happened with Cassie and being in the realm that had only existed in stories before. I hadn't questioned his weak excuse. But now my only concern was him. 'You said it took too long to heal from a fatal poison. But I've seen you heal from a stabbing. It took seconds. Even if poison was more complex, surely it wouldn't have taken much longer.'

Callum's gaze dropped to where his fingers interlaced. 'I thought I'd be able to heal myself. I was wrong.'

There was truth there. Perhaps he had gone in thinking he'd heal himself and Jaxon easily enough. But it wasn't the whole truth. I hadn't seen him use his healing in months. 'Why weren't you able to?'

'It doesn't matter.' There was no room for pushing, no invitation to press more in his tone. It was pure, solid stone.

Unfortunately for him, I had never been much good at bowing to authority. I shifted forward, studying his expression – the pallor that crept into his cheeks, the tension through his body.

'Something's happened, hasn't it? Has Vitus somehow blocked your access to your Gift?' Callum's jaw feathered in response. I continued, not ready to give up. 'You wouldn't use your Gift at the brothel – you even sent for ungifted healers.'

'Leave it, Chiara.' His voice was shadows and warning. The turmoil of emotions in his eyes warned me of the edge he was teetering on.

I wasn't sure what would be at the bottom if he fell.

But sometimes, falling was necessary to face the darkness that lurked below. I'd learnt that for myself, and it had been Callum who'd hauled me out afterwards. 'Then it's true. You can't use your Gift. I take back what I said before. Travelling to the godly realm wasn't just reckless. It was idiotic!'

His eyes met mine. 'I don't see why you're getting so worked up over this. Surely that would've been an ideal ending for you? Me taking care of without you having to lift a finger.'

The words – well-deserved, I knew – slammed into me like shards of ice, cutting deep. My hand pressed to my chest as I inhaled raggedly. Callum smiled, ice coating his expression. I recognised the look in his eyes. Not angry, as his tone suggested. Sad. Lost. A little broken. The same look as I had worn for months.

'Or were you worried my death would interfere with your plans?'

'Of course not,' I snapped.

Callum's hands fisted. 'Don't worry. I've made sure Deana can—'

'You idiot,' I whispered, my rage guttering. And with it, my defences crumbled. I might not deserve Callum and the clear care he had for me. But he deserved someone to care for him. To help him shoulder his pain, just as he had done with me. And while I might be the absolute worst choice for the role, I owed him this much. The silver of my Gift did not disappear. Instead, it reached out – not in an attack, but simply as though it wanted to tether him to me. 'It's because I care about *you*.'

Callum's smile faltered, his eyes widening. 'Say that again.'

My cheeks heated, but I did not back away. 'I care for you, Callum.' I stepped closer, reaching for him, but not quite touching. Not yet. 'I know I have no right to say that, not after everything I've said to you in the past, but it's true. And you not having access to your Gift *terrifies* me. What if Evania hadn't come for you today?'

'But she did,' Callum said with a patience that only made my panic grow.

'What if Liam or Vitus go after you, and you're hurt?'

'Then I'll recover the normal way.'

Fury flared alongside the panic. For once, I didn't allow it to consume me. Not yet. 'And what if he does worse than just hurt you? What if he takes someone else I care for—' I broke off, my throat growing tight.

'That won't happen,' Callum said, taking my hand in his. I hadn't realised I'd begun shaking until then.

'You don't know that!' I clung to his hand as though it were my lifeline. It should've made me feel weak. It didn't. 'If Vitus can block your Gift, all it'll take is a lucky strike! Gods, it doesn't even need to be Vitus who strikes you. It could be anyone!'

'Vitus hasn't blocked my Gift,' Callum said quietly.

I froze. Blinked. Stared. 'What do you mean?'

He inhaled deeply. It was his turn to hold tightly onto me. 'Vitus hasn't blocked my Gift,' he repeated, his voice thick with emotion. 'It's me.'

I shook my head, my chest tightening. 'I don't understand.'

'I'm the one who's blocking my Gift, Chiara.'

The words speared through me. Again, anger threatened, my Gift sparking beneath my skin. But I recognised it for what it was this time. It was fear. Bone-deep terror that I'd lose Callum. Swallowing, I clung to whatever scrap of calm I could find as I said, 'Explain.'

'Do you remember what I told you of my father?' Callum asked. His gaze had turned distant, his expression blank, but his hand continued to hold tight.

I nodded, my eyes lingering on the scar that slashed over one side of his mouth. The only lasting sign of the damage his father had done, the rest forcedly wiped away by Callum's own Gift. And there were other things he had been forced to do as well –

ways his Gift was used to allow the torture of others to stretch on.

'Every time I had the slightest mark, a bruise, a cut, anything, my father forced me to wipe it away.' He twisted the hand wrapped around mine, showing me the back of it. 'See this?' The gentle light of the room revealed nothing but smooth, unmarred skin.

'There's nothing there,' I replied, glancing down at the contrast of my own scarred skin, woven from the tapestry of what I had endured.

'My father broke every finger in my hand once. Another time, he drove a dagger through each just as you did to that creature. When I was five, he even cut off a finger for having a grass stain on my trousers.' He pointed at the scar that split one side of his mouth in two. 'I told you about this one in the Niguran forest. This is my only mark. My only rebellion.'

I said nothing. Sometimes, that was all that was needed.

'I was kept in a room for three weeks for the single scar. My arms, my legs, were flayed. Every bone in my hands and feet was broken and shattered. I would've died at least a dozen times if I were not able to heal myself. I tried not to, but I wasn't strong enough back then. Every time I lost consciousness, that curse of a Gift would rise and make me as good as new.' Callum took a deep breath. There were no tears in his eyes. No horror in his face. But I could see it nonetheless – the scars that weren't worn on the skin. 'And after he bored of that, he drove a blade through me.' A ghost of a smile curled his lips upwards. 'I refused to heal it.'

My heart twisted as I thought of the child Callum, bleeding from his father's own hand. 'Why?'

'It was the only rebellion I could accomplish.' He tapped a finger to his scar. 'Just like this, only greater. Without an heir, a king's reign is threatened. And do you know what I thought when he stabbed me? I thought, *good.*'

There was a moment of silence, a shared understanding between us. The bastard of a prince and the monster of a girl, who learnt the world hated them far too young, and decided to hate it back. Two children who had found ways to bite and kick and claw even when the walls of their cages were too tight to move, refusing to yield any sliver of control they had. Even if that sliver of control meant death. And when they bit those hands that had held them down, and clawed at the skin that sought to beat them back, both had found they liked the taste of blood.

But that understanding passed, and the fear rolled back in. I could've lost him before I'd even known him. Would've gone through life without knowing the vital piece that was missing if he'd succumbed to his wound.

Callum's laughter was hollow. 'But he assured me that my Gift could heal it – left me in the dark and told me he'd come back once I'd lost consciousness and my Gift smoothed away the wound. He was too arrogant, though. He left the room unlocked, thinking I'd be unconscious in moments. I was a stubborn brat back then.

'I somehow managed to stumble my way out of the palace, through a small tunnel underground that no adult could get through. It was how I met Jaxon. I still can't decide if it was fortune or not that had me collapsing at the door of one of his gambling dens, semi-conscious and demanding that he kill me. He locked me in a room and told me I could heal myself or die.'

'You chose to heal yourself?' I asked carefully.

'I didn't have a choice once I fell unconscious. Now, my Gift will often wait till I actively control it – or am on the cusp of death. Back then, it didn't. Jaxon offered me passage out of the city, but I'd regained my senses enough by then to remember I'd left someone behind in the palace. A girl who didn't acknowledge my existence.'

'You idiot,' I sighed, echoing my earlier words. He'd escaped the palace. Had had a taste of freedom, yet he'd come back. For me, before we'd even properly met.

His lips quirked upwards. 'Perhaps about other things, but not when it comes to this. I don't regret going back. Not if leaving meant I'd never see you again.'

'I wished you hadn't.' I bowed my head, pressing my eyes shut. He'd come back to a nightmare for *me*. 'You should've run.'

'Even back then, I knew the only place I'd ever run to was wherever you were.'

Emotion swelled, thick and messy. I pushed it aside for now as I lifted my gaze to his once more. 'That still doesn't explain why you can't heal yourself.'

Callum's head dropped forward. Silence settled upon us, long enough that I believed he wouldn't explain. And did I have any right to push? To pretend I could help when I could barely help myself? Just as I began to pull back my hand, Callum spoke. 'I … remember it. Feel it.'

I stared at the top of his golden head. Even with his head bowed, there was a quiet strength to him. A king, shouldering his pain along with everyone else's. 'Remember what?'

His shoulders shuddered with his next breath. 'Every break of my bone. Every cut of my flesh. And every time I healed the same injuries away from someone else. When I try to use my Gift – when my father isn't here to force me into it – that pain all rears up, and I just … *can't*.' He lifted his head, the desperation in his eyes painful to look at. 'All my Gift has ever been used for is to bring more pain. And the one time I could've used it for some good – when I could've kept you from grief by saving all those lives in the throne room – I failed. I couldn't save a single one. Not the guards. Not the servants. Not your sister.' His lips pressed into a thin line. 'And, worst of all, I can never use it to help you.'

I closed my eyes just long enough for the sting of tears to fade. Inhaling deeply, I opened them and knelt before Callum, the rug soft beneath me. Pressing my hand to his cheek, I waited until his eyes found mine. And then, in the fiercest voice I could muster, I uttered the words it had taken seeing Cassie's soul for me to believe. 'It's not your fault.'

Surprise flared in Callum's eyes, and it hurt to see – to think that he would be shocked to hear such a thing. 'But I chose—'

'You chose to save me,' I said, fending off the trembling that threatened to take hold. He needed to hear this. I needed to say it. 'It's not your fault she died.'

'If I'd chosen differently, there might've been a way. Something I could've done to save you both.'

'Maybe, or maybe we all would've died.' I shrugged. 'There's no telling what might've happened if you'd made a different choice. But you didn't. You did the best you could in the moment, and it was cruel of me to hate you for your choice. To even ask you to make that promise in the first place.' That had perhaps been the greatest cruelty of them all – asking for a vow I should've known Callum would've been unable to keep.

'I happen to like your cruelty,' Callum said, a hint of a smile curving his lips. His hand lifted, curling a lock of my hair around his finger. 'I find it endearing.'

I scoffed. 'You found it endearing for me to threaten to kill you?'

'Absolutely.' He leant in, amusement flickering to life in his eyes. 'Especially when we both knew you wouldn't do it.'

My brows rose. 'You don't think I was capable?'

'Oh, I know you're perfectly capable, Captain.' He crooked the finger wrapped in my hair, drawing me closer. The hand in mine slipped free, only to rise and hold the one on his cheek in place. 'But I would've been dead before you left the throne room that day if you'd truly meant it.'

I considered his words as the warmth of skin against mine

flooded through me. There was truth to them. Days ago, that would've terrified me. Now, I only smiled.

Callum's smile ticked up for a moment before it faded. He pressed my hand harder to his cheek. 'I don't know if I can use my Gift. The pain that finds me when I try to use it, or if it's activated unconsciously…' He trailed off, a shudder running through his body. 'And even when I prepare myself to endure that pain, it refuses to answer me.'

I studied him. 'You're not sure you'll be able to take on Vitus's power,' I said. 'That's why you wouldn't give Evania the answer she wanted.'

'I want to. What I saw in that vision…' He shook his head, horror filling his eyes. 'But I've been trying to draw on my Gift. Trying to see if it even works anymore.' He gently pulled my hand away from his cheek and held out his hand.

Before I realised what he was doing, he'd pulled a knife off the table at his bedside and dragged the edge across his palm. I pressed my lips together, fighting the urge to berate him as thick blood welled. Together, we watched it gather, the darkness spilling over his skin.

Closing his eyes, Callum inhaled, his body stilling. A muscle twitched in his jaw. His lips pressed together and pain began to pale his features. But there was no flicker of shadows. No sense of his Gift tugging at my own as it tended to do. The cut remained as it was – bleeding with stubborn tenacity until it began to drip over the sides of his palm. At last, he let out a shuddering breath. His eyes flew open, echoes of agony still apparent. An agony, I sensed, that didn't belong to the present.

I stared at the cut. 'Did you need to make it so deep?'

There was a pause. 'I feel you've missed the point.'

I swallowed. No, I hadn't missed the point. Callum was vulnerable in a way he hadn't been before. Even if he believed his

Gift would kick in when he was at the brink of death, it hadn't seemed to do that with our visit to the godly realm.

I could lose him. This revolving truth made my breathing shallow.

'What is it?' Callum asked, voice gravelly with the remnants of pain as a shudder tore through me.

'You...' I trailed off, my attention consumed by the blood. So thick and dark it seemed to almost be made of the same shadows as his Gift. 'You could die.'

A hint of amusement returned to his voice. 'Yes, Chiara. As we've already discussed, I could die. So could anyone else in this realm.'

'I don't like it.' I hadn't realised I'd spoken until Callum huffed a short laugh. I glared. 'What?'

'This is what it means, Chiara. To be mortal.' He paused, then added, 'To care for a mortal.'

I let out a breath. 'Mortals are far too breakable.' Blood stained my fingers as I closed my hand over his injured one.

His fingers folded over mine. 'I'm not as fragile as that, Captain.'

It wasn't just his fragility I was worried about. It was mine. I was something that had been reforged too many times, and it wouldn't take much more to shatter me. And I suspected my shattering if Callum died wouldn't be gentle on the realm.

'What is it you want to do? About Vitus,' I asked.

'I need to take on his power,' Callum said.

'Is that what you truly want?' He began to answer, but I held up a hand. 'You. Not the gods.'

He laughed, but it was a hollow sound once more. 'Want? No. I want to be rid of this damned Gift. I want to live a life free from pain. I want—' He broke off, his eyes trailing over my features, his gaze growing intense. The look faded as he sighed. 'But that was never my fate. The only path forward is for me to figure out how to handle Vitus's power, or die trying.'

Die trying. The words thundered through me, sending my mind spiralling with all the possible ways that could happen. There were too many. Too many ways a mortal body could be shattered. No matter what he believed, there were too many ways I could lose him. Lose Jaxon, Deana, too, who had somehow slipped through my defences and cemented themselves as my friends.

'And you?' Callum asked, tugging lightly on my hair to draw my attention back to him.

I smiled, bitterness lacing my voice as I said, 'I suppose I need to figure out how to kill Vitus. And Liam.'

It was the vengeance I'd been seeking all these months, yet the words I spoke felt more like a burden. I wanted Vitus and Liam dead. Needed it, even. But perhaps that wasn't all I wanted anymore. But Callum and I were trapped in a game of gods, and we had no choice but to move according to the rules of that game. Every path left open to us was flooded with danger and suffering. Suddenly, I was tired of it all. Exhausted of being forced down such a path. Of seeking blood over comfort, pain over peace.

'What else?' Callum asked. My brow furrowed and he clarified. 'Aside from your vengeance. What else do you want?'

There were so many desires I could speak. Ones that I had pushed aside again and again until I could barely recall what they were. Some simple, like wanting to spend a day buying the food in the market and gorging myself on it. Some impossible, like wanting to know what it was to live without the fury that consumed me.

It was none of those words that came out when I finally broke the growing silence. Only one pressed to the front of my mind as Callum stared down at me, his fingers still curled around my own. Only one that mattered in this moment. 'I want you.'

That was all the invitation he needed. Callum lifted my hand to his mouth, pressing my palm to the gentle curve of his lips. His eyes remained on mine, the green seeming to deepen with desire. The touch was nowhere near enough to satiate me. I rose from where I knelt, pressing my hands to his shoulders. Callum leant back in his chair as I leant towards him, fingers curling around his cheek. His hand slid to the back of my head, tangling in my curls.

There were pressing matters to attend to. The Ankuran, the Archinian king, Vitus and Liam. But Callum consumed all of my focus. I needed him. Needed his touch. And when our lips met, I feared I might break apart from the consuming desire that raged through me. My hands fisted in his shirt. Wrapping his arm around my waist, Callum tugged me down so I was sitting on him. Our bodies pressed together as our kiss deepened.

Safe, my Gift sung, settling calmly into my bones in a way it never had before. *We're safe.*

I didn't feel safe. I was a fuse ready to blow, and Callum was the fire needed to start it. The press of his fingers into my side, his lips against mine – everything about him was dangerous. A sweet corruption to every bit of common sense. And gods, did I want to be corrupted. Desire built just as Callum pulled away. I made a sound of protest, the corner of Callum's mouth kicking up in response.

'Impatient,' he chided, his eyes raking over my features in a way that seemed almost as desirous as the press of his lips was. His eyes brightened as he held firm against my attempts to pull his mouth back to my own. Shadows threaded through his voice as he said, 'You're a goddess.'

'Half,' I corrected automatically, skin prickling with heat. Callum's answering smile was enough to send that heat up a notch.

'Not to me,' he murmured. 'Nothing quite compares to you, divine or otherwise. Never has, never will.'

The hand around the nape of my neck tightened, pulling my lips to his once more. Every touch was steady and sure, a feeling of rightness I had never realised had been lacking with any other fleeting partner. The need of him only mounted further. Silver rushed over my skin, seeking him out and bathing him in its glow. As before, it didn't seek to hurt him. It only wanted *him*. Wanted him in the same way I did. All of him, every inch of power and grace and sheer force of will that was Callum.

And I would have him.

I pulled him as close as humanly possible. My fingers reached down, tugging at his shirt with an almost animalistic desperation.

'Off,' I mumbled against his lips. 'Take it off.'

'Of course, my lady.' My eyes narrowed at the amusement in his voice, but he acquiesced. The shirt was gone, and I was staring at bare skin and muscle.

My eyes trailed over every ridge, every part of him, over the smoothness of his skin, where mine was covered with lines and scars. A trickle of sorrow interrupted the fire burning through me. What story would his skin have told had he not been forced to wipe it away? The story of a survivor, I thought. A fighter. A king deserving of his crown.

Callum caught my fingers in his. 'Don't,' he whispered. 'Don't worry about me.'

My eyes traced over his hand, his arm, up to where the only marks sat on his neck. 'I'm not worried.' A lie. Gods, my heart twisted at the thought of the pain he felt whenever he tried to use his Gift. I'd become too soft when it came to him. And yet, I couldn't bring myself to shut those emotions down.

I began to look away, and he caught my chin, not allowing me to escape. 'Ignore what I just said. Emotions don't make you weak.' Callum lifted my fingers, kissed them lightly.

'Just like all the times you've been openly concerned about

others?' I asked archly, pulling away just enough to stare him down.

'All I have time for is concern for you.' He smirked then, and my breath was robbed from my lungs. Gods, he was beautiful. 'I can tell you it's been a full-time job. I barely have time for kingly duties.'

'Could've fooled me,' I murmured, eyes roaming over him. 'Seems you've been doing a far finer job than your father at ruling.'

'I want to.' His voice was stripped bare. 'But I'm not sure I'm enough for this kingdom.'

I paused in my perusal of him, meeting his gaze. The shadows were back in his eyes. 'You are, Callum.' My hand lifted, pressing to his cheek. 'If anything, the kingdom's not enough for you.'

Callum's eyes drifted down from my face to where I was still clad very much in clothes. 'This doesn't seem fair.' His fingers followed his gaze, touching, trailing, sending shivers across my body even as each touch burnt like fire. 'Here I am, defenceless against your wiles, and you get to keep your shirt?'

I raised an eyebrow at him. 'If you want my shirt, you're going to need to take it from me.' His eyes lit up at the challenge. He began to pull the hem up. I didn't shy away from his eyes as they traced my scarred skin, and he did not flinch at the sight. If anything, his gaze seemed hungrier, devouring me in their intensity.

'Goddess,' Callum breathed again.

'Watch out for the knife,' I warned as his finger trailed up my stomach, lifting the shirt higher.

Callum's hands froze, eyes shooting to me with eyebrows upraised. 'Really?'

I shot him a look. 'Of course. I never joke about knives.'

The low chuckle Callum gave was one of the loveliest sounds I had ever heard. It was filled with a light I didn't know he still possessed. I wanted to capture it in my hand, imprint it as a memory to drown out all the bad ones.

His fingers slid over my skin, the shirt not yet coming off. 'I didn't know this was something I could have.'

'What?' I asked, trying not to let my frustration at his languidness enter my voice.

He lifted his eyes to mine. 'Happiness.'

My breath was snatched from me, warmth flooding my body. *Yes*, it seemed to cry in jubilant agreement. *Yes, that's what this is.*

It almost seemed a cruelty to experience it, even for these moments, when I knew how quickly such things could be shattered.

Yet I didn't dare move away as my hand lifted, fingers curling into his hair at the back of his head. I leant down, my kiss slow. Teasing.

'For a king,' I whispered, our noses near brushing, 'You're rather sappy.'

His chest vibrated with a deep laugh underneath me. 'Apologies, Captain, but I'm afraid I won't be stopping anytime soon.' His fingers curled at my waist, shifting me closer to him. 'Even if no words will ever do you justice, I'm still going to try.'

'Unlike you, I'm not much a one for words.' My lips found the corner of his. He tried to twist into the kiss, but I tightened my grip on his hair, not allowing him to. A deep sound emanated from his chest. 'I'll have to find other ways to show you how you make me feel.'

'Such as?' Callum said, his lips ticking up.

'Such as—'

A sharp knock came at the door.

Callum made a sound of annoyance. Without letting his fingers slip or his eyes slide away from me, he ground out, 'I'm busy.'

The pounding came again, and then Deana's voice called out

in a panicked voice, 'Come on, Callum. We need to fetch Chiara.' It was Deana.

Callum groaned, his head falling back. 'Can't it wait?'

'No—' Deana's words died beneath the sound of the doors being thrown open, replaced with a vitriolic curse.

Jaxon strode into the room like he owned it. His usual ease had vanished. His straight back and furrowed brow were enough to send me clambering off Callum's lap. 'You chose quite a time to finally quit being stubborn fools,' he said. 'But you'll need to pause whatever it is you're doing.'

Deana, surprisingly, did not disagree as she swept in behind him, resplendent in a violet gown that glittered with threads of silver. Matching gems studded her hair, sweeping it off her face.

'I thought you had enough sense not to come back for a while,' Callum said sharply, glaring at Jaxon.

Any smile dropped from Jaxon's face. 'I would've loved to stay away, but I ran into a slight problem on my way out.' He glanced over his shoulder. 'You have some uninvited visitors.'

'Nobles come to meet me?' Callum asked. He'd slipped on his shirt impossibly quickly, his sword held in the hand that had only recently been pressed against my skin.

'Of a sort.' Deana's voice was steady, but her knuckles whitened as a knife flickered into existence in her hand before vanishing in a swirl of red mist. 'We have visitors from Archin.'

The mention of Archin was enough for us all to fall in behind her as she headed back out of the room. 'Did you get what you needed?' she asked over her shoulder, a strand of hair falling across a pale cheek.

It took me a moment to realise she was asking about the godly realm, not about what had just passed between Callum and I. I flexed my fingers. The power roiled beneath the surface. Focusing, I let a few strands slip free of my hold. Soft silver light spilled from my palm. 'I think so.' I fisted my hand, quenching the light with ease.

'Good.' She fell into silence as we twisted through the corridors.

We came to a stop outside a set of tall, foreboding doors. My eyes flicked to their shape, to the way they loomed over us with more than just height. Deana barely paused, swinging open the doors and striding in. Jaxon followed after, ignoring her mutters that whatever lay inside didn't involve him. But Callum and I both stopped, tipping our heads back to stare at the throne room doors.

Ice began to crawl over my skin. It had been a few months since I'd walked through them, Callum by my side and the chains of the gods in my hands. I swallowed, fighting the urge to flee. 'I haven't been here since…' I trailed off, throat closing up.

Fingers slipped into mine, holding tight, as though Callum knew I needed something to tether me to the here and now. 'I haven't, either.' His chest rose in a deep inhale, chin lifting. 'But we're ready for this.'

I stared at the golden light spilling from the throne room. Would the stains still be there, forever marring the marbled floor? Or had the lives lost been wiped away, as though nothing had ever happened? I inhaled deeply. Fear still coiled around me at what I'd see and remember in there, but… I'd seen Cassie. Heard the peace in her voice, the light of her soul. Helped her move on to what awaited her beyond the Gates. And I would not let what Vitus, Kane and Liam had done break me. Nor would I allow it to break Callum.

'Ready?' I asked, glancing over at Callum.

Callum gave a sharp nod. We strode into the throne room together.

It was almost exactly as I remembered the very first time I'd entered it as a child. Gold flecks on the floor glinted in the too-bright light. Where they had once seemed an offensive show of wealth, the way the gold seemed to seep into the white, overrunning the floor with its garishness, now seemed a taunt from Vitus himself. Crystals glittered overhead, hundreds of tiny stones interweaving together before dripping down. Small candles and Illusionist lights were embedded in the spaces in between. Ahead, the two thrones loomed over us garishly like twin monoliths of evil. The slighter, silver throne was no longer as pristine as it had once been. Dust coated the arms and cushions, matching the thin coating on the larger throne next to it.

My steps faltered for a heartbeat at the emptiness of the throne. Some of the tension in my shoulders released. I'd known the throne would be empty – that the tyrant who'd once ruled from his golden seat was far away – but it hadn't stopped my mind conjuring images of cruel eyes and twisted sneers. Callum stilled, taking a fraction longer than I to recover himself before he guided me to a curtained alcove to the left. Deana and Jaxon already stood there, their backs to us. Jaxon's hand rested upon his blade. Red flickered in Deana's hand, forming various weapons before dispersing. They seemed to be guarding someone I couldn't see.

My recently settled heart began pounding once more. Whoever was in there was unlikely to be a welcome surprise. I withdrew a dagger, comforted by its familiar weight in my hand. The scarlet of the bound curtains was stark against the white walls. For a second, the gauzy material became splatters on the walls, on the floor, on everything. A blink, and it was gone. I sucked in a breath, grasping hold of the present while allowing the memories to wash over me. I wouldn't forget the past, nor the wrongdoings committed. But I wouldn't drown in it, either.

Callum leant towards me, his whisper loud in the silence. 'If you decide to wreak your vengeance on whoever our guests are, please warn me first so I can get out of your way.'

I shot him a sidelong glare. 'I'm not going to go on an

indiscriminate killing spree just because I find this room unpleasant.'

'I know you won't,' he said, his smile more genuine. 'You're very discriminate with your killing.'

'I'm not going to kill anyone!' I protested as Deana twisted, her brows raising.

Jaxon flashed a grin over his shoulder. 'I wouldn't say that yet, Chiara. You haven't seen who our guest is yet.'

Deana and Jaxon peeled apart, allowing Callum and I to stop between them. I froze at the sight of our 'guests'.

On the ground was a girl a few years younger than me. Her delicate features were smeared with blood and dirt, skin unnaturally pale. Once, she might've been described as pretty. Now, with her matted hair and torn gown, she was a mess. Her brown eyes locked onto Callum, then slid slowly to me. I froze at the tiny flecks of gold within the brown irises.

Ankuran, Jaxon had called Vitus's creatures.

Bleeding lips twisted into a mockery of a smile. 'Little raven,' she cooed in a voice made of gravel and ice. 'You've come to see me.'

Callum threw an arm out as she lunged at me, drawing his sword. Before she could collide with him, ropes binding her to the chair behind snapped taut. She fell back, teeth bared with frustration.

It wasn't the girl, though, that sent me staggering back a step, grip tightening on my dagger and rage calling silver to my skin. It was the man bound next to her. A man with familiar brown hair and bright blue eyes, his features deceivingly boyish. A man whose name I hissed with enough hatred to scald my insides. 'Liam.'

Chapter Twenty-Five

'Not Liam.' He rose to his feet, the ropes binding him far looser than those of the girl's. I lifted my dagger, pointing it at him.

'Don't take another step.'

He stopped, glancing at the dagger warily. 'Not Liam,' he repeated, his voice holding the gentle melody of an Archinian accent. There was a familiarity to his voice that echoed the one that had mocked me moments before Cassie died, but there were also clear differences. A depth that Liam did not possess. A polish around the edges of vowels that hinted at a tongue practised at sweet-talking others. He lifted a smooth-skinned hand, offering it towards me. 'Brayden. Liam's brother.'

I eyed that hand, but made no move to take it. Brayden dropped it.

'Brayden,' I repeated. 'The Archinian crown prince, who has just walked straight into the enemy's castle with a girl trussed up like a cow for the slaughter.'

Brayden's eyes darkened at my words, his fingers curling

tighter around the rope he held. 'Not prince. Not anymore.' He glanced at Callum, back straightening and chin lifting. 'King.'

The only sign of concern on Callum's face was the slightest crease between his brows. 'I heard the king was Liam,' he said, his attention shifting to the girl. The crease deepened. 'And this is your ... pet?'

Brayden's cheeks reddened, his hands balling at his side. Before he could say anything, the girl's lips peeled back from perfectly straight teeth. She laughed. The golden flecks in her eyes grew, becoming tiny shards.

'Tali,' Brayden hissed, glaring down at her before raising his eyes to Callum. 'Apologies. She was injured in her escape and hasn't been quite right since. I think she might've hurt her—'

'Quiet,' Callum snapped before turning his attention back to the Ankuran princess. 'Speak. Why are you here?'

The girl focused on Callum. 'I am no one's pet, King of Nothing,' she hissed. Her voice was made of two – one, ancient and powerful; the other, far weaker but still with a hint of arrogance. A god and the king he'd taken over. 'I am a soldier in a war soon to come. A weapon to make all mortals pay for their treatment of the divine.' Brayden opened his mouth as though he would reprimand her again. At Deana's warning look, he snapped his mouth shut.

'What's your plan?' Callum pressed, crouching down in front of the girl. She merely smiled.

'Luc and Kailey found them wandering the palace courtyard,' Deana explained as the silence stretched thin. 'According to him'—she tilted her head towards Brayden—'they appeared in the palace corridors, and seemed to think it was a *wonderful* idea to go for a stroll.'

Brayden flushed with indignation. 'That's not— Tali looked unwell. I thought some fresh air would be a good idea before we met with the king.'

From the shifting of his eyes, that was only part of the truth.

Callum cut a look towards Deana. 'And where were our palace guard during all this? The ones stationed at the doors and in the corridors.'

'They claimed they were royal guests. Apparently, one of the guards recognised Brayden, and didn't have the sense to realise that an Archinian prince might not be welcome in our palace.'

'Where's this guard now?'

Deana's lips tightened with displeasure. 'No one seems to know.'

There was a moment of silence, then Callum pushed himself to his feet, swinging to face Brayden. He didn't say anything. He simply stared expectantly.

It seemed even Archinian princes couldn't withstand Callum's quiet authority. Brayden ran a hand through his hair, pushing it back from his face, when the resemblance between him and Liam diminished. 'Archin has fallen.' His face paled. 'A few small towns were destroyed first, but Ballaronia quickly followed. I know of no survivors.' His eyes shut as the girl at his feet chuckled softly. 'The bodies – there were whole families. Children. Towns reduced to rubble.' He swallowed. 'And it was all my brother's doing. I was north when he came home a month ago. I don't know the specifics, but I know there was a feast. One that ended with my family's blood and the city gates being opened.'

The words settled heavy in the air. Archin had long been an enemy. All I'd wanted a year ago was for the Archin to fall so that my sister and I could each have our freedom. Now, I wished desperately for that war.

A war between mortals would be kinder than a war of gods.

Tali clapped her hands in delight, straining against the ropes as she leant forward. Gold crept through the skin at the corner of her eyes. 'Mortal throats slit so very easily. Even those of kings and queens.' Her eyes flicked to Callum, and I tensed, hand dropping to my knife. Callum brushed his fingers over mine. 'You're all so very ... breakable.'

A shudder ran through me, the words an eerie echo to what Callum and I had spoken of not long before.

'Tali,' Brayden hissed, glaring down at her. She didn't take her eyes off Callum. Not until I shifted closer to him. Then, she grinned, a monstrous curve of her lips that cracked her skin with gold.

Brayden glared accusingly Callum's way. 'I was told it was your father who came once Liam opened the city gates, with an army of my own people.'

Callum regarded him coldly. Deana stood at his right shoulder. A king and the captain of his guard, immovable against the accusation. Tension built as the two kings surveyed each other, waiting for the other to crumble. Before that could happen, a small, throwing blade whizzed past me, skimming past Brayden's cheek.

Brayden startled, hand flying up to a line of red as he swung towards the origination of the blade. Jaxon raised his brows. 'Are you done with the useless chest-puffing?'

'Is this how you let your subjects treat nobles?' Brayden asked, indignation spreading across his features. His arms folded over his broad chest, his lips twisted into a distasteful frown. Tali cocked her head, eyeing Jaxon curiously.

'Oh, I'm not his subject.'

Deana shot Jaxon a glare. 'You are, and you will treat the king with respect.'

Jaxon smirked as he stared at Deana from across the alcove. 'Darling, I'm no one's subject but my own.'

Deana's mouth tightened, her eyes darkening with annoyance. She took a step forward.

'Enough. This is not the time for your arguments,' Callum said, voice low. Deana settled, though her features were still pale with rage. Surprisingly, Jaxon did, too. Callum turned his impenetrable stare at Brayden. 'Continue.'

Brayden cleared his throat, any haughtiness dripping away from his features as he continued his tale. 'I snuck into the palace with some help upon my return, and spied on Liam there, bragging to a prisoner.'

I frowned, exchanging a look with Callum. Something was off about his story. A single man – a prince who, by all accounts, was more accustomed to gambling and women than he was to any sort of stealth – had managed to get into the palace unnoticed.

'My parents were dead, had been for some time, and were displayed like trophies. My…' His voice became choked and we waited as he regained composure. 'One of my sisters, Armania, had been sliced into so many pieces that I could barely recognise her. And Taliana…' His attention drifted to the girl at his feet.

Ice filled my veins. With the gold not yet fully entrenched in her, it was easy to see the girl she had once been. To see the same straight, thin nose, high cheekbones and brown hair. His sister.

'I thought she was dead.' Brayden's voice was barely a breath. 'She'd been beaten and strangled. There were three gathered around her body. Liam, King Kane and another man – the one Liam had been bragging to. He wasn't there willingly.'

'Was he bound in chains?' I interjected. 'Ones that might've felt … strange to be around?'

Brayden glanced at me, surprised. 'Yes.'

My chest tightened. It had to be Dearil.

'Kane touched my sister. His skin glowed golden, and when it did, she … she came back.' Awe mingled with the fear in his voice and he glanced at the Ankuran. A flicker of uncertainty crossed his face as he spied the gold veining that'd been creeping across her skin. It was chased away in moments. Nothing was quite as dangerous as the sort of hope love caused. The sort that blinded one from the truth. 'The king left with Liam, dragging the third with them. I grabbed Taliana and ran.'

Brayden's cheeks turned ashen. He twisted his hands together, looking away from all of us. The skin around his fingers was red, as though he had been wringing them for hours. 'Except, once we left the room, Tali wasn't the girl I knew. She was vicious.' He looked at us desperately. 'Tali wouldn't hurt a fly. Not normally. She must've hit her head when she was attacked or been forced to drink something that altered her mental state. She tried to attack me as we ran down the hallway. It slowed us enough that Kane and Liam caught up to us.'

His eyes turned to stone at the thought of his brother. It must be hard, to have been betrayed so utterly by his own family.

'Liam tried to kill me.' His hand pressed to his midsection. 'I thought I was about to die. I *would* have died, except...' His brows drew inwards. He faltered, lips pressing together before he spoke. 'I blinked, and we were here.'

Jaxon, Callum and I turned disbelieving stares on him. Brayden's hands rose, palms facing outwards. 'I swear it,' he said earnestly. 'I barely believe it as well. We appeared in the corridors, and then—'

Deana nodded, breaking away from the glare she was giving Jaxon. Jaxon slumped as her gaze moved away. He seemed almost disappointed.

'It tracks with the stories Luc and Kailey gave me,' she said. 'He wandered out of the palace, not into it.'

'Tell me what happened just before you vanished,' I demanded.

Some of Brayden's arrogance returned. He stared down his nose at me, eyes running over my crumpled clothes and scarred skin. His lip curled. 'Who are you to be asking such a thing?' he asked, cold disdain entering his voice, 'Servants don't speak to royalty that way. They don't even *look* at royalty that way.'

Maybe it was simply the haughtiness of the word. Maybe it was sneer coupled with the blue eyes and brown hair that reminded me too much of another prince who had tried to do unspeakable things to me with the same look in his eye. A prince who had stolen everything from me. Whatever it was, it was enough to wake my slumbering Gift once more. Power roiled beneath my skin, pushing and testing for a way out. I could feel it, the living power that sparked at my fingertips. It was ready and willing, as it always had been. This time, though, I was in control.

A single step. That was all I took. All I gave the inordinate rage that rushed through me, sending silver veins pulsing against my dark skin. It clashed with the golden freckling in the marble underneath my feet. Overpowered it.

Callum spoke before I had a chance to do anything. 'Do not forget,' he said in a deceptively mild voice, 'that you are in my palace. You are under my rule. Any power you think you have is a lie. And I will gut you and send your head back as a present for my father and your brother if you ever think to speak to Chiara that way again. Do I make myself clear?'

Brayden nodded stiffly.

My Gift receded, a strange satisfaction curling through me at Callum's intervention.

'Good. Then continue.'

Brayden's feet shifted, his knuckles white where his hands gripped his knees. 'I was mostly focused on the sword about to disembowel me, but I remember Kane looking furious. He'd dragged the chained man along with him, and he...' Brayden hesitated, before saying in an almost embarrassed tone, 'he waved at me.'

I frowned. Waving was not something I could picture Dearil doing. Offer disapproving looks and unwanted advice, absolutely. But *wave* at me? Captive or not, I couldn't see him lowering himself with what I was sure he'd consider an undignified gesture. Callum's brow creased as I exchanged a look with him.

Jaxon laughed. 'Those precious chains don't work quite as well as our golden friend had hoped. The only way these two got here was if the threads of the realm were pulled together to transport these two.' He was careful not to mention the gods, undoubtedly seeing the same thing I did in Brayden – a man on the verge of breaking. 'What does it matter if this…' he raked his eyes over the Archinian king, 'boy knows. If Vitus has his way, soon the entire mortal realm will be destroyed.'

Slowly, all four of us turned to look at Tali. She blinked back at us, her irises now fully corrupted with gold. I knew as we locked eyes – that it was not a princess who looked back at me. It was a god.

'Your plan,' Callum said slowly. 'I've already asked once. I won't ask again.'

'Oh, I have so many things planned, false king.' Her head tilted to one side, strands of hair brushing the ground. Brayden went rigid as gold swirled under her skin, a beautiful corrosion of her humanity. 'Your father misses you terribly,' her – *its* – gaze swung to me, 'as does yours, little raven.'

I pressed my lips together, not allowing a shred of emotion to cross my expression. Bad enough that I'd come to care for a king. To care for a god – even if that god was my father – was downright foolish.

The Ankuran girl leant as far forward as her constraints would allow. 'His screams are delicious, child. He screams for you, for your help.' A pink tongue darted out, swiping over cracked lips.

'A lie,' I said. Dearil was far more powerful than I could dream of being, and he saw me as nothing more than a tool. A god's pride would never allow him to ask for help from a halfling.

The gold eyes brightened. 'Oh, I won't kill him yet. I need him for something far more important.' The Ankuran straightened.

It was a jittery motion as though the body was tiring of being yanked around by her puppet master. 'Don't worry. You'll see him soon enough. Him and sweet Cassie.'

Every muscle in my body jolted and tightened. Only the press of Callum's hand on my back kept me from turning the Ankuran to ash. I dug my nails into my palm until there were sharp stings of pain. 'You do not get to speak her name,' I said, voice low.

The Ankuran laughed. 'Touch a nerve, did I?'

I ignored it – ignored the god behind the mask. Turning, my eyes met Callum's. I did not let my voice waver as I said, 'We need to hold her elsewhere.' Anywhere but this throne room, where every mention of Cassie's name had me trembling with rage. There might have been some release from seeing Cassie's soul, but hearing her name spoken with that cruel voice had me balancing on the precipice of an all-consuming fury.

'Hold her?' Brayden lunged to his feet. 'You can't mean—'

A sword manifested in Deana's hand, its surface glinting red. She held the tip to Brayden's throat. A drop of sweat trickled down his neck. 'Careful, Your Highness. You're in His Majesty's palace, not your own.'

'You may go with her,' Callum said, with barely a glance at Brayden. 'But she's a danger to my people. Until we've figured out what to do with her, she stays locked up.'

Anger simmered in Brayden's eyes, but he had enough sense to nod.

'Corin,' Callum called. Moments later, the throne-room door opened, a carrot-haired guard poking his head in. 'Fetch three more guards. Able-bodied ones, please. You're to take our two *guests* to one of the more secure rooms. Do not let them out of your sight.'

Corin nodded before disappearing. Minutes later, he returned with the requested guards. Together, they hauled the Ankuran to her feet. As they dragged her from the room, her eyes locked with mine, lips stretching into a wide grin.

'You squander my power, false king,' the Ankuran called. 'Give yourself up. I will spare your friends if you do. Perhaps I will even grant the little raven a quick death.'

Callum tensed beside me, but he did not move. A chill ran over me as the doors swung shut behind her. That final grin the Ankuran had shot us hadn't been one of pure amusement. It had seemed to be one of victory.

Chapter Twenty-Six

'What now?' Deana asked as we strode for the throne-room doors, Jaxon collecting the knife he'd thrown at Brayden.

'Give him a chance to simmer,' Callum said, pausing as a guard rushed to pull open the doors. We left the hollow vastness of the throne room, stepping out into the sterile corridor. The quiet sent a chill of unease through me. 'Brayden's a proud man. He was when we met as children, too. He's also hot-headed, though, and not the brightest. Once he's had a chance to think things through, we'll be able to gather more information about him.'

'You could just get rid of him,' Jaxon cheerfully suggested. 'Or —' He broke off, frowning as he glanced to the side. 'Strange place to have a nap.'

I followed his gaze. A small window, too small to see much but a square of ground, sat to the right. Fallen flowers littered the stones around a woman sprawled on the stone, facedown and hair splayed around her head. The window was on the eastern side of the palace, the paths there infrequently used due to the lack of sun that reached it.

Callum cursed softly as he spied the darkness beneath the man at the same time I did. The woman wasn't slacking on her duties. She was dead.

'That's Teresa,' Deana said grimly, striding over to the window and staring down. She glanced over her shoulder at us. 'The guard who spread the word that Brayden was a royal guest.'

Leaves moved and shadows shifted. I leant in, brows drawing together. 'Is that—'

A child appeared, hair in two long braids, the hem of her dress stained. She meandered through the blood, bare toes turning crimson as she halted. Slowly, her head turned until she was staring directly up at us.

I inhaled sharply. Golden veins spindled over skin, the child's eyes bright with divine power. The Ankuran's lips crept upwards into a smile, too wide for the child's small face. Flesh cracked, and more gold spread.

She raised a finger in our direction. 'The little raven,' she hissed, her voice easily penetrating the palace, 'Or the false king. Bring one to me.' Her head tilted, braid spilling over its shoulder. 'Or I shall come to fetch you myself.'

And then she was gone, scampering down the path.

I whirled around, my mouth dry. 'Which way does that path lead?'

Deana paled. She might not know what Ankurans were, but she was sensible enough to guess from our reactions that they were nothing good. 'The front courtyard.' She hesitated, then added, 'And the entrance to the palace.'

'How many guards on duty?' Callum asked, twisting and heading down the corridor.

Deana fell into step beside him while I took up the rear with Jaxon. 'Thirty,' she said brusquely, the knives she'd manifested shining red. 'Or, there *were* thirty. Who knows now.'

Callum nodded, his shoulders tense. 'Who's the most experienced amongst them?'

'Commander Lena would be ideal, but she's training new recruits out at the barracks today.' The quiet of the corridors echoed our footsteps back at us as we turned a sharp corner. 'The guards are all green. We've been stationing the more experienced guards in the city and some of the towns nearest to Archin, as you ordered.'

'It seemed like a good idea at the time,' Callum muttered, his knuckles whitening on his sword. He paused at a set of double doors, turning to face Deana. 'If not the most experienced, then who has the calmest head?'

Deana's brow scrunched. 'Possibly Brent? He's the oldest of the lot, but he has a limp that slows him down. Arley's not bad, though he tends to rush into decisions. Or Kailey—'

'—Kailey,' I interjected.

Callum twisted to appraise me. 'Why do you say that?'

'She's the only one brave enough to speak with me every time I pass her, but still possesses the sense to be on guard.'

'Kailey, it is.' He returned his attention to Deana. 'How many guards are stationed in the courtyard?'

'Five.'

'Send someone for Kailey with the orders to take ten more to guard the gates. They're to keep the Ankurans from leaving the palace grounds.'

'You mean to trap them in here with us?' Jaxon tapped a finger against his sword hilt. 'Don't know if you noticed, but that Ankuran seemed rather desperate for royal blood.'

'Better in with us than out with the defenceless people of the city,' Callum answered. 'Have Luc gather anyone else in the palace and take them to the food cellars. Ten of the remaining guards should go to guard them.'

Deana nodded before disappearing through the door.

'Will you go out to them?' Jaxon asked, his normal laggardness replaced with alertness.

'Perhaps, but we need to see what's going on. Walking out blind might worsen the situation.' Callum smiled grimly. 'Facing ten Ankuran is very different to facing down a hundred.' He glanced at us. 'We should find a window with a clear view of the courtyard.'

I nodded in grim agreement. My heart hammered as I yanked one of my knives free. Fighting and killing were two things I excelled at. When I killed, there was no room for uncertainty – no room for confusion. Only me, my opponent, and the dance of death. And Vitus had just offered me the perfect playthings. This time, though, it wasn't just anticipation that forced my pulse to quicken. There was fear there, concern over the number of lives that might be lost today should we fail. Dread came next as my Gift warmed my body.

Death had found someone nearby.

Callum led the way, Deana finding us as we turned down a shadowed corridor. 'Kailey's headed out,' she explained brusquely as we moved. 'Corin's gone to fetch the others and relay your orders.'

Callum nodded, throwing open a door to the left and shoving aside baskets of dirty laundry. Jaxon slipped past him, beating him to the opposite side of the room. Yanking open a set of crimson curtains, he leant forward, his reflection showing in the panes of glass as he stared out into the night beyond. It caught the shift in his expression in perfect clarity – the widening of his eyes accompanied by a sharp inhale. Jaxon spun, lurching to the side and pressing a palm to the wall as his other hand fisted at his mouth.

Callum approached the window next, and I forced myself to

move into the space next to him. To ignore my instincts screaming at me not to look, to turn and run from whatever horrors awaited.

I'd never been one to cower before blood.

Illusioned lights cast a white glow across most of the area below. Body parts littered the courtyard. Even from our height, I could make out a chunk of a torso, flesh raw and bloody. A head, lips twisted into a scream, eyes plucked out from the skull. A scrap of a guard's uniform, black and embroidered with gold, barely staying on a dismembered arm. Entrails strewn out like a toddler's artwork, bloody and gory. A foot tossed into a bush with what looked like several toes missing.

At the large gates, ten guards fought off at least three times the number of Ankurans. I recognised the one at the forefront of the group – Kailey, her hair pulled from blood-splattered features as she swung her sword through the neck of an Ankuran. The creature toppled. His place was immediately taken by another, who lunged at Kailey with a child's hands and an innocent smile. The sword swung again. This time, it slammed into the Ankuran's arm. The creature that had once been a child reached out with gold-veined hands, fingers wrapping around the sword. Kailey's features paled. She twisted the sword, severing tiny fingers.

Behind her, another guard stumbled away as a second child came for him. Kailey drove her sword through the Ankuran's chest as she twisted. Even through the glass her voice rang clear. 'Do not falter! Protect the gate and the city! These are no longer people.'

The young man who had staggered glanced between Kailey and the Ankuran child. His hold on his sword trembled.

'Come on, Damien,' Deana muttered, pressing her fist to the glass as though she were considering launching herself through it to get to the fray. 'Now's not the time to hesitate.'

There were three types of people who stepped onto a

battlefield. Those that fought like Kailey, her head held high as her sword cut through Ankurans. Those that fled. And those that froze. People usually discovered which they were far too late.

Damien was the latter. He shook his head, retreating another step only to find his back to the closed gate. Deana's head fell forward, her eyes squeezing shut. I didn't let myself look away as the Ankuran made its move, surging forward, fingers curled. With strength no child should possess, she grasped hold of Damien's throat. His mouth gaped open in a scream that never reached us. Kailey whirled, as did a few other guards, but there were too many Ankurans, any path to the man blocked. With a vicious wrench, she ripped Damien's throat free, and blood sprayed through the air.

One of the guards – a younger woman with a nasty wound to her shoulder – screamed. She twisted towards Damien, a desperate hand reaching for him. Before she could get to him, though, Ankurans fell upon the dying man. His body disappeared beneath grappling hands and exposed teeth.

Nausea swelled. Deana inhaled sharply, staggering back a step.

'Leave him!' Kailey shouted. She grabbed a handful of gold-stained hair and shoved her sword through the neck of an Ankuran man. 'He's dead. Focus on the enemy!'

Something cracked nearby, loud enough to echo through the room. None of us reacted, all too focused on the gruesome display below.

The child Ankuran who'd killed Damien turned around. It was the same one that'd spoken to us before. Wearing the same smile as it had then, it shoved the gory mess of flesh between its lips, red smearing across gold-veined skin.

'Gods,' Deana whispered. 'He was only sixteen.'

As though hearing her words, the Ankuran tipped her head back. Golden eyes stared at the window we were behind. Her bloodied lips twisted into a gruesome grin as she pushed the rest of the flesh into its mouth.

'They're eating him,' Callum said, voice hoarse.

It was Jaxon who explained. 'Ankurans are dead creatures brought to a half-life. They crave life, want it more than anything.' He straightened, his expression haunted as he stared out the window. 'Eating the flesh of the living is the closest they can come to experiencing life.'

'Gods,' I murmured, nausea roiling through me as the Ankurans rose from where Damien had been. All that was left were bones and bloodied smears of leftover flesh. There was no time for plans and strategy. No time for worrying about numbers. 'We need to get down there.'

'That's not our only problem.' Tension thrummed in Jaxon's voice. He stepped up beside me, pointing down. 'That's where the cracking noise came from earlier.'

I followed his point, keeping my eyes as far away from the ruin of flesh as possible. Two oak doors had fallen onto the marble steps, splintered and caved in. Streaks of gold coated the surface, as though the Ankurans had thrown themselves at the doors, their bones cracking and flesh breaking, until the doors had given way.

Callum whirled to Deana. 'The servants?'

'If Brent acted quickly, they should be barred in the food cellars by now,' Deana replied. 'It's deep enough in that it's the safest part of the palace.'

Safe, until monsters came knocking and there was nowhere to run.

A scuff of feet on tiles sounded nearby. Not close enough to be an immediate worry, but loud enough that it soon would be. Callum twisted to stare down the corridor before saying, 'Brayden. We need to find him. He knows Archin palace's layout. If Vitus is holed up there, we'll need that information.' Callum headed down the corridor, Deana following behind.

'Do we have to?' Jaxon asked. I shot him a look. 'Don't tell me you weren't thinking it. He's an ass.'

Despite everything, my lips twisted into a ghost of a smile. I had been thinking it.

'Come on.' Callum and Deana were already halfway down the corridor. The shouts and rings of steel sounded from outside, masking the sound of our footsteps. A human scream echoed. Jaxon and Callum stiffened while Deana flinched. I only raised my knives higher. Screams were as familiar to me as birdsong. I couldn't let them distract me now.

We almost reached the bend in the corridor when a familiar carrot-haired guard careened around the corner. His face was bone-white, fingers trembling where they clutched his sword. Deana stepped forward, catching him by the shoulders before he could crash into Callum.

'Corin—' she said sharply, the guard's eyes swinging around wildly. His breath rose and fell in ragged gasps. 'Did you do as I asked?'

'I-I killed one,' he gasped out, his sword shaking. Golden blood slashed across the metal's surface. 'It was – gods, I killed a child. Th-they were trying to attack a servant who'd hidden, and th-there was no one else there and I—'

'You did the right thing, Corin.' Deana moved aside to allow Callum space. He clasped Corin's shoulder, steadying him. Corin blinked as he stared at the king. 'For the servant and the child.'

'I—'

'The right thing,' Callum said again, firmer this time. Corin swallowed, then nodded. 'Where did you run into them?'

'Near the palace entrance, Your Majesty.'

'They're still a distance from the food cellars,' Deana said. 'Even so, Brayden was placed in the guest quarters. If we go looking for him, then there's every chance the Ankurans will reach the servants before we find them.'

'Then Brayden will have to fend for himself,' Callum said. 'Let's—'

A laugh, filled with mocking glee, cut Callum off. I turned, my skin prickling.

Ankurans stood at the end of the hall, each wearing eerie smiles. Tali was at the front, blood dripping from wounds and hands coated in red. A small boy clutched a bloody foot in a hand, digging his teeth into the flesh as though it were a piece of chicken. A woman gripped a baby to her breast. The babe turned its head, fixing us unnervingly with too bright eyes. An older man, at least fifty, stood holding a pitchfork in one hand and a knife in the other. More bunched behind them, seeming to fill the entire space with their gold-veined bodies.

All of them staring at us with hungry eyes.

'Run,' Callum commanded.

We fled from the growing horde of Ankurans, hurtling around corner after corner. Callum led the way, every turn confident from the years he must have spent walking these very corridors. Deana, Jaxon and I followed easily enough. At every twist, one of us would reach out to haul Corin with us, the youth stumbling in his fright. Behind us, the hallways seemed to groan under the weight of all those feet scampering after us. It was no longer the sounds from outside that echoed around us. It was the laughs and shouts, the whispers and jeers, each echoing with the same cruel power.

'Little raven,' one crooned, the malice discordant with the youthful voice. 'Come here and we'll stop.'

'Or give us your false king,' another called. 'His life in our hands will have the same outcome.'

I didn't waste breath on any response as we took a set of stairs, two steps at a time. Wood groaned beneath us. I fixed my eyes on the closed door below. If we could get through, we could bar it. Give ourselves some precious seconds to plan. Callum hit the landing first. He slammed into the door, a heavy *thud* echoing back at us. The door did not open.

'Godsdammit!' Callum slammed his fist into the door. I spun to the yawning expanse of shadow at the top of the stairs as he asked, 'Where's the key?'

'Corin?' Deana asked, panting heavily. 'You were meant to keep hold of a set.'

Fear had Corin in its clutches, his entire body trembling. 'B-Brent has it,' he stammered, his feet shifting. 'We thought it'd be best if he took it to the food cellars. To lock the creatures out if needed.'

It would've been decent-enough thinking we were facing a siege from mortals. But these Ankurans were not mortals. They felt no pain, experienced no fear. They would batter bodies until they were left in pieces if it allowed them to get to their victims. Locking the doors would only give them – give us – seconds. Seconds that would be nothing but extra moments to drown in terror for those in the food cellars. Seconds that might've been the difference between survival and annihilation for us.

'We have to go back up. Now.' Jaxon began ascending the stairs.

But Deana grasped hold of his shirt, hauling him back. 'Too late. I can hear them around the corner.'

Insidious power began to trickle through the air. It wrapped around me, the hairs at the back of my neck rising. My Gift pounded against the temporary restraints I had placed it in. *Let me out*, it seemed to cry. *Soon*, I promised, adjusting my grip on my knives as Deana shoved Corin towards the door.

A hand appeared first. It curled around the doorframe, cracked nails digging into wood as the Ankuran hauled itself around to the top of the stairway. The mother and babe, a curve to the lips that seemed little more than an impersonation of a real smile, on both of their faces. Their eyes fell on Callum, then me. Gold veins bulged beneath papery skin as their mouths gaped open in unison. 'We would have had one. Get one, and the other will follow,' they intoned. 'Now, we will have both.'

They did not rush to descend. We had our backs to a door, and more Ankurans were flooding the space behind them. There would be no more fleeing.

We were trapped.

Chapter Twenty-Seven

'Callum?' Deana hissed, her eyes never leaving the Ankurans. 'Any luck?'

Another muffled curse was her answer. I risked a glance behind to find Callum spinning around, blade poised, ready to kill, fury in his eyes. 'No.'

Jaxon heaved a sigh. 'Must I do everything around here?' Sheathing his blade, Jaxon pulled out a set of lock picks. He unceremoniously forced his way past Corin and Callum, kneeling in front of the door and glancing back at me with a smirk. 'Glad you kept me around?'

Cocky bastard.

'Cut down any that slip past us,' Callum ordered Deana.

'I should be at—'

'That's an order.' Deana's brows drew inwards, but she didn't argue. Callum shifted his attention to me. 'We'll take the front.'

'What about me?' Corin, staring up at the slowly approaching Ankuran, asked. He couldn't have been any older than twenty. Older than me, perhaps, but young by a guard's standard.

'Keep guard with me,' Deana said, tugging him into place beside her. His sword trembled in his grasp.

Callum glanced at me, a challenge in his eyes. 'First to ten wins?'

'You're depraved,' I muttered back. Adrenaline was rising high, my body itching for battle. 'Besides, are you sure you want to lose against me again? Remember what happened last time.' He'd suggested a competition when we'd been surrounded by mercenaries. I'd won by a healthy margin.

Callum smiled. 'Last time it was people. This time it's not.'

'What do I get when I win?'

Callum's smile widened. His sword arced out, slamming into the throat of the approaching Ankuran. Gold spattered as the woman fell backwards, her throat slit so deeply it was a wonder her head stayed attached. The babe in her arms fell onto the stairs, a sickening *crack* sounding. Gold pooled beneath the child's head. Corin whimpered behind us.

'When I win,' Callum whispered, 'the only thing I demand is a kiss.'

'Fine.' I tried not to look at the babe that had once been mortal. 'When I win, I want ten gold pieces and the finest necklace in your possession.'

Callum shot me a sidelong glance. 'I believe the finest necklace in my possession is missing. Your friend back there, perhaps?'

My shrug was quick, fingers tightening on the hilt of my knives. 'Second best, then.'

Callum had no chance to respond. A twisted laugh cracked through the air, dragging my attention to the babe. Half-open eyes of gold stared up at us as its tiny limbs waved in the air. A mockery of the innocence of an infant.

The laugh acted as a command to the other Ankurans. They surged forwards in a wave of bared teeth and bloodied fingers. A woman leapt over the body of the mother, lips pulled back in a grin. Her fingers stretched for Callum's eyes, ready to claw them out, should she get the chance. Callum raised his sword, calm seeming to ripple from him as he collided with the Ankuran.

There was no chance to check if Callum had it under control. Another Ankuran launched himself towards me, his age-spotted skin freckled with blood. This one came armed. He swung a dagger at my throat in a wild arc. I stepped backwards, the air shifting in front of me as the blade flew past. Another Ankuran lurched past us as I twisted, Deana grunting as she engaged it behind me.

Acting on years of honed instinct, I lunged forward before my opponent could bring the blade back the other way, my knife sliding between his ribs. Hot blood spurted over my fingertips, the stench of decay suffocating. The Ankuran shuddered, but didn't stop. He fell atop me, nails digging into my shoulders as I struggled to retain my footing. I struggled to breathe through the smell as I yanked the knife free. Golden eyes set on mine, lips curving into a smile as blood dribbled from between its lips.

'Little raven,' it whispered, lifting its weapon again.

Heart pounding in my ears, I drove my second knife into his eye. A sickening wet sound accompanied the spray of liquid that spattered over me and dribbled down its cheek. Twisting, I shoved it away, using its plummet to rip both my blades free of it. It fell. The smile never left his face, even as his neck twisted at a sickening angle, dark lines ringing it. His true death.

Jaxon cursed as the body tumbled the last few stairs, knocking into his heels, but he didn't stop working at the lock. I whirled around as another Ankuran lurched towards me. My knife flew up, catching the shaft of a spear and deflecting it to one side.

'Have you changed your mind about killing me?' Callum said as he twisted away from the spear's path, dragging the Ankuran he'd been facing down a step to take his place. The spear plunged through her neck. She jerked, the golden veins fading from under her skin. With a twist of his body, Callum shoved the spear-bearer down the stairs. Corin cried out, swinging his sword in a surprisingly polished movement through the Ankuran's neck. Deana and Lena had trained him well.

'I figured you'd need the extra kills.' I slammed my boot into the Ankuran Callum had killed, sending her rolling down the stairs to join the other. 'We both know I'm going to win our little competition.'

'We'll see,' Callum responded as he thrust his sword forward, taking down the next Ankuran.

I tilted my head to survey the cluster of Ankurans before us. There were at least twenty crammed onto the stairs. More behind. I should have been afraid. Should've been ready to turn and run the second Jaxon had the door been open. Instead, I felt alive.

I lifted my knives in silent summons to the next Ankuran. The threads of gold desecrated nearly every centimetre of his exposed skin. He lunged forward, his movements far quicker than the previous Ankuran. A rusted dagger thrust for my left side. My knife dropped, batting the blow away as I spun. His other hand flew up. It caught on my shirt, yanking me forward. Cloth ripped as I pulled myself back, my breaths quickening with the adrenaline. He smiled. His hand flew up again, this time pressing to a patch of bare skin.

The single touch was all it took for pain to flare. Fiery agony ripped through me, my breath snatched from my lungs. Through the pain, I was vaguely aware of Ankurans making it past me; of Callum, Corin and Deana fighting. In front, the Ankuran's flaxen surface bulged, cracking through paper-thin skin in several spots and sending thin rivulets of blood streaming down his cheek. He cocked his head to the side. 'Foolish child. You cannot even withstand the touch of my power.'

Gods, I was quickly learning to hate the smooth voice that pealed out of these throats. I forced in a breath through my too-tight throat. I couldn't move my weapons, my muscles locked up from the pain. But I could think. And if I could think, then I could draw on my Gift.

Shoving aside the agony, I reached out for the roiling power in my veins. A beckoning to death. It responded eagerly. Silver roared to the surface of my skin, making the Ankuran's golden veins writhe as the silver surged into the knife I held. The agony in my body abated, as though Vitus's power was repelled by my own. My body sang with my Gift as I drove the blade upwards. A tiny nick of skin, a droplet of gold forming, and the power launched itself forward.

I had believed Ankurans incapable of pain. But as soon as the silver brushed over his skin, the Ankuran's head jerked back, veins at his throat straining as he screamed. His dagger clattered to the stairs. Silver flames wreathed his body, illuminating the space with their incandescence. The closest Ankurans halted. Callum didn't. He plunged his sword into the chest of a small Ankuran child, whose eyes didn't even glance at the sword as she toppled over, her eyes locked on the screaming Ankuran as he sunk to his knees. The flames covered his whole body, until only the glow of golden eyes remained. The gold flashed, throbbed, and then in an instant, disappeared entirely. Another flare of silver, and all that was left were ashes where there had once been a man.

'Show off,' Callum murmured as he faced the next creature. His sword swung, dismembering a middle-aged woman and leaving her body to rot. 'That's three.'

I had no time to spare breath for a rebuttal as a young Ankuran boy stepped in front of me. 'You can only hold this up for so long,' he said, 'then you'll tire. And when you tire, you'll be mine.'

I hissed out a breath, hesitating a moment too long at the sight of his young face and the shock of red hair. It was almost the exact same shade as Cassie's. He grasped hold of my wrist. I couldn't contain the scream that ripped out of me at the contact. The touch was both fire and ice, one following the other in an endless wave. My legs shook with the effort of keeping myself upright.

'Chiara!' Callum shouted nearby, followed by a curse as steel rang against steel.

I needed to muster my Gift again. To destroy the Ankuran in front of me. But the pain was more intense than it had been before, spearing through my chest and twining around my limbs. *Come on*, I pleaded with the elusive power. It flickered.

Before it could surge forward as it had before, wetness splattered over me. Swiping my hand across my eyes to clear them of the stinging gold, I blinked up at Callum.

'Are you hurt?' he asked, even as he swung his sword at the next one. A few fingers dropped next to me. A knife flew overhead, taking down an Ankuran before disappearing in a haze of red. I didn't need to look back to know it'd been Deana's kill.

'Fine,' I leveraged myself against the wall, straightening. 'Vitus's Gift pairs as well with mine as yours does.'

Callum frowned as though taking personal offence at the comparison to Vitus. His next swing was particularly vicious, lopping several inches off a middle-aged man, who fell on top of the bodies already there. I grasped the wrist of another creature, flinging it unceremoniously down the stairs before it could push Vitus's power into me. Corin managed to plunge his sword into its chest.

'Gods,' Deana cursed, 'These things are never-ending.'

'Jaxon?' I shouted, ignoring the beginning ache in my arms. 'Any progress?'

'Yes, Chiara, I've managed to open the door and just forgot to mention it.'

Deana muttered something cutting about him before calling up, 'Just a few more minutes.'

I wasn't sure we had that. I swung, again and again, losing

myself to the rhythm of the fight. A slice here, a body fell. A thrust there, another body down. A twist, and an Ankuran was flung to meet their end at Deana or Corin's hand.

Callum and I danced in perfect unison, our movements a complement to one another. When he faltered, my blades took his place. When one of them managed to touch me, he cut them down. It was like a song – a melody and a countermelody. If not for the horror of the bodies we cut down, the number of children among them, it might even have been beautiful.

My arms ached with every swing as body after body fell. Even my Gift was fatigued, the weight of battling the Gift of Life overwhelming it. Every time I called the silver to my blade, it flickered a little less vibrantly, took a little bit longer to bring them to their knees. Sweat soaked my skin, Callum showing similar signs of flagging. And still, there was no sign of the horde stopping.

A click sounded behind us, followed by the squeaking of hinges.

'It's open,' Jaxon called up to us, his voice just barely breaking through the thrumming of my heart amidst the swinging of my blades. 'We can go.'

I didn't spare a glance back as Callum ordered, 'You four first.'

'Callum—'

'Don't argue, Deana,' Callum snapped. 'You're wasting time.'

He didn't voice what I knew. We couldn't leave or switch our positions without risking a weapon in the back. They were still coming, thick and fast. Any more squeezed onto the stairs with the bodies piling at our feet and I feared the entire structure would crumble beneath us.

'Your Majesty,' Corin called up, his voice recovered from its earlier trembling. 'I can take some down. I'm good with a—'

'Deana,' Callum snapped, fingers closing around an Ankuran's throat and sword plunging into her chest. 'Take him and go. I'm not losing any more people today.'

'String me up for treason later,' Deana said with equal force. 'We're not leaving.'

'Dammit,' Callum bit out. 'Fine. Jaxon, you go on. Check on the servants. Make sure no Ankurans slipped our notice.'

There was a hesitation, then Jaxon's light tread raced away.

I caught a glimpse of Deana lifting her sword in defiance, Corin mirroring her movement, before I spun under a wild blow, straightening in time to sink my knife into the chest of the attacking Ankuran. My feet almost slid upon the stairs. The wood was coated in blood and gore, the air rank with the stench of rot. Taking advantage of my distraction, fingers grasped hold of my loosening bun and wrenched me upwards.

Grunting, I swung one of my knives through the wrist of my attacker. The tension at my scalp loosened as a hand fell at my feet. My next blow slid across the neck of my opponent. He didn't stop, didn't drop, until I had plunged my knife through the bloody throat again. Every breath burnt, my throat dry and chest painful. Beside me, Callum hissed in pain.

'Callum!' Deana shouted, but then there were more Ankurans pushing past us. Moving purposefully, I realised, to isolate us from the others.

I risked a glance at Callum, fear icy upon my skin. Red spilled under where his fingertips pressed to his side. The flow was fast, but he did not slow. He went low, drawing his blade across the back of the girl's legs. She laughed as she fell.

He didn't have a chance to finish her before a mountain-sized Ankuran stomped towards him, moving at a speed that didn't seem possible for a man that size. Callum moved faster, though. His sword plunged into the man's chest, the Ankuran swinging his own weapon at the same time. Callum ducked, dodging the blow as the Ankuran stumbled to the side, his wound bringing him down.

The red gushed fast from Callum's side, dripping upon the ground and panic clawed at my sense. I stepped towards Callum, ready to drag him away from the fight. If we could regroup for a moment – if I could somehow convince Callum to heal himself – then we could face the remaining Ankurans without much trouble.

Callum straightened, his eyes meeting mine. He grinned. 'I believe I'm winning our—' His eyes widened as he glanced over my shoulder and he lunged for me, sword clattering to the ground as he fisted my shirt. In a quick movement, he wrenched me around, placing himself between me and the top of the stairs.

'What are you do—' My words dried up as I stared at Callum's chest. At where the tip of a blade protruded, crimson rapidly blooming across his shirt. Behind him, the Ankuran girl he hadn't had time to kill grinned at me. She jerked the knife out again, Callum's body jolting with the cruel movement. He fell to one side, barely catching himself upon the stair rail.

Something inside me drew taut, dragging out all my wrath and fear as the girl drove the knife towards Callum's exposed back once more. I did not think past the roaring in my ears. She'd stabbed Callum. Callum, who had jumped between us, taking a blow aimed at me. It was unforgivable.

I collided with the girl, dragging both of us onto the stairs. Ankurans screeched as we rolled into them, sending a few tumbling into the hoard that surrounded Deana and Corin. Pain flared as my hand pressed to her throat, holding her down, but my fury was greater than any agony Vitus might try to give me. Callum was hurt. Badly, from the sound of his ragged breathing to one side. And I would make the Ankurans pay for daring to touch what was mine.

There was no mercy in me as I drove the dagger down, again

and again and again, until gold dripped off my cheeks like tears and the girl was nothing more than an empty carcass.

There was no sound behind me. No movement.

Don't look. I ordered myself as a wet cough came from where Callum had fallen. Not yet. Not even if everything in me pulled me towards him, begging me to check he was all right. I feared if I did – if I saw the wound again, saw the damage he'd taken because I'd been fool enough to allow myself to be distracted – then I wouldn't be able to focus on the fight. Either that, or my panic would consume me.

I didn't need that fear right now. I needed my fury.

'Give him up, little raven.' The words were a mix of voices, every one of the Ankurans on the stairs above me speaking as one. Jaws clicked as they opened too wide, shut too fast, the movements jerky. 'He's gone anyway. The pathetic child does not use the Gift I gave him. He will die, just as you wished.'

'Why?' I forced out. 'Why would you go after him?'

The closest Ankuran smiled. 'If the false king dies, then you will be mine anyway, in the end. So broken that you will not care to defy me.'

I will not allow it. The thought pounded through me. Not at the thought of being Vitus's, but of letting Callum die.

A trembling began in my fingers. It grew quickly, sliding up my arms, down my legs, through every part of me. There were too many Ankurans for me to beat with my blades alone. My strength was fading, exhaustion threatening to send me staggering back to the ground as I straightened. I had no idea how long we had been fighting – seconds, minutes, hours. All I knew was that Callum wasn't moving, and these creatures – this spiteful god – was to blame.

My Gift prickled beneath my skin. Kerta had told me that acceptance was the key to controlling my power. She was wrong. It was not acceptance that raged through me as silver sprung to my skin. It was defiance. A refusal to accept the path set for me. Rebellion against Vitus, the divine, the godsdamned realm if need be.

There was only one future I would accept. One path I would follow. And that was one where Callum survived.

'Give in,' Vitus's voice crooned from a different Ankuran as they bunched forward, crowding me. 'You'll suffer less that way.'

'No.' My voice was not loud. It did not fill the room, nor did it shake the floors.

Instead, it silenced. Every cackle of laughter, every shuffle of feet against stairs, fell away. My skin glowed, silver that was brighter than starlight flooding out of me. It burnt with my fury, with my resolve. The Ankuran nearest me fell back, screaming, as the silver brushed her skin. Within moments, she'd been rescinded to ash. The other Ankurans lurched backwards, the first flickers of anger showing in their golden eyes.

Good. Let their master be angered. Let him see me and wither with fury.

An adolescent Ankuran lurched to the side, attempting to get past me. My hand shot out. Silver crackled as my fingers closed around her throat. 'You will not touch him.'

The silver lashed out with the violence brewing in my voice. It speared through the Ankuran, her back arching as she shrieked. Then she, too, was gone, her ashes dusting my hand.

'Enough of this.' The Ankuran who had once been Brayden's sister stepped forward from where she'd been watching from up high. She was barely recognisable as mortal anymore, her flesh cracked and bleeding gold where the veins had split through skin. Red smeared across her lips. I didn't want to think about what remained of the guards who'd taken her earlier. 'Give him to me. He is of no use to you. Join my side and we can rule the realms together.'

I finally glanced at Callum. He stared up at me with half-open eyes, pain tightening his features as his hand pressed to his chest. There was so much blood – enough that it had begun to drip down the stairs and soak into the wood. Yet, his lips curved upwards, his eyes alight with awe.

'You're wrong.' My Gift crackled, my voice echoing with power. 'I have every need of him.'

The sweet smile on Tali's face shifted into a scowl. 'Then I shall have to kill him myself.' The air grew heavy, power brewing as the golden veins in the Ankurans broke through flesh, skin taking on the same sheen as the eyes. My skin prickled at the power.

I smiled. My hand raised, and power exploded outwards.

Chapter Twenty-Eight

Silver light flared.
Every single Ankuran was coated in it, features unrecognisable beyond the glow except for the gold of the eyes. And the screams that cracked the air were filled with traces of the god who controlled the creatures.

I relished it all.

The Ankurans fell to their knees, nails dragging down their faces and tearing through flesh. Where golden blood spurted, silver launched to embrace it, swallowing it whole. My chest filled with the warmth of death as the space lit up with the glow of my Gift. Only Callum, Deana and Corin remained untouched, my will guiding my Gift. *This* was power. Not just the ability to take lives, but to decide whose lives would be lost.

It completed me. Filled me. Urged me on, a ravenous need for death overwhelming me.

'You!' The Archinian princess shrieked as she staggered away from where the rest had succumbed, the screams dying off one by one. When those eyes fixed on me, they were filled with deep hatred. 'You dare—'

'I dare to do far more than this.' I stepped forward, and the silver moved with me. The air was thick with ash and the stench of death. Another step. Another backwards stagger from the lone Ankuran. How much did Vitus see behind those eyes? How much did he feel? I hoped it was everything. 'You should never have killed my sister. And you should never have gone after Callum.'

Her eyes flickered, gold sparks spearing off her. The silver lapped them up greedily, and my power hummed in satisfaction. I nearly hummed along with it as I grasped hold of more of it, sending a bolt of silver lancing for Tali's heart. Again, the satisfaction of wielding such power thrummed through me.

Yes, everything in me whispered. This was who I was. Death's daughter, in all her vicious glory.

The Ankuran princess barely twisted to the side. 'You will regret this. I am the king of gods. You will bow before me.'

'Even gods must bow in the face of death.' Another step. Another surge of power. My smile widened as I lifted my hand once more, directing a single finger towards the Ankuran. 'And you are no king of mine.'

Her hand lifted. It was useless as my power barrelled towards her, a wall of inescapable silver. It stretched from ceiling to floor, carrying the scent of jasmine and smoke with it, the smell overpowering that rot around us. Energy crackled through, the world around turning incandescent with brightness that shattered shadows and overpowered any other light. Corin murmured a prayer to the gods behind me as Deana gasped. But the silver was not done yet.

It stretched under our feet, a lake made of starlight. Above, it curled with the threat of a wave readying to crash. It curled around me, turning my skin that same shining silver. The wall was beautiful. A barrier of power, built from my fury. From my hatred. From something far more powerful than either.

And the Ankuran – the creature who controlled it – would not pass. They would not lay another finger on Callum. On Deana, or Jaxon, or any other in this palace. Because this place – the kingdom, the people, the king – they were mine to do with as I liked. Mine to protect or damn.

Not Vitus's. Not any of the god's.

The power sang through me. *Death* sang through me. It was utterly unlike Dearil's power, which had always been the calm of a peaceful passing. No, there was no calm here. There was hatred and love; happiness and despair. It was death brought by an enemy's blade or a lover's hand. Death brought to win wars or to end hardship.

This Gift was *me*. Every death I'd brought. Every death I'd feared.

And I revelled in it. Despised it. Feared it. Loved it.

Became it.

All it took was a single thought. A shift of my will. An order of my heart.

The silver crashed downwards with all that malicious, lovely power. There wasn't even time to scream before the Ankuran was swallowed whole. And just like that, the Ankurans were gone. The silver pulled back into me, sinking into my skin as exhaustion settled over me. It curled up like a pleased cat, its sleepy contentment humming through me as I staggered to the side. My shoulder collided with the wall, trembling legs barely keeping me upright. A breath shuddered through me.

Our first battle against the god. And we had won.

The jubilation of victory faded as I forced my aching body to whirl. We'd won, but at what cost? Placing my weight on the stair rail, I half walked, half fell down the stairs between Callum and I. The knife I'd retained hold of clattered from my hand as I dropped to my knees beside him. My breathing shallowed as my Gift lifted its sleepy head, warmth flooding through me. A warning that death was approaching. Terror wrapped around my throat like a noose as I grasped at Callum, rolling him onto his back. His eyes were shut, skin pale and clammy. Bloodied smears tainted his skin as I pressed my fingers to his neck.

'Don't you dare die on me,' I whispered, heart lodged in my throat as I waited for a pulse.

Nothing, nothing, and then – there. Thready, weak, but there.

I exhaled, relief slumping my shoulders as Callum's eyes fluttered open. He stared up at me, a weak smile curving his lips upwards. It disappeared the moment I slammed my hand down on his wound, pressing hard to staunch the steady bleeding. 'You don't get to smile,' I said, my heart tumbling at how much blood spilled between my fingertips. 'Not after pulling a stunt like that.'

He blinked slowly. His hand raised, bloodied fingers trembling as they wiped away droplets of gold from my cheek. 'You're magnificent,' he breathed. The words cost him, a cough racking his body seconds later. Red speckled his lips, his chest faltering under my hands.

'Heal yourself,' I demanded. He was too pale, his skin too cold. I'd treated wounds like this before. Knew them well enough to realise the likely outcome.

Hesitation flickered across his expression. 'I can survive without—'

'No, you can't. And I know what I said,' I snapped. Gods, the amount of blood – it was too much. Had Cassie bled this much as she'd died? I didn't think so. 'That you could have a choice with when to use it. That remains true for anyone else. Save everyone, leave everyone to die – I don't care. But you don't get a damned choice when it comes to your own life.' I leant in. 'Use your Gift. Now.'

'I—' Callum broke off, exhaling before tilting his head in a barley-there nod. 'As you command.'

His eyes shut, his body stilling. The pain already there intensified as shadows began to curl under his skin. What horror was he recalling? Something he had healed another from, or what his father had done to him? The shadows lanced down his cheeks, smoky tendrils weaving beneath his collar. I removed my hand from his wound, letting the shadows weave their magic. His features tightened further, fingers blanching where they pressed into the ground.

I reached for his hand, biting back a gasp as the sudden pain from his Gift hit my skin. His fingers curled around mine, squeezing tight as his back arched. I didn't know if he even realised I was holding him. I knew what it was to be trapped in memories of violence and pain, and to have no tether back to the real world. So, I held on, ignoring the fiery agony of his Gift, ignoring my own aches and pains, as he endured his torment. As he chose to face it to live. At last, Callum released a long breath. His eyes flew open, pain clearing as he struggled up onto an elbow. The wound at his midsection was nothing more than a faded pink line. I stared at in wonder. His Gift wasn't simply healing. It was rewriting fates. Changing the deaths that were meant to be.

A perfect complement to my own.

The fingers in mine tightened. I jerked my head up, finding Callum staring at our joint hands with quiet horror. 'Were you touching me while I was using my Gift?' When I didn't reply, he lurched onto his knees, his hands grasping my shoulders. 'Why? You knew the pain it would cause you. Why did you—'

'I didn't want you to be alone,' I said softly, finding the frankness of my words strangely comforting. My eyes raised to his. The green was still fractured by shards of black. 'You used your Gift.'

A slow smile spread upon his lips. 'I did.' He paused, then added, 'It might've kicked in once I was moments away from death. You could've just let it be.'

I shifted my gaze away. I'd been aware of that, but...

I remembered what he'd done. How he'd forced me to face that which was plaguing me when everyone else was too scared to. How he'd moved me from my stagnancy and given me purpose when Deana had first found me in the slums. How patient he'd been when I didn't deserve it. But I wasn't quite ready to share all that with him. 'Can you stand?'

Callum nodded, slowly rising to his feet as he heavily leant on the wall. Deana and Corin kept their distance behind us as he winced, hand pressing to his wound. 'That was nowhere near as pleasant as getting stabbed by you.'

My fist swung out, catching Callum in the chest.

He stumbled back a step, brows rising in surprise. 'What was that for?'

'For scaring me, you idiot.' I folded my eyes, glaring furiously up at him 'I thought you might die. Why did you jump between me and the Ankuran? I could've taken the blow. What if Vitus had been able to fully block your Gift? What if the wound had been more severe and you'd bled out while the Ankurans were still there? You'd be dead just like—' My voice broke off. I raised my hand again, debating whether hitting him once more would knock some sense into him.

This time, Callum caught my hand in his. His fingers interlaced with mine, pulling my palm close until it rested against his chest. 'I did it because it would've been you bleeding out if I hadn't. This, I can survive. But if it had been you – I can't use my Gift on you, Chiara.' Our hands were a match of gold washed skin. 'But I'm still here. He didn't win this time.'

For a while, I stayed there, frozen, feeling his heartbeat, his hand curled around mine. There was blood on my shirt and my pants and melded into my hair. Rot and decay surrounded us, and there was so much to do, too many things to prepare for, but I didn't care.

We were alive. We had beaten Vitus.

And we would again.

It took us some time to stumble down the corridor, Deana and Corin going ahead to check on the state of those in the food cellars.

Callum was still affected by the memory of pain lingering in his flesh. I wasn't much better, my body wanting to fall into an exhausted sleep. It wasn't unlike the times I had walked off a battlefield, bloody and bruised, collapsing onto my litter for whatever sleep I could steal. But sleep was a luxury we couldn't afford at the moment. Instead, with Callum's arm slung over my shoulder, we took slow, staggering steps into the kitchen and through the door on the other side.

'You owe me ten gold pieces and a necklace,' I said. My voice was laced with the same weariness that wracked my bones. 'I won the bet.'

'You cheated. I was winning before you unleashed yourself.'

'It's not cheating to use my Gift.'

His lips shaped into a smile that wasn't quite as wicked as it usually was, fatigue tugging at the edges. 'I had the common decency to wait until after the battle was over to use mine. It most certainly is cheating to use your Gift, even if it is the most exquisite thing I've ever seen.'

We staggered around a corner. I pressed my hand to one of the walls, leaving a golden handprint behind when we moved on. 'I disagree. It's a natural part of fighting, particularly when it comes to fighting gods.'

'I'll adorn you in whatever jewellery you want.' His lips quirked up, and my eyes narrowed in anticipation of whatever was coming next. 'Though I do think a crown would suit you best.'

Before I could do more than blink at the unexpected statement, bootsteps sounded from down the corridor. We froze, but neither of us drew our weapons. The steps were too sure of themselves, and we were too tired to do much more than stare in the direction they were coming from. If it were to be enemies, our best hope would be to turn and flee. The shadows appeared first, two long, slim ones that reached half of the way towards us before their owners showed. Deana and Jaxon appeared.

Jaxon lowered his tightly clutched weapons when he saw us. 'Deana said you'd killed the Ankurans, but I thought she might've been trying to convince me to run back and get myself killed.'

I narrowed my eyes. 'And where were you in all that?'

He grinned. 'Doing the very important job of guarding my own life.'

Deana scowled, but she grudgingly said, 'A few Ankurans had found another way in. Jaxon apparently fought them off with the guards.' Her eyes swung to Callum. They caught on the blood staining Callum's clothes, drenching the legs of my pants, and then on his still pale face. 'I thought you healed—'

'I'm fine,' Callum cut in. He straightened, removing his arm from my shoulders. I pressed my arm to the wall to stop myself falling at the sudden change in balance. 'Just a small scratch, anyway.'

I shot him an incredulous look. At the flaring of panic in Deana's eyes, I forced my rebuke down. He wasn't dead. That was the best outcome for any soldier coming off a battlefield. There was no sense worrying her further. 'It was. Nothing more than a scratch.' I forced a smile. 'He made a bigger deal of it during the battle than it actually was.'

'And the Ankurans? What did you do with them?' Jaxon's eyes narrowed. He stared into the darkness behind us, waving a hand. One of his yellow lights flew down, illuminating the corridor behind us. All it caught in its glow was the white walls and infrequent smears of gold or red blood from Callum and I. 'Deana was too set on getting back here to tell me.'

'Gone.'

'Gone, as in gone back to their master? Or gone, as in dead?' Jaxon paused, lips twisting into a frown. 'Or, I suppose, more dead?'

I gestured at the amount of gold soaking through my clothes. 'You can take a look past the kitchens if you want.'

Jaxon's lip twisted in disgust as he caught sight of the hand. 'I'm good, thanks.'

Callum leant forward slightly. One hand braced against the wall. I saw the tremble in it, as though one slip and he would tumble down. He straightened as much as he could. 'Has anyone seen Brayden?'

Jaxon shrugged. 'I was rather hoping he ran into one of the creatures we'd missed.'

I glared at him. His lips curved into a smile. 'Jaxon.'

'Again – don't tell me you weren't thinking about it.' And again, I didn't answer. I didn't think anyone deserved to be torn to shreds and *eaten*, but I also wouldn't mourn his loss. Not when it was his actions that had led to the events of today.

Deana shoved in front of Jaxon. 'One of the guards found him hiding in a guest room. Apparently, the guards who'd taken him and his sister had told him to run when Tali attacked.'

'Coward,' Jaxon muttered. That he was the one who said it spoke volumes.

'I'll need to speak to him at some point. I'm beginning to suspect it wasn't Dearil who sent him and his sister here.' Callum sighed, dragging a hand over his face. 'But not today.'

'Then what's next?' Jaxon asked. Together, we looked expectantly at Callum. He needed rest, as did I, but it would have to wait. Today was only the beginning. A deep foreboding warned me that the battle that had just occurred would be mere child's play to whatever Vitus's next steps were.

Callum's eyes filled with shadows. 'We count our losses,' he said. 'We bury the dead. All of them.'

'And then?'

'Then, we make a plan.'

'To do what?'

Callum smiled grimly. 'To kill a god.'

The clean-up took some time. The Ankurans outside had been defeated once reinforcements arrived from the city, and the stench of death soaked the air outside the palace. Seven guards had been killed – the five on duty at the gate at the time of the initial attack, Damien, and one of the reinforcements. Of the five, only the latter had a full body to burn by the time the fighting was done. The burial rites took hours, the sun painting in pinks and oranges as dawn found us standing before the blazing fires of the bodies we could recover. The families of the dead had been informed, several trudging into the palace grounds with grief-stricken faces. Servants, guards and civilians gathered before the pyres. Tiny embers twisted through the air as distraught sobs sounded around us. As the last of the bodies was burnt to ash, Jaxon lifted a hand. His eyes glowed an intense yellow as his Gift poured into the air around us. From the dirt in front of the crackling flames rose dozens of ornate stones, each covered in blooming flowers of shades of yellow. The flowers budded, then spread their petals to the sky. The centre was dotted with vibrant orange.

'They'll last until proper ones can be crafted,' Jaxon said quietly to Callum.

Callum nodded his thanks before going to speak to the grieving families in hushed tones. A mother collapsed at his feet, wailing as she clutched at his dirtied trousers. Twins, the spitting images of Damien, flinched when Callum approached, while a husband of one of the fallen slammed his fist into Callum's cheek. Callum simply stood there and took it all, his shoulders rigid, a sharp word to Deana was all it took to keep her from lunging in front of him. Jaxon and I leant against the palace walls. Callum's father had never once done such a thing in his reign. Unexpected pride blossomed in me. This was what it meant to rule. To create a kingdom worth protecting.

When Callum and Deana turned back to the palace, expressions haggard, Jaxon and I joined them in silence. None of us spoke as we staggered towards the palace, each of us struggling to maintain a decent pace. Stepping over shards of wood scattered upon the marble steps, Callum's bootsteps echoed like a warning of the growing cloud of anger that surrounded him. He did not march off to his room and collapse in his bed as he should have done. Instead, he led us all back to one of his meeting chambers.

At the entry to the room, he froze.

Golden stains spread across the carpet, the splotches deep and wide and matched with the crimson that splattered over the walls. One of the guards must have been cornered here. I only hoped that gold meant they had their chance of revenge in bringing down their killer.

'They attacked my people.' Callum's voice was quiet. He did not move from the doorway, standing still. So perfectly, unnervingly still. 'People whose only crime was protecting my palace. Protecting me.'

I squeezed between him and the doorway, turning to face him within the meeting chamber. Any discomfort at touching him so candidly before Jaxon and Deana disappeared as his eyes met mine. There was rage there, yes, but there was also pain. Pain and guilt. 'It wasn't your fault.'

His jaw tensed under my fingertips. 'I'm king. Every death in this kingdom from war is my fault.'

War. It was a harsh word. A word I had detested for year after year, that had ripped me away from Cassie and forced me into servitude for a man I despised with every fibre of my being. But I had never dreaded or feared the word as much as I did now.

Not for myself. Never for myself.

For what, given the chance, it could do – would do – to the man before me. I could see it in the angles of his face and shadows in his eyes. Every death would be a blow that Callum would bear. The ones he wouldn't be able to save, no matter how well he ruled.

'Cheer up, Cal.' Jaxon slid between Callum and I, forcing me away. He wrapped an arm around Callum's shoulders, pushing him into one of the chairs. Jaxon wore a smile, but I recognised it for what it was. It was as much an armour as the rage I wore, as much a mask as Callum's stony quiet now, as much a weapon as the dresses and pretty laughs Deana used. 'We can always switch places. You can live in the slums, and I can live in this fancy palace. Then you won't have to be king anymore.'

Deana did not offer Jaxon any cutting words or even look at him. Instead, she watched Callum carefully. A royal guard protecting her king, understanding that Jaxon's provocation was the distraction Callum needed, to save him from himself.

Callum inhaled slowly before giving Jaxon an equally mocking smirk back. It didn't reach his eyes. 'And see this palace stripped bare of all its riches in a day? I think not.'

Jaxon raised an eyebrow. 'You think it hasn't already been stripped?' He reached into his pocket, hand flourishing like a street performer I had once seen perform magic tricks. His fingers flicked out. Two hooks curved around his finger, the ends glittering with jewels. A set of diamond earrings I could have sworn Deana had been wearing earlier. Deana's hand flew up to her ears. At the smooth skin under her fingers, she hissed out a curse and held out a hand. Jaxon shrugged. The earrings were tossed into the air, disappearing into her pocket the moment she caught them.

I slid into a chair next to Callum. Golden blood crusted under my fingernails. My skin itched with it – with the reminder of what we had managed today. Of what we would face. Picking at it, I watched as tiny flecks drifted to the carpet. 'A plan.' I repeated the words Callum had spoken earlier. 'A plan to kill a god.'

'We do what Kerta and Evania suggested,' Jaxon said, as though it was that easy.

Callum shot him a deadpan look. 'Their plan wasn't far off throwing Chiara at Vitus and hoping it would be enough.'

'It needs some refinement,' Jaxon allowed. 'But the idea is there. Chiara managed to overpower those Ankurans today with her Gift. The principle is the same – she simply needs to get close enough to strike, temporarily incapacitate him and then unleash her power.'

Simply. There was nothing simple about it. There were too many ifs – *if* I could get close enough. *If* my Gift was strong enough to overwhelm an ancient god. *If* Vitus didn't kill me first.

'You're forgetting something,' I reminded both men. 'We're assuming that I'm strong enough to cause Vitus to lose hold of his power. Ankurans are nothing more than puppets. Vitus is a god – one of the most powerful in existence. I'm only half of one.'

Callum considered me. 'You're strong enough.' There was no uncertainty in his tone. Just unyielding faith. 'That's not what I'm worried about. I'm worried about the fact that, if rumours of Archin are true, there are thousands of dead bodies between you and Vitus. Dead bodies Vitus can mould into his own personal army.'

I shuddered at the thought. We'd just faced dozens. We had won, but I could feel the cost. My body was drained, my Gift flickering like a flame as the wick died down. I was exhausted. Facing thousands of those creatures would be near impossible.

There was another thought that thrummed underneath all that. Between us and Vitus, there would be Liam. But it was not fear that hummed in my blood and in my bones. It was hunger. Rage. Vengeance.

I wanted Vitus to fall, but I needed Liam to suffer. To feel every drop of pain that had been wrought out of me over the past few months, the hopelessness and the despair. He would be on his knees before the end, and he would know it was me who reduced him to such a state. And for that, I would gladly destroy thousands of Ankurans. I would destroy the god who controlled them. Even, quite possibly, destroy myself.

'I just need a way past them,' I said, half to myself, mouth twisted in concentration. My fingers pushed my dagger around idly, sending it spinning on the table. 'Some way to get around them all without Vitus noticing.' I considered the problem, studying the way light danced off my dagger, seeming to jump from one spot to the next. An idea occurred to me. A ridiculous, dangerous idea, but the only one I had. I met Callum's stare. 'Brayden.'

Callum's eyebrows rose. An amused smile found his lips. 'I agree that throwing him to the creatures would be ideal, but at most it would only distract three of them.'

My fingers slammed onto the spinning blade, bringing it to a halt. 'He arrived here from seemingly nowhere, right?' Deana nodded. 'Then either Dearil or Vitus sent him here. Could we find a way to do the same?'

'My money's on Vitus,' Jaxon said. 'The timing of the Ankuran girl letting in all the others was too convenient. My guess is that Dearil tried to send them elsewhere, but Vitus got in first and sent his spy straight into our palace.' His expression darkened. 'That means his power is beginning to return to its full strength.'

Callum frowned contemplatively. 'We don't have Dearil to transport us from one place to another. Kerta was also clear that the other gods would not be able to assist.' His tone was not dismissive. He was contemplative, a strategist at work, figuring out how to break down that barrier.

I silently cursed, my brilliant idea evaporating. I'd forgotten Kerta said that.

Jaxon grinned. 'We don't need Dearil or the goddesses.' The yellow in his eyes glowed in the light, showing his glee. 'We have something just as good.' His eyes slid to me. 'Dearil's daughter.'

Chapter Twenty-Nine

My first response was a look of mute horror. My second was a *no* – so vehement that I felt it down to my bones.

'Why not?' Jaxon countered, a challenge in his voice.

I refused to rise to the bait. 'Why not?' I picked up my dagger, slamming the hilt into the table as I leant forward. 'Do you not remember what happened to that book in the godly realm? You were the one who suggested I not try it with an actual person.' Deana's eyebrows creased in confusion. I filled her in. 'It was a mess. I tried to transport the book like the goddesses told me and it ended up in hundreds of tiny bits.'

Jaxon heaved a sigh. 'That was a book. Your heart wasn't in it. Besides, our situation is a little more dire now than it was.'

'Or maybe I can't do it, and if I tried with *people*, it would be bits of us decorating this room. Or the Archinian palace. I'm sure Vitus would love that.'

Jaxon propped his feet up on the edge of the table. 'It won't happen.'

I narrowed my eyes at him, staring pointedly at every feature that hinted at ethereality. The yellow eyes, the too-smooth skin, the sharp points of his features, not unlike my own. 'I'm not the only one who is half-god. Why can't you do it? You're supposedly much older than me.'

'Not that anyone would've guessed,' Deana chimed in.

Jaxon's chair fell with a thud, softened by the carpet underneath. 'I'm not a—' His lips pressed together for a moment before he started again. 'My dearest mother is strong, but your father is one of the two most powerful gods alive. At one point, before Vitus's betrayal led to his imprisonment, Dearil ruled the gods. Even Tarina struggles to transport more than just herself. Barely half of that trickled down to me.'

I didn't want to believe him. Didn't want yet another thing to be my responsibility, my failure should everyone be killed. Not when all I wanted was vengeance. Or, at least, it had been. Caring about others, about the lives of those I knew and those I didn't, was a burden I had never cared for, and one I wished to shed myself of now. But I could not, and there were far too many lives at stake for me to not even consider what he'd suggested.

'Not yet,' I finally said. 'Let's think of something else first. Another plan before we go to that.'

'I could go into the city,' Jaxon suggested. 'Ask around my contacts, see what information they have and bring it back here. They might be able to give us a way to get to Archin safely.'

'You've got to be kidding,' Deana said flatly.

Jaxon rested his elbow upon the table, propping up his chin with his fist. His smile turned sharp. 'What's that supposed to mean?'

'What do you plan to do once you've gotten that information? Will you try to extort a new deal out of Callum, just like you did when he came to you for help after his father had stabbed him?' She rose to her feet, fists pressing into the tabletop as she loomed over Jaxon, her expression furious. 'Or will you be running away like the coward you are?'

'Gods, you're still upset about that?' Jaxon sighed. 'It's called *business,* love. I gave our king seven precious years between when he asked me to kill him – which, I'd like to point out, I didn't do – and when I asked for a trade.'

'A trade?!' Deana exploded. Callum and I both leant back as she jabbed a finger in Jaxon's face. 'You extorted him! Your exact words to me were, *either your pretty boy prince lets me do what I want, or I go and tell the king what his little heir planned to do that day.*'

Jaxon straightened, his smile falling away. 'We all have to find a way to survive, Deana. My way was to find a way to escape an execution. And don't pretend that you're upset about that part of how things ended up, and not the two years we spent together prior to—'

'Do not finish that sentence.' Deana snarled. Clearly, something had happened between them. And to then threaten Deana's prince… I knew enough about her to know that was the gravest offence Jaxon could have committed, a betrayal that would have destroyed any trust between them.

'We're not going to get anywhere right now,' Callum cut in before things could escalate. He dragged a hand over his face, deep shadows under his eyes. He struggled to his feet, swaying slightly as he did so. 'We're all exhausted. And no matter how urgent planning is, doing so now will only lead us to be reckless. Let's get what sleep we can and meet again when we're not likely to go at each other's throats.' He winced. 'My body's still replenishing the blood loss, so I definitely need a few hours to recover.'

'Blood loss?' Deana's head jerked in his direction, suspicion narrowing her eyes. 'I thought you only had a small scratch.' She shook her head, annoyance flaring in her eyes. 'I *knew* it looked more serious when you got injured.'

Callum smiled. 'You know how fragile my body is. A few drops of blood gone, and I'm as weak as a kitten.'

Deana sighed heavily, her eyes dropping to his stained shirt. 'I've sent the guards who fought away to rest for a few days and doubled the number stationed at the gates. I don't know the ones guarding your rooms as well as those typically on rotation. It'd be best if I came with you and—'

'No,' Callum interrupted, tone firm. 'You were guarding our bodies while we were in the godly realm. You need sleep as much as any of us do and, trained as you are, I'm well aware of how difficult it is to rouse you once you're asleep.'

Her jaw set. 'I'll be fine. I've trained to stay awake and—'

'It wasn't a request.' His expression softened at the unease in Deana's eyes. 'I need you at your best. Besides, I've already chosen the perfect bedside guard.' His eyes slid to me, a smile curving his lips.

'Absolutely not!' Jaxon declared, finally rising to push himself in front of me. I raised my eyes skywards. 'You kids are not—'

I dug my elbow into his side. 'We're not kids and stop thinking whatever it is you've got in your head. Look at Callum. He's at the edge of collapse.'

Callum frowned at this appraisal but didn't protest. Out of the four of us, he did seem the worst off. It was no wonder, given the wound he'd survived.

'It's fine. I'll use his chair and catch a few hours of sleep while I'm there. I'm not a heavy sleeper.' Years of being constantly on edge had trained me to wake at the smallest disturbances. Before any other protests could be made by Jaxon, I offered Callum my arm and we began the slow stagger to his bed chambers.

Callum barely managed to mutter something about how I should take the bed before he collapsed on the floor of his chambers, sleep finding him enviably quickly. He did not stir as I struggled to drag him onto his bed, giving him enough accidental knocks that he'd likely wake with extra bruises. Sinking into a soft armchair to the side of a small table, I heaved out a sigh and began working through the tangles of my blood-matted hair, flakes of red and gold drifting down as I painstakingly pulled the curls apart. Cassie used to love this job – me sitting before her, her fingers working far more deftly than mine did. The whole time, I stared at Callum. Checked for the rise and fall of his chest, my heart stuttering every time his breathing hitched.

Those breaths had been too close to stopping today. And I didn't want to consider the damage I might've wrought had that come to pass.

Desperate to distract myself, I brushed my fingers down the spines of a pile of books teetering on the table to my left. Most I didn't recognise. Reading and writing had been a skill my mother had forced upon me from a young age, one of a myriad of others. The courtesan she'd been grooming me to be knew how to please in all ways. If a customer demanded to be read poetry, then the courtesan better be able to read poetry. At least that particular talent had served for more than my pain. The king, however, saw little value in my literacy, aside from reading missives from him or deciphering letters containing my commands for the next battle. Anything more was a risk to a control wound so tight I didn't know what freedom tasted like.

Callum had had no such boundaries imposed by his father. Or perhaps he'd found his own ways to dodge those boundaries, hiding books from King Kane's sight. The books ranged from massive tomes detailing histories that most would never know, the pages pristine, as though rarely touched, to slimmer novels with pages so worn it was a wonder they hadn't disintegrated. I carefully eased one out of place. A small piece of paper poked out of the top, a nearly illegible scrawl trailing the white sheet as it held his place in the book. I stared at the paper, my cheeks warming. I recognised that writing – the way I would've quickly scratched the letters across the page before heading into a battle. The edges were worn down, the message referring to a battle two years prior, right when I started with the last unit I'd captained. How had Callum gotten his hands on this? And why? His tasks were always ones done in the shadows – torture, assassinations, threats and bribes. Political manoeuvrings to serve King Kane, dealing with internal conflicts where I dealt with external. He'd have no use for war updates.

Placing the paper to the side, I eased the book open and began reading. I'd forgotten the simple joy of stories. While I hadn't read much, I'd loved creating stories for my sister. Stories of the gods and the past, some fact and some fiction, that whirled off my tongue with silver-spun words. This story was not otherworldly or about gods and wars. It was sweet and simple, a tale of a boy and a girl born so far apart in life that they should never have met, let alone fall in love. Every so often, I glanced surreptitiously at Callum, surprised that he had read this. My eyes would inevitably be dragged back to the page, shutting out any noises from the world beyond as I lost myself to the words.

'Good choice.'

Startled, the book dropped from my fingers, shutting closed. I flicked my eyes from it to Callum, who struggled to push himself upright. 'You made me lose my page.'

Callum smiled, though the expression quickly turned into a wince when I brought out the paper that had been marking the page. 'Ah. You found that.'

'I did.' I raised my brows. 'Care to explain?'

A hint of heat tipped his cheeks. A smile twitched at my lips. I rather liked seeing him flustered. 'I might have collected a few of your missives after you were sent to war.'

'How many is a few?'

Callum rubbed the back of his neck. 'All I could get my hands on before my father burnt them. Probably around fifty.' I blinked, the paper almost dropping from my grasp, and he laughed. 'I was rather enamoured with the fierce girl who caused chaos wherever she went. I wanted to know you were alive. To read about all you'd done.'

'But you kept them,' I said, waving the paper. 'For years.'

He shrugged. 'Like I said, I was enamoured.' With a sly look, he swung his legs around the side of the bed and leant forward. 'And am even more so now.'

It was my turn for my cheeks to heat. 'Well.' I cleared my throat, trying to keep my gaze from sliding away again.

Callum's grin widened triumphantly at the offbeat response. His eyes darkened with something heated and wicked as he leant forward slightly. His shirt had been slashed open enough that it barely held on at the top, revealing every inch of skin underneath. 'You know,' he murmured, voice deep and throaty, 'I rather think I enjoy seeing you flustered.'

It was almost an exact echo to my earlier thought about him. 'I rather enjoy seeing you not being killed by a hand that wasn't mine.' I pushed myself off the chair, wincing at the stains my filthy clothes left behind. At least I wasn't the only one covered in blood, grime and who knew what else – Callum's golden hair was matted with blood, sticking to his forehead, his white sheets stained with the same. Poor servants. They were going to have a nightmare of a day when they next came to clean this palace. 'And now you've had your beauty sleep, I'm going to go.'

Before I could turn, Callum lurched to his feet, his fingers curling around my wrist. 'Don't go.' I hesitated, eyes moving between Callum to the door and back again. I shouldn't stay. Shouldn't give in to the softness in his eyes, the tiny cracks of vulnerability showing in his usual calm demeanour. I'd told myself time and time before that this – whatever existed between he and I, what could exist there – was more than I deserved. My resolve weakened as he added on a soft, 'Please.'

'Why?' The question was not as blunt as I had meant it to be. It was an invitation – an opportunity for him to convince me. Because, godsdamn me, I wanted to be convinced.

'Because I don't want you to go.' He leant forward, half twisting where he had propped himself up. 'And I don't want you to stay because you feel you have to, or because you think it will aid you somehow in your quest for vengeance.'

'Do you want me to stay simply because you're the king?' I asked, eyebrows drawing inwards.

'Gods, no.' Callum choked out a laugh. 'And I imagine if I ever did make a demand of you as the king, you'd be gone before I could finish blinking.'

'Then why do you want me to stay?'

'I want you to stay because—' He paused, his throat working in a swallow before he continued. 'I want you to stay because you want to. Because you want to be here, with me.' He leant forward, his forehead resting against mine as his eyes shut. 'I want you to stay because I want *you*. Want to treat you as the magnificent woman that you are.' His breath skated over my skin, warming me. 'And because we deserve it. We deserve our moments of happiness, even amongst everything that's going on. And this – *you* – are the greatest happiness I could ever achieve in this life or any other.'

I saw, in that moment, what I could do with his fragility. The million ways I could shatter him irreparably, just as I had once thought I wanted to do. All it would take would be pulling free from his grip. And in doing so, the million ways I could destroy myself. But I did not want to do that. I did not want to destroy either of us. I wanted to be here, with him, for however long we had left.

I allowed him to draw me to the bed. His hand twined behind

my neck, our breaths mingling as he pulled me closer. I let go of any remaining uncertainty, any hesitation, any fear that I would ruin everything – ruin him. Let him see all my vulnerability as we lay on the mattress, learning each other in ways that I had never known anyone before. I let myself give in to all of that. Let myself live in a way I thought I hadn't deserved.

I stayed.

Chapter Thirty

We didn't spend long in Callum's chambers. No matter how glorious the time we stole was, there were too many threats that lingered on the horizon. I used the passage between our rooms to slip into my own, pulling on a black tunic and trousers before heading out, meeting Callum in front of our rooms. My hair was freshly braided, any trace of blood gone from the ends. Two knives sat in my boots, three at my waist and two long, wicked hair pins that would do some serious damage if driven into someone's throat worked into my hair.

Callum was similarly dressed for battle. His boots were polished clean, gleaming black in the morning light. The simple make of his shirt sat well upon his frame, a coat embroidered with silver designs pulled over the top. His sword, cleaned and sharpened, hung at his side. A simple silver circlet adorned his head, golden strands pulled back from his face.

Every part was carefully curated, simple yet brutally devastating in the way it accentuated every sharp feature, every curve of muscle. The message was clear. Today, he was not simply Callum. He was the king.

The sound of Jaxon and Deana arguing met us as we rounded the corner to the corridor. Jaxon leant against the doors, the unfamiliar guards eyeing him mistrustfully as they maintained their stiff-backed positions to either side. Deana stood opposite him, hands on her hips. Both silenced as Callum cleared his throat, Deana spinning and Jaxon straightening. She smiled at Callum's garb. Jaxon smirked at mine.

'Who are we planning to kill today?' he asked. I stared pointedly at his own sword, his hand hovering close by. As cavalier as he might pretend to be, he was as rattled as we were by the battle.

'It's far past time to have a word with Prince Brayden,' Callum replied for me. He turned towards Deana. 'Bring him to the throne room.'

She nodded sharply, offering Jaxon one last glare before heading to collect Brayden. We reached the throne room quickly, the corridors even quieter than usual. Inside, the marble floors and high walls were immaculate, free from the gold and silver dust that covered other sections of the palace. It was a stark contrast to my memories of the place, most of which had seen the floors soaked in red.

Callum did not hesitate as he strode towards the throne. He settled himself into it. There was no mistaking that he had been born to rule from there. The shadows behind him darkened the floor beneath his feet, the light in front playing off the sharpness of his cheekbones and the hardness of his eyes. He didn't need a retinue of guards standing at the bottom as his father had always had. He was frightening enough by himself. Even more so with the smirking criminal who seated himself on the bottom stair, sprawled out like a sunbaking cat.

Still, it would only take one impulsive blow from an idiotic Archinian king to fell Callum. I stalked towards the shadows beyond the throne. Callum had once taken up that position behind his father, wearing a cold mask I had once loathed. A silent warning against those who might attack. I would be that for him. The nightmare that lurked in the shadows. I had once become a monster for my sister. I would gladly do it again for him.

As I brushed past the ornate throne, he caught my wrist. 'Not behind,' he murmured. 'I don't want you to ever stand behind me.' He tugged gently until I was beside him, staring out at the empty throne room. 'Stand with me.'

It was hard to pull my eyes away from his, even as the doors opened. With some effort, I tore my eyes from Callum and regarded Brayden as he strode in, an annoyed looking Deana behind him. Brayden had the sense to look nervous and the bravery to stand up straight, red-rimmed eyes fixed on Callum. Callum's face revealed nothing. He stared down the Archinian king, waiting for him to approach the dais. A few feet from the stairs, Jaxon shifted, hand casually falling on the hilt of his blade.

Brayden stopped, swallowing nervously as he tracked us – Jaxon, whose casualness was underlaid with brimming violence; Deana, who knelt to Callum, hand dangerously close to her wicked necklace; Callum, who barely shifted as Brayden wisely dropped to his knee, and me, who offered a slow, wicked smile. He seemed to finally be realising he had escaped the massacre of his kingdom only to run straight into the den of blood-starved wolves.

Callum tensed as Brayden's eyes stayed on me for a moment. Word travels quickly in a palace of bored servants, and he undoubtedly knew it had been me who'd turned his sister's body to ash.

Callum spoke before Brayden could say anything that would end in bloodshed. 'I warned you what would happen if you so much as breathed towards Chiara the wrong way. Don't forget it.' Brayden's attention snapped back to Callum. He blanched but nodded. There was no pity, no softness in Callum's voice as he continued. 'Tell me exactly what happened when you came to Naruzia.'

Brayden stiffened. 'You can't—' Callum raised his brows, and Brayden flinched. 'As I said, we appeared in your palace from Archin. Tali was feeling unwell, and I thought the stress of meeting an enemy king would be too much, so we made our way through the palace—'

'Did you suggest going outside, or did Tali?' Callum interrupted.

'Tali did.'

'And how did you know which way to go?' Callum's finger tapped upon the throne's arm. 'Palaces aren't so easy to navigate that you might've ended up outside by pure chance.'

Brayden frowned. 'Tali led the way. She found a passage that led out to an unguarded exit to the eastern side of the palace.' He hesitated, then added, 'I headed for the back side of the palace. Tali disappeared, and when I found her, she was out the front.'

'It must've been Tali who let the Ankurans in,' Deana said. 'Kailey reported the gate had been unlocked from the inside. None of the guards would've done that, but a seemingly innocent girl who could slip past the guards' defences certainly could.' She shook her head, anger warring with the sorrow of those she'd lost. 'It seems my guards need retraining.'

'You didn't find it suspicious that your younger sister, who's never been to Naruzia, somehow knew the way?' Callum asked.

'W-well…' Brayden glanced to the side. Callum stiffened, and my Gift leapt in my veins, eager to turn my anger into lethality. 'She really did seem unwell.'

'I see. So, you knew something was off – you must have, given she attacked you in Archin – and, when you arrived in my palace, you decided to ignore your suspicions because your sister claimed she was unwell?' Callum's eyes narrowed. 'Or perhaps you thought you might make it out through the palace gates without anyone discovering your presence.'

Brayden winced. 'It didn't seem to be a good idea to wait around. I recognised the palace, and I remember you, Your Majesty. You've never been one to show mercy.'

'You're right. I'm not.' Callum shook his head. 'I suspect that Dearil tried to send you someplace else, but Vitus got to you both first, sending you directly here. This was all a set up from the moment you entered that damned Archin palace.'

'Dearil? Vitus?' Brayden laughed, his hands trembling where he pressed them to his legs. 'You're crazy. Those are the—'

'Do not test my patience, Brayden,' Callum warned, his circlet glinting in the light. 'You're a royal without a family or a kingdom. No one would miss you if you disappeared.'

Brayden shifted where he remained kneeling. 'What would you do in my position? Naruzia is our enemy. For all I know—'

'No,' Callum cut in. Deana straightened at the creeping chill in his voice. I smiled. 'Those who destroyed Archin are your enemies. And you led one of those straight into my palace. Let her open our gates to more of them.'

'I—'

'You have cost me good men and women. Men and women whose recovered bodies were no more than pieces and I had to refuse their families the right to see them. Men and women who did nothing to deserve the death your idiocy brought.'

Brayden cast his gaze down, shame reddening his cheeks. His trembling fingers pressed to the floor. 'I'm—'

'Do not look away from me.' Callum's voice lashed out more viciously than any whip could, the first glimmer of anger breaking through that expression. 'You brought a creature of a god who wants us dead in here. It was her who opened the gates. Every one of those deaths are on you.'

Brayden jerked as though slapped. 'My sister—' he began indignantly.

Callum leaned forward. A slight movement, but the rage in his face sent Brayden staggering to his feet, hands lifting in front of him. 'Your sister is dead. Has been since before you came here. You knew that, deep down, I think. Knew it and chose to believe a lie because it was *easy*. Chose to risk my people for some useless hope that you might be wrong. I could have you executed for that.'

Brayden tried to take a step back, but Deana was behind him. 'Don't,' she warned, and he froze.

Callum continued. 'But if I do, the next in line for the throne is your brother. And you may be worthless, but your brother is something worse. In return, I expect information.'

Brayden's throat worked on a swallow, the candlelight sending flickers of yellow across his pale features. 'Information?'

The air seemed to turn icy as Callum said, 'Yes. The layout of the Archin palace. How many people used to live in the city. Any secrets your kingdom might hold.'

Silence settled as Brayden stared up at us. Even if he was nowhere near the man Callum was, he was still royalty. Loyal to his kingdom above all else. To reveal Archin's secrets to us must seem a betrayal.

But he must've had some semblance of sense, because he slowly dipped his chin. 'All right.'

'Good. You will meet with Commander Lena and Kailey and relay any information they ask for. If I sense you're lying, then that'll be the end of any safety you have in my kingdom. And trust me when I say I *will* find out if you're lying.' Brayden nodded again, his fingers locking together, I suspected to hide their trembling. 'Then we have a deal. You will live, and I will have my information. Once this is over, you can return to Archin and do with it what you wish.'

'Then I'll—'

'I'm not done,' Callum interrupted. 'There may not be a throne left soon. Until we win this war that's beginning, you will stay here. If Naruzia falls, then so will you. If one more of my people is harmed by your actions, then I will see you dead for it. If you try to leave the palace, I will kill you myself. And you will leave this world knowing the same suffering my people did because of you.'

'You're imprisoning me here?'

'Think of it as an extended visit.' Callum smiled coldly, straightening. 'Right now, your kingdom is little more than corpses and a cruel god who would see every mortal dead or enslaved. You're safer here.'

Until you step out of line did not need to be spoken for everyone to hear it. We left Brayden to Kailey, the man shaking with a mixture of indignation and fear in the middle of the throne room, and followed Callum down the corridors to a large, empty space. The room was easily as big as The Den. Every wall was lined with weapons – bows and arrows, axes, swords of every variety, daggers, and more. It was a familiar room to me, one where I had earnt many scars from the brutal training I had been put through.

'What are we here for?' I asked, eyes scanning the room.

Callum's smile did nothing to reassure me. 'We're here to train.'

'I'm perfectly capable of using these weapons, thank you.'

His grin widened. 'Oh, not that sort of training.' He stepped closer. 'You're not confident you can deliver all of us intact to Vitus? We're going to make sure you are.'

I backed away, shaking my head. 'You're going to lose some perfectly good blades.'

'I won't, because you're not going to be trying with weapons.'

My stomach dropped. He had to be joking. I voiced this, and Callum merely stepped into the centre of the room and spread his arms in silent invitation.

'Callum,' I tried again. 'You're the king. When I manage to pull your body into lots of little pieces, there will be no one left to rule.'

'So don't fail.'

Chiara and Jaxon had backed away to the wall, having the same amount of trust in my Gift as I did. Callum didn't shift from his position. I folded my arms across my chest, glowering at him. 'I could try it on Brayden.'

Jaxon spoke up. 'Actually,' he said slowly, eyes flicking between us, 'doing it with Callum is a good idea.'

'Why? Because I want him dead less than I do that idiot?'

'That,' he allowed, 'but also because of the other connection you share.'

I turned my glare on Jaxon. 'What are you on about?'

Jaxon's expression was speculative. 'Kerta told me that she saw something between you when we went to the godly realm. It's faint, given one of you—' He stopped and stared pointedly at me. 'One of you has refused to fully accept it, but it's there. There's a bond between the two of you. A soul-bond.'

I scoffed, shaking my head in disbelief. 'Like between Kerta and Evania? They're both gods. I'm nothing more than a halfling, and Callum is fully mortal.'

Jaxon leant forward. 'Maybe so, but it's there, nonetheless. Why did you not kill Callum when you had the chance? Or at any point over the years? It would have been the perfect vengeance on King Kane.'

'Because my sister would've been killed.' True, yet not. There had been opportunities to seek justice against the king by taking away his son. Times when it could have been done, made to look like an accident. Time on the road to the Niguran forest. Times when I could have let fate do its work.

Yet I never had. Jaxon smiled knowingly at the scowl that crossed my face. Callum merely looked on, seeming unbothered by Jaxon's words.

'And after, when your sister had died?'

'I—' I frowned. I'd had my hand wrapped around his throat at one point, yet I'd let go. And I could've tried to end him that day in the throne room. 'I stabbed him in the chest once,' I argued, folding my arms and thinking back to the night in the tavern with Liam a few doors down when I had driven my blade through his flesh.

'She did,' Callum confirmed, grinning with a baffling amount of pride.

'And yet, he's not dead.' Jaxon leant forward. 'Tell me, Chiara, how many times have you stabbed someone with the purpose of seeing them dead, only for your blow to not be fatal?'

Aside from when Liam had been saved by Vitus, none.

'It's not possible,' I tried again. 'I would've known. I would've realised.'

'Would you have? Most gods don't find their linked soul until at least their second century. They often don't realise the truth until the third, or until something so cataclysmic happens that the soul-bond either pulls taut or rips entirely. You didn't even know soul-bonds existed until we went to the godly realm.' He tilted his head, studying me. 'And I hate to point out the obvious, Chiara, but you're not the most ... attuned with your own emotions.'

I shook my head again, as much to shake my thoughts free of their panicked swirl as in denial. 'What do you know about soul-bonds?'

Jaxon's smile dropped away. 'Plenty. I had one.' He turned away, striding towards the wall of weapons. His fingers skimmed each one, pausing upon a finely crafted arrow. 'And I took it for granted up until someone tore that bond away from me in the cruellest way possible.'

'Who?'

'A young halfling warrior. I met him in my third decade of life in Axania. Did you know the Empire of Axania has a different understanding of gods to us?' Jaxon glanced over his shoulder. He was smiling, but deep sorrow filled his eyes. 'Where we see gods as little more than stories, they see the gods as beings to devote oneself to. Their priests and priestesses have high authority within the empire, their understanding of Gifts being that they're a divine blessing for those destined to be devout believers. Our lands are a place of faithless fools to Axanians. It's why so few ever leave the shores of the empire, for fear that if they are tainted by our ways, the empress will exile them forever.'

He plucked the arrow from the wall, twisting it between his fingers. 'I met Garrett when he was beginning to realise the world was not as small as their empress would have them believe. Garrett was a halfling, the son of Kyrah. We halflings travelled between the two realms far more easily than gods could. But where I was trapped in the godly realm for most of my childhood, Kyrah had sent Garrett to live with his father in Axania. He thought me a heathen, to speak to the gods with such irreverence. I thought him naïve. When we eventually got past our differences, I believed it to only be love. Never thought it was more than what existed between two mortals. Kyrah was the one who eventually told Garrett the truth of the bond between us. She could always see those sorts of things. Kerta had the talent, too – after all, bonds like that often bring about the wars her power thrive in.'

Jaxon shoved the arrow back into its slot before turning to face us. 'We were happy, for a time. We opened small forges in different towns every ten years, so no one grew suspicious of how we didn't age.' His finger tapped against the hilt of his curved blade, the one he had told me was made by a master forger. When he continued, his voice became brittle and cold. 'My mother didn't approve. She went to Vitus and asked him for his assistance. Vitus hated Kyrah for siding with Dearil when the barrier was initially brought down. He had little reason to refuse. One day, I left to travel for more supplies,' he paused, muscles feathering in his jaw, 'by the time I reached our home, it was too late. Vitus ripped my husband's heart from his chest in front of me.'

Jaxon took a step towards me, hands fisting by his side. 'Trust me when I say I know a soul-bond when I see it. And trust me when I say you and your Gift will do everything to prevent it from snapping. Your soul knows what your mind does not. It knows that surviving the severing of a soul-bond with the rest of you intact is impossible.'

You're not the only one wronged by that god. You're not the only one seeking vengeance. Words Jaxon had once spoken rang through my head. It was that which had me relenting a fraction. Not at what he was saying about the bond, but in understanding of the combination of grief and rage in his eyes. This wasn't only my vengeance.

Yet a soul-bond ... it was too much. Another binding tying me to someone.

Even if it didn't feel like a binding should.

'But...' I glanced at Callum, and then away. A strange warmth flooded me. A rightness I didn't dare acknowledge, old fear rising to beat it back down.

Callum said nothing. When I looked back towards him, he was watching me. Observing. Waiting.

'You knew,' I realised, shock flickering through me.

He inclined his head. There was warmth in his expression, in the small upward slant of his mouth, the slight relaxing of his shoulders. All those little tells I hadn't realised I'd been collecting from him.

But there was also fear. Not the same fear I held. Callum had never had the sense to fear being bound to me. This was a fear, I thought, of rejection.

My chest tightened at how easy it'd be to deliver exactly that. To shatter him.

'I guessed,' he corrected. 'Evania told me a little of soul-bonds, and it made a strange sort of sense. And then when I was returning to the mortal realm – I told you about the silver cord I grasped hold of. How it felt of you.'

My thoughts swirled. There'd been a cord present on my journey to the godly realm, too. One of silver wrapped in black. One that'd been startlingly familiar.

As familiar as Callum himself had become to me.

'It's a binding.' I hadn't realised I'd spoken the words aloud until Callum shifted towards me.

He brushed his fingers over my cheek before tucking loose strands of hair behind my ear. My breath hitched at his closeness. 'It's whatever you wish it to be, Captain. You decide what to do with it. Whether we act on it. Ignore it.' He paused, and there was a flicker of pain in his eyes before he said. 'Or spend the rest of our lives after all this far, far apart.'

The thought of that was more terrifying than any bond. I'd only just found him. Only just *let* myself find him. To give him up now would be like tearing away some vital part of myself.

But staying might chain you to him forever, an old part of me whispered. The same part that used to resent being bound to this kingdom and the king that had come before.

Callum was not that king.

'I don't want to ignore it,' I whispered. Fragile hope blossomed in Callum's smile. 'But I don't know what I want with it. Not yet.'

'That's fine.' Callum bent his head, pressing his lips to my forehead. Warmth flushed through me even as Jaxon sighed. Callum and I both ignored him. 'Take all the time you need. And whatever decision you come to – I know it'll be the right one.'

He'd accept it, too. Even if I told him I never wanted to see him again.

I swallowed past the dryness in my mouth. It wasn't just fear that thundered through me. It was something else, too. It was warmth, rightness, and the sense of some vital understanding clicking into place. I couldn't voice that yet, though. Not until I'd had a chance to sort out my thoughts.

Later, I promised myself. When there wasn't a god after our blood and a war brewing, I could think on it further. Decide what I wanted, and what I would accept.

The warmth grew as I met Callum's eyes, finding endless patience in that fear. As though he knew me well enough to know what I needed. That I needed time. Needed to come to the decision on my own. That he'd endure his worry for me.

Perhaps a soul-bond wouldn't be so terrible, I thought.

'I'm not saying I agree it's a soul-bond,' I started, tucking that thought away for later, 'but even if it is, that doesn't mean my Gift will be enough to do what you're suggesting.'

Callum smiled, and it threatened to snatch my breath away with its wickedness. 'How about a challenge?'

'A challenge?' My guard was instantly up. Callum's challenges, I was coming to realise, tended to involve some form of mortal danger. 'What challenge?'

'You try this. If you manage it, I'll owe you a favour. Anything you ask of me, I'll do.'

I tapped a finger upon my knife hilt. 'If I don't manage it, then, what – you die?'

'You'll manage,' Callum said with a confidence I did not possess. 'If you don't try, though, then I'll take the fastest horse I can find and ride out by myself. We both know I'm the better horseman, so there's no chance of you catching up.'

I jerked. The fear that was missing at the mention of the soul-bond flooded through me. Memories of Callum bleeding out on the stairs, his revelation that Vitus could block his Gift, him facing both the god and Liam alone... A chill clawed down my spine. 'Do *not* even joke about that. You'll die if you go.'

Callum shrugged. 'Exactly, so you might as well give this plan a try.'

'I—' I cut off my words, shaking my head sharply. There was some temptation to call his bluff, except I knew him well enough to know that he wasn't bluffing. He held the same regard for his life that I did for mine.

He raised his brows as he waited for an answer.

'I'll try,' I finally gritted out, breath tight in my chest. 'I don't want a favour from you.' I suspected Callum would do most things I asked with or without a favour. And that which he didn't – the things that might put me in danger – he would disregard any previous promises to keep me alive. Instead, I turned to Deana. 'I want a favour from you instead.'

She blinked. 'Me?'

I nodded. 'I already have a favour from Jaxon, courtesy of our fight in the Den. I have a feeling that having one from the king's right-hand woman would come in handy.' And I suspected Callum would grant me almost any favour if I asked for it, deal or not, while ignoring anything I asked that might place me in danger, regardless of favours owed. She considered it before nodding. I sighed, turning back to Callum. 'Any sign that it's not working, and we think of a new plan.'

Everyone nodded. We all knew, though, that there was no other plan. This was our only option. I would succeed, or there was every chance that Vitus would tear the mortal realm to shreds before we could act.

Deana and Jaxon left with my insistence. Their curious eyes made my palms sweat and breaths shallow. Failing was not something I was accustomed to, and I didn't plan to become familiar with it now. And I was also afraid – *terrified* – that Jaxon was wrong. That my Gift would not do as it was supposed to. That, in the end, it would be me that destroyed Callum. I stared at him from across the room. He watched me back, giving nothing away. He did not push me to try, nor did he try to offer advice. He simply waited.

'I don't think this is a good idea,' I warned him for the tenth time, my hands veining with silver before the colour flickered away.

A smile formed on his lips. 'I never said it was a *good* idea. It's our only idea. Just try taking us to the kitchens.'

I huffed out a biting laugh. 'Great. I'm about to commit regicide because we're that desperate.'

Callum made his way across the room, stopping before me. He grasped my hands in his as the silver crackled over my skin once more. Raising one to his chest, he pressed my palm flat. 'Feel that?'

I eyed him sceptically. 'Your heartbeat?'

He remained unperturbed at my unimpressed tone. 'Yes. Do you know what you're going to feel after you try this?'

'Whatever pieces of you I manage to sprinkle around the room?'

Callum's eyes narrowed, but his lips twitched at the corner. 'Pessimistic today, aren't we?' I scowled, attempting to pull my hand away. He held me fast. 'No, Captain. You're not going to do that. Once you try this, you'll feel this very same heartbeat.' His smile broadened to a more roguish one. 'And, if you're lucky, I'll let you feel whatever else you want.'

I swallowed my laughter, some of my trepidation fading. 'Who said I want to feel anything else?'

Callum smirked, eyes tracing the flush that stole across my cheeks and down my neck. The prick of his eyes only served to deepen that flush. 'I think we both know you do.' His smile fell away, gaze becoming more intent. 'I trust you, Chiara. You need to trust yourself.'

Trust. Such a delicate thing. So easily broken. I'd learnt that from my very first memories, and yet … yet, when Callum looked at me like that, like I was the only thing that made sense in this chaotic world, I felt it. Felt what trust should be, the small kernel of warmth that settled in my chest. Felt what it might be like to trust in myself as much as he did.

'I promise you, you will do fine,' Callum murmured into the quiet. 'And I've learnt not to make promises I can't keep.'

Sighing, I gave in, letting his touch centre me. Power crackled beneath my skin. Silver light flickered at my fingertips, spreading in size until it enveloped my whole hand, then my whole body, then Callum, too. *Imagine where you want to be*, Kerta had told me. Closing my eyes, I pictured the kitchens, warm from the cooking fire, the scent of bread surrounding me. Pull the fabric of the realms together and step across to where I wanted to go. The Gift did not feel like a creature caged in my body this time. It felt like a hand holding mine, like the press of lips that obliterated all else around, like the gentlest of words whispered in my ear. It felt like warmth and hope. It felt like Callum. Suddenly, he was all I could think about. Him holding me last night. His fingers tangling in my hair, his lips against my skin.

'Focus, Chiara,' Callum whispered, his fingers tightening in mine. 'And remember to trust yourself.' So, holding him tight, I did. I stepped. Dizziness washed over me, my eyes cracking open to a whirl of silver. Within seconds, the silver died away, the dizziness disappearing with it.

'This doesn't look like the kitchens,' Callum murmured. I stared around the room, recognising the rumpled bed we'd left unmade and the pile of books upon his table. 'Did you mean to bring us here?'

'Yes.' I put as much conviction as I could into the word.

'Liar.'

I didn't deny it, letting a smile play on my lips. 'I think the fact you're not dead should forgive me any missteps.'

'What now?' Callum asked.

The Broken

'Now,' I said, voice resolute, 'we do it again.'

The next few days fell into a routine. The days were spent training – transporting Callum and I until I could bring us to any place in the palace, then the city, then around Naruzia. Kerta had been right when she had spoken of the limits of transporting people. I could move books up to ten times without breaking a sweat. But with people, every trip exhausted me, my Gift flickering weakly until I had rested for a while. The most I could manage was two consecutive times, and that nearly knocked me off my feet.

Once I was confident enough, I brought Jaxon, and then Deana, along with me. It seemed, though, that the pool of my power only extended to the four of us. We tried surreptitiously to add in a guard – one of the seven who had replaced those who had been slain – without them noticing. My Gift didn't even make a showing. I also couldn't manage it unless I had physical contact with all I was transporting. Any distance between us and it was a choice – me, or them.

The training always held an undercurrent of urgency. We couldn't rush into action, not when we didn't know the extent of Vitus's forces. Deana sent a small group of her finest spies to Archin. We should wait at least three weeks, she told us, to see if we could sneak out any information before making our next move. Even so, we were all aware the god would only wait so long before making his next move. Callum met with the nobility and generals within the army, giving commands to station guards in every town and keep an eye out for golden-veined people. He only gave the necessary details. There was no telling the panic that would ensue if people learnt we faced the threat of a god.

The tension of the days was balanced by the moments we

managed to snatch away together at night. When Jaxon and Deana retired to their rooms after practice and plotting, Callum and I retired to his. Sometimes, we simply curled up on the bed together, his breath soft against my neck as we fell asleep. Other times, we didn't do much sleeping at all.

On the fifth morning, the first news of war reached the palace halls. Kaliksa, a town on the outskirts of Naruzia, had been ransacked and pillaged. Only one survivor remained to bring news to the king. The man the guard brought into the throne room, a butcher nearing his sixtieth year, came in with a hacking cough that brought up blood. An old illness, he told us, that had persisted for two years. The warmth that spun through my belly told me he had little time left. I could imagine Vitus laughing at us at the irony. The only survivor was a man days off his death, golden lines carved across his chest.

The story the man told was a horrific one. Young girls – ranging from three to twenty years old – had been going missing sporadically over the past few months. The town's guards set off in search of each. Wherever a girl was last seen, a patch of blood and new growth of grass or flowers were all that remained. When they'd come back a week ago, it was considered a miracle from the gods. When they began tearing out the throats of their families, gorging themselves on blood and flesh before turning on the rest of the town, they all realised it was a nightmare.

The man spoke of a golden-armoured man with the face of a king, and the brown-haired lad who rode with him. How they strolled through the carnage. How they gave him a message for the current king after carving lines into him on how this would be the fate of all if we did not deliver ourselves to the Ballaronia palace.

I shuddered at the news, nausea roiling through me. Deana turned away, tears shining in her eyes, while Jaxon stormed from the room. Only Callum maintained his calm, nodding and urging the man to continue. When he'd finished, Callum attempted to heal him, my hand on his back as he shuddered with the agony of his memories. His shadows shot forth, crossing the man's skin. We waited a heartbeat. Then another.

The man had reeled back with a yelp, golden light flashing across the wounds on his chest.

Not wounds, I realised as I stared. Markings of some kind. Something that was preventing Callum from using his Gift.

'It didn't work,' Callum said, staring at his hands and blinking. The man let out a chesty cough, illness still racking his body. Nothing had been healed, I realised.

At last, Callum stepped back.

'Go to the nearest healers. Tell them that anything they charge will be at the Crown's cost,' he ordered.

The man stared for a moment at Callum before shaking his head. 'Thank you, Your Majesty, but I ain't going to do that.'

'Why not?'

''Cause there's no one left to live for.'

The man left before Callum could reply. Callum's whole body tensed as he seemed ready to chase down the man.

'Let him go.' Deana was the one who spoke. 'He needs to heal wounds that are deeper than that sickness. A king chasing him down and ordering him to get help will do nothing.'

Callum stared stonily at the space where the butcher had stood, shaking his head slowly. 'I couldn't do anything,' he whispered into the quiet, voice hoarse. 'I'm finally able to use this damned Gift, and I couldn't heal him. It was like there was a wall between me and it.'

'Vitus.' Jaxon guessed. His eyes were also trained on where the man had stood. 'Your bloodline is Gifted by him. And those markings on the man's chest – I recognised them.'

'And you didn't say anything?' Deana demanded.

'It's been a while since I've seen them, so it took a while to recognise. He glanced at Callum. 'Those are wards. Wards designed to stop any Gift from entering his body. It wasn't your Gift's failure. It was Vitus's plan to stop you healing anyone.'

It was a cruel thing to do. Incredibly cruel, and incredibly calculated. Vitus had offered Callum a survivor, let him hope that one good thing could come out of the massacre of the town, only to tear it away.

On the sixth day, the smaller town of Porias suffered a similar fate. All children were Ankuran, all between four and five. This time, the survivor came with a death wound through her abdomen, a gaping wound where a clear baby-bump showed. From the size of it and the way she clutched her belly and cried, refusing to speak of it, it seemed that the unborn babe had been ripped from her while she was still alive. She shouldn't have lasted so long. None of us believed it a miracle, though. As soon as Callum tried to heal the woman, it was as though whatever had granted her extra life crumbled away. She collapsed dead at our feet.

On the seventh day, Callum called two of the army generals and Commander Lena to the throne room.

'What's the status at the border, Jakob?' Callum demanded, staring down at a gruff-faced man of thirty.

'Not good, Your Majesty.' General Jakob rose from where he'd knelt upon entering. His clothes held signs of days of travel, dirt smudging the coarse fabric. The crooked bend of his nose and the scar slashing across a milky eye suggested he was the type to lead from the front – a stark difference to the generals I'd served under, who'd always given commands from the safety of the rear. 'I stationed two companies out there under Captain Henri and Captain Jadea. Jadea reported in a day ago. There's no active pushing of the border like there was during the war with Archin, but it seems the enemy has been employing guerrilla tactics, often targeting the smaller squads or slipping past and attacking the northern towns.'

'That doesn't make sense,' Callum said, his finger tapping the arm of his throne. 'Their forces should be ample enough to engage in full-on war. Why use that approa—'

'Fear,' I cut in. The word echoed through the throne room and everyone turned to me. The second general, General Olisker, narrowed his eyes, his neatly trimmed beard seeming to bristle with irritation at my interruption. I ignored him, focusing on Callum as I continued. 'Our enemy hates mortals. He doesn't simply want to wipe out this realm. He wants us to suffer. What better way than spreading fear? If he targets those towns – drags out a few, sends them back as Ankurans – it won't be long before families and friends stop trusting one another.'

'Vitus also wants the barrier down before he proceeds with his plans,' Jaxon added. 'He's not at full strength, and he's the sort of god who doesn't engage unless he's sure of his—'

'God?' Olisker let out a biting laugh. He turned to Callum and his clear disdain had me stiffening. Callum laid a hand on my arm, stilling me before I could step forward. 'Your father always said you were prone to flights of fancy, Your Majesty, but believing a god is—'

'What of Henri?' Callum asked sharply, cutting Olisker off.

Jakob scratched at his chin as Lena smirked at the rage mottling Olisker's cheeks at the interruption. 'No word from him, Your Majesty. There hasn't been in three days.'

'Henri's typically prompt with his communication,' Deana murmured to Callum's other side. 'If there's been no communication—'

'Henri is nothing more than a commoner,' Olisker sneered. I took in his pristine uniform and unblemished skin. Next to Jakob, and even Lena, who bore several bruises along her jaw, he seemed more like a man playing dress-up than a true general of the army.

'You can't trust someone like him. Allowing commoners to rise in rank in the army was one of the few mistakes your father made.'

'My father made many mistakes,' Callum said, voice crackling with ice, 'But that's not one of them.'

'I understand why you'd think that.' Olisker's voice dripped with false sympathy. 'Your father didn't have time to teach you all he should've, but there's a reason his council only consisted of nobility.' He stared pointedly at Jakob, Lena, me and then over to Jaxon. 'I think—'

'That will be all for today, Olisker. You may go.'

Olisker's jaw dropped, indignation flaring in his eyes. 'Your Majesty, you must take the counsel—'

'*Silence*,' Callum commanded, and both Lena and Jakob shifted a step away from Olisker. 'I am not here to deal with your petty gripes. You only retained your position because of your links to the nobility, and it was less work than dealing with the fallout of your exile or execution. Do not make me second guess that choice.'

'Your M—'

'Guards,' Callum called. The doors to the throne room opened, and Corin and Kailey stalked forward. They crossed an arm over their chest and bowed low to Callum. 'Please escort Olisker out of the palace grounds.'

'Your Majesty!' Olisker cried, outraged. 'You must consider the ramifications—'

'What I must consider is my people.' Callum rose, his shadow looming down the steps of the dais as he descended them, striding slowly, coming to a stop before Olisker. 'I must consider the threat brewing, and how to best protect my kingdom. I do *not* need to consider your feelings or that of the nobility.'

'The nobility hold much of the power! If you anger me, you anger all of them.'

'That's fine,' Callum said, a smile spreading. For the first time,

Olisker flinched, finally seeming to realise that the man before him was not some poor imitation of the tyrant king who'd preceded him. No, Callum was the sort of ruler to protect those he'd sworn to by any means necessary. And when it came to his enemies, he would be far, far worse than Kane ever could have been. 'If angering you angers the nobility, then I suppose I'll have to remove the threat altogether.'

'Your Majesty—'

'Perhaps I should start with you.' Callum rested a hand upon Olisker's shoulder, fingers squeezing tight enough that Olisker paled with the pain. 'What do you say? Should we find out what colour nobility bleeds today?'

'N-no, Your Majesty. I will take my leave and do as you say.'

Corin and Kailey lead a terrified Olisker from the throne room as Callum walked back up to his throne and reseated himself as though nothing had happened.

'Your Majesty,' General Jakob began slowly, 'I'm not sure upsetting Olisker was the best move. He's a bastard, but he does have power over the other two generals.'

'I know.' Callum drummed his finger against the throne's arm. 'He'll no doubt run to them and speak of my threat. I know their sort – they followed my father because of their fear. There's no time to win them over now, so that fear that I'll be the same will have to keep them in line until we stop the threat of Vitus.' Jakob smiled for the first time, a hint of respect showing upon his features, as Callum turned to Commander Leda. 'What of the city guard?'

'They've been doing their best to search for any with signs of the golden infection, Your Majesty,' she said, snapping to attention. 'Most seem willing to believe it's a sickness that turns people feral.'

We'd decided that only those with high enough ranks needed to know the threat we faced. Panic was as insidious a beast as any force could be. There was no telling the havoc news of what we were facing could wreak. 'Have they brought many in?'

Lena shook her head. 'Only three so far. It seems the targets are currently the towns rather than Alluvite itself.'

'Keep an eye out. The last thing we need is for an outbreak of Ankurans to run rampant in the city.'

Jakob and Lena bowed low to Callum before exiting the room. The moment they left, Callum sighed, his stiff posture slumping. Deep shadows were carved under his eyes. I'd woken that morning to find him gone from his room, despite the sun only just beginning to trickle its light beyond the horizon. He hadn't returned to the rooms until late in the night, too.

'Why do you think Vitus isn't targeting Alluvite?' Deana asked, turning to us.

'The same reason he's not attacking us head on. To show us he has complete control over the situation,' Jaxon said, seating himself upon the ground. He bore the same signs of fatigue we all did, though not as bad as Callum. 'He manages to get Ankurans through the city to the palace, yet hasn't attacked anyone outright in the city. He's trying to show there's no point in defying him.'

Before any of us could answer, the throne room door cracked open once more. Kailey appeared, her features pale. 'We've had one of those ... visitors, Your Majesty. The ones you told us to bring to you if they appeared at the gates.'

We all tensed. Callum pressed his lips into a thin line before nodding. 'Bring them in.'

Kailey opened the door wider, Harris and Corin standing to either side of a boy of around eight. Golden veins twisted their way through smears of blood. Red stained his hair, his thick, dark lashes, even his teeth. There were rotting, lumpy bits stuck to his shirt, like he had feasted on a carcass and not bothered to clean himself up. I tried not to think too much on how he smiled knowingly at us, and said in a sweet, soft voice, 'My little sister wanted a hug when I came home,' when he spotted us staring at the gore.

Corin blanched while Harris visibly shuddered.

'Leave us,' Callum ordered. The guards quickly complied as the Ankuran came forward.

He dipped into a mock bow, eyes glinting with amusement at the stony expressions we all wore. 'You should protect your villages better, Your Majesty.' The boy straightened, his body going eerily still for a child of that age. The previous traces of Kane's voice that had been present in Vitus's puppets had all but disappeared, leaving only the god's domineering tones behind. 'Carmile's villagers were so happy to see their sons returned to them alive. Ecstatic, even, until the moment we tore into them.'

'If that's all you came here to say, then I've heard plenty already,' Callum bit out. He glanced up at Deana who stepped forward, a sword appearing in her hand.

The Ankuran clicked his tongue. 'So *impatient*, false king. You should listen to my message first.'

'I have no interest in—'

The Ankuran paid Callum no heed, turning his golden eyes to me. 'Little raven,' he crooned, taking a step towards me, 'How high you have risen. One step from the false king; at his side.' He grinned, baring those bloody teeth as he shifted his attention back to Callum. 'And who will you rule, false king, once all your people are dead?'

Callum's features tightened, his hand dropping to the pommel of his sword. 'Enough of your games.'

Any pretence of civility dropped from the child's face. He snapped his teeth like a wild animal before saying, 'We will be at the Archinian palace tomorrow evening. We know you've been practising using that lovely weapon that stands at your side, and she can get you there. If you and your raven woman aren't there, then the rivers of blood your pathetic kingdom drowns in will be of your own doing.'

A flicker of hopeless rage flickered into Callum's eyes. I did not hesitate when I saw it – the fury and the guilt as Callum stared at the child who had once been his citizen. I struck, my blade slamming into the child's forehead. Gold spattered on the marble. The smile remained even as the child toppled backwards, his skin rotting with the time that had passed since his death. By the time he hit the floor, he was little more than bones and decaying flesh, spread across the tiles like a gruesome artwork.

Callum stood, hands clenched at his side. Without a word or a glance, he strode through the doors, leaving the throne room echoing with his absence.

Hours later, Deana, Jaxon and I argued in one of the smaller rooms.

'It's a trap.' Jaxon said yet again, fists pressed against the tabletops 'We'd be fools to go.'

'Clearly, it's a trap,' Deana snapped back. She was on her feet, pacing the length of the room. 'But what are we supposed to do?'

'We need to—' I started, leaning forward in the chair. Before I could finish my sentence, the doors swung and Callum strode in.

'It is a trap,' he agreed. Any trace of guilt was wiped from his expression, his face a mask of brutal resolve. 'Which is why I'm going in alone.'

The three of us stopped our arguing, Deana halting her pacing mid-step to gape at Callum. My heart skipped a beat, a combination of anger and fear curling tight around me. Silver began to crackle upon my skin, my Gift riled up by my emotions. 'You can't be serious.'

Callum didn't look at me, keeping his eyes firmly fixed on

Deana and Jaxon. 'I am. We know he wants Chiara dead. We know he wants the wall between his realm and ours down. We know he expects us to either ignore him completely or all appear in that palace.' Callum took a deep breath. 'Which is why I should go alone. I am not the one he truly wants, but maybe I can get close enough to hurt him. And if I don't, if he slaughters me, it doesn't further his plans in any way.'

'We don't even know his plans!' The words lanced through the air, filled with rage. It was not my usual sort of anger – the sort made of ice shards and knives. This was hot. Wild. Desperate. I pressed my fingers into my palm, trying to wrangle control over my emotions. 'All we know is he wants us dead or captured, and that he's trying to bring down the barrier between our world and his to reclaim his power. For all we know, maybe he needs to sacrifice the life of one of his own Gifted.'

'Chiara.' I bristled at the gentleness in Callum's voice as he finally looked at me. 'If he needed that, he would've killed Liam already. He's had no qualms about killing everyone else.'

'That doesn't mean you won't end up dead! He might be trying to take back his power from you by killing you. Did you consider that?'

'I did,' Callum said in the same aggravating tone. 'And I still believe this is the best option.'

'You haven't explained why you think your idea is a good one, or even a real option at all.' Deana said, ice coating her words.

For the first time since entering the room, ire rolled across Callum's expression. There was a shakiness to his next words as his clasped hands tightened, whitening at the knuckles. 'Because,' he said, voice low, 'If I don't go by myself, then you'll all go. And we haven't come up with any plan that will end with us all alive.'

'No one likes a martyr, Cal,' Jaxon drawled.

'Maybe not, but Chiara is our last chance against Vitus. If she goes, if she falls into his trap, then this realm is doomed.'

I sucked in a breath that was half laugh, half choked gasp for air. Fear turned me cruel as I spat out, 'It's about saving this realm, then. Sacrifice yourself so I can sacrifice myself at a later date.'

Any impassivity dropped away entirely as Callum exploded to his feet. The chair he had been sitting on rocked back, crashing to the floor. 'Gods, Chiara!' he shouted, and I flinched at the words. Flinched at how the anger in them struck me more surely than a fist could have. 'Of course it's not about the fucking realms. It's about you. It's about how, when Evania showed me the future, it wasn't the death of the world that shook me to my core. That made me go against every vow I'd made to myself and try to use my Gift again. It was your death at Vitus's hand that I saw first. It's about how every breath I take, every time I close my eyes, every time my heart even beats, it does it for you. It's about how every time I think of Vitus and my father, every time I even think Liam's name and about how he used you, I want to let this world burn if it means you'll be safe.'

He took a step towards me, shadows churning in his eyes. 'I would ruin myself for you, Chiara. I will let my soul be dragged into the Dark if there's even the possibility that you'll be safe. So, no, it's not the realm I'm going for. It's you.'

Silence followed his words as his chest heaved raggedly. He wasn't avoiding my gaze anymore. He was staring right at me. Letting me see my own pain, my own fear, reflected in him.

'I take back most of the things I said about him,' Jaxon whispered in my ear, elbow nudging into my side. 'You have my blessing to be with him.'

I wasn't capable of looking away from Callum, but Deana knew what I needed all the same. She hauled Jaxon from the room just as I stepped towards Callum, closing the distance between us.

'And you don't think I would do the same?' Heat laced my words as I jabbed my finger into his chest with every word. 'You don't think I would sacrifice myself, curse myself to a miserable existence, for you?'

Callum's eyes flared, but he shook his head slowly. 'Chiara, you don't have to… I know you care for me, but it's not the same.'

'The same as what?' I challenged.

He ran a hand through his hair, fingers catching in golden-blonde strands. When he spoke, his voice was quiet. 'Love. It's not the same as love.'

My heart faltered in my chest. I stared up at him, warmth and sorrow mingling in a confusing combination. I'd known, I realised, for quite some time. Had recognised that the way he treated me – the way he protected me, even after all my moments of selfishness, after all the horrible things I'd done – had to be more than simply caring for me. But I hadn't wanted to admit it. Not because I didn't want him to love me, but because I knew what love made a person do. Knew what I'd done for Cassie, what I'd allowed myself to turn into.

And now all my fears were being realised with this foolish plan of his. 'You shouldn't.'

'Why not?'

I wanted to look past him, at the wall beyond. When I tried, though, I found it impossible to look away. The words I found, clear and logical, were not the ones that burst out. 'Because I won't see you ruined for me! Love is a burden, Callum. And I don't know if I can bear it.'

'This isn't about you loving me.' Callum's face was not its usual mask. It was a window, every tic of his jaw, every movement of his lips, revealing far too much. 'This is about how I feel. How, when I am away from you, I feel as though I've been ripped in two. It's about how, when you were gone, I didn't go one minute without thinking of you. Not of what kissing you might feel like, or holding you, but of *you*. Of your smile, your laugh, how unforgivingly strong you are. It's about how I would be lost if you were to be taken from me. It has nothing to do with what you feel for me.'

'But it does.' The words fell from my lips like raindrops fell from white clouds – soft, barely there, and entirely unexpected. 'Because if what you feel is love, I must – I'm a mirror when it comes to this, Callum. Everything you said is—' I broke off. I couldn't yet speak those final words. Couldn't tell him what I had come to recognise – that, at some point, I had fallen hard and fast, and there would be no coming back from it.

Callum reached for me. His fingers traced the shape of my jaw, lingering under my chin as he gently tilted my head so I was looking directly at him. 'I don't expect you to say anything. I just needed you to know. To understand.' He sighed, shaking his head. 'That's not what we were talking about, though.'

'No. We were talking about how you're being an idiot.'

Callum smiled as though I was being endearing. 'It's the only logical choice, and you know it.'

Any of the rawness of moments before vanished, replaced by a fresh flood of anger. 'I *don't* know it. You are the king. It's your job as king to use the tools at your disposal. To put others on the front line.' I gestured at myself, at the silver I brought to the surface of my skin. 'I was taught by your father to be a weapon. I hated it, but I'd accepted it, and then you had the gall to show me that there's more to me than just death and destruction. That there are people in this realm who deserve to be saved. This is something I need to do. This is how I can do some good with my Gift – by destroying the monsters who took my sister from me.'

Callum closed his eyes, forehead furrowing. 'Chiara…'

I cupped his cheeks in my hands. *Love.* Such a simple word for the unthinkable force it was. Enough of a force that something had tangled inside me, tightening to the point of strangulation at the thought of him going alone, of him dying and leaving me behind.

Callum's eyes opened, meeting mine. 'You have to let me help. We will go together. We will fight him together.' He opened his mouth to interject, but I shook my head fiercely. 'No. Promise me. Promise me that you'll let me have my vengeance.' *That you won't face this alone,* I added silently.

I could see the hesitation in his eyes as he took in my words. 'You do help,' he murmured. He took one of my hands, pressing his lips to it. 'In every way that matters.'

'So do you,' I said fiercely, trying to make him believe.

'Fine.' He sighed. 'I will promise you that, if you promise me that you'll forget any notion of selflessness and will save yourself if things get too heated.'

'They won't.' I set my jaw stubbornly, staring him down. He did not balk at the ferocity of my gaze, meeting it with the same intensity.

'Promise me anyway, Captain.' A thumb brushed over my cheek, featherlight. 'For my own peace of mind.'

I rolled my eyes, even as something warmed within me at his words. 'Fine. I promise I will be the most selfish, horrible person there is if things go to shit.'

'Thank you for that gracious vow.'

I scoffed in response, shifting away from him, but Callum held me in place. He was gentle enough that I could easily break away if I wanted to. His eyes drifted down to where he held me as if he, too, realised that. And realised that I did not move away at all. His smile was a beautiful thing, unfolding on his lips and bringing light into his eyes. 'Gods, I love you, Chiara.' I opened my mouth to object, but he shook his head. 'No. Let me finish. I have loved you since the moment I saw you. Loved you in a way that stole my breath and hurt my soul. And I would've loved you for a thousand years, a million years more if you'd let me.'

My breath hitched. 'And now?'

The smile Callum gave me was full of an ache so earnest it seemed it was my soul that throbbed with the pain of it. There was a hint of something else there in the slight tightness at the corner of his mouth, the way his eyes darkened, not just with want but with a deep regret. 'And now I would love you for that long if this world allowed us.' His fingers trailed a fiery path down my skin. 'But if there is anything I have learnt, it's that time holds for no man.'

I leant forward, pressing my forehead to his. For all I cared, we could have been in the middle of the marketplace or back in the Niguran forest. In this moment, there was Callum and there was me. There was peace.

'I don't deserve your love,' I whispered in the quiet between us, 'but I'm glad for it all the same.'

'I've told you before, Captain. You deserve everything.' Callum's lips pressed against my forehead, tender and sweet. My body shuddered with the sensation as those gentle kisses trailed lower and lower, over the bridge of my nose, every kiss ruining me. As he hooked me in his arms, I was complete. It was me and Callum and no one else. Nothing else existed except us.

For a while, I allowed myself to fall into the peace of Callum's embrace. Time trickled by, slipping elusively through my fingers as I attempted to force it to halt. But, as Callum had said, time holds for no man. At last, I shifted, angling my face towards his. 'I'm sorry.'

He pulled away from me, his hand sliding down to my waist. 'What for?'

'For blaming you for Cassie's death.' I lifted my hand, cupping his cheek. 'I should've apologised a long time before.'

His exhale tickled the underside of my wrist. 'You don't need to—'

'I do,' I said firmly. I knew we'd spoken of it before – knew he'd moved past it long before I had – but I'd never properly apologised for it. 'I wasted so much time between us. I wasn't the only one who lost things that day. You did, too. And then you were thrust into a throne you didn't want, faced with a war unlike any this realm has ever seen, and I wasn't there for you.'

Callum turned into my hand, pressing a kiss to my palm before shifting onto an elbow. 'Grief does terrible things to us all.'

'I'm fairly certain most people don't grieve by threatening kings and committing violent acts throughout the city.'

'You've always been special.' He twisted a lock of my hair around his finger, giving it a light tug. 'And I happen to love your particular brand of violence.'

My chest warmed at how casually he threw in that word – *love*. Callum settled back down, tugging me over so my head was rested on his chest. 'If memory serves me correctly, I wasn't the only violent one in the months that followed. Didn't you execute a number of your father's men? And you were the one who sent the rest to me.'

His fingers traced circles on the back of my shoulder. 'I'm the king. It's within my rights to do so.'

I tipped my head back, lips curling upwards. 'Legal violence is still violence.'

'Are you saying you disapprove?'

'No,' I said, settling back on him. His chest rose and fell evenly beneath me, his warmth wrapping around me. 'I happen to love your brand of violence as well.'

My cheeks darkened as I realised what I'd said – how easily the love had slipped out. Callum made a satisfied noise, his fingers dipping lower to trail along my back. 'You should get some sleep. Gods know you've had far too little of it in recent weeks.'

'You're one to talk,' I retorted, rising yet again and pointedly staring at the shadows under his eyes. 'You're always gone before I wake.'

He smiled, his cheeks dimpling. 'Kings don't need sleep.'

'Kings are as mortal as the rest of us.' I paused, then corrected, 'And more mortal than some of us.'

'Mortal or not, you look exhausted,' Callum said, tugging me back down. 'I'll sleep when you do.'

I snorted. 'Knowing you, you'll slip out to complete whatever duties await you the moment I sleep.'

'I promise I won't.'

'But—'

His hand slid over my eyes, blocking out all light. With anyone else, I would've leapt away. There was something comforting about the darkness with Callum's arm wrapped around me, though. Something safe. 'Sleep, captain.'

I huffed out a breath but allowed my eyes to close all the same. There were a few long moments of silence before I shifted, Callum's hand remaining where it was as he sighed. 'People are usually still when they sleep.'

I pried his fingers apart, just enough that I could catch a glimpse of him between them. 'After all this is over, I'm going to tell you.'

'Tell me what?'

'How I feel.' I closed his fingers again, encasing myself in the warm darkness. 'But not until I'm sure I won't lose you.'

The mattress shifted under me as Callum lay down, his arm wrapping around me. There was an odd note to his voice as he said, 'All right. After everything's over, then.'

Smiling, I curled into his side, letting the gentle sound of his breathing lull me into the hazy zone between wakefulness and slumber. I could spend an eternity like this, I realised, as my thoughts began to muddle. Could spend the rest of my life alone with Callum, listening to the rhythm of his heart and allowing myself to relax in a way I never had before.

My mind began to drift off, seeking the serenity of sleep. It wasn't until I teetered on the precipice of unconsciousness, too far gone to haul myself back from it, that I realised Callum's omission. He'd never promised me he wouldn't go to Vitus alone.

Chapter Thirty-One

I woke to an empty bed and a tight knot of dread.
I've learnt the hard way not to make promises I can't keep. Callum had spoken those very words to me only a few days ago. He hadn't made a promise not to go off by himself yesterday. Instead, he had distracted me with beautiful words and gentle touches. *He wouldn't*, I tried to tell myself as I quickly freed myself from the sheets. I yanked my clothes on, not caring about their crumpled state as my heart pounded in my chest.

He wouldn't, I assured myself as I yanked open the doors, nearly colliding with two surprised-looking guards. When I questioned them, one turning pale at the harshness in my voice, both told me they hadn't seen the king.

He wouldn't, I pleaded to myself as I raced down the corridors, questioning every servant and guard I came across only to have apologetic shrugs meet my questions.

But I knew Callum. Knew what he was willing to sacrifice for me. And I knew he most definitely would.

'Kailey!' I called, spotting the young guard stationed at the doors to the throne room. Slamming to a stop, I forced my Gift back, its frenetic energy threatening to break free. 'Have you seen the king?'

'Afraid not,' she said apologetically. 'Shift change was two hours ago. The guards from earlier might know where he went if he left. Marcus should be back by midday if—'

'Jaxon and Deana,' I interrupted, urgency thrumming through me. Midday was too long. Every minute I wasted here was too long. 'Where are they?'

'I think the commander is in the kitchens,' Kailey said. I whirled, sprinting off without another word. It took me mere minutes to slam into the kitchens, a startled kitchen girl letting out a scream as I burst past her and through the doors. Deana sat at the table, her head tipped back and a laugh pealing. The grin on Jaxon's face near split his face in two, his eyes gleaming as though making her laugh was the greatest achievement he'd accomplished in three hundred years. Both looked up as I entered.

'Finally, you've—' Jaxon began.

'Where's Callum?' I demanded, eyes raking the room as though I might find him lurking in the shadows. All I found were a small collection of dishes, a fire that crackled every few breaths I took, and a pot bubbling away over the top. My breathing quickened.

'I thought he was with you?' Deana asked, eyebrows pinching together.

I shook my head once, the haphazard braid I had done in a rush already coming loose. 'He didn't promise,' I said, the words punching free. My fingers trembled as I tried to order my thoughts into coherent words. 'I asked him to promise me, and he didn't, and I didn't notice, and now—'

'Chiara,' Jaxon said firmly, half risen from his chair. 'Slow down. What's happened?'

Dull pain throbbed where my jaw clenched. I glared at him. 'I can't slow down! There's no time to slow down.'

'Make the time.' Jaxon grasped my shoulder and forced me onto a stool. As soon as I sat, restlessness settled in my limbs, begging me to stand again, to take action. He slid across from me, pushing an apple that I ignored over the table. 'Now, tell me what's happened.'

I took a fortifying breath, pressing my eyes shut. He was right. We would get nowhere until I managed to explain in a way that they understood. My battlefield instincts slammed into place, the panic separating from my mind enough that I could speak. 'Yesterday, I asked Callum to promise me not to go by himself to Vitus. He didn't promise anything. When I woke up this morning, he was gone.'

'That's all?' Jaxon asked.

'No, that's not all!' I burst out, my eyes flying open. I couldn't quite explain it — how something in me had pulled taut, taut enough that I feared it would snap with the lightest of touches. That I knew Callum would have promised me if he hadn't planned to go off on some half-brained plan to spare me. I jumped to my feet, silver sparking around me. Jaxon and Deana backed up a step as I glared. 'If you don't believe me, then I'll head to Archin by myself. That must be where Vitus has him.'

'We believe you!' Deana raised her hands as silver began to swirl around me, ready to transport me to Archin. 'But if you go by yourself, you'll just be playing into Vitus's hands.'

I pulled the power back to me but did not let it fall away entirely. 'Then what do you suggest?' Frustration built. 'Every moment we waste here is a moment where Callum is alone.'

'First, we need to figure out how he's gone to Archin,' Jaxon said, eyeing the silver warily. 'It's unlikely he's reached Archin yet — it's more than a day's ride to the border. If you use your Gift to travel there, there's every chance we'll have to save you instead of Callum.'

Deana launched to her feet, her expression falling into cold calm. 'He must have taken a horse. We should head for the stables, see what time he left.'

I nodded brusquely, even as everything inside me itched with the need to take action now. Deana took the lead. We were close to the entrance to the palace when the first wave of pain hit. The tautness I had been feeling since waking up pulled tighter, spreading a sharp, shooting wave of fire through my abdomen and up to my chest. It was agonising, like something was trying to tear free of my very soul. I pressed a splayed hand against the stark white wall, my breaths coming in shallow pants as the pain slowly ebbed. Black spots blurred in my vision as I fought to regain my strength. Jaxon and Deana had halted, turning back to look at me with concern.

'Everything okay?' Deana asked, taking a step towards me.

I shook my head, straightening my body slightly. The pain was gone, but the tautness was not. 'It's like my Gift is being ripped free, or perhaps trying to keep something from tearing away,' I said, forcing my breaths to slow and steady. 'It's gone n—'

Another wave of pain, this one more intense. Breath hissed between my teeth as I struggled to get any air in. Gods, this was agony. It was like acid being poured over my skin, into my blood and veins. Everything was burning. I sank to the floor, muscles trembling. My fingers blanched against the floor, barely managing to stop me from toppling. My vision wavered I had been wrong. This wasn't simply my Gift acting up. This was a shattering. A wrenching of me, towards something – someone – else. I could barely breathe, barely *think* past it as it engulfed me. Then light was flaring in my vision, forming a long thread before me. I squeezed my eyes shut, but even in the darkness I could see it – a silver rope braided with shadows. The rope shook and trembled, the agony seeming to roll down its length to collide with me. The shadows within it writhed, shuddering as though they, too, could feel my pain.

Again, as suddenly as it had come on, the pain disappeared. I gulped down a breath before carefully unfurling myself from my position. My muscles ached. Deana knelt beside me, a steadying hand pressed to my back. She glanced up at Jaxon. 'Do you think it's Vitus?' she asked, her voice thrumming with anxiety. 'We need to catch up to Callum. Maybe you can transport us to Carishmere or one of the other towns so we can intercept him. Even if he can't heal you with his Gift, he'll know what to do.'

My stomach hollowed out at the paleness of Jaxon's face, and the way his eyes flared with worry. And that pain – that consuming, wrenching pain – was nothing compared to what his words brought. 'We won't find Callum riding towards Archin,' he said hollowly. 'I've experienced this before.'

Deana frowned. 'What do you mean?'

Jaxon didn't need to answer. I had seen it in his eyes the moment I had locked mine with his. My voice was hoarse as I spoke. 'We won't find Callum because he hasn't ridden off by himself.'

Jaxon nodded grimly, bending over to offer me a hand up. I took it, steadied myself with the touch as I hauled myself to my feet. 'It's the soul-bond,' he explained. Terror unlike any I had experienced before raked through me, and it was only Jaxon's grip on me that kept me from crumpling to the ground. 'Something's happened to him. The soul-bond is threatening to break.'

I did not talk as we searched for any sign of how Callum might have left. All horses were in the stables, according to the stable hand, and no guards had seen any sign of Callum leaving. Even the servants hadn't seen him. The pain came and went, less intense each time. My body seemed to be getting used to it, the agony of whatever was happening to Callum. With every step, my heart thudded faster and my breathing became shorter. I was stuck in my own head, in all the imaginings of what could be happening.

He's going to die.

A step.

They're going to kill him like they killed Cassie.

A breath, too shallow to do much good.

I won't survive this.

A beat of my heart, too loud in my ears.

He was going to be taken from me, and I wouldn't ever have the time to sort through everything I felt. I wouldn't get to tell him I loved him, all because I'd convinced myself to wait. I forced my eyes to focus on our surroundings as we stalked through the gardens. Flowers were beginning to bud, their petals peeking open to reveal shades of red, blue and lavender. Small insects buzzed in the chill morning air. One landed on a flower, the stem bending but not breaking as the bee made its way to the centre of the bud.

It was all so normal when I could feel my world imploding.

My eyes narrowed as I watched a dark shape squirm its way through the foliage. It moved jerkily and unnaturally, several flowers crushed between its weight. 'Is that...' I whispered, pointing to the shape amongst the flowers.

Deana paled. 'I think so.'

Together, we approached it, Jaxon claiming he was *quite content watching from a distance.* When we were five steps away, the squirming stopped. The stillness was even more unnerving as golden eyes glared at us from in the darkness, and lips pulled back from sharp teeth. I recognised the Ankuran – a young gardener whom I had seen several times in the early morning light tending to his flowers and trees.

The gardener, face and body covered in dirt, stood up from where he had been lying amongst the flowers. I swallowed hard as I spotted stains of something else on his chin, and the red smears where he had been lying on the ground.

'Little raven,' he hissed, laughter in the mocking tone. 'I have something of yours.'

I stepped forward, hand on the hilt of my dagger, but Deana held me back. 'Wait,' she hissed. 'We need to find out where Callum is.'

I clenched my fists but stopped. 'Where is he?' My Gift surged with my fury, silver wrapping around my fingers and sparking in the air.

The gardener laughed again, a chilling sound that echoed with malicious humour. 'He came willingly. Thought he could kill me with his pathetic sword. I cannot come directly to your palace in my frail state, but my creatures can. And the ones who came with me move swifter than any horse could. They can travel distances you could only dream of in hours, even with the valuable package they bore.' Another smile, another sinister laugh. 'Your precious king is mine now.'

'Let him go,' I demanded.

The gardener cocked his head to the side, twisting his neck far enough that I waited to hear a crack. His tongue darted out. This time, when he spoke, it was not the god's voice that echoed through. It was one that made me rage even more. 'I don't think so, Chiara.'

'Coward,' I spat out, brandishing my blade. 'Relying on a god's power to hide behind a corpse. I suppose I should expect nothing less of you. If you were a true prince, you'd face me yourself.'

It was Liam's laugh that came through the dead man's mouth this time. My lips curled. 'I am not an idiot, Chiara,' he said, voice as soft and gentle as it had been when I thought him to be a different kind of man. The kind who did not kill little girls just so he could have a pretty title and a crown to match. 'I know how much you would love to kill me.'

I stepped forward, shaking free of Deana's grip to snarl at him. 'I won't just kill you. I'll skin you alive first. Let you bleed and cry before the end.'

Liam shook the gardener's head, tutting softly. 'You're the one being foolish now,' he crooned, dipping his vessel's hand into a grime-coated pocket to throw something at my feet. 'Don't forget I've got something of yours. I would hate to see him end up like dear, sweet Cassie.'

I tried not to look. Tried to keep my eyes glaring at the man who stood somewhere far away, puppeteering this gardener with the help of Vitus. My eyes, though, moved on their own, drawn down by the glint of red and gold in the light.

My breath caught in my throat. A short lock of hair, golden and matted together with blood. My eyes shot up to the gardener. 'If you hurt another hair on his head...'

'Threats are useless now.' The Ankuran leant in, mouth gaping into a horrific smile. His hot breath slammed into me, the stench of decay nauseatingly strong. 'If you want to see your king again, you will come to my palace. Tonight. I know all about your little trick.'

'Tell me.' I stepped closer to the walking corpse and the prince who spoke through it, 'Do you feel anything in this body?'

'Why, want to try something?' The Ankuran smirked, but it was an identical twist of lips to the smirk Liam had given me. 'I'm sure I'll feel something if you want to give it a go.'

I let the sweet smile turn sharp as I reached into my hair, sliding out one of the sharp pins I had hidden in my braid earlier. 'Good.' Without any other warning, I slammed the several centimetres of metal into the side of the Ankuran's neck. The eyes flared with surprise and pain as golden blood spurted over me, and the creature dropped to its knees.

'Bitch,' the Ankuran gargled through Liam's voice as the gold fled from its face, a stab wound appearing at his chest from his true death. I revelled in the stickiness of blood upon my skin. Revelled in the pain I had heard in that final word, in knowing an echo of pain had found its way to Liam.

Jaxon wrinkled his nose at the mess. 'You could've ended it cleanly.'

'I don't care.' I wrenched the pin from the man's neck and wiped it clean before shoving it back into my hair. I was beyond angry, heading into the darkness that lay past the wrath. The same darkness I had let myself slip into following Cassie's death beckoned me, called for me. Begged me to burn those who hurt those who were mine to ash.

Vitus had made a fatal misstep today. He had threatened the one person who had held me back from truly becoming a nightmare, who had been the logic to my vengeance. Now, there was little to stop me from tearing him apart, piece by piece. 'Let's go get our king.'

Our plan was a simple one.

I would get the three of us in. Jaxon assured me I could use Brayden's description of the palace in Archin's Capital, Ballaronia, as a tether, holding it in my mind as my Gift flared to bring us to Callum. Vitus would've created wards around the city, he warned, which would block us from travelling all the way to the palace itself. The shifting between the fabric of the realms could be used outside the wards or within the wards, but they could not travel through the wards. Even so, in Vitus's weakened state, the wards wouldn't be far from the palace he resided in. Then, all we had to do was make our way to the palace, grab hold of Callum and jump to the edge of the wards before slipping through. If there was a chance, I would do as Kerta had told me and incapacitate Vitus long enough for someone to free Dearil from his bindings and chain Vitus. If there wasn't a chance, then we could worry about dealing with Vitus later. My priority was Callum.

'If he's hurt, he'll be able to heal himself once he's away from Vitus.' It was the sixth time I had repeated this.

'He will,' Deana reassured me.

I tugged the cloak cowl over my head, tucking strands of hair into it. The metal chestplate, a match for Deana's silver one, was a familiar weight – one that I'd almost come to miss in the months since I'd stepped onto a battlefield. My fingers brushed over the hilts of the blades strapped to me, enough to supply an entire army unit.

Deana and Jaxon were similarly dressed for battle, Jaxon bearing his swords and Deana with her garrotte and red Gift flickering at her fingertips. We looked ready to reign chaos upon a god. Wordlessly, I offered a hand to each of them. There was no hesitation as they grasped hold. Closing my eyes, I pictured Ballaronia's palace: a towering stone spire with windows that stole any sliver of light and reflected it tenfold. Gardens overflowing with wiry bushes and scraggly trees that coped well with the dry Archinian climate. Gates flanking every side, iron twisting together to form vine-like shapes. As I'd done in all my practising, I pulled the image towards me, letting my Gift envelop us. Then, we stepped through the fabric of the realm.

Chapter Thirty-Two

When I opened my eyes, it was not to gently sloping stairs or wild gardens planted in dry soil. Instead, it was to a dark sky and too-quiet streets. Around us, buildings huddled together, an odd assortment of shapes and sizes. Some crouched low to the ground, rooves sagging enough that I might have been able to brush them with my fingers if I tried, while others stretched into the air. In the near distance, the shape of the palace I had been picturing loomed high.

Jaxon scuffed at the ground with his boot, drawing my attention to the golden markings that stretched across the ground, similar to those that'd been carved into the man Callum couldn't heal. A faint light shimmered. 'The wards,' he explained. He stepped past the markings, the air shimmering for a heartbeat. I followed. A shiver coursed through my body as the air pressed down on me, my Gift roiling in protest. As soon as I passed to the other side, the sensation disappeared.

'Does anyone know the way?' I asked, eyeing the streets warily. They were less uniform than those of Alluvite, narrow streets twisting in various directions. Despite the guide of the palace spires, there was no clear path to take.

'It's been a hundred years or so, but I have. I'll lead us.' Jaxon turned left, heading for a darkened alleyway.

Deana grabbed his arm, hauling him the other way. 'And I came here ten years ago. Plus, I had Lena relay the information Brayden gave her on the city's layout,' she snapped. 'I think the streets have changed in the time since you've been here.'

Jaxon and I followed behind Deana, eyeing the space around us. It was a city of the dead. There were no lights in windows, no smell of cooking winding its way out of windows, no sounds of laughter or shouts. Even the wind seemed to be quieter here than in Naruzia. Every so often, we would pass a doorway that was cracked open. When we did so, we all covered our noses, the stench of rotting meat permeating the air. The odour only thickened as we progressed further into the city.

'I don't like this,' I muttered, eyeing an open door. Red stained the threshold, and the vague shape of an outflung hand could just be made out in the darkness beyond.

Deana made a sound of agreement. She had used her Gift to conjure a small knife, the surface shimmering with red. Silence lapsed again. It became thicker, heavier, as we walked, unease skittering over my skin. After a few minutes, Jaxon slid his sword free of its scabbard. His eyes darted over the street. 'There must be some who still live in the city.'

None of us voiced what we already knew – that if there were people left alive, then we would have surely seen some sign of life by now. Instead, there wasn't even the call of birds or the scurrying of rats in darkened corners. It was the god of life's domain, yet death ruled the streets.

The narrow street we crept down broadened out into a square, the sort that would once have been bustling with people and stalls, street performers weaving through the crowds. I wish that was the sight that greeted us.

Deana came to a sudden stop, Jaxon and I nearly crashing into her back. 'Gods,' she whispered hoarsely.

Lines upon lines of Ankurans stood before us. All were perfectly straight. They didn't breathe. Didn't blink, either, staring out with their unnaturally gold eyes. There had to be at least two hundred of them. Some were barely taller than my knee, others in their prime of life. I spotted a young mother next to a girl no older than three and a boy of about eight, each perfectly distanced from each other as though they were no relation at all. Their skin was all webbed in gold, vines creeping across their faces and beneath bloody clothes.

'Are they … aware?' I breathed, my heart pounding. My Gift rose, but I held it back, staring at the Ankurans. There was a far deadlier enemy in the palace to save my power for.

Jaxon shrugged. 'Only one way to find out.'

The fact that Jaxon had survived for centuries was nothing short of miraculous. He strolled out in front of the lines of corpses, sword hanging casually from one hand. None of the Ankurans so much as flinched. He turned back to us, shrugging, then stretched out a finger towards the nearest body. 'See? Perfectly—'

The Ankuran he'd pointed at whipped her head around, hand snapping up to catch Jaxon's hand in hers. Her lips pulled up into a smile. 'I know you,' she whispered in a flat voice. 'Tarina's whelp.'

Deana muttered something that sounded like a prayer to save her from fools and ran to Jaxon, ripping him away from the Ankuran's grasp. The girl's smile dropped, face sliding back into blankness.

'Are they revived by touch?' Jaxon muttered, tugging away from Deana and heading towards the next closest Ankuran.

'Idiot,' she muttered, shoving him back to my side. 'Don't even think about touching any more.'

Jaxon rubbed his shoulder, still looking far too intrigued at the mindless bodies. 'Shouldn't we check? If they're reporting to Vitus or have any sentience, best we know before we head to the palace.'

Deana didn't get a chance to respond. At the back, a child began laughing. The sound rippled outwards. Two more did the same, then four, then eight, the sound spreading until the entire group of them were filling the space with their eerie laughter.

Jaxon yelped, jumping backwards. He shot a look at Deana and I. 'It wasn't me, I swear.'

'I feel you, little raven,' the group crooned as one, jaws clicking and lips moving in unison. As soon as the words fell away, I heard an echo of the words somewhere far off to the left. Then another behind. One closer to the palace. Again and again and again, groups of Ankurans we couldn't see echoing the god's words.

'Shit,' I cursed, immediately regretting speaking as all those golden eyes snapped to where I was swathed in shadows. My skin prickled as grins grew, golden fissures cracking away at skin. Power roiled through the air, thick with Vitus's essence.

'Found you,' they whispered. All of them took one step forward. Two. Three. Coming closer. Eyes fixed solely on me.

'What do we do?' Deana asked, knuckles white around the hilt of her knife.

I couldn't use my Gift here. Couldn't risk expending it, or harming Deana or Jaxon. 'Run.'

I spun from the Ankurans. Deana and Jaxon turned with me, hurtling down the alleyways as cackling laughter and heavy steps followed us. We twisted sharply around a corner, narrowly avoiding colliding with a wall. Our feet pounded in unison, my heart hammering and chest burning. We were running in the dark, in a city none of us knew well. The palace turned in and out of view as we ran, the Ankuran's feet echoing behind us – never gaining on us, simply there, following our path.

'This way,' Deana lunged for a dark alley. I followed, Jaxon taking up the rear.

'The palace!' I shouted as we turned away from it once again. 'We need to get to it!'

The others didn't reply, too focused on survival. My legs burnt as I pushed them. A combination of fear and fury fuelled me. Sweat soaked my back, the Archinian heat turning brutal as we sprinted through another open courtyard. Two streets lay ahead.

Deana skidded to a stop, her head swinging between the two. 'Which way?'

Jaxon took the lead, rushing for the sun-soaked street to the left. 'It doesn't matter. Just *run*.'

I dared a glance behind, finding golden eyes locked on me. The girl Ankuran at the front smiled, golden fissures running through her cheeks. The momentary pause had cost us, the Ankurans were closer than before. Cursing, I faced to the front once more. The street veered off suddenly to one side, the width of it narrowing and pressing inwards. The buildings surrounding us began to press together, their different heights and shapes making the layout a confusing maze. The palace disappeared from view, situated somewhere behind us, as Jaxon headed around another corner. My feet didn't adjust quickly enough to the turn, and my shoulder collided with stone as I careened into the wall, sending a hiss of pain out of me. Wasting no time, I shoved off the wall, sprinting once more. My breaths were little more than ragged gasps, Jaxon and Deana in much the same state. None of us gave in to our exhaustion. There were only two options – keep going, or let the Ankurans catch us.

Failure is not an option, I repeated to myself as my muscles ached, every breath burning. Deana stumbled over a divot in the road. I reached out, grasping her shoulder and tugging her upright before she could fall.

'There are too many for us to fight.' Jaxon panted, swiping hair and sweat out of his eyes. 'We need to find somewhere to hide and then sneak past them.'

I nodded, eyeing the junction in the road ahead. Jaxon twisted to the street to the left, glass from a shop window crunching underfoot. Deana lunged forward, grasping a handful of his shirt and yanking him back.

'Not that way,' she said grimly.

'No,' Jaxon agreed, staggering back to us. 'Definitely not.'

We stared at the line of Ankurans standing before us. They stared back.

I shifted to run, but Deana didn't move. 'They're not doing anything.'

I blinked. She was right. The golden-eyed creatures did not shift towards us. Instead, they stood as still as the ones in the marketplace initially had, completely lifeless.

'Do we try to get past?' Jaxon suggested, taking a step towards them. He quickly staggered back as the Ankurans snapped their heads towards him. 'Or not. Do we go back the way we came?'

I twisted around, searching the darkness for any sign of the Ankurans, who had been trailing us. I couldn't make out much – the vague outline of what might have been a body, shards of glass, some empty bottles. No Ankurans to be seen.

My pulse quickened as dread-soaked confusion swamped me. I jerked my head towards the other end of the street in silent suggestion. Jaxon and Deana nodded, and we were once again running back the way we came. As soon as we reached the juncture we'd been at before, Deana cursed. Again, a line of Ankurans blocked off one of the streets – the one we'd originally run up. Our decision was made for us once more.

It was at the third crossroads that Deana realised what they were doing. We came to a fork in the road, one side teeming with bodies, the other empty. 'They're herding us,' she whispered, trepidation seeping into her voice.

'Like sheep to the slaughter,' Jaxon murmured.

I didn't respond, my fingers tightening around my blades. His words felt far too prophetic.

We all knew the easiest solution. I'd transport Deana and Jaxon back to the boundary created by the wards. No matter how fast they moved, no Ankuran would be able to beat us back there. Then we could run. That, though, was not an option for me. I wouldn't leave Callum behind. Wouldn't allow Vitus and Liam to take another person I cared for.

Failure is not an option, I repeated to myself. Callum would return to Naruzia alive. That left only one choice – allowing ourselves to be herded.

Every time there was a choice in the road, one path would be blocked. We were forced left, then right, then straight across an intersection of roads. Alarm built with each forced choice. Vitus was leading us to something, and we were willingly allowing ourselves to be led. Insects trapped in a god's game. With every turn and twist, the palace loomed higher and higher until it blocked out views of almost anything else. It was exactly where we wanted to be. The way we had arrived, though, was the opposite of what I'd wanted. There was no secrecy, no surprise. No chance of sneaking in and reaching Callum before the god noticed us.

We stopped outside iron gates, the spikes glinting dangerously under the sun. I pressed my hands against my knees. My breath came hard and fast, sweat running in rivulets down my back. I allowed myself the space of three heartbeats to regain my breath before straightening, staring up at the palace. Resolve settled over the dread, shoving it away. Behind us, the Ankurans halted in a semi-circle. I didn't bother sizing up their numbers. There were too many to fight without wasting my Gift and trapping us in this city.

'What are we supposed to do now?' Jaxon asked, adjusting his grip on his sword as he glanced over his shoulder.

Deana shrugged helplessly. 'I don't think we have a choice.'

Beyond the iron gates, two massive doors hung open. A disturbing invitation that we accepted with unease, walking up the stairs and into the palace. We didn't linger in the oddly decorated front hall, passing garishly coloured tapestries without a second glance. The Ankurans followed behind. For every step forward we took, they took the same. Never close enough to touch, but close enough to be a warning. Any misstep, any straying from the path, and they would be there, as attached to us as our shadows were.

My dagger was warm in my hand as I stared down the seemingly endless corridor we passed into. There were doors lining each side, all shut tight. Dark stains spread beneath our feet, soaking into stone floors. I glanced down, swallowing hard. For all the strangeness of the palace, there was one familiarity. The sensation of death. Not the physical smells, that of rot and decay or even of blood, but the lingering heaviness to the air that called to my power. A scent that almost reminded me of smoke and jasmine.

'Should we check each room?' Deana whispered, sending a nervous glance over her shoulder at the Ankurans.

I shook my head. 'Too many. We don't have the time to waste.'

'And I don't think we want to see what lies beyond these doors,' Jaxon said grimly, eyeing where red pooled beneath one of the doors.

'We should—' I broke off, suddenly overwhelmingly aware of the tug in my gut. It had gone from a dull ache to a sharp pang; less the agony of before and more a pulling down the corridor. I stared at a single door at the end, gilded in gold. The gold seemed to shimmer and twist, rolling down the door in constant movement. From Brayden's information on the palace's layout, I knew it to be the throne room. 'Callum's there.'

They looked to where I pointed, hands instinctively tightening upon their weapons as though they could sense the same malevolence seeping from the door as I could. The gold seemed to pulse like a heartbeat as we stared. I met Deana and Jaxon's stares. There was no hesitation in either of them. We knew entering was a bad idea. One that might end with us all dead, and this realm primed to fall to Vitus. But Callum was behind that door, and I would not leave without him.

Taking a breath, I closed my hand around the unnaturally warm door handle. The metal seemed almost eager, starting to twist before I had a chance to. With barely a nudge, it cracked open. I snatched my hand away as soon as golden light spilt from the room. An imprint of my fingers remained upon the handle. The gold roiled and swallowed up the imprint, leaving behind smooth metal.

I pulled a second dagger into my hand before summoning my Gift. The metal gleamed silver, power crackling upon the surface. The power I'd once hated was now a comfort as I stepped into the room that awaited us.

It seemed a separate world to the palace corridor. Instead of colours and odd trinkets, the room was bare. Every wall was coated with the same gold as the doorway, all the way up to the domed roof. The space was vast enough to be a throne room but with no sign that it had once been one, aside from the raised platform at the other side. No light entered through the two arched windows to one side, unnatural darkness blanketing the glass. Not the darkness of night, but the darkness of finality. Of endings.

'Beautiful, isn't it?' The voice was laced with malice, its power filling the room. This time, it did not come from the mouths of the dead that closed in behind us. The gold on the wall opposite parted like curtains, a man striding through. Gold clung to his skin like armour for several moments before dripping away to reveal the face beneath.

Deana gasped and Jaxon took a step back. Outwardly, I did not react at all. Inwardly, I oscillated between horrified at the god's appearance and vicious satisfaction at the fate of the king who had called Vitus to our realm. King Kane had never been an impressive-looking man. He was cursed with a handful of mediocre features and a cruel personality. He'd never truly been an ugly man, though. Average, definitely, but passable. The same couldn't be said now.

I could barely identify any familiar features of the old king. Where there had once been lines of age, carved deep into his skin, there were now golden cracks that seeped brilliant lights. His eyes were a startling mix of burst vessels and flaxen veining, a combination of red and gold seeping from the corner of them like tears. In several places, his skin seemed to have flaked away, leaving gaping spots of gold in their place.

Those hateful golden eyes turned to me. 'You seem disgusted.'

I stiffened as Vitus's voice filled the space. 'You were easier to look at last time we met.'

'This body has served me well until now.' The rich tone of his voice was little more than a poorly worn mask of warmth that cracked at the edges, revealing the rot beneath. 'Alas, the soul who so generously leant me this body disintegrated a month ago. It seems his body is beginning to follow suit.'

My stomach hollowed. I'd hated King Kane with a passion nearly as deep as my hatred for Liam, yet ... if such a despicably powerful man could be wiped from existence so easily by the thing before me, then what did that mean for us? For this realm?

Later. I would dwell on all that later. Only one thing mattered right now.

'Where's Callum?' I bit out, the silver seeping into my weapons intensifying with the wrath that twisted inside.

Vitus smiled. 'Patience, little raven. You will see him soon.'

I wanted to scream, to lunge at the god and tear into him until he told me where my king was. His smile grew as though he sensed my desire. As though he wanted me to do exactly that. My hands clasped tighter around the hilts of my blade. I didn't move, rooting my feet to the ground.

Vitus's eyes flicked to the silver covering my blade. They narrowed, then crinkled with genuine amusement. 'How sweet.' He took a step closer and the entire room shifted, gold stripping away from the walls to reveal grey stone and marble floors veined with brown. The gold rushed at Vitus. It fell on his shoulders, forming a cape, and circled his head in the shape of a crown. 'You think that little trickle of power can do anything against me?'

A blink was all it took for Vitus to move from the other end of the room to directly in front of me. His smell hit me. Too-sweet roses mixing with the rotting flesh that housed him. It overcame that scent of jasmine and smoke, the scent of death, as though even a force like that hid from the malevolence before us.

Run, my body begged me. *Run. Run. Run.*

I couldn't. Not without Callum.

Vitus's smile dropped when I failed to stagger back, to flee as every sense was screaming at me to do.

'You think you can do anything against me when your father failed?' Golden light flickered around us, the very walls seeming to shake with his wrath. 'You aren't even a full god. You're a halfling. Weak. Pathetic. And so very breakable.'

His power enveloped me, my chest tightening until I could squeeze in no air. All I could see was gold, that sickly scent suffocating me. My head swam as my Gift churned inside, oscillating between leaping to my skin and drawing back. Then, just as I feared I would collapse, Vitus stepped back. His smile returned, a perfectly crafted mimicry of human emotion. I tried to swallow. Tried to force my heart to slow. Tried to feel anything but fear as the god touched a flaking piece of skin like a child might pick at a scab. The skin peeled away, a horrifically large piece disappearing into nothingness.

'Where's Callum?' I asked again, hoping he didn't hear the quaver in my words.

'Your precious other half. I only wanted him so you would come running.' Vitus tilted his head, considering me. Behind me, Jaxon and Deana shifted. 'I had thought to kill you both, but I am not wasteful. You, little raven, will serve me, one way or another, and I need you alive for that.'

'I will never serve you.'

'We'll see.' Vitus leant in close once more. His fingers curled under my chin, forcing my head up. Forcing my eyes to meet those bottomless pools of hatred. 'Tell me, did it hurt you when we cut him? When I suppressed that precious kernel of power I foolishly Gifted him?' His eyes deliberately dropped down, down, down, until he was looking at the floor. His hand shifted to the back of my head. Before I could react, he shoved my head to bow.

Don't look. Don't look. Don't—

Oh, gods.

There was blood. Blood I hadn't seen beneath the ever-shifting gold. Enough to fill a large kitchen pot, splashed out on the floor, trickling into crevices and along the tiles. It was still wet. Fresh. Enough to kill a weaker man.

My fingers tightened around my blades, head snapping up as Vitus's hand fell away. The fear disappeared, replaced by a rage that belied the malice in his eyes. 'I'm going to kill you,' I said softly. 'I'm going to make you suffer, and then I'm going to send you to whatever forsaken place gods go to when they die.'

Vitus chuckled – *chuckled* – at my words, sending the beast of fury snapping through my body. I raised a dagger, tensed my legs, poised myself to lunge at him and sweep the crackling silver metal across his decaying throat.

'I wouldn't,' Vitus warned, still smiling. He lifted a hand – a hand covered in fresh, red blood – and pointed to behind me. 'If you do, your little friends will die.'

I froze as the muffled sounds behind slammed into me. At the lack of commentary from Jaxon, who rarely knew when to shut up, and Deana, who would never stand silent if Callum was harmed. Slowly, I turned.

I had been too focused on Vitus, failing to realise that the Ankurans had separated them from me. Five held Deana. Jaxon had been forced to the ground, at least eight sets of hands pinning him to the ground where he struggled. A hand wrapped over both of their mouths to prevent any sound escaping. Deana looked enraged, but Jaxon – he looked ready to massacre them all as he stared at the Ankurans holding her.

Trembling with fury, I turned back to Vitus. 'Let them go.'

His lips twisted, more golden light spilling from the fissures on the face. 'You do not give the orders here, little raven.' He eyed me, then the floor. The floor littered with Callum's blood. 'Kneel.'

I bared my teeth at him. 'Never.'

'Kneel, or your friends will find themselves food for my pets.'

Nausea mingled with my trembling anger, forming a toxic mix. I would not kneel to save myself, but to save my friends – to stop them being torn apart like the palace guards had – I would gladly prostrate myself. Never taking my eyes off the god, I forced my knees to bend. It was near impossible to make them go down, to let the knees of my pants soak with still warm blood. Gods, there was so much of it. The next breath I took raked through me.

'Does it make you feel strong, to have me kneeling at your feet?' I asked softly, staring up at Vitus. 'Does it make you feel *powerful?*'

Vitus laughed. 'There was never any place for someone like

you, except at my feet. There is no power in this, only nature.' He lifted a hand, flicking it towards the gold wall from where he had emerged. The gold shifted, sinking inwards to shove another form out. '*This* makes me powerful.'

I stared at the man who had emerged, wrapped in chains. Dearil. Gone was the straight back and immaculate dress. He looked like a shadow of the father I knew. Dearil had always been ancient, but he had never looked so old. Every feature was lined with the pain of the chains binding him, the toll of remaining in his true form in the mortal realm weathering his skin and greying his hair. Golden lines carved into his skin, mimicking those of the wards we'd crossed over to enter the city. Their light was diminished, however, as though even the chains couldn't keep Dearil's true power from suffocating them.

Only his eyes remained the same. Silver pits of endless power that first looked to Vitus before sweeping past him, taking in the Ankurans and my friends. He inclined his head slightly to Jaxon, always regal in bearing, even when captive. Vitus watched hungrily as Dearil's eyes dropped away, lowering to the blood before rising to stare at me. He blinked, just once. It was the only reaction my presence received. From the smile that spread across Vitus's lips, it was enough.

My knees were going numb from pressing against the hard floor as Vitus said, 'Does it displease you, my old friend, to see your daughter kneeling at my feet?'

Dearil did not respond. He barely shifted, standing perfectly still despite the weight of the chains wrapped around him.

'Go on, then.' Vitus gestured at me. 'Greet the child as a loving father would.'

Dearil was slow in shifting his gaze. He stared at Vitus for several long, tense moments. Vitus's features tightened, anger beginning to crack through just as it had when I'd refused to flinch before him. Finally, Dearil spoke. 'What you seek to do is a mistake.'

Vitus made a disgusted sound, turning his back to me. 'You always told me that. It's a mistake to try to rule. It's a mistake to test my power in new ways. It's a mistake to love a halfling. Everything was always a mistake!' The last word was a roar, once again shaking the foundations of the palace. Golden flames lit at the tips of his fingers, the walls seeming to surge closer together. Power crackled through the room.

I swallowed, fear a bitter taste in my mouth. We were at the mercy of a god who seemed to be hanging by a thread of sanity. And Callum had been here since the morning.

'Do you know what was a mistake?' Vitus stepped forward, the marble splintering under his foot. 'Refusing me the right to stay in the mortal realm. Allowing Alexia and my children to pay the price of your stubbornness.'

'Your presence in this realm would have upset the balance,' Dearil said in that calm way of his as they were discussing nothing more exciting than the weather. 'The mortal realm faced destruction.'

'It deserves to be destroyed!' The gold flared brighter. I winced, shutting my eyes against the stinging of the light. The Ankurans shifted behind me, agitated by their master's fury. 'The mortals are little more than selfish insects, yet here you stand, still trying to protect them.'

'It is our duty to protect them.'

Vitus's cold laugh rang out. 'Always so sure, even when this is your doing. If you had allowed me to stay, or allowed Alexia to live the centuries she would have had with me—' He broke off, exhaling. My eyes opened as the light diminished, but the uncomfortable pressure of his power did not yet abate. 'You did do one thing right. You allowed your halfling child to live and, in doing so, gave me the winning hand.'

He moved so quickly I didn't have time to raise my dagger. His bony fingers grasped a fistful of my hair, wrenching it painfully upwards. He yanked me to my feet and shoved me in front of Dearil. I couldn't stop the gasp of pain that slipped out.

His fist only grasped tighter. 'You will not bring down the barrier to save me from this cracking human body, nor yourself. But will you do it to save your child?'

I expected the next word. Knew it was coming, knew it was the right answer if this realm was to survive. Knew that, even if the realm wasn't at stake, Dearil wouldn't bend to anyone for my sake. It still didn't stop the sting of it.

'No.'

Several strands of hair snapped under the tension in Vitus's hand. 'I expected that of you. Always the hero. Always so *righteous.*' The word was spat as though it had a foul taste. 'What will you do, though, after days of her screams? Weeks of them? *Months?*'

A single push of Vitus's power through my body was all it took to tear a scream from me. Agony roiled and my Gift tangled inside me as it collapsed inwards, desperate to escape the golden glow. My legs weakened, Vitus's grasp the only thing keeping me upright. Gods, it *burned*. I had believed the agony of his Ankurans' power was bad enough. This was a thousand times worse. It felt like being pulled into a thousand tiny pieces, each doused in flame so hot it singed the very sky. For the second the power pulsed through, I was nowhere and nothing but pain.

There was a moment of relief as the power abated. I had time to suck in a desperate breath and hear the muffled shouts of my friends before it came back again, more vicious than the last time. Gods. Oh, *gods*. I couldn't breathe, could barely think.

Once again, the pain receded, but the shock of it did not. Dimly, I was aware of Vitus letting me go. My legs were trembling so hard I couldn't even stand. My hands slipped on the blood-slicked tiles, sending me sprawling. I shouldn't have come. It was an idiotic journey, spurned only by my need for Callum. Vitus was a *god*. I was barely half of one, barely worthy of even being called a mortal.

And yet … and yet, I had no choice when it came to Callum. I had to have him back. My fingers pressed into the tiles as I moaned, trying to regain the strength to stand. Callum. I needed to focus on him. Needed to get to him so we could escape. Which meant I had to somehow get away from the god who towered above me.

I closed my eyes, waiting for the spin of pain to back away enough that my vision was no longer tinged with darkness before opening them again. I took stock of my surroundings, of the barriers in my way.

One – a wrathful god who wanted to see my father suffer.

Two – at least a hundred animated corpses surrounding my friends.

My fingers curled around the daggers that had clattered free from my grasp as I had gone down. Two obstacles. Two things to get out of my way if I wanted to see Callum.

I could work with that.

I spared a glance back at Deana and Jaxon. Their eyes were on me. *Be ready*, I tried to communicate through nothing but the set of my jaw and the steel of my eyes. Neither dared nod, but both tightened their grips on their respective weapons. There were too many creatures to fight off. However, if they could hold them off just long enough for me to stick a dagger deep into Vitus – just long enough to break any hold he possessed over the creatures – we might get out of here.

My next glance was at Dearil. He did not look at me. I might be able to get to him, get him out with my friends. But with my current power levels, it would be a choice between my father and Callum. That was no choice at all. To get to Callum, though, I needed a distraction. And Dearil was currently serving as the perfect diversion.

'It's almost sweet,' Vitus said as I slowly unfurled from my curled-up position. 'She came for a mortal. Her *soul-bonded*, if you would believe it.' I didn't attempt to deny his words as Vitus stepped around me, approaching Dearil. 'Do you remember what it felt like to have a soul-bond?'

I positioned my feet under me, making sure my legs would support me when I rose to stand. Dearil quietly replied, 'She is still my soul-bonded.'

Vitus laughed derisively. 'You were always weak. Even after she betrayed you so thoroughly you seek to defend her.' I studied his back – the scrawny shoulders of the now-dead king, the proud tilt to his head. As though he felt my stare, Vitus's head whipped around, eyes locking on me. 'Just like your daughter. Pathetic, really, coming to find that false king.'

I forced my fingers to loosen around the hilt of the blades. My eyes dropped to the ground, submissive and quavering beneath the weight of his eyes. Deana had once told me that being seen as weak could become as dangerous as any blade, should I use it right. I understood that now, as Vitus snorted with disgust, turning back to my father. It was clear how Vitus saw me. A halfling. Insignificant, helpless against the divine power before me. And it was because of these things that he missed the curl of my lips as I drew in a deep breath, readying myself. He was underestimating me. Good. Let him underestimate me. Let him learn what that would cost him.

I cast one last look back at Jaxon and Deana. They were both standing, tense and perfectly still, entering that killing calm. My look conveyed what I could not voice. *Now*.

Then I attacked.

Chapter Thirty-Three

I pushed off the floor, powerfully enough to propel my body forwards the few steps between myself and Vitus. My body moved in perfect unison with my weapons, performing a dance I had learnt long ago. One arm raised defensively. The other aimed low. It was time to see what colour a god bled.

Vitus's last-second twist was the only thing that saved him from the knife driving straight through his back and the very mortal heart his host body possessed. His flesh gave way surprisingly easily as I drove the blade in deep, blood turning the hilt slick. With a vicious shove of my Gift, I sent more power surging through my body and down the blade, straight into Vitus.

The god let out an almighty roar of pain. Smiling savagely, I twisted the blade deeper. Gold-flecked crimson flowed hot and fast, spattering over the blood that already soaked the floor. Behind me, his Ankurans echoed his roar, followed by the sickening sound of blades pulling free of wet flesh. I couldn't spare Deana and Jaxon a glance. I only hoped it was the sound of their weapons I heard under the grunts and the screams of the creatures.

'Worthless creature,' Vitus snarled, a thread of agony thrumming through his words. His hand flared with golden power. I fed my Gift my anger – the one thing I'd always had in ample supply. Vitus's golden light flickered, silver corrupting its core. My body crackled with energy as sparks flew in the air around me, his flesh flaring gold wherever those silver specks fell. With every push of power, his features reflected the agony I knew all too well from his own power. 'You *stabbed* me.'

My smile grew. I yanked the blade further upwards. Flesh tore beneath the blade, silver cracks veining out from the edges of the wound. 'I hope it hurts.'

Vitus bared his teeth in return. He tried once more to gather his power to him. I wouldn't let him. Every time gold glowed at his fingertips, my silver attacked. I could feel my Gift inside me, swelling and pulsing with something that felt akin to pleasure. *Good*, it seemed to whisper as strands of hair in the corner of my vision turned silver. *It's good when you don't fight me.* And it was. It was glorious, feeling that power coursing through me. Seeing what it could do to the god before me.

He was shaking now, knees bending. His fingers closed around my shirt as though to keep him from falling. I wrenched the blade free, drove it in again, higher this time. The god roared once more, his grip failing as he collapsed to his knees. The weight of his power cracked the marble underneath, sending gold veins spiralling through the room. His back arched in pain as the golden walls around us roiled with his agony.

'I hope you suffer,' I ground out, driving the blade in again. And again. And again. 'Just like you made my sister and Callum suffer.'

Callum, who had to be alive. I wouldn't allow myself to think otherwise.

Vitus knelt at my feet just as I'd knelt at his. A divine being, prostrate before me. Still, he didn't fall, no matter where my knife struck. That was fine. I could do this, over and over, making him bleed and scream, for the rest of my life if I had to. Could enjoy it forever.

With a hissed breath, Vitus forced his head up. His entire body shook with the effort of raising his eyes to meet mine. There was a burning fury in those golden eyes. Fury, and something else. Something far worse.

Victory.

My heart thudded as I realised his body wasn't shaking from the effort. It was shaking from wild, crazed laughter. My elation fell away, my stomach dropping.

Oh, gods.

I had miscalculated. Missed something vital.

I ripped the blade free, driving my boot hard enough into Vitus's side that he crashed to the ground, still laughing. My eyes swept the room. Deana and Jaxon were still fighting their way forward – swathed in golden blood, bodies littering the floor, but alive. Winning, even. Dearil remained wrapped in chains, face grave as he watched. But his face was pale, his eyes sad. He did not look like a god about to receive his freedom. Ice trickled down my spine. And then there was Vitus, slowly getting to his feet, the dripping of his blood slowing. Everywhere my knife had touched, the wounds were now closing, threaded together with golden power.

'That was pointless,' he wheezed, his skin more pallid than it had been. 'I am the god of life. I cannot die by mortal blade.'

I narrowed my eyes at him, lifting my blades once more. 'You can die by another god's hand.'

He brought his hands together, clasping them like a delighted child. There was still an edge of deep, unrelenting anger in those eyes, though. 'But you are not a god, are you?' His eyes swept over me. Any hint of pain vanished, the only sign of his wounds the blood he left behind. 'And you have forgotten something.'

Another sweep of the room. Deana was now bleeding from a gash in her arm, her back pressed to Jaxon's. There was fatigue in their movements, the swings getting slower, the dead taking a little longer to fall. They were getting closer, though, to breaking through the front line. Jaxon caught my eye for a split second, nodding grimly.

We're fine.

'Not them,' Vitus said, voice soft. 'You're forgetting someone else.'

Callum wasn't in here, but I knew that already. I'd hoped to bring Vitus down before seeking him out so the god couldn't interfere. And everyone else was here except…

The floor dropped away from my feet. I was an idiot. An idiot, to not wonder where *he* was. I was so focused on getting to Callum, on tearing this palace apart, that I hadn't thought of the second person I had promised vengeance against. My palms grew clammy as I spat out my next words, 'Where's Liam?'

Vitus's smile promised pain. 'Finally, the right question.' A hand waved through the air, the golden walls shifting once more. Liam stood beyond the parting, every bit as perfectly put together as I remembered. I had forgotten how handsome he was with his boyish looks, twisting and corrupting every memory of him through the lens of hatred. The only sign of imperfection was a few red droplets of blood that sprinkled his left cheek.

He smiled when he saw me, a curve of the lips that mimicked Vitus's. 'Miss me?'

I opened my mouth to snap something at him, but a clink of a chain caught my attention. My gaze fell upon the metal links looped around his hand. I couldn't blink, couldn't even breathe, as I followed the chain's length to where it sunk into the gold that masked whatever lay beyond. Liam followed my gaze, the smile growing a little harder, a little crueller. He gave the chain a sharp, hard yank.

I froze as Callum fell through the golden part, crashing to the ground. His face was a mess, barely recognisable save for the sliver of familiar green that gazed out from swollen eyes. Everywhere I looked, there was a cut or a bruise, fingers that bent the wrong way and red clothes that had once been near white. I let out a sound that was half a gasp, half a choked sob. Behind, the sounds of battle had died away, Vitus forgetting Deana and Jaxon as he watched with clear pleasure.

'Callum,' I whispered, taking a stumbling step towards him. Vitus swung his arm out, catching me in the chest.

I didn't look at the god. I couldn't look, not when my attention was consumed by what had been done to Callum. His shirt barely clung to him, and his back – oh gods, his back. I recognised the mess of raw flesh, the stripes of gashes lining them. A whipping.

'It was a challenge,' Vitus began conversationally, 'to figure out how to supress the Gift I gave him. Gods, for all our power, can't take away what we gave, and I didn't want to see the false king dead until I had you in my hand. But I perfected it after some time.' He tilted his head, his smile growing. 'It's hard to get wards right on such an unwilling canvas. Not strong enough to deflect any true god's power, of course, but for a single seed? They do their job.'

It took a few moments for me to comprehend. To see, beyond the mess of red, the golden shapes that circled Callum's wrists. The same as those the man who'd been ill when he'd come to the palace, bring news of Vitus's attack, had borne. The ones that had flared when Callum had tried to heal the man, only to fail.

'You carved wards into him,' I breathed, the words tasting of blood and bile. He hadn't just harmed Callum. He'd *marked* him, like he was no more than an object to play with.

Vitus studied me, his malice turning to delight at the horror I wore. 'Wards act as a boundary to a god's power. Ineffective, perhaps, in bottling up the full extent of divinity. But what do you think they do, little raven, when cut into a mortal body?'

I couldn't find the breath to answer.

'It was my power I Gifted him. It seems only right that I should be the one to lock that Gift away.'

I stared as blood trickled across Callum's skin. There were too many wounds. Wounds he should've been able to heal if it weren't for the wards. My body seemed to recognise that pain, the bite of a whip tearing through skin and the burn of a fist pounding into flesh. I'd been right upon seeing the amount of blood upon the floor earlier. Any lesser man would not be alive.

Somehow, Callum managed to raise his head off the ground. Horror wrapped its tendrils around my throat, choking me. There was a chain around his *neck*, like he was a goddamned animal. It rattled as he looked straight at me, rasping out, 'You shouldn't have come. Gods, Chiara, I hoped you wouldn't come.'

Suddenly, I wasn't horrified. I was furious. Furious at what they had done to Callum, furious at Vitus for repressing his Gift when he so desperately needed it, furious at the world for putting us here. Furious at myself for being so blind before, for wasting precious moments with Callum, and being so godsdamned stubborn when I'd known – *always known* – how I felt. And furious, *wrathful*, even, at Callum, for thinking himself unnecessary enough to face Vitus on his own.

I looked at Liam first, let him see that fire of anger, then turned it on Vitus. 'Hurting him was a mistake,' I said, almost gently. And there was a flicker of something – of unease, maybe, or even a flicker of concern – in the god's eyes before he slid on an oily smile.

'I don't think it was.' He flicked his eyes behind me. There was a rumble, the corpses waking once more. 'Lower your weapons or your precious king dies.'

A pause, and then the sound of a sword being sheathed. Deana's weapons likely returned to the same red mist they'd come from. Vitus lifted a hand, pressing golden-coated fingers under my chin. 'You keep forgetting what you are,' he whispered, his nails biting into my skin. 'You are nothing. Your king is nothing. The only reason you still breathe is because I need your father to get in line.'

I wrenched my head away from those fingers. 'Let my friends go,' I snarled. 'And you can have me.'

I heard Deana take in a breath behind me, heard Jaxon's choked '*No.*' I felt rather than saw Callum's eyes flick up, heard the rattle of his chain as he somehow, impossibly, forced himself to his feet. Liam did not shift to stop him, his eyes set hungrily on me.

'Chiara, *don't.*'

I look away from Vitus at the breaking in Callum's voice. Let him think he had won. Let him send my friends away, send Callum to safety, and have me. Let him forget the thing I had been forged to be – a weapon. And once my friends were safely away, I would unleash myself onto him. He would not survive my fury.

Vitus stared at me for several, long seconds. His golden eyes studied every movement, every flicker of emotion, every breath. Finally, his lips parted. 'No.'

The word bounced around the room, setting my ears ringing.

'No?' I echoed, disbelief ringing through me.

Vitus's smile was grim. Certain. 'No, little raven.' He stepped forward, coming too close. I did not shift back, though. The closer he was, the easier it would be to end him. 'You might be insignificant, but you are your father's daughter. I have no doubt you would seek to undermine my plans at every turn. And your power is sizeable enough that that would be annoying.'

My heart was beating too fast now, dread tightening like a

noose as Vitus continued, his words a chilling caress. 'I only have one set of chains to bind a god's power. But there are other ways to bind a Gift like yours.'

My brow creased. I had never heard of ways to bind a Gift. There was certainty, though, in Vitus's eyes. Certainty. Malicious greed.

'Did you not question why my Ankurans sought to take your king?'

'Because you're a greedy bastard,' I bit out. 'You couldn't let him keep the power you'd given him.'

Vitus laughed, the sound spearing through me. 'Why would I bother with a measly seed of my power? Mortal lifespans are so terribly short. It would have returned to me in no time.' My body locked up at his words. He was right. What was a century to a god?

The god nodded as though he'd seen the understanding in my eyes. 'I took him because of that precious bond between the two of you. Get one, and the other will follow. Tell me,' he murmured, pinching my chin between two fingers and forcing me to look at Callum, 'Who would you choose? Yourself, or your soul-bonded king?'

Several dozen of the Ankurans broke away from Jaxon and Deana, coming to form a barrier between Callum and I. They held the points of their swords up at me, every single face painted with an eerie smile.

Don't do it. I might have screamed the words, might have whispered them, might have just thought them. They were powerful enough, though to make my ears ring and my blood roar. I tried to pull away from Vitus, but his grip didn't shift, fingers digging into my chin hard enough to bruise. I shifted my attention to Liam, staring at him. At the sword he now held. 'Please.'

There was begging in my voice, but I didn't care. I would get on my knees if I had to. Whatever it took so I didn't have to watch someone I loved die again.

Vitus yanked my face towards his. He smiled, a look of pure satisfaction. 'Time to make a choice.'

'I will not,' I whispered, choking back tears. Behind Vitus, Callum began to struggle. Chains clanked, and then Liam snarled with annoyance. The sound was enough to send a surge of energy through me. Vitus freed me as I twisted back to Liam and Callum. I screamed as Liam raised his sword and lunged for him. Vitus's arm caught at my waist. My Gift surged, spurred on by my desperation, but he did not relinquish his grip. Instead, he merely laughed through the pain he surely must've been feeling. I could do nothing but watch as Liam swung his sword.

Callum staggered backwards. It was not with his usual speed, the cruel wounds draining him. Still, he dodged the first blow, and the next, dodging the ring of steel. But his skill could only last so long in such conditions. I had to reach them before Callum's wounds took their toll. As Callum moved, so did I. With a cry of rage, I plunged my nails into Vitus's flesh, tearing through skin and bringing up blood. Startled by such a mundane attack, his grip loosened. I shoved my Gift towards him again. This time, his breath hissed out of him, and I tore myself away from his hold.

There was no time to waste on strategising. I threw myself into the midst of the Ankurans. Silver crackled along my skin, but it was faltering, too weak to destroy all of them at once. Instead, I directed it into my blades. I sliced through the stomach of the first in line. They disappeared in a cloud of ash as I whirled on another. But there was none of my usual elation, no sense of brutal victory, as I fought, cutting down Ankuran after Ankuran. Not as I whirled, catching a glimpse of Callum behind the hoard. Not as I saw him falter.

On any other day, there would be no contest between the two

men, no matter who held the blade. Liam was taught from books on technique. Callum was taught by years of brutal experience. Today, though, with Callum weighed down by chains, in pain and pale from blood loss, there was little he could do to dodge the blows that came. He stepped to one side for a wild swing at his head. The next, a more feral swing of annoyance from Liam, sank into his side. Red blood sprayed but Callum did not fall. He staggered backwards.

'Callum!' I screamed, throwing myself with more vehemence at the Ankurans.

He met my eyes. 'It's okay,' he said, his words reaching me through Vitus's laughter and the sounds of renewed struggle behind as Jaxon and Deana fought to get to us. 'It's okay. You need to go. Remember your promise.'

No!' I plunged my dagger through the throat of an Ankuran woman, lunging forward before her body even hit the ground. It wasn't okay. I wasn't okay. And perhaps I never had been, but this – this would be my undoing. The breaking from which I didn't return.

'Please, Liam!' I shouted over the din, pulling my blade deep enough across the throat of one Ankuran that his head tipped back away from his body. 'Don't do this. I'll stay here. I'll do whatever you want. Just let Callum go.'

Liam turned, locking eyes with me. His shone with cruel satisfaction. 'I'll get what I want from you, regardless. Right now, *this* is what I want.'

Callum dodged the swipe of Liam's blade. There were only a few more Ankurans between us. All I had to do was kill them, and I would be there. If I could get to Callum's side, everything would be fine. I slammed my elbow into the face of one, driving my knife through the eye of another. I could do this. I could reach him.

But then Callum's feet caught in his own chains. He cried out as he fell, slamming onto his back. Liam did not waste the opportunity. He drove his sword downwards, no hesitation in the movement. A scream lodged itself in my throat as Callum jerked, the sword stabbing through his stomach.

'No!' I screamed as Liam wrenched the blade free.

Callum blinked, his head lifting weakly as he stared at the blooming red with surprise. And then his eyes shifted to me, an apology written in them. *I love you.* Three words, mouthed as blood dribbled between his lips. His lips curled upwards as he fell backwards, his head cracking off marble. I felt it in my stomach then. The warmth of impending death, seconds away. The fraying of the silver rope that tethered us.

No. *No.*

This was not our end. I would not allow Liam, nor Vitus, to tear Callum away. Even as I felt the warmth of death grow, as that same pain that had sunk me to my knees in the Naruzian palace flared even stronger than before, I reached out. Not for Callum, who was still painfully far. Instead, I reached out for my Gift.

I pulled every ounce of my power into me, recalling it like one might call back a pet. Any trace of my Gift that remained in Vitus, anything that might have been stifling his power raced back to me as I summoned it. It draped over my skin, cool and smooth, spreading until every vein was lit up with that silver light. I did not stop fighting, did not stop mowing down the Ankurans as I did so, even as they began to circle behind me as well as in front. Callum would not die today.

Vitus's laughter turned to that of victory. I did not care. Let him win. Let him take me, use me, kill me. Dearil would never fold to the god's demands. My father didn't care enough about me to sacrifice a world for me. But I – I would not allow Callum to leave, because he was mine. He was not allowed to abandon me.

There was little life left in Callum's eyes. His head was resting on the floor, hand outstretched as though he was trying to reach me. I let the world fall away – Vitus's hard fingers, Liam's smugness, the Ankurans pushing in on me, even Deana and Jaxon's cries as they broke free of the mass, running too late to Callum's side. No one stopped them. There was no point. Not as I felt his soul surging upwards, trying to leave. Not as the brightness in his eyes turned dull, as his chest stopped moving.

Not as he died.

Chapter Thirty-Four

I screamed, and it was not the scream of anything belonging to this realm. It was a sound made to rent worlds in two, fury and agony welded into something tangible. It was the part of me that had lost, time and time again, and refused to lose again.

Dearil's gaze scorched my skin as I took hold of those last few vestiges of strength that I had gathered up, sending as much of it as I could spare towards gripping the bond as tightly as I could and the other towards my fingers. My hands flared silver as I pushed them across the golden scarred faces of two of the Ankurans. They fell to dust beneath my fingers. The silver light did not halt there. It burst outwards, rolling with a strength it had never possessed before. Streaks of silver crackled across the ground at my feet. It had always been a hungry power, but now it was ravenous as it surged for every Ankuran in the room. The silver swallowed them whole, one by one, until there were dozens of bodies covered in incandescent light.

As quickly as the silver enveloped them, it rolled away, leaving clouds of silver ash floating through the air and sprinkling the gold marbled floors. I didn't allow the ash time to settle as I pushed myself forward, feet grappling for purchase on the blood-slicked floor. They slipped and I fell, knees crashing painfully hard into the tile. I did not feel the ache as I scrambled to my feet once more. I felt nothing but desperate rage.

'Stop!' Vitus shouted behind me, complete authority in his voice. I ignored him as I raced for Callum, falling heavily to my knees beside him.

'Callum,' I whispered, a sob breaking through as I pressed my palms to his chest. Deana and Jaxon appeared, their expressions distraught as they slammed to a stop opposite me. I didn't say anything to them, too focused on where I touched Callum. There was no answering thud of a heart, no breath warming my skin. 'No.' I pressed bloodstained fingers onto his cheek. 'No, no, no.'

'It's what he deserved.'

I froze at Liam's voice. He stood near Callum's head. Deana let out a wordless cry of anger, lunging towards him, but Jaxon caught her. He pulled her back, whispering something in her ear that had her relenting, focusing on Callum once more.

Liam held up the sword that had driven through Callum. Blood dripped from the tip, splattering across the floor and Callum's cheek. *Drip. Drip. Drip.* It fell as my sister's blood had, each splatter hitting the ground painfully loud.

'You.' I breathed as I slowly lifted my head. My fingers curled where they touched Callum. I couldn't risk doing anything to save him until Liam was dealt with.

Drip. Drip. Drip. Liam had dared to draw Callum's blood. He'd killed him, just as he'd once had a hand in killing Cassie. Slowly, I rose to my feet, my eyes fixed on the prince.

'Don't come any closer,' Liam warned, the point of the sword aimed towards me. 'Vitus might not want you dead, but I can injure you badly enough that you can't move.'

'You,' I repeated, louder this time. My voice shook with the force of my anger. 'You did this.'

'I—' This time, his throat bobbed as he swallowed, and I smiled. There was nothing human in that smile. Behind, I could hear the footsteps of a god approaching, slow and unhurried. Vitus was confident in his ability to restrain me when he was ready. He would be able to, I knew. My Gift flickered weakly, only a few scraps remaining, whilst his body was still awash with gold.

I needed to move quickly. I took a step forward, and Liam flinched.

'Don't,' he warned again, lifting the blade higher.

Liam didn't have time to move as I lunged forward. My forearm slammed into his throat, sending him careening towards the floor. The back of his head hit the tiles with a meaty *smack*, the blade clattering off the floor. I fell on top of him, straddling his quaking body. My goal had been for Liam to suffer for days, or perhaps even years. I had dreamt up countless ways to destroy him. I wanted him to break, like I had done.

But now, Callum needed me. I would sacrifice my chance at vengeance if it meant I could save Callum. Liam's death would be quick. Quick, though, didn't mean painless.

'Don't.' The word was a plea this time, weak enough I might've delighted in it had it not been for the terror consuming me.

'You shouldn't have touched him.' I didn't bother with blades or power, not for Liam. I wanted to see the terror in his eyes, to see that he remembered who I was in his final moments. The woman he had betrayed. The nightmare he had helped forge. A half-god born of wrath and blood.

It would be his blood that wet my hands next.

My hand thrust forward, fingers sinking into his throat like talons. I wasn't sure if it was all the anger brimming inside of me, or if it was the divine blood fuelling my movements, but it was surprisingly easy to rip through layers of skin and muscle and flesh.

'I hope you rot in the Dark,' I whispered as I pulled, wrenching a chunk of his throat free. Blood sprayed, hitting my cheeks and stinging my eyes. Liam's eyes widened as he gurgled. Red bubbled in the space where flesh had once existed.

I stood, dropping the piece of skin and muscle I held on top of his chest. I did not watch him suffocate in his blood. He did not deserve that dignity. Something warmed in my stomach, a tug at the shadowed silver cord I had been holding tight since Liam had turned on Callum. A warning that time was running out.

Spinning, I fell to my knees at Callum's side. My fingers pressed against his cheeks once more as I stretched out towards the glowing presence at the end of the bond between Callum and I. For the briefest of moments, my eyes connected with Dearil's. His were shadowed with a melancholy I did not understand, but he made no move to halt my movements as I lifted my hands, balling silver between them. My fingers grasped onto the bond that connected me to Callum, holding tight as his soul tugged towards what awaited.

No, I ordered that thread, yanking back. *You don't get to do this.*

I sensed a smile that did not appear on those too-cold, still lips, and I could almost imagine the words that he would say back to me if he could. *There are some things even you can't stop.*

Maybe. I pulled again, gathered the specks of light that were Callum's soul. Forced them back to where they belonged. And watched. Waited for his chest to move. *But this isn't one of those.*

Vitus was still standing there even as the warmth lessened in my stomach. Not much – not enough for death to not be a looming threat. But enough that with a gasping, shuddering breath, Callum's chest rose. My Gift focused solely on holding his soul in, the crackling power of it diminishing. There was little else I could do as Vitus shifted forward, finally grabbing me. His grip closed around my throat, pulling me to my feet and wrenching me away from Callum. I didn't resist. I didn't have the strength to, even as he dragged me away from Callum.

Live, I silently ordered Callum as his eyes blinked open then widened in horror at the sight of me held in Vitus's clutches.

I could almost feel his silent refusal shooting back at me. *No. Not if it means you do not.*

The tether between us pulled taut, as though Callum were trying to break free of it. Trying to free me, free my Gift that was now bound so tightly. I gritted my teeth, narrowed my eyes, and pulled right back. *Don't you dare, you bastard.*

There was still a flicker of power in there, as there had always been. Enough to reduce a man to ash, but not enough to bring a god to his knees. I pulled that power to my core.

'Such a foolish choice,' Vitus whispered.

I dug my nails into his hand. 'Would you call it foolish if you could've done the same for Alexia?'

The fingers at my throat dug in harder. I cried out as Vitus's power surged through me. 'You do not speak her name.'

I did not respond to the god, focusing on Deana and Jaxon instead, croaking out, 'Leave.'

Callum's eyes flared, his expression twisted with panicked desperation. 'Don't! Keep your promise. Let me go. Save yourself!'

There was blood all over him – on his face, his neck, his chest, pouring from wounds that refused to heal. That Vitus would not allow to heal as long as Callum was here.

If he didn't leave, then forcing his soul back into his body would only be a delay of his death. He was bleeding out. And if his soul left again, my Gift would not be strong enough to pull it back. I could sense the death looming near, could feel it pressing at the tremulous bond I fought to keep in place.

No. I whispered fiercely to that brilliant, burning soul that was Callum. *You will not leave me. Not now. Not ever.*

'Leave, Chiara!' Even as Callum's soul fought me, his body

clawed at the ground, fingers stretching to where Vitus held me. He was dying, yet he was dragging himself, bit by bit, closer to me.

Stop. I begged him through my desperate gaze, a reversal of the words we had traded only moments before. *Go. Leave.*

Callum's eyes contained a mixture of terror and fury. Fury at Vitus, yes. But I knew there was also fury at me for doing this. For choosing him over myself. I could hear his voice as clear as if he spoke next to me. *I will not.*

Go. If I could have cried, I would have. I would have sobbed and screamed and shouted until Callum understood. Until he saw that I was doing this for me as much as for him. He'd been right the night before. I deserved this – deserved him. And I'd be damned if I was going to lose him now.

'You don't get to do this, Chiara.' Callum's movements were slowing, the blood flowing faster. He had minutes, if that. Still, he edged closer to the golden barrier between us. 'You don't get to choose this nightmare. I won't let you do this.'

Something in me twisted, even as I forced my eyes to find Jaxon and Deana. 'Your ... favours,' I choked out from where Vitus gripped my neck. Vitus merely laughed, unbothered by everything that was happening as I flicked my gaze between my friends to Callum.

Deana understood first. Her face paled as she reached for Callum, grasping hold of his wrist. He tried to shake her off, but he was too weak to do so as her head dipped in a sorrowful nod. Jaxon caught on moments later, his eyes widening with horror. Horror and understanding that this was the only way that some of us survived today. He waved his hand, hundreds of him, Deana and Callum coming into existence out of a bright yellow light.

Vitus's fingers tensed as his laughter cut off abruptly. 'What are you doing?' He threw me to the ground, breath exploding out of me as I crashed onto the floor. 'Answer, girl. Do you think you'll manage to escape me?'

I did not answer, scrambling away from him. Clicking his tongue, Vitus raised a hand. The gold wall split, Ankurans flooding into the space once more. Half of them lunged at the replicas of Deana and Jaxon, fingers slashing through them. The replicas they touched disintegrated into nothing. It would not distract them for long, but it would be enough.

The rest turned on me as I rose to shaky feet.

'Chiara, please!' Callum cried, wrenching my attention towards him. I caught a glimpse of his golden-blonde hair through the Ankurans that circled me.

The first lunged towards me. I caught it under the jaw, slamming the blade upwards while I kicked out at a second Ankuran. I didn't seek to get to Callum and the others. There were too many, my Gift too depleted. All I needed was to distract Vitus and the creatures for long enough to gather what remained of my power.

Even as I fought, Callum's voice seemed to ring through my head. The soul-bond. It had to be. *I will never forgive you if you do this.*

I pushed my thoughts down the soul-bond as I fought, hoping I was right and that they'd reach Callum. *You have a kingdom to run. Countless will die without you there to lead them to war. You need to survive.*

'They won't escape, little raven.' Vitus's voice rumbled behind me.

I ignored him as an Ankuran lunged at my exposed side. I barely dodged the woman, staggering into a large male Ankuran. He wrapped beefy arms around me. With a grunt, I drove my hand backwards, sending my dagger plunging through his torso. The Ankuran's arm sprang free and I twisted, cutting his throat.

'You promised!' Callum screamed and my heart cracked at the

anguish in his voice. If he sensed we could use the soul-bond to communicate – if he'd even received my words – he didn't show it. 'You promised you'd run. You promised you'd leave!'

A bitter laugh scraped out of me, the falsity of it almost painful. But I needed him to be able to move on as I gathered the leftovers of my power. I needed him to forget me once he made it out of here. Digging my fingers into the throat of an Ankuran child, I called back, 'Promises are nothing other than prettily wrapped lies. You taught me that, Your Majesty.'

The words hit as hard as I meant them to. Callum flinched back just long enough for Jaxon to tighten his hold around his body.

Live, Callum, I ordered silently as I pictured the edge of the wards where we'd arrived, pulling the fabric of the realm to meet the spot where Callum, Deana and Jaxon huddled in the midst of the Ankurans. Silver spread, lancing across the ground towards the only three in this realm I cared for. It did not attack the Ankurans as it had before. It swept under them, then pooled around its targets.

'No! Chiara, don't you godsdamned dare!' It wasn't just anger that caused the volume of Callum's words. It was terror. Bone-deep terror, the sort that could slice a person in two.

His fight against Jaxon resurged, even as the blood continued to pour, slick across his skin. I cocked back my arm, heart twisting at the pain in his voice as I threw my dagger into the forehead of an Ankuran reaching for them. My second knife found the chest of another. A third fell as I reached upwards, jerking its head to one side until there was a sharp crack.

There were too many, though, my body and Gift too tired. Something hard slammed across my back. I cried out, staggering forward. Before I could regain my footing, another blow rained down. My knees slammed into the floor, hands splashing into blood.

Callum screamed my name again. A shadow fell upon me. Not an Ankuran, but a god. Even as my heart seized with fear, I didn't hesitate. I yanked one of my last remaining blades from my hip, lunging upwards and shoving it through the god's chest. He stumbled back, staring down at the blade with a perturbed expression. His interruption gave me the chance I needed. Turning to Callum, I flung the last piece of my power towards him, and mentally shoved them through the fabric of the realm.

The silver sparked, crackled, flew towards the trio. There was a flare of light, bouncing outwards and turning the nearest walking corpses to dust. One last thought rose that would never be spoken aloud to him. Words that I should've said long before.

I love you.

There was a final agonising scream from Callum, a wordless cry of a pain so deep it sliced to my core. And then, it cut off. When the light disappeared, there was nothing where the three had been, except blood and a chain that clattered to the ground. They were gone. Safe.

And I was alone with a wrathful god.

Vitus ripped the blade free from his chest, tossing it and then me onto the floor at his feet. The impact snatched my breath from me.

'That,' he said, 'was nothing more than annoying, little raven. It has only delayed the inevitable.' He reached for me, brushing back tendrils of my hair. The movement was almost tender, almost gentle, until he grabbed a fistful of it. 'Though I rather enjoyed seeing the way your king's forced exit broke him.'

I didn't cry out. I refused to as he dragged me through his blood, through Callum's, and deposited me at the feet of Dearil. Ankurans hovered behind Dearil, replacing the ones that now dusted me with silver ash.

I mustered the energy I had to glare up at him, eyes hard. 'I will kill you.' The whisper was weak, but the words were not.

'I don't know when and I don't know how, but if it's my last act in this world, I will pull your beating heart from your chest and crush it.'

Vitus smiled, and I smiled back, two wolves sizing each other up. He was the bigger one by far, but I was a cur with the taste of blood in my mouth. I was not as breakable as this god thought I was. I would suffer here. Maybe for months, maybe for years, maybe for an eternity. But I had suffered for my whole life. And I would cling to an existence that was worse than death, if it meant I could keep Callum alive while doing so. And in my pain and suffering, I would be damned if I didn't drag Vitus into the depths of the Dark with me.

Vitus's shadow loomed over me as he nudged me with one foot, hard enough that I jerked. 'Will you help me bring down the barrier?' he asked.

Dearil did not look at me. 'No.'

The smile on Vitus's lips was a nightmare of a thing. He crouched once more, pressed a finger against my temple, and *pushed* his power into me. It hurt, far worse than it had before. And yet, I did not allow my lips to part. Did not allow a single sound to escape, a single tear to fall as I writhed on the floor. I would not have been surprised if my skin had been flayed from my bones from the intensity of that pain, but I did not scream.

Vitus seemed mildly displeased at my lack of sound as he withdrew his finger. 'Now?' he asked.

Dearil did not speak this time. He merely stared stonily ahead.

Vitus shrugged, letting out a disappointed breath. There was a glimmer to his eyes, though, that betrayed excitement. 'You have always made me work hard for what I want.' His eyes flicked to where I was sprawled. 'That's fine. We have plenty of time to break your daughter into so many pieces that there won't be a soul left when I'm finished with her. And you will break, too, old friend.'

Dearil did not move as Vitus turned to one of his Ankurans.

Callum is safe, I told myself as Vitus instructed the Ankuran to give me a proper welcome.

Callum is safe, I told myself as the Ankuran smiled, an eerie echo of Vitus's. I could feel Callum, somewhere at the end of the bond. Feel the sorrow and pain that was far more severe than anything physical could be. Revelled in what it meant – that he was alive.

Callum is safe, I told myself as the Ankuran put on a metal glove, flexible enough that he could form a fist, plated with unyielding iron at the knuckles.

Callum is safe, I told myself as the first blow landed, knocking the air from my chest. It left me coughing, curled around my stomach.

Callum is safe, I told myself as the blows kept falling, as blood began to paint the floor almost prettily at Dearil's feet. As something snapped in my side, and darkness edged my vision. I thought it to myself as I forced any sound deep, deep down. Forced the cries of pain to only be inside my head.

Callum is safe, I told myself as I felt my grip on my silence slip, just for a moment, and internally reached out for something, *anything*, to tether myself to.

Callum is safe. I repeated the words as I grasped onto that tether – onto the bond that not only tied Callum's soul to his body but tied me to him. A soul-bond.

Callum is safe. I thought it to myself as my consciousness pulled away. It would be my shield, the one thing that no one could take away from me. As long as Deana and Jaxon kept him away, I could hold onto it. *Did* hold onto it as I sank into nothingness.

Callum is safe.

Chapter Thirty-Five

Callum

It had taken all of Jaxon and Deana's strength to pull him through the wards. All of their strength to pull him away from Chiara, even as he bled out on the stones.

'Come on,' Deana hissed. 'You need to get past the wards. If you don't—'

He quieted her with a look. It was one of rage and pain and a heartbreak so deep he didn't know what to do with the pieces that were left. 'I have to get her.' There was blood on his face mingling with the tears, blood and tears and sweat and none of it mattered. What mattered was who they had left behind. 'I have to get her.'

'You idiot!' Deana snapped, wrestling with him as he managed to get an arm free. 'You'll only get yourself killed!'

'I don't care!' His throat was raw from screaming, his head light from blood loss, but the words managed to snap out of him. 'She didn't say it out loud, but I heard it. Heard her. She—' He choked on something – a sob, or blood, or the utter desperation.

He'd heard those three words – the ones that had cut through him more painfully than any wound given by a blade. *I love you.*

'I don't know what you heard, but you've lost too much blood. You're delirious, Callum!' There was a combination of hopelessness and anger in Deana's voice as she pulled him further back.

Callum shook his head mutely. He might have believed her, if he had not seen Chiara's eyes. Her expression had been cold, but Chiara had never been able to master control over that which showed in her eyes. It was why his father had despised her so much. Every time she looked at King Kane, there had been a hatred in there, a rebellion, that no amount of whipping had been able to beat out. She might have bent her head and bared her back, but those eyes told the truth. She had never been broken. Not once.

What he had seen in those exquisite eyes before had not been anger or coldness. It had been the feelings encompassed in those words. Rage. Sorrow. Regret. Love.

'The bond.' Jaxon's voice was emotionless, as though he had been fully drained of it. 'It is possible – if the bond is accepted by both sides, then sometimes strong thoughts, strong feelings, can get through.'

Jaxon's words hurt more than any physical wounds could have. Chiara had chosen him. In the end, despite everything that had passed between them, she'd chosen him. She could have gotten out. She could have gotten to Deana and Jaxon and gotten them all out, left him behind. She should have done that.

In the end, though, he had seen the calculations in her eyes. Whose life was worth more.

She had gotten the calculations terribly, fatally wrong.

It had been Jaxon who eventually got Callum past the wards with a swift blow from his sword's hilt to the head. By the time Callum emerged from the blackness, they had ridden hard and fast upon stolen horses, his arms wrapped in bandages from where Jaxon told him he'd had to burn away the wards Vitus had cut into him. He was injured enough that his Gift had taken its time re-emerging, taken his time healing his broken body.

As soon as he cracked open his eyes, he knew it had failed to heal his soul.

Callum recognised the bed he had been laid upon. The sheets were white, pristine, as clean as his skin. Someone had taken the time to bathe him and redress him. Every mark, every wound, had been wiped away, even the ones on his neck that he had so carefully left. A clean slate, his Gift had clearly decided. He hated his Gift in that moment in a way he had never hated it before.

Deana and Jaxon had been in briefly to visit. They had filled him in – Archin was virtually impenetrable now. The border was lined with a mix of Vitus's creatures and a mortal army led by his former General, the only way in or out either as a corpse or with a god powerful enough to do so. With the attacks on the outer villages continuing, they had too much of one and not enough of the other.

The only news they had of the god and Chiara was that the palace in Ballaronia was now empty.

Callum tried to care about the matters unrelated to Chiara. He tried to slip on the mask of a king. That was what everyone was expecting of him. He had even managed it for a moment or two, until a pain so sharp he lost hold of his breath rang through his bones.

It hadn't been his.

Now, Callum sat alone in his chambers. His room still smelt of Chiara – of smoke and jasmine. The bond was still there. It had been there in unconsciousness, a silver line interwoven with his shadows. The silver was stronger, holding the shadows in place even as they tried to untangle. Callum remembered the way her voice had sounded in his mind – the softness to it, the steel that always underlined every single one of her words. He closed his eyes, probing experimentally at the bond.

Chiara? he tried, imagining his voice spiralling down the length of the bond.

A silence, and then – *Callum.* Weaker than he would have liked, a thread of pain he could tell she was trying to shield from him, but there. Alive. Conscious.

What's happening? Where are you? How do we— His words broke off halfway as a burst of pain flew at him down the bond. It held an intensity he wasn't aware pain could have, simultaneously burning and icy. A gasp escaped his lip, slipping down that line to where the other half of his soul rested. A pause in the pain and then, like steel gates slamming down, the connectedness of the bond stopped.

Callum's heart faltered. She wasn't – she couldn't be—

No. She couldn't be dead. If Chiara was dead, then his soul would no longer be tethered to his body. He would have died, too.

Unconscious, then?

But that didn't ring true either. When he was unconscious, the bond was a sharp presence in his mind. Now, it felt dull. Muted. Like if he stared at it, he could only see his half, the other half bathed in darkness.

Realisation shot through Callum, and he let out a curse violent enough and loud enough that a maid in his receiving chambers let out a muffled squeak next door. The bond wasn't gone. Chiara must have found a way to block it. Sensed he felt her pain and stopped it going through.

'Godsdammit, Chiara,' he hissed. He was well and truly furious. When he got his hands on her, he would let her know exactly what he thought of everything she had done. She had promised to be selfish. She had told him she would save herself over anyone else in that room.

And yet, she was not here. She had done none of that. She had saved him and cursed herself in the same process. And now, on top of all that, she was blocking him out, trying to spare him her pain when his ill-fated idea had led her to her current situation.

He should have known she would do exactly that. Chiara liked to pretend that she hated everyone and everything, that she would burn the world down and laugh in its ashes, but she was not as selfish as she wanted everyone to think. Not when it came to those she cared about.

She should never have let him in. She never should have loved him.

At least then she would be free.

He barely realised he had gotten to his feet, or that he was pacing the room like a caged animal. Shadows grew at his fingers – the shadows Chiara had helped him regain – seeking to heal the deep ache that it could not touch. There was a crack inside him. A deep, deadly crack that was draining him of his life and of his soul. No wretched Gift would be able to heal it. The only person who could was trapped, alone with enemies who were cruel and callous and would hurt her until even Chiara, with all her strength and resolve, warped and broke. He would not allow that. He would not allow her to leave this world thinking she was less than him, than anyone, when she was so much more.

It didn't take long to hunt down Jaxon and Deana. He didn't care when Deana forced Brayden along, the landless prince somewhat less sulky than he had been the last time Callum had seen him. Deana was stone-faced. Jaxon looked angry at the world. The expression suited him far more than his smiles did, Callum thought. And rage would serve them well.

They all looked at Callum expectantly. 'So?' Jaxon prompted, crossing his arms over his chest.

'Vitus wants to bring down the barrier between our worlds. He brought war to us. It's time we brought war to him.' Callum's smile felt like a wicked slash across his face. 'We will hunt down each of his foot soldiers. We will burn down his kingdom, bit by bit. We will destroy any creatures, mortals and gods who are loyal to Vitus.' There was no room for mercy in his voice. Not even Brayden flinched at the cavalier mention of destroying his homeland. A homeland of ghosts and corpses was no use to anyone, and right now, it was in Callum's way.

'And?' Jaxon asked.

Callum turned his gaze to stare out the window, over the roof tops and fields and beyond, to where that half-shadowed bond urged him to go. Chiara had sacrificed herself from him. Now he would do the same for her, if it meant she was returned to his side.

'And we get her back.'

DON'T MISS THE EPIC CONCLUSION IN *THE DIVINE*

I wouldn't be done until I held the heart of a god in my hand.

Chiara is a captive of Vitus, the god of life. He plans to kill her and in doing so shatter the barrier between the godly and mortal realms. If he succeeds, everything Chiara knows and loves will be destroyed. More than that, she will lose Callum.

The daughter of Death, Chiara has only known darkness. She is a monster. A weapon. A killing machine. And – if she can escape Vitus – the mortal realm's only hope.

But even hope might not be enough when it comes to war with the gods. For Chiara and Callum to win, Vitus must die and only a god can truly kill a god. It seems nothing can save them, except perhaps Death itself…

AVAILABLE IN PAPERBACK, EBOOK AND AUDIO

Acknowledgments

I would like to thank my mum, Fiona, who has been my biggest support from day one. Thank you for all the time you've spent reading, editing, and asking me when you're going to get the next one (one day, I promise!). Thank you to my dad, John, who never fails to encourage me. To AJ, who has spent five-hour road trips listening to me talk about the plot of each and every book, and Josh and Bec, for always asking how my writing is going.

Thank you to my friends, who have to put up with me talking about my books (especially Lauren, who bears with me during work hours and outside of them). A huge thank you to everyone at One More Chapter. To Charlotte Ledger, who has been such a massive support from day one. And, to the readers, thank you for taking a chance on this series – your support means the world to me!

The author and One More Chapter would like to thank everyone who contributed to the publication of this story...

Analytics
Imogen Wolstencroft

Audio
Fionnuala Barrett
Ciara Briggs

Contracts
Laura Amos
Inigo Vyvyan

Design
Lucy Bennett
Fiona Greenway
Liane Payne
Dean Russell

Digital Sales
Laura Daley
Lydia Grainge
Hannah Lismore

eCommerce
Laura Carpenter
Madeline ODonovan
Charlotte Stevens
Christina Storey
Jo Surman
Rachel Ward

Editorial
Rosie Best
Kara Daniel
Charlotte Ledger
Jennie Rothwell
Sofia Salazar Studer
Caroline Scott-Bowden
Emily Thomas
Helen Williams

Harper360
Emily Gerbner
Ariana Juarez
Jean Marie Kelly
emma sullivan
Sophia Wilhelm

International Sales
Peter Borcsok
Ruth Burrow
Bethan Moore
Colleen Simpson

Inventory
Sarah Callaghan
Kirsty Norman

Marketing & Publicity
Chloe Cummings
Grace Edwards
Katie Sadler

Operations
Melissa Okusanya
Hannah Stamp

Production
Denis Manson
Simon Moore
Francesca Tuzzeo

Rights
Ashton Mucha
Alisah Saghir
Zoe Shine
Aisling Smyth
Lucy Vanderbilt

Trade Marketing
Ben Hurd
Eleanor Slater

The HarperCollins Distribution Team

The HarperCollins Finance & Royalties Team

The HarperCollins Legal Team

The HarperCollins Technology Team

UK Sales
Isabel Coburn
Jay Cochrane
Sabina Lewis
Holly Martin
Harriet Williams
Leah Woods

And every other essential link in the chain from delivery drivers to booksellers to librarians and beyond!

One More Chapter is an award-winning global division of HarperCollins.

Subscribe to our newsletter to get our latest eBook deals and stay up to date with all our new releases!

signup.harpercollins.co.uk/
join/signup-omc

Meet the team at
www.onemorechapter.com

Follow us!

@onemorechapterhc

Do you write unputdownable fiction?
We love to hear from new voices.
Find out how to submit your novel at
www.onemorechapter.com/submissions